The Adventures of Chase Manhattan

A Trilogy

Part One:

Breakthrough

Stephen Tremp

iUniverse, Inc.
New York   Bloomington

BREAKTHROUGH

The Adventures of Chase Manhattan

Copyright © 2007, 2008 by Stephen T. Tremp

All rights reserved. No part of this book may be used or reproduced by any means, graphic, electronic, or mechanical, including photocopying, recording, taping or by any information storage retrieval system without the written permission of the publisher except in the case of brief quotations embodied in critical articles and reviews.

iUniverse books may be ordered through booksellers or by contacting:

iUniverse
1663 Liberty Drive
Bloomington, IN 47403
www.iuniverse.com
1-800-Authors (1-800-288-4677)

Because of the dynamic nature of the Internet, any Web addresses or links contained in this book may have changed since publication and may no longer be valid. The views expressed in this work are solely those of the author and do not necessarily reflect the views of the publisher, and the publisher hereby disclaims any responsibility for them.

ISBN: 978-0-595-47400-4 (pbk)
ISBN: 978-0-595-71070-6 (cloth)
ISBN: 978-0-595-91677-1 (ebk)

Printed in the United States of America

iUniverse rev. date: 12/16/2008

Dedication

For my beautiful wife, Deena, and my family, who have supported me while I took this past year off to research and write *Breakthrough*.

Acknowledgements

I WOULD LIKE to sincerely thank the following people for their constant encouragement and feedback that significantly contributed to the writing of this book. I thank my parents, Duane and Joyce Tremp, and the creative DNA I inherited from them. Thanks also to my brother and his wife, Scott and Sandy Tremp, and my two sisters, Debbie Sack and Theresa Dayton, who have offered invaluable, unbiased feedback beginning with the first rough draft. Without you all, this book never would make it to the bookshelves. Thank you.

THANKS TO PAULY Kotin for sharing her literary expertise and insight. Thanks to Yvonne Wittstock, who gave timely and constructive feedback at a time when I needed it. Thanks also to Anna McDowell, who took time from her busy schedule to give me insightful input into the character's personalities. Thanks to Sandy Peoples, and I hope to see you publish one of your books soon. Thanks to Dr. Virginia Trimble, professor of physics at the Department of Physics and Astronomy at the University of California-Irvine, who helped critique my understanding of the basic concepts of Einstein-Rosen Bridges. She reminded me, although this is a timely and exciting subject, I am still writing in the realm of science fiction. Or am I?

Thanks to Guillermo Puig for allowing the use of his picture of Boston for the dustcover. Thanks to Jeremy Tremp and Adam Kragt for their creativeness in designing the dustcover. Finally, thanks to the tenacity of my two proofreaders, Cindy Beatty at www.proofpositivepapers.com and Alanna Boutin at www.youreditress.com, who took this diamond in the rough and polished it into the gem of a story that you now hold in your hands. Enjoy.

PART ONE

Chapter 1
Las Vegas

He carefully opened the door of the floor safe in the Salon Suite on the fifty-eighth floor of the Wynn Hotel, one of the newest five-star mega hotels on the Las Vegas Strip. Inside: a single item he had been hired to retrieve from an anxious and panicked research scientist in San Jose, Calif. The risks were high—not only for his client, but for himself. He understood that if he were caught, there would be no leverage for negotiation. He would be killed quickly, and his body dumped somewhere out in the middle of the Mojave Desert, like so many other unfortunate, nameless souls over the decades who now called this vast wasteland their final resting place.

There was also the risk that this item could again fall into the wrong hands. He was being paid handsomely to retrieve the stolen nanotechnology—a breakthrough in transferring information that could soon replace the use of wires and printed circuit boards in computers. This development was one of the Holy Grails of the Information Age, *exponentially expanding the amount of information that could be stored and the speed at which it could be processed.*

He needed to return the breakthrough information to its rightful owner quickly since the possibilities for this discovery were endless and could usher in a new paradigm for how data is input, stored, manipulated, and retrieved. In the wrong hands, it could be used by rogue nations to exponentially enhance the performance of weapons of mass destruction.

Reaching down, he took out the flash drive containing 585 pages of PDF documents outlining how to build this new breakthrough from the bottom up. The thieves who stole the flash drive had set off a small bomb in one of the bathrooms of his client's three-story office building. Then they called, threatening to blow up the entire building—solely to create the diversion they needed to steal the flash drive. The operation was an inside job masterminded by a trusted colleague whose betrayal Chase's client never foresaw.

The thieves made a quick stopover in Las Vegas to hand off the flash drive to a third party and throw off anyone who might be on their trail. The flash drive was scheduled to go to Arlington, Va., to the individual who paid to have it stolen. He would, in turn, sell it to an agent for an Eastern European group, who wanted to sell it on the black market to the highest bidder, regardless of their intentions.

Chase Manhattan gently placed the flash drive in his jacket pocket, closed the safe, and swiftly exited the posh 1,950-square-foot suite. He wore dark, loose-fitting khakis, a gray long-sleeved hooded sweater, a Dodgers baseball cap, a five-day growth of facial hair, and makeup that made him look Hispanic so that the cameras in every hallway, elevator, and stairwell would not be able to identify him. Chase even took the extra measure to change his hair color from light brown to dark black.

It was just past midnight on Sunday evening, and the thieves sat in one of the Wynn nightclubs on the first floor. They were negotiating the final details of their agreement to transfer ownership of the flash drive for a cool $5 million.

Now, all Chase needed to do was exit the hotel and drive through the night, return the flash drive to its rightful owner in San Jose, and collect what he liked to call his "finder's fee." He entered the elevator and pressed the L button. He was confident that in a few short minutes, he would be in his rented Cadillac DTS driving across the heart of the Mojave Desert, through the San Joaquin Valley in central California, and into San Jose around eight o'clock in the morning. It would be fun to stay and admire the hotel's extensive art collection and maybe play a round or two of golf in the morning, he thought. But these luxuries had to wait for another day. He needed to get out of the hotel and out of Las Vegas as quickly as possible—his life depended on it.

At the twenty-second floor, the elevator stopped. Chase didn't give it a second thought, thinking a guest was on his way to the casino or one of the nightclubs. Instead, three young men in their early twenties entered. They seemed menacing to Chase, and he was immediately on guard. One of the men—with a shaved head and a blue-and-green webbed tattoo that covered his scalp and the right side of his face and neck—stood to Chase's left. A second, thin man, almost as tall as Chase and wearing a dark blue Armani business suit and white oxford dress shirt, wore his black hair combed straight back and held in place with a styling gel. He and the third man, who was considerably shorter but much thicker, and who wore casual clothes, positioned themselves to his right.

Stepping out of the elevator just as quickly as the three men stepped in, Chase walked briskly down the red-and-gold-carpeted hallway toward an exit sign forty feet away. After only a few steps, he sprinted for the stairwell. He didn't need to look back to know the three men were behind him in close pursuit. Chase had at least six or seven strides on them. Reaching the stairwell door, he stopped, turned, and made like he was pulling out a handgun. Although Chase had a permit to carry a gun in public in California, he did not have this privilege in Nevada. But the ruse bought him a few additional seconds and he made it through the exit door, beginning his hasty descent down to the lobby by jumping over the handrails and clearing each flight of stairs in a couple of leaps.

The stylish leader yelled to his partners, "Chase him down the stairwell. I'll take the elevator to the first floor. There's an extra ten grand for you to split if you get the flash drive before I do." The two young men burst into the stairwell and duplicated Chase's leaps over the stairwell railings while quickly closing the gap between them.

On the sixteenth floor, Chase knew he had to stand and fight. With webhead only one floor above, he stopped, took a deep breath, and waited for his first pursuer to meet him.

"That was really stupid of you to steal that flash drive. Forget about taking you out to the desert; you're going to die right here in the stairwell," the tattooed man yelled as he cleared the final steps that separated the two men.

"You're way out of your league tonight," Chase responded confidently as he quickly sized up his attacker.

The assailant led with a kick to his chest. Chase crouched, grabbed the man's ankle with his left hand and thigh with his right, and used his momentum to spin him around and throw him headfirst down the stairs toward the fifteenth floor. To Chase's surprise, webhead landed on his hands, pushed off, and performed an aerial somersault before landing on his feet.

The second assailant was right behind the first, hurling himself over the staircase railing and attempting to land on top of Chase, who anticipated the move and grabbed him by his shirt, throwing him against the wall. Using the momentum, the man ran six feet up the wall, performing a near-perfect backflip, and landing in front of Chase while entering into a roundhouse kick. Chase easily ducked underneath the strike, again picked him up by his shirt, and threw him into webhead, who was running back up the stairs, knocking both assailants down to the landing.

Chase understood these thugs were urban ninjas, more skilled in acrobatics and stunts that involved running attacks rather than experienced in the traditional martial arts. Leaping halfway to the landing, Chase faked an attack, then jumped over the railing. Webhead anticipated the move and jumped to meet Chase as he was landing on the midpoint of the stairs, tackling him as both rolled down to the next landing.

Chase gave him a stiff palm to the jaw, momentarily stunning him. The shorter assailant jumped down onto the landing and delivered a roundhouse kick directed at Chase's head. Chase ducked under the kick, leaned against the railing, and slid down to the next landing, ran halfway down the stairs, then proceeded to jump railings again.

"Give us the flash drive, amigo, and *maybe* we'll let you live," the short assailant shouted down the stairwell as he picked up the pursuit. He yelled at his partner, "Get up. After him—*now*."

At the eleventh floor, the short, stocky thug caught up to Chase, who threw a punch directed at the thug's throat. He grabbed Chase by the wrist with both hands and spun him down hard to the cement floor, almost breaking Chase's forearm in the process. "Give me the flash drive *now*," he demanded, "or I'll break your arm in three different places."

Chase delivered a kick to his ribs that loosened the grip and allowed him to pull his arm free. He stood back up as webhead jumped on his back and grabbed him in a choke hold. "Just hold him. I'll kill him," the shorter attacker yelled at his tattooed partner while pulling out a folding switchblade knife from his pocket. As he began to thrust the four-inch blade towards Chase's abdomen, Chase planted his left foot on the cement landing and rammed his right foot into the short, thick man's forehead, knocking him down a half flight of stairs.

Gasping for air, Chase faked like he would ram webhead into the wall behind them and instead, spun around and fell over backward on the stairs. Webhead landed on his back with Chase on top of him. The impact knocked the wind out of him for a few seconds, giving Chase the opportunity to escape his deathly tight grip, get up, and clear more railings on his way to the bottom of the stairwell. Webhead stood up, pulled out a 9mm handgun, and zeroed in on Chase as he crisscrossed the line of fire while jumping rails. The other assailant caught up to him before he could pull the trigger. "Don't shoot in here, you idiot. There are cameras everywhere, and the sound would bring security."

On the fourth floor, the short, thick man caught up to Chase, pulled out his knife again with his right hand, jabbed at Chase's chest and slashed at his neck, then lunged at his stomach. Chase shifted his legs two feet back to create space between him and the knife while grabbing his attacker's wrist and redirecting the strike to his right. He reached out and raked the fingers from his left hand across his attacker's eyes, then hooked the same arm around the back of assailant's neck and pulled his head back by his jaw, still holding onto the thug's right wrist. Quickly Chase slammed him level to the floor, holding his wrist that grasped the knife at a ninety-degree angle perpendicular to the thug's body.

Then he raised his left foot to squash the thug's head when webhead jumped onto the landing above him, pulling out his 9mm handgun. "No more messing around. I'm ending this now," he yelled. Chase had no choice but to let the thug go and continue leaping the railings to the bottom of the stairway. He heard a deafening boom echoing down the stairwell and felt the bullet ricochet off the handrail, barely missing his left hand.

"You idiot, I said not in the stairwell; that's going to bring security for sure," the shorter assailant yelled up to his partner.

Chase ran down the final two flights and burst out of the stairwell on the first floor and into a corridor leading toward the boutiques, restaurants, and nightclubs while the two assailants regrouped and continued their hurried descent. Chase ran toward the elevators when one opened, revealing the tall, thin, well-dressed man who stepped out. He seemed more surprised to see Chase make it to the first floor than Chase was to see him.

The man blocked his path, causing Chase to stop. "The flash drive. Give it to me now, and I'll let you live," he demanded.

Chase stood in a free motion fighting stance, left side facing forward, his weight shifted to his right foot, knees slightly bent. He balled his right hand and raised it in front of his face just below his eyes. "You have two seconds to make your move. Come and get it, slick."

Chase heard a click and saw a glimmer of light reflect off a switchblade knife that the attacker pulled out of his pocket. He lunged at Chase's neck with a fast slash. Chase blocked the strike with his left forearm and punched the assailant in the nose hard with his right fist, breaking it as an explosion of blood sprayed in all directions. The assailant reeled back into the elevator, bouncing off the wall. Then he stumbled back toward Chase, who kicked him in the chest, causing him to fall back again into the elevator wall and slump onto the floor. Quickly, Chase pressed the fifty-eighth floor button and the elevator doors closed, increasing his odds of survival by one-third.

He ran down the hall and into the first open business he saw, the *Bartolotta Ristorante di Mare*. Only a few strides behind him were the two thugs, who had made it to the first floor. They were just a little faster than he was and were closing in. The short, thick man took over the lead role. "Fan out to the left side," he shouted to webhead, directing him to form a pincher.

Although it was off-season in Las Vegas, the night was alive with guests and there were still more than twenty tables hosting late-night diners. The maitre d' and waiters stopped in midstride to stare as Chase and the two attackers ran through the restaurant.

Picking up dinner plates from an empty table, Chase hurled them at his closest pursuer, webhead, who was closing in on his left. Two plates found their mark, one shattering off his forehead, which momentarily caused him to drop to his knees. However, the short man was closing in fast, leaping over tables and knocking a waiter to the floor, his tray of four entrées flying off in four directions.

Chase sprinted into the kitchen, weaving through the maze of tables, stoves, and ovens, toward the back door. The short thug leaped up onto and over the counters, then landed on the floor in front of Chase as he rounded a series of cooking stations on his way to the exit. Chase pulled out his final ace and yelled in Spanish, *"Ayúdeme por favor. Estos hombres malos están intentando robarme,"* meaning, "Help me. These bad men are trying to rob me."

The Hispanic chefs, already staring intently at the chase unfolding in their kitchen, dropped their skillets and saucepans and quickly surrounded the assailant, jumping on him and pummeling him down to the floor. This was just the diversion Chase needed. He got down on his knees and swept out the pots and pans stored in the open space underneath one of the center counters, thrust his body through headfirst, and landed awkwardly on the floor on his right shoulder. Jumping to his feet, he ran toward the back door.

Webhead was right behind him. He grabbed the top of the counter and hurled himself through the same opening feetfirst, coming out the other side in a full sprint and gaining on Chase, who raced out the back door of the kitchen and into the parking lot with webhead in close pursuit.

Just then, the tall, thin man burst through the swinging kitchen doors. His nose was severely broken, angled horribly to the left, and already a deep purple. Blood had flowed down his face and stained his teeth a dark scarlet. The top of his white oxford shirt was soaked in blood, as were his coat sleeves as he wiped blood off his face. He pulled out a Smith & Wesson M&P 45 and fired off one round into the ceiling. The noise boomed and echoed throughout the kitchen as the employees stopped beating his partner and dove to the floor seeking cover.

The stocky thug stumbled to his feet holding his head as blood gushed from an open wound. The tall, thin man shouted, "Let's go, man! Out the back door. Let's get this guy before he escapes into the night. If we don't retrieve that flash drive, we're dead men."

Leaping over the pile of bodies on the floor, the tall man ran toward the back door. As he looked back at his half-dazed partner, one of the chefs picked up a pan of boiling water and threw it in his face as he turned around. He let out a loud scream as the skin on his face immediately began to blister. A second chef picked up a pan of hot garlic sauce and threw it on the tall, thin man's face. The steaming sauce streamed down his neck, producing second-degree burns on his skin. As he wiped his face and neck with his sleeves and tried to open his eyes, he felt the sharp, excruciating pain of a chef's knife penetrating deep into his left thigh.

Letting out another agonizing scream, he lifted his Smith & Wesson and fired off three more rounds, hoping to hit anybody near him. Then he managed to pull the knife out of his thigh as he stumbled backwards toward the exit, still trying to wipe the scalding sauce off his face and neck. Just before he exited, one of the cooks hurled a small cast-iron skillet, hitting him in his right eye and immediately causing it to swell shut.

Inside the kitchen, the shorter thug stumbled and tried to regain his composure. He leaned against a stainless steel table to keep his balance, knocking pots and pans onto the floor and slipping on spilled sauces and foods that now covered the tile floor. The chefs and cooks once again pummeled him to the ground as two security officers ran into the kitchen. Tipped by hearing the gunshot in the stairwell and having picked up the excitement on hidden eye-in-the-sky cameras, the two security men dressed in dark blue business suits, retired L.A. police in their late-forties, entered the kitchen with guns drawn.

The first to enter shouted in Spanish to the chefs, "Get off of him, *now*." He ran to the semiconscious assailant and rammed the barrel of his gun hard into his thick neck as he tried to stagger to his feet. "If you so much as breathe, I'll blow your freakin' head off," he shouted as he shoved him hard back onto the floor.

The second security officer, gripping his gun with both hands, quickly broke down the kitchen into quadrants and scanned it for the other three, then asked the chefs, "Where did the others go?"

They pointed in unison toward the back door.

He yelled into his shoulder radio, "We have one assailant secured. The other three ran out the back door into the parking lot. Request additional security outside the facility."

Outside, Chase made his way around to the front of the hotel and ran toward the Las Vegas Strip, jumping onto and over luxury cars, SUVs, and limos parked in his way, incurring the wrath of the valet drivers and the wealthy owners.

Chase was losing ground to webhead, now just twenty yards behind. It was midnight and the moon was only half full. He looked for any shadows where he could hide and increase his chances of losing his pursuer. But the lots and valet stations were too well lit and there were still a few dozen guests and hotel employees mingling outside. With webhead closing in, Chase jumped up onto the pedestrian catwalk that crossed Las Vegas Boulevard from the Wynn Hotel to the shops and restaurants across the street.

But webhead was too fast, and Chase knew he wouldn't make it to the other side. A little more than halfway across, he jumped up onto the ledge and looked down at the traffic below flowing at 40 mph. To his right, he could see his rental car parked at a steakhouse on the other side of Las Vegas Boulevard. He considered his options as he looked back, thinking his attacker might not be so tough after all. Then he saw webhead stop and pull out a gun. Chase looked down at the traffic again, saw the cab of a semitruck coming into view in the southbound lanes, and jumped. The sound of three shots echoed through the night as he disappeared from sight.

Chase landed awkwardly in the middle of the trailer with a loud thud and rolled to the passenger side. The driver, hearing and feeling the impact, made a two-lane change to the far right. The lane change caused Chase to roll over to the driver's side of the trailer, his right hand grasping the lip of the top of the trailer as he rolled over the side. The driver looked out his side mirror and saw Chase dangling and bouncing perilously off the side of his trailer. He pulled over to the curb and jumped out of the cab, a tire iron in his right hand and his left hand clenched into a fist.

"Hey, you idiot! What the hell do you think you're doing?" he yelled at Chase.

Two more bullets whizzed by, barely missing Chase, and ricocheting off the pavement a few feet in front of the truck driver. The driver jumped back in the cab, and drove off. Chase dropped to the pavement, cars speeding by and just missing him by inches.

Webhead sprinted down the sidewalk toward him. He must have run back to the beginning of the pedestrian bridge and taken the sidewalk. He was fast—faster than Chase—and he was catching his second wind. Chase had no choice but to run into the oncoming traffic that was flowing freely on Las Vegas Boulevard between Stardust Lane and Country Club Road. He crossed the median and ran straight up the four northbound lanes, weaving in and out of the oncoming cars. His rental car was now a half mile away.

Running down the middle of four lanes, two semitrucks came at him, horns blaring. Traffic split on both sides of Chase and came to a screeching halt. The sound of screeching rubber on asphalt and twisting metal was loud as cars crashed into each other. Chase looked behind in time to see webhead running up to him. Passengers began to get out of their cars and circle around Chase and his assailant. Some were angry and cursing, while others just seemed to be thankful they were still alive.

"Give me the flash drive, amigo, and you can walk away. Or you can die right here. It doesn't matter to me either way," webhead shouted, his blue-and-green web-tattooed head adding a hint of madness to his threat.

Then he pointed the handgun at Chase. The drivers and passengers watching began to disperse, screaming and running to get away. Just before he could fire the gun, the same truck driver whose trailer Chase landed on stepped out from the dispersing crowd and swung his tire iron, connecting with the back of the webhead's neck. The blow knocked the gun out of his hand and sent him sprawling facedown onto the asphalt.

"You son-of-a-bitch. I don't know who's right or who's wrong here, but I'm going to clobber somebody tonight, and I'm starting with you, you freak," the trucker yelled with a thick New Jersey accent and a half-smoked cigar protruding from the right side of his mouth.

There was a brief moment of silence as the crowd began to gather around Chase, the truck driver, and the unconscious webhead lying in the middle of Las Vegas Boulevard. More people stopped their cars on both sides of the median and added to the crowd. Four young drunk men on the sidewalk ran over to the scene and started yelling at Chase. The truck driver began cursing him, too. "What the hell's your problem, pal? Looks like you're the cause of all this mess."

Chase looked around as traffic on both sides of the boulevard was jammed. It was difficult to see exactly what was going on around him as the glare of headlights shone directly into his eyes. But he could hear the once-silent crowd turning into an angry mob.

"Hey, mister," shouted a very angry lady, "I have to be in L.A. tomorrow morning for an important business meeting. Look at my car. The whole front end's smashed."

"I say we beat him senseless," yelled another man as his friends cheered in agreement.

More people began surrounding Chase and closing in on him while shouting and cursing. It was time to exit, but the circle of angry and intoxicated people closed off any avenue of escape.

With pavement around Chase quickly disappearing and an angry mob drawing closer, Chase thought he would have been better off fighting the three thugs in the elevator. Just then, the boom of three rounds fired from a Smith and Wesson M&P 45 echoed through the night. The crowd began scattering in all directions, screaming and stumbling over each other in mass hysteria. People ran across the median, jumped into their cars on the southbound lanes, and sped off.

Through all the confusion in the restaurant kitchen and on Las Vegas Boulevard, Chase forgot all about the tall, thin leader of his assailants with the broken nose. He looked a world apart from the dapper dresser Chase saw in Wynn Hotel. He was half-running up to Chase with one good leg while squeezing the bloodied knife wound on his left thigh, the Smith & Wesson gripped tightly in his right hand. Chase was stunned as he looked at the man's face. He limped badly into the headlights of the tangled mess of cars. His face and neck were badly burned and blistered and his right eye was swollen shut. His nose was grotesquely deformed and his face was so badly bruised and swollen his own mother wouldn't have been able to recognize him. Dark-red bloodstains coated his teeth and his once-white shirt.

He staggered across the asphalt, raising his gun at Chase, and fired off a round that missed by three feet. "I'm going to kill you. Forget about the flash drive. I'm going to shoot you dead!" He fired off two more rounds at Chase as he darted toward the sidewalk, this time the bullets missing him by only one foot.

Chase didn't have anywhere to hide on the northbound side of the street, and he desperately needed to get out of the line of fire. He did the only thing he could do—he ran through the maze of crashed cars and across the median to the southbound lanes where traffic had once again begun to move. He saw the traffic light turn green fifty yards away, and the cars and trucks moved toward him, quickly speeding up to 40 mph.

His pursuer followed. Drivers swerved and honked their horns. The side mirror of an SUV struck the tall, thin man on the side of his head, shattering the glass and knocking him hard to the pavement. He quickly stood back up, but was so disoriented he could not walk between the lanes of traffic. He stumbled across two lanes of oncoming cars toward the curb.

Miraculously, Chase made it to the other side and onto the sidewalk safely. His final pursuer was not so fortunate, however. Chase heard the blaring of a horn, followed by screeching brakes, and then the loud cracking sound of a leg and pelvis being struck and shattered by a large pickup truck. He looked over his shoulder to see his last assailant airborne, flying ten feet into the air over him, and landing in a crumbled heap on the sidewalk. The man was not dead, but Chase knew he would *not* be getting up. He was now free to run back to his rental car. He quickly sidestepped the groaning, mangled body sprawled in front of him, and in less than three minutes, he started the engine and drove southbound on Las Vegas Boulevard toward Interstate 15.

Chase glanced at the car radio. It read 12:47 a.m. in a gold-and-black glow. Removing his hat, he began wiping the makeup off his face with towelettes. Driving past the area where he almost lost his life, Chase looked at the crowd gathering around the tall, thin man lying on the sidewalk. Traffic was still jammed on the northbound lanes due to the cars that crashed, but southbound traffic was moving quickly. He could hear the sirens of police cars and ambulances approaching the scene. A dozen security officers from the Wynn Hotel gathered on the sidewalk trying to put together what just happened. He was certainly glad he asked for a rental car with extra-tinted windows.

Driving past the Venetian, the MGM Grand, the Luxor, and Mandalay Bay, Chase saw that the Las Vegas Strip was alive with life, even on a Sunday night during the off-season. Pedestrians strolled up and down the sidewalks, watching the outdoor spectacles of the fountains at Bellagio, the volcano at the Mirage, and the Treasure Island show. Neon filled the night with every color of the spectrum, and there was no shortage of limos lined up in front of the scores of casinos that dotted the south end of the Strip. Las Vegas was alive with a spectacular nightlife. *New York isn't the only city that never sleeps*, he thought.

He had two phone calls to make. Although Chase was a young, single man who was independently wealthy, he still had accountability responsibilities. First, Chase called his good friend Fred Merrill, in Laguna Beach, Calif. It was Sunday night, and he knew Fred would not be playing in his band. Fred was originally from Detroit and moved to Orange County a few years earlier after selling his interest as a managing partner of a high-profile corporate investigation firm in Chicago. Fred was exceptionally gifted in searching and locating information that other people tried very hard to destroy or cover up.

Fred's girlfriend, Nancy Hudgins, picked up. "Hello," came the anxious voice on the other end. Chase was happy that Fred had met such a nice girl who shared the same interests. At age thirty-five, Fred had confided in Chase he was worried he might never find the right person to settle down and build something special with. But when Nancy recently entered his life, all of that changed.

"Hi, Nancy, this is Chase calling in to let you know that I'm on my way home."

"Chase," Nancy shouted into the phone with relief and excitement, "Fred and I have been so worried about you. Are you okay?"

"Chase," Fred said as he had picked up the extension, "how did it go? Are you leaving Las Vegas?"

"I'm actually on my way to San Jose. Then I'll be driving back to Orange County in the morning. Everything went according to plan. Well, almost everything. Honestly, I couldn't have done this without you two. Thanks again."

Breakthrough

"We're glad that you're okay. Now listen to me, Chase. This is the last time I'm going to do something like this for you. The only reason I crossed the line is because you convinced me that this information could not fall into the wrong hands. I'm officially retired from the business. That's it, my friend. No more."

"I understand. And thanks again, Fred. I'll see you when I get back."

Chase ended the call, and had one more to make. He needed to contact his best friend, Bennie Knowles. Chase had known Bennie since the sixth grade when they attended a private Catholic school in Newport Beach. Feeling sorry for him when bullies pushed him around at recess, Chase came to his aid countless times. Chase was not a tough guy in the bully sense. But he was a martial arts expert at a very young age, and bullies quickly found out that on any day, Chase could hold his own against two or three of them. Chase would take out one bully right away, usually the biggest one, then the second, leaving the third one to rethink about making any move. Bennie recognized Chase's number on his caller ID.

"Chase, I sure hope you're either at the airport or leaving the Las Vegas city limit. How did things go tonight?" Bennie asked with great concern. "Julie and I have been worried about you."

"Julie? Who's Julie? Never mind." Chase looked once more at the flash drive in his right hand and placed it carefully in his jacket pocket. "I'm just entering the 15 freeway now. I should be in San Jose before breakfast."

"I'm glad you made it out alive. But listen to me, Chase. I'm going to hold you to your word. This is your *last* adventure. You finally have a new career, and you need to leave the superhero lifestyle behind you starting right now."

Chase let out a long sigh of relief. He accepted the fact that he needed to slow down and start conducting himself like a responsible adult and begin settling down.

"I will, Bennie. I promise. Once I drop the flash drive off to its rightful owner, I'm on my way back to Orange County to stay. I'll get a good night's sleep and be back at the university before you know it."

"Okay, Chase. I'm going to bed now that I know you're safe. I have a huge meeting with some clients in Irvine early in the morning. I need sleep," Bennie said through an exaggerated yawn.

"I'll only call if something important comes up. Otherwise, I'll see you in a day or two."

"Get a cup of coffee before you leave town," Bennie suggested through another extended yawn.

"I have one and its full strength. I went through a McDonald's drive-thru right before I got on the freeway. Get some rest, big guy. I'll see you soon."

Chase ended the call, sped up to just under 70 mph, and drove toward the California border with a sense of a new day dawning for him even though he still had six hours of darkness ahead. The southbound freeway was alive with the glow of red taillights leaving Sin City as the last remnants of tourists, gamblers, and weekenders made their way back to California and Arizona. Chase was wide awake. His adrenaline was still pumping from the battle, and he had a large cup of hot coffee for the ride. He put his right hand in his jacket pocket and held the flash drive one more time, then took another drink of his coffee and started thinking of the new "normal" lifestyle awaiting him.

Chapter 2
The Professor

THE FIRST MAJOR STORM of the winter struck Massachusetts and surrounding New England with a vengeance. The storm was reminiscent of the Blizzard of 1978 that immobilized the city of Boston for nearly a week. November through January had been mild compared to historical records. Global warming was on everyone's mind, from politicians and end-times prophets to global corporations wanting to "*go green.*" The recent mild spell seemed to support everyone's personal agendas, but this storm challenged their theories.

Despite the blizzard, Prof. Nicholas Fischer left his house at 5:00 a.m., drove his midnight-blue Range Rover across the Harvard Bridge, past Memorial Drive, onto Massachusetts Avenue, and into the Massachusetts Institute of Technology campus in Cambridge. The storm made driving hazardous for the few motorists brave enough to drive on the streets and highways. As he approached the East Garage parking lot, visibility was barely one hundred feet. Fierce winds whipped the snow into a swirling vortex of bitter freezing cold and icy flakes, severely punishing anyone foolish enough to venture outside. The snow was driving hard in all directions, and it was difficult for Prof. Fischer to tell what direction the wind was blowing.

The stiff, unrelenting winds drove the snow against his face as he stepped out of the warmth and safety of his SUV and into the unforgiving elements. The wind blew the snow hard enough to make the skin on the exposed parts of his face red and raw. Running faster than he had in years, he sprinted from his Range Rover to the front door of Eastman Laboratories in Building 6. His cashmere sweater and wool overcoat were no match for the biting cold that easily cut through his clothes and numbed his skin.

Shivering violently and barely able to grasp the keychain from his right coat pocket, Fischer unlocked the front door of Building 6 and quickly stepped inside. He struggled against the wind to shut the door, as if the storm were pursuing him into the lobby to wreak as much havoc inside as it was doing outside. Brushing the snow off his coat, he looked around the deserted and dimly lit lobby. He knew no one else would be there this early and thought the entire campus would probably be empty for the rest of the day, if not the remainder of the week. Fischer looked back outside through the window in disbelief as the fury of the storm increased in its intensity. It was still pitch-black outside and the streetlamps struggled to emit their feeble light through the snow as the storm picked up strength.

Nicholas Fischer was compelled to work today regardless of the conditions. The U.S. Postal Service had nothing on the good professor. He was on the verge of a breakthrough that would not only redefine physics, but the way humankind perceived reality and the very universe they lived in. No snowstorm, no matter how violent and unforgiving, could stop him from moving forward with his discovery.

Nicholas Fischer, or Nicky, as he was known since his youth, was captivated by building blocks, Lincoln Logs, and then, chemistry sets. Although he made friends easily as a child, he was most comfortable playing in the basement with his science projects, mixing chemicals and anticipating their reactions. He was usually correct in his assumptions of their outcomes. Usually. But it was those unexpected reactions that stimulated his curiosity and fed his insatiable desire, his unfulfilled lust to discover and unlock the secrets of the unknown universe.

Fischer possessed two traits that served him well in his quests over the past five decades: knowledge and imagination. He believed that both sides of his brain were in intense competition to outperform the other, to be the first to discover new things, whether physical or metaphysical, and to see how quickly the two could possibly interact with each other.

The storm outside only intensified his anticipation. He interpreted nature's fury as a challenge from a Higher Source that was commissioned to stop him from uncovering a secret hidden since before the beginning of time itself. It was a secret that the Higher Source would only reveal to a worthy soul who, through dedication and self-sacrifice, would use the discovery for the betterment of humankind, and Prof. Fischer believed he was that soul.

To say that Fischer was ambitious is an understatement. He grew up in a lower-middle-class neighborhood of Boston. Although his family of six always had a roof over their heads, clothes on their backs, and food on the table, they had to do without most luxuries. He worked his way through college on his own ticket, a scholarship from Columbia University in Manhattan. He held two part-time jobs and took out a few small loans to get through his Ph. D. degree at the University of Michigan.

But now he wanted more than just the nice house, two new cars in the garage, and college funds for his three children. As a young man, his passion was to lead highly specialized teams researching and developing new technologies and their practical applications. He had countless breakthroughs and patents that were used by corporations and common people that made him a wealthy man. But he was now entering a midlife crisis. He coveted what his peers were now achieving—the fame and fortune at the next level of his professional career.

He had known for more than ten years that he was onto something big—something truly monumental that would change the world and forever secure his name as one of the greatest scientists the world had ever known. His name would be spoken with the same degree of respect that Newton, Galileo, and Einstein had achieved. For ten years, he had overcome obstacles and barriers that would crush most other scientists' careers and suffocate their vision. He lacked the prerequisites one needs in a large New England city—like a family name with credentials. And he faced a blockade of state funding originating from a state senator who did have a family name with credentials. These were the largest and almost insurmountable barriers for Professor Fischer to overcome.

But the winds of change had recently been most kind to the good professor, and he no longer needed the blessings of Sen. William O'Connor III, or the money he controlled. O'Connor publicly ridiculed Fischer often, saying his projects were foolish boondoggles and a waste of taxpayers' money. *Boondoggles, indeed.* Fischer had to laugh out loud at the thought. This was from a man who threw away more money than almost any other politician in state history.

The network of friends and colleagues he had built over the decades was finally paying huge dividends. Gloria Newcombe, a colleague and friend from the University of Michigan with whom he had stayed in contact over the years, was a brilliant physicist and twenty-year veteran at Globalized Dynamics' Infrastructure Unit, specifically the energy and transportation industries. Gloria was deeply involved with their *Green Revolution* initiative, which envisioned a "greener" world where major global conglomerates would act with ecological responsibility while earning large profits for the company and its shareholders. She was assigned the nearly impossible task of finding ways to transport large generators, locomotives, and massive prefabricated building materials around the globe at a fraction of their current transportation costs, and, of course, in a *green* manner.

Fischer and Newcombe had collaborated on numerous projects in the past, but nothing as significant as this current project. Globalized Dynamics had committed a significant amount of seed money to Fischer and his small team of assistants and students regarding breakthroughs in Einstein-Rosen Bridges. Although Fischer knew this was possible and could someday become a reality, he also understood that most people would scoff at this idea out of ignorance and fear of the unknown. Globalized Dynamics, though, decided to roll the dice and for at least one more year keep Fischer and his team funded, all under the watchful eye of Dr. Newcombe.

The latest installment from Globalized Dynamics hit the department's account yesterday morning and Fischer was very anxious to get to work. Inwardly, he mulled over the rumor that William O'Connor III was running for the U.S. Senate. *That man,* he thought, *is a greedy and incompetent buffoon who lives in the past glories of his family's heritage. He throws money away on "boondoggles" like the Big Dig or social programs destined for failure before they leave the drawing board. The man has no vision for the future. He has no vision for the present. He has no vision for change.* Not that any of that mattered now. Prof. Nicholas Fischer would see to it that William O'Connor III never made it to Capitol Hill. He would see to it that he would never practice politics again.

Chapter 3
William the Great

WILLIAM S. O'CONNOR III was a career politician who believed he was God's gift to the world, or at least to the good ol' U. S. of A. He was born and bred to be a politician, and a good one at that. His father, William O'Connor, Jr., was the governor of the Commonwealth of Massachusetts during the 1970s and early-1980s. A beloved and respected leader, he would go down in state history as one of the best governors of the state of Massachusetts. The patriarch of his family, William O'Connor Sr., was a state senator during the 1950s through the 1970s and was still alive and active in retirement. He brought about the history and tradition that began his family legacy that still endured to the present generation.

Upon retirement in 1988, the family torch had been passed from William Junior to "William III," as the media liked to call him. William III had been a state senator for twenty years and had decided that at the age of forty-four, he needed to take that next step up the political ladder while he was relatively young and still had much of his thick, dark, wavy hair. As president of the 185th General Court of the Massachusetts Senate and House leader for the past nine years, most of the political analysts had all but voted him in as the next governor of Massachusetts.

William III, however, had loftier aspirations. He would soon announce his candidacy for the U.S. Senate. He knew the incumbent would not be easy to unseat. But he had a political machine of his own along with his family's legacy. His advisors were confident they could displace the incumbent. He also had the support of his wife and his twenty-year-old daughter, Cecilia. He believed that he could conquer the world if necessary.

On this bitterly cold and dreary Tuesday morning, William III was too excited to sleep in to his normal time of seven o'clock in the morning as he wanted to get an early start on the day. He was to meet with his advisors in his office at the State House on Beacon Hill, hone the strategies concerning his campaign, and set a day when he would go public with the news of his intent to run for the U.S. Senate.

He showered and quickly put on his robe as the frigid air of the incoming February nor'easter storm had already overwhelmed the single-family town house's heater. William kissed his beloved wife of twenty-two years on the cheek, the only visible part of her body that escaped the warmth and security of their down comforter. She started to lift her head to say something, but he gently stroked her hair, and in a deep and seductive voice, tried to croon her back to sleep.

"Thanks for letting me go back to sleep, sweetheart," she said with a soft and sultry voice through a shy smile, peeking up out of the blankets and comforter. "I'll make it up to you at dinner tonight, even if you won't be home until very late."

"I'll eat something on the way to the State House, Helen. You just close your eyes and sleep in."

"I'll slow cook a pot roast for you. I'll even break with your diet and bake a loaf of homemade sourdough bread."

William kissed her on the forehead. "Maybe you could thaw out the frozen peach pie," he suggested.

"Anything for my future senator husband," Helen replied, still smiling with her eyes half-closed.

Last night, William had made up for lost time due to his recent, hectic schedule, and he knew that with his calendar filled for the next two weeks, he would not have another chance to redeem himself for a while. He thought he had better give his beautiful trophy wife a night to remember, and he did. Even at the age of forty-four, William

III felt like William the Great in his bedroom, the living room, the kitchen, and everywhere else their inebriated, entangled bodies ended up throughout that erotically passionate night.

Before falling into a satisfied slumber a few short hours earlier, Helen had promised William she would wake up early and prepare his favorite breakfast: pancakes, Italian sweet sausage, and fresh fruit along with gourmet coffee and cream. However, on this bitterly cold and unforgiving morning, Helen wasn't about to give up the warmth and security of her bed. Instead, she pretended to slip back into a suspended state of slumber. Such are the games couples play when it's too cold to get out of bed.

Helen watched her almost nationally famous husband slip into his pin-striped boxers. She giggled as he slipped his shorts up over his sexy tush and did a little shake for the half-open green eyes he knew were watching him. Helen slipped a hand out from underneath the warmth of the comforter, reached over to the nightstand, and pulled a fifty-dollar bill from William's wallet. She discreetly rolled the bill up and slid it into the elastic waistband of his boxers.

Trying desperately not to laugh at her amorous gesture, William performed a reverse striptease as he dressed himself in one of his many power suits that filled a closet the size of most of his constituents' bedrooms. Such are the games couples play when intoxication lingers from the night before.

Chapter 4
Death of a State Senator

WILLIAM S. O'CONNOR III knew he had to arrive at his office early since this storm threatened to drop as much as three feet of snow up and down the New England coast over the next three days. Skipping his morning workout, William arrived at the State House, the oldest building on Beacon Hill, just past six o'clock in the morning. The bitter cold instantly froze his face as he stepped out of his black Cadillac Escalade, and he wondered if he should have stayed home, gone back to sleep, and waited for Helen to make his pancake breakfast. At least he had the foresight to have a few members of his advisory board, the ones who lived outside of Boston proper, stay at a local hotel so the storm would not prevent them from attending the morning meeting. Rain, sleet, snow, and the advancement of a political career waited for no one.

Flipping his collar up over the back of his neck and bunching his coat as far up his body as he could, William ran from the parking garage to the front door of the State Building. Entering the historical building and passing through the security checkpoint, he took a moment to say a few kind words of cheer to the lead security officer, Sam McGowan, affectionately known for more than thirty years as "Sam the Security Guy" to everyone in the State House. Sam was a wiry man who stood five feet six inches and weighed 168 pounds. But he displayed a hint of a hostile temperament to those who did not know him well, and even at the age of fifty-six, he looked as if he could still win a few bar fights. Sam grew up in the Deep South and served two tours in Vietnam. He met his wife after returning stateside and moved to Boston, where she was born and raised. One peculiarity about Sam was that he always wore sunglasses, even at night.

Since Sam started work at the State House in 1975, there had been a revolving door of new security officers stationed with him. The newest was young, clean-shaven Erik Davis, who was hired a few weeks earlier. Erik, still in awe of his position and the deep history of the State House that sat beneath the golden dome, didn't say anything to the senator when he entered. He merely stood at attention, looking at Sam for cues whether to speak or remain quiet.

"Good morning, Sam. How are things with you and your family these days?" asked the aspiring U.S. senator with genuine concern and enthusiasm. William III was a natural politician, able to network with the local and national power brokers, while still connecting with Joe Constituent.

"I can't complain at all, Senator," Sam replied with a hint of his native Alabama accent. He quickly stood up from his slouched position in his chair, took off his sunglasses, and laid them on the table. "I didn't expect to see too many people come to work today with this weather we're having, especially this early in the morning. What brings you in so early today, Senator?"

"I'm just trying to tie up some loose ends on a few matters, Sam. I can't keep the wonderful citizens of the greatest state of our union waiting for progress to happen on its own."

William genuinely liked Sam. He liked tradition and things that stood the test of time. Sam began working at the State House when William, twelve years old at the time, came to work with his father. William observed his father demonstrating a tremendous amount of respect for Sam. William had come to know Sam well over the years and gave him the respect he would give a member of his own family.

Erik Davis, however, had to earn the right to be acknowledged by the state senator. It seemed there was a new security officer manning the second chair of the security checkpoint every month, and William did not like the constant change. *It's too difficult,* the senator thought, *to conduct business with so much change.* Maybe in a year, Erik would earn the right to be acknowledged.

Walking through the spacious marble-floored corridors of the State House, William looked at the pictures of past governors and other famous personalities in the long, prestigious history of Massachusetts, his father immortalized among the distinguished leaders of the state he so loved and cherished. Massachusetts had a deep and unique history that was unmatched by any other state in the Union. Its heritage was reconstructed in pictures and murals that made its history and contributions speak about complex stories in single images to all those who were graced by its centuries of recorded past. William was always in awe as he walked down the corridor to the elevator. He was honored that his family's name stood among the John Adamses, Benjamin Franklins, John Hancocks, and the Paul Reveres. He was proud to be a citizen of this state and proud to serve its citizens to the best of his ability.

William took his time as he strolled past the Senate Chamber directly below the golden dome. As president and majority leader, his time spent sitting at the rostrum under the golden eagle would soon end another illustrious chapter in his family's history.

He took the elevator to his office on the second floor and settled into his traditional Boss black leather executive swivel chair. His office consisted of five rooms shaped like a cross. He utilized the largest room farthest from the hallway, using the other four rooms as a buffer from the activity and distractions that his office seemed to attract like a magnet. His secretary, Margaret Adams, held down the front office and was his first line of defense. The middle office acted as a small conference room for those private meetings that were better off held away from the larger conference rooms shared by other state legislatures. There were two smaller rooms to either side of the conference room, the room on the left used for storage and the room off to the right held a twin bed, reading chair, and a small table and lamp. Even state senators needed an occasional afternoon nap.

Although a bit smaller than many of the other rooms in the State House, William's were some of the more prestigious and desired offices. His personal office had a rich history and was home to some of the most famous politicians to grace the state. The polished mahogany lining the walls dated from the early 1800s. The desk, guest chairs, and most of the furniture were even older. William took great pride in the historical and traditional décor. He had little interest in the modern makeovers desired by many of his younger colleagues who had paid interior decorators to renovate their offices.

Leaning forward in his high-backed leather chair, William reached across his thirty-day planner to turn on his computer. Then he leaned back in his chair and pulled out the rolled up fifty-dollar bill from his shirt pocket his seductive wife had playfully slipped into the elastic waistband of his boxer shorts an hour earlier. Rolling it back and forth between his fingers, he tried to decide if he would keep it as a keepsake or buy lunch with it. His stomach would dictate the outcome in a few hours. The result would be a formality as large amounts of alcohol and sex the night before made a man very hungry the following day.

After his computer booted up, William started opening his e-mails. Sixty new messages had arrived since he left the office the previous night. This seemed strange to William. Typically, less than ten new e-mails came in overnight, and most of these were spam messages promising him hair he did not need, or a longer penis that he did not need. At least that's what he certainly thought.

He quickly deleted the spam and opened more than a dozen other e-mails, all from different addresses but with the same brief message, *"You cannot put new wine into old wine skins."* "What the hell does that mean?" he wondered aloud. William was a scotch and microbrew drinker with little taste for wine. If not for his wife's preference for finer French wines, there would not be any in his house at all. Continuing on, he opened a dozen more e-mails—all containing the same message, *"You cannot put new wine into old wine skins."*

Being in politics and receiving odd e-mails is part of the business, something every politician has to tolerate. But receiving this many e-mails—all with the same message but all from different sources—startled the senator. A bit shaken, William quickly stood up to regain his thoughts and focus on the morning's agenda with his group of advisors.

That's when he saw the dark, unwelcome figure at his office door wearing a tight black outfit covering the entire body. Glaring green catlike eyes were the only things visible on the intruder, who wore a *shinobi shozoku*, the wardrobe traditionally worn by practitioners of the Japanese martial art of *ninjutsu*.

Stunned at the sight of the intruder, William looked the perpetrator up and down in disbelief. The black head covering was two pieces, a black hood and a black mask tied behind the head. The pants were tied at the knees and the ankles with a piece of thin black cloth. The boots were split-toed. The hands held a sword. The shoulders were relaxed and stretched slightly forward as the sword was held upright at a 45-degree angle. The intruder was in a balanced stance without bias to one side or the other. Upon closer inspection, he could make out decidedly feminine curves on the slight frame. Shaking his head and blinking his eyes, he was dumbfounded someone had sent him a female assassin.

William knew he needed to act quickly. He had always wondered what his thoughts might be if he knew he was about to die. Now he knew. He thought of his wife, naked in bed on a bitterly cold Massachusetts night, with a wine glass in her hand and a glass of scotch in his as he lay beside her. This brought little comfort to William as he quickly shifted back to reality and wondered how this intruder had eluded security. He was even more bewildered as to how she had gotten the sword through the metal detector.

But William wasn't intimidated. He looked the assassin directly in the eyes and said, "I don't know who the hell you are, but you chose the wrong person to pick a fight with."

Dropping the money still clenched in his fist onto his desk, he reached for his .38 Ruger that he kept strapped to the underside of his desk. The dark figure struck with blinding speed, taking two leaps to cover the distance between the office door and the large desk, then pounced onto the top of the desk in a strike position. Feeling only the aged leather strap dangling underneath his desk, William realized the intruder had already removed his main line of defense. His backup plan, yelling for help, quickly disappeared as the assassin struck with her right foot into his throat, crushing his larynx into his esophagus, and slamming poor William the Not-So-Great back into his chair.

William couldn't talk. He couldn't breathe. Shocked, he could only sit and look up into the unblinking sea-green eyes staring at him out of the slit of the mask. Plan C was simple enough—run for help! But as soon as William sprang out of his chair and tried to run around the right side of his desk, the assassin leaped onto the floor in front of him and planted her right foot into William's left knee, crumpling his breathless body onto the plush red-carpeted floor.

Bred to be a quick thinker and make snap decisions, William could not grasp what was happening to him in these fifteen seconds, but he did know that he was about to die. He could not protect himself, he could not yell, and he could not run. *Hell*, he thought to himself, *I can't even breathe.* William understood his killer had no intention of negotiating. Again, he thought of Helen and her warm body lying alone in the comfort and safety of their bed, and how she would react to the news of his death.

Reality quickly set in as William stared up at his killer. The soft, tight skin surrounding the still-unblinking eyes was the only clues to her identity. William looked the menacing figure up and down, noticing the curves that formed around her breasts and hips. It was hard for him to grasp his killer was female. That, along with the excruciating pain, blunt trauma, and lack of oxygen almost caused him to pass out.

Finally, the assassin spoke. "I'm not going to tell you who I am. But I will tell you that I'm going to kill you because you have been thwarting the progress of a new breakthrough that will usher in a new era in Western civilization, which will rival anything in the annals of history. You should not have interfered with Professor Fischer's projects. Now you must die, as you've become an obstacle that needs to be removed."

The assassin, with the softest and most graceful of footsteps, circled around William as he lay on the floor, placing one foot over the other in a side-to-side manner while holding her sword over her right shoulder. William quickly ascertained that his killer, with her catlike features and mannerisms, wanted to play with her prey before killing him. William, never one to back down from a challenge, wanted to play too. He reached out with his right arm, trying to grab her behind her left knee and throw her on her back.

But she anticipated the move, even posing in a stance with her left leg in front of him, daring William to make the move. He did, and she struck with her sword in a swift, arcing motion, severing his arm just above the elbow in one smooth, quick slicing move. As a swooning dark gloom began to overtake his consciousness, William decided the only thing he could do was to leave clues as to whom his killer was. He tried to direct the flow of blood streaming from his severed arm in such a way that the assassin would step in it and leave footprints. Footprints that would leave clues of her foot size, weight, and height. Footprints that would show what direction she took after she left his office.

But once again, she anticipated his action, sidestepped the senator, and planted her left foot on his shoulder to steer the flow of blood away from her and the senator. In the same movement, she grabbed William's head and twisted it 180 degrees. The snap was loud yet short, and then it was over. William's heart stopped pumping, and the blood flow from his severed arm slowed to a trickle.

The assassin placed her sword—with its twenty-six-inch double-edged blade—back into the scabbard strapped to her back. Walking around to the front of his desk, careful to avoid stepping in any of the senator's blood, she leaped onto its surface and created a new e-mail on his computer. She typed a quick line then clicked the send icon. Noticing the rolled up fifty-dollar bill lying next to the mouse pad, she picked it up, rolled it playfully across her fingers, and placed it in a small pocket on her right thigh.

Her work done, she moved silently to the senator's small bedroom from where she came and knelt down in the middle of the floor. She pulled out the small silver suitcase she brought with her and hid underneath the twin bed. She opened it and programmed a few coordinates into the keypad. Laying the suitcase on the floor, she took two steps back, picked up the original black suitcase she used to bring her there, and held it tightly to her breasts with both hands. Within a few seconds, a corona of bright orange-and-yellow light appeared in front of her. She took a deep breath and boldly stepped directly into the luminous aureole as if she were walking through an entryway into another room. In a moment, the encircling ring of light and color disappeared, and the assassin and the black suitcase were gone.

Chapter 5
The Office

ON THE START OF YET ANOTHER beautiful day in paradise, Chase woke early to enjoy the sunrise making its way over the canyons and mountains to the east and shining its rays on a new day on the West Coast. He jogged along the beach as he had recently begun to do a few mornings each week. However, on this particular day, less than a half mile into his run, he came upon a group of Asian tourists engaged in tai chi and stopped to join them.

After twenty minutes, the group finished its routine and Chase walked the rest of the way back to Main Beach in Laguna Beach, where he had parked his car. He enjoyed watching the town awaken from its slumber. He found few things in life were more interesting than the different and unique nuances in human behavior displayed by every person. Chase was convinced that if he hadn't become a physicist, he most likely would have become a psychologist.

It was Tuesday, and already the promise of a new day radiated fresh hope in Southern California. Having lived on the East Coast for extended periods with his parents and siblings, Chase knew what winter could be like in February. He loved cities like New York and Boston, but he would forever spend his winters in beautiful, sunny Southern California with its deep blue skies and balmy weather.

Breakthrough

Driving down Coast Highway with the top down on this clear and sunny morning, Chase felt like this day was created especially for him. He had three things going for him. First, he was getting back into shape after a year of physical inactivity. Second, he was excited to continue his controversial and interactive lecture regarding potential breakthroughs in Einstein-Rosen Bridges with his students at the University of California-Irvine later that morning. Finally, he had a date with Susan Anderson. Susan was one of the most beautiful and intelligent girls that Chase had ever met. He hadn't seen her since high school, and even then, he hadn't known her very well. He remembered she was attractive and kept her appearance simple. She was the quiet type who made school her highest priority and social interactions a distant second.

Chase met and became reacquainted with Susan at a party the previous week at a mutual friend's house in Newport Beach. She was definitely what you call a "late bloomer." They talked and immediately formed a bond. Her radiant smile, her self-confidence, and the way she carried herself was too much for him to walk away from at the end of the evening.

Continuing south on the highway, Chase was confident and excited about his immediate prospects. He was content that he had achieved everything he wanted to accomplish by the age of twenty-six. He had left his previous life of adventure behind, begun a new career as an associate professor of physics at a local university, and struck a new relationship with a girl he honestly believed he could settle down with and build something special. He wondered what could possibly go wrong with the scenario.

After taking a detour home for a quick shower and change of clothes, Chase drove north on Coast Highway toward Newport Beach. He looked at all the magnificent new million- and multimillion-dollar Mediterranean-style, red-tiled roof houses in Crystal Cove that dotted the landscape. There were thousands of them on the hills on the north side of the highway that, just a few short years ago, were empty fields of grass and wild flowers. He wondered how young couples could afford to move into the area and buy homes.

Making a right onto Newport Coast Drive, Chase passed Pelican Hill Golf Course and Resort. He knew he had to take up his friend

Bennie Knowles' offer to play a couple rounds of golf, have a few beers, and eat steak and shrimp at the clubhouse until they burst at the seams. Continuing along the snaking, six-lane boulevard, he ascended the steep hill in his silver Mercedes-Benz SLK350 hardtop convertible while barely shifting into third gear.

Passing five-star resorts and impeccably manicured landscapes, Chase reached the top of the hill where inland Newport Beach, Costa Mesa, Irvine, John Wayne Airport, and the UC-Irvine campus opened up to him in a beautiful sweeping vista. The San Gabriel Mountains on the horizon were capped with a fresh new layer of white snow that descended below the 4,000-foot level due to the recent storm that dropped three inches of rain along the coast and twenty-four inches of snow in the mountains. It was a crystal clear day and the air was still crisp and cool since the sun hadn't kissed Orange County yet.

Chase crossed over the San Joaquin Hills Toll Road, made a right on Bonita Canyon Road, and entered Irvine. Making a left on Anteater Drive, the namesake of the local college sports teams, he entered the campus from the south. How the school adopted the name Anteaters was still a mystery to him, as anteaters are not indigenous to the area. He felt foolish for not knowing this and was too embarrassed to ask anyone. For the hundredth time, he made a mental note to put this on his to-do list.

Chase was amazed at how quickly Orange County had developed. Bonita Canyon Road was under construction, being widened from a sleepy two-lane road to a busy six-lane boulevard. New housing, dorms, and university buildings were going up left and right. How times were quickly changing. He remembered driving with his father through Irvine when he was a child, seeing mile after mile of orange groves and strawberry and lima bean fields.

Now Irvine didn't have any crops to boast of. Chase missed the way things were, but he also embraced the rapid and hurried change and the opportunities and new discoveries that were approaching seemingly at the speed of light—discoveries not just at UC-Irvine, but at other universities, corporations, and governments around the world. He had access to many things that were happening domestically and globally, things that he should have knowledge of and some things that he probably would be better off not knowing about.

UC-Irvine is a diverse campus, not only in the nationality of its students but particularly, in its cutting-edge discoveries in nanotechnology, biological sciences, chemical and biochemical engineering, and especially physics. These were the areas that Chase excelled at as a modern-day reverse archeologist, seeking out opportunities and discoveries of tomorrow, and discovering them just a bit earlier than anyone else.

Chase held a Ph.D. in physics and astronomy from UC-Irvine, and as an associate professor at the School of Physical Sciences, he was lecturing for a professor who had fallen ill. Entering the Physics and Astronomy building, he stopped to talk to a few of the students who were also arriving and on their way to get a cup of coffee before his class. He arrived at his office at 8:30 a.m., giving him thirty minutes to sort through his e-mails, return phone messages, and check up on the day's latest headlines before lecturing in front of eighty-seven students regarding Einstein-Rosen Bridges and some of the obstacles to breakthroughs facing science. Chase was well prepared for his discussion. He had spent the past ten years studying wormholes and was excited to continue his lectures that he began on Tuesday and Thursday mornings.

Sitting in his small but comfortable office, he poured his remaining Starbucks coffee into a UC-Irvine mug and warmed it up in a little black microwave he kept on top of a filing cabinet. He didn't have the catchy phrases that other people have on their coffee cups, magnets or picture frames like *"Caffeine isn't a drug, it's a vitamin!"* However, some of the wisest words he had ever heard came from a song, and he had them printed, matted, framed, and posted on his office wall:

You've got to know when to hold them

Know when to fold them

Know when to walk away

Know when to run

These words of wisdom got Chase out of countless bad situations throughout his life, and he knew that they would continue to do so countless more times.

Just then, his cell phone rang, jarring him out of his thoughts. It was Bennie Knowles. Chase knew Bennie was going to ask him to lunch at the Pelican Hill restaurant.

"Bennie, what's up, big guy?" Chase asked as he scrolled through his e-mails and sipped his reheated coffee.

"Are we on for lunch today, Chase? I really want you to see this place. This is one of the best courses and resorts you'll ever come across. The north nine looks out over the bluffs onto the ocean. Terrific sunsets, too. I know how much you like your sunsets. It's like a bent dick, Chase. You can't beat it."

"Ha ha ha." Chase tried not to laugh but couldn't refrain.

"Trust me, Chase, this is exactly what you need to help you transition to a more domesticated lifestyle. Remember, you promised no more traversing the globe and chasing down new adventures."

"I remember, Bennie. I'm happy with my new position here at the college and the prospects of settling down."

"Speaking of settling down, are you still going out with Susan tonight? She's so hot."

"Yes, I am. We'll talk more at lunch. I have to get ready for class, Bennie. See you in a few hours," Chase said, still grinning at Bennie's immature comment. Chase had heard Bennie use that line countless times, but it always seemed funny the way he said it.

Chapter 6
The Lecture

BY THE TIME CHASE walked to the front of the class, his students were already talking about the murder of Sen. William O'Connor III 3,000 miles away. Although the family had been notified of his death, the news was not yet public. But details of the event had been picked up on police scanners and were quickly posted on Internet blogs. Text messaging further spread the story across the country. Chase made a mental note to follow up on the story as soon as class ended.

He walked out on the stage in a pair of dark slacks, a dark-blue pullover collared shirt, and a charcoal-gray sport coat. He rarely wore a tie and never brought one to work. He did, however, have a tie hanging from a thumbtack pressed into the wall of his office for emergencies. To date, he had experienced no such crisis that would warrant him wearing the uncomfortable nuisance.

"Okay, let's get started," he began as he slowly paced back and forth across the stage. He liked to move around when he lectured, rather than sit at a desk or stand behind a podium. He preferred to make use of the entire wall of chalkboards during his lectures, rather than use an overhead projector, writing complex equations as he progressed through his lecture. He also encouraged, and, at times, demanded that his class of eighty-seven bright and gifted undergraduate students in applied physics participate in lively discussions. He accomplished this by making a full twenty percent of their grade dependent on attendance and class participation.

"Last Thursday, we left off in the middle of a heated argument regarding certain applications of the space-time continuum—more specifically, the potential and practical application of Einstein-Rosen Bridges, or wormholes, as people today like say. To reiterate, the term 'wormhole' gets its inspiration from the idea of a worm traversing from one side of an apple to the other side. The idea is that if a worm could tunnel through the apple to the other side, then a shortcut would be established. In the same sense, a wormhole through the space-time continuum could theoretically allow matter, including people, to be transported through a hole from one point in the universe, such as Earth, to another point in another universe, such as a planet that could support life in a distant galaxy."

Victor Villanueva started the debate, as he usually did every class, by standing and posing a question that challenged the instructor's premise. Victor came from extreme poverty, growing up in a small town of less than 100 people in the middle of the Sonora Desert in southeastern California. Victor earned his way into UC-Irvine on a scholarship. He used hard work, a few published articles on applied physics and astronomy in major publications, an innovative mind, and one of the highest IQs on the campus to gain acceptance into the physics program.

"Professor Manhattan, aren't these theories and concepts just that—theories? It's been ninety years since Einstein proposed his general theory of relativity and Hermann Weyl propagated the concept of wormholes. Why haven't there been any breakthroughs in the area of wormholes? We've split the atom, and we have the ability to destroy the earth's surface thousands of times over. Yet, still no breakthrough in wormholes. Why not?"

"Thank you for getting us started, Victor. First, Einstein's theory of general relativity supports the possibility of wormholes. Many theorists today believe that wormholes already exist, only on a subatomic scale. They theorize that it is possible to identify and enlarge these existing wormholes and make them stable enough so that they will not collapse when matter, including people, travel through them. But that's the tricky part—making the wormholes stable so that they will not collapse and destroy whatever is passing through. But you're still young, Victor. You may yet live to see the breakthrough and the practical use of wormholes in your lifetime."

A student with long brown hair streaked with blonde and wearing sunglasses, who Chase wasn't even sure was paying attention, stood and asked, "So, how does this all work? I mean, how can a wormhole exist or be created?"

Chase thought this guy would have to do more than ask a generic question to pass his class. He addressed his answer to the entire class. "Theoretically, Einstein said that if it is possible to distort space and bend it, it is also possible that space can be folded in half. When space is folded in half, it is possible to punch a hole in both sides of space, thus, creating the shortcut, or wormhole, to travel from point A to point B almost instantaneously."

A girl in the front row named Erica asked, "What can be used to bend or fold space? To bend space for time travel would require a tremendous amount of force and energy, right, Professor?"

"That's right, Erica. Bending space for time travel would require a source of tremendous energy and power, such as objects with great mass, like a collapsing star. But even a planet the size of Earth rotating around the sun can bend space."

"And that brings us to gravity. How does gravity factor into the equation, Professor?" asked a brilliant and very imaginative young Asian girl who looked like she shouldn't have a driver's license, yet, as a senior in high school in Oceanside, Calif., could pick any college she wanted to attend.

Chase thought of answering the question, but decided to ask his class to elaborate. "There are four known forces in our universe: electromagnetism, strong nuclear force, weak nuclear force, and gravity. Can anyone tell us how gravity relates to and affects the space-time continuum?"

Raymond Sutter, a tall and lanky eighteen year old with curly red hair from the Inland Empire, responded, "I remember one of my high school professors had us take a sheet, fold it in half, and then loosely hold it horizontally. A guy from the football team then dropped a football in the center, causing the two halves to come in contact with each other. Another student then dropped a golf ball onto the sheet, and the ball rolled into the indentation that the football made in the folded sheet."

Chase added, "It was the mass of the football that caused the indentation in the sheet. Gravity, according to Einstein's general theory of relativity, results from the curvature of space caused by energy and mass. It is the gravity that we experience that draws the golf ball to the indentation in the sheet caused by the mass of the football."

The next question was expected. JuliAnna Sommers, a freshman from Downey High School, just outside Los Angeles, asked, "What about time travel, Professor? Is it theoretically possible to travel back and forth in time? Can a person go back five years and change events that they regret?" The question received a chorus of laughter from the other eighty-six students, as they imagined the possibilities that would create.

Chase had performed due diligence on the topic and was current with what the foremost theorists on wormholes thought about this topic. "Again, although the existence of wormholes has never been proven, Einstein's Theory of Relativity supports such an idea. Theoretically, wormholes can traverse both space and time, although many theorists today believe time travel is not possible, at least, not as we perceive it. If a person were able to use a wormhole to go back in time, he would actually end up in another universe that is similar, but certainly different and separate from ours. He may be able to change events in this parallel universe; however, he would not be able to change events in his own particular universe. In other words, people could not travel back in time and meet themselves."

JuliAnna continued the argument. "But isn't it true, Professor, that astronauts actually travel to the future when they go into outer space?"

"That's true. While the Newtonian theories have evolved into the current dominant cosmological theories, such as quantum physics, we find that there are two concepts of time. There is internal time and external time. In our own personal world, internal time and external time parallel each other—they coincide. However, a time traveler experiences a significant difference in internal and external time. Newton said that time is singular and uniform throughout the universe, whether you were experiencing time on Earth or in a distant galaxy. Yet Einstein, influenced by Ernst Mach and his theories on the development of mechanics, challenged Newton's consistencies of time. He said distance and time are not absolute. They are influenced by motion and mass, and that is where the difference resides."

The student with long, brown, blonde-streaked hair and sunglasses interjected, "This is what Einstein referred to as time dilation."

Chase wondered if perhaps he had been paying attention after all. "Time is relative to space. However, if you were able to travel as close to the speed of light as possible, or 185,999 miles per second, the clocks on your ship would actually slow down while time remains constant here on Earth. So if you travel to our closest star, Proxima Centauri, at 4.3 light years, spend three weeks orbiting the star, and then return to Earth at the same speed, your onboard clock would slow down and record that you had been gone only 24 days, 4 hours, 9 minutes, and 28 seconds, while in actuality, 8.66 years on Earth would have passed.

"So, theoretically at least, an astronaut could travel in space for a specified period of time at a fraction of the speed of light. How closely the astronaut travels at the speed of light would determine the amount of elapsed time here on Earth, which could be seconds or centuries. But at this point and time, the subject of time travel can be filed under gedanken experiments.

"But it is possible to travel in time, right?" asked a student in the third row.

"According to Einstein, the problem with time travel is that as you approach the speed of light, objects increase in size, so much so that they can ultimately become infinitely massive. So even if time travel is possible, it is not practical."

"Unless some of the laws of physics are broken," interjected a young man from the back of the auditorium.

"That's right," Chase responded with a smile. "And that's where wormholes enter the realm of possibility. Even if it is not practical to travel back and forth in time, we could, theoretically, use wormholes to travel in space from point A to point B, almost instantaneously."

The conversation between Chase and his students continued for the next ninety minutes. He tossed his lecture notes aside and allowed the students to dictate the direction of the day's lecture with their questions and responses. Some were skeptical and outright hostile to the idea of wormholes, while others passionately took the view that a breakthrough could be imminent and happen at any time, even during their lifetime. After more heated discussion, Chase glanced up at the clock on the wall which displayed 10:58 a.m. He had two minutes to wrap up his lecture.

"Okay, in summary, wormholes, or Einstein-Rosen Bridges, are theoretical, hypothetical, topological, short-lived, stable, thin constructs created as needed. They are temporary, spherically symmetric static flux tubes that have two mouths, or portals, and stretch between two points, and traverse space and time. But it's important to understand that wormholes do not break matter down into particles or subparticles. Rather, they transport matter as a whole.

"We'll pick up this thread again on Thursday. So read your books and be prepared for another two hours of controversial material. See you all then." Chase deviated from his normal routine of talking to students after class and made his way back to his office, where he could go online to read about the terrible news coming out of Boston regarding the death of one of Massachusetts' state senators.

Chapter 7
Pelican Hill

CHASE MET BENNIE in the parking lot of Pelican Hills Golf Club, south of downtown Newport Beach, on his way home to Laguna Beach. He arrived early at 12:45 p.m. and Bennie, as usual, was late by about fifteen minutes, which made the time 1:15 p.m. when he finally arrived. Chase strolled around the front of the clubhouse, taking in the size and the stunning beauty of the new resort that was still expanding. He thought to himself, *Just when I thought Orange County could not accommodate another new five-star resort, somebody comes in and one-ups everyone else.*

Bennie pulled up in his silver BMW 6 Series convertible, cruised around the parking lot once trying to look as cool as a slightly pudgy, slightly short, and slightly balding twenty-eight year old could. Top down, sunglasses on, right hand on the wheel, and left elbow resting on the driver's side door, Bennie hoped that somebody—anybody—would notice him as he circled in front of the clubhouse. Unfortunately for Bennie, everybody who was going to be at the clubhouse was already seated for lunch. His hopes dashed, he parked toward the back of the lot in the middle of three open parking spaces, because he was always afraid somebody would open their car door and dent his Beamer.

Bennie, still wearing a suit with a yellow power tie, walked briskly up to his friend. "Chase, glad you could finally make it. What's it been—almost a year since my first invite?"

"This place looks great, Bennie," Chase said in an almost sedated tone, turning in a 360-degree circle. "I had no idea how beautiful the scenery is here."

"I know that you're more into the scenery than the ambience, prestige, and the women, Chase," Bennie exclaimed with an excited look of anticipation on his face that only a successful supersalesperson could display when he was about to close a deal. Bennie sold commercial real estate in south Orange County, and he could sell a toothbrush with only one bristle on it to a dentist if he had to. "But, wait until you see the rest of this place. I have a golf cart reserved. We'll take a quick tour around the course and then come back for something to eat. Sound good?"

"I'm ready, Bennie. I think I'm really going to like this place," Chase responded as they stepped onto the path leading toward the golf shop.

They picked up the golf cart at the pro shop just behind the clubhouse. Bennie did the driving. It took him a while to make the rounds since Pelican Hill stood on 504 acres of prime Orange County real estate on both sides of the coastal highway. The grounds were a classic, five-star sanctuary reminiscent of classic northern Italy. Bennie first drove Chase around the new 204-room resort and 128 custom villas that were still under construction. Signs were clearly posted *Construction Vehicles Only*, so Bennie and Chase incurred the wrath of a few hard hats as they drove through. Next, they headed down the paved paths toward the links on the coastal side.

The Ocean North Course itself resembled the classic Scottish links that meander along an elevated plateau. Chase looked out on spectacular views of the Pacific Ocean and Newport Harbor to the north. The clear blue skies, temperate weather, and calm seas of sun-sequined water brought out dozens of sailboats that dotted the China-blue expanse up and down the coast.

The design incorporated the beauty of the natural landscape into a course that was unparalleled in its magnificence. Expansive two-, three-, and four-story residences lined the bluffs facing the ocean. They would capture the magnificent sunsets over the Pacific horizon. The Ocean

South Course was a challenging 18-hole, par-70 course that featured arroyos and bluffs as part of the scenery. After impressing Chase with one of the most stunning and beautiful golf courses on the West Coast, Bennie drove the cart back to the club restaurant.

"Take a look at this, Chase. The golf carts are equipped with laser range finders, and an onboard computer displays the distance to greens and hazards."

"I'm really impressed, Bennie. Sign me up."

"Now, let me show you the club restaurant. The food is absolutely terrific. The surf and turf is on me, my friend."

Driving to the clubhouse and looking in the windows at the dressed-up patrons, Chase replied, "Is there somewhere else we can go where we can get a sandwich and a couple of beers? I'm not in the mood to sit with this type of crowd today."

"No worries, Chase. We can sit on the patio, eat a couple of roast beef sandwiches, and drink Newcastles on tap," came the reply Chase wanted to hear.

Bennie took off his tie and unbuttoned his top two buttons. "Okay, now I'm dressed for the patio."

Sitting out on the patio, Chase never tired of looking at the ocean, listening to the surf crash against the rocks, watching surfers, or observing tourists who were just as fascinated at seeing the beach for the first time as he was at seeing it every day. He had seen the sun rise and set over the four corners of the earth. Traveling with his parents throughout his childhood to every continent except Antarctica, he had witnessed more daybreaks and twilights from the twenty-four time zones than just about anyone else living today.

Chase lived very close to the ocean, although he was on the inland side of Coast Highway. On stormy nights, he could hear the waves crashing against the cliffs. On balmy summer evenings, he watched the sun set over the Pacific on its path to the Hawaiian Islands and points beyond, painting a swirling picture of bright orange, pink, yellow, purple, and red, and creating a different scene every night. Nature kept Chase in daily suspense, and he always wondered what masterpiece it would paint for him next.

Sitting at a small, round white table looking out onto the azure-tinted Pacific, Bennie asked, "What do you think of the Angels this year, Chase?"

"The Angels are looking good, Bennie. We'll definitely go to some games. I already have my calendar cleared for when the Tigers come roaring into town."

A young, pretty waitress, close to six feet tall with her blonde hair pulled back into a ponytail, approached their table. It was obvious she knew Bennie.

"What can I get you two today? Sorry, but trouble is *not* on the menu, so don't even *think* about asking."

"Two Newcastles on tap, sweetheart. This is my good friend, Chase Manhattan. That's right, Chase Manhattan," grinned Bennie.

Smiling at Chase and showing a little more cleavage than she probably should have, she winked and said, "I'll be right back with your beers, guys. Don't go away."

"So what do you think, Chase?" Bennie grinned. "Can you see yourself in a place like this?"

"Bennie, I'm sold. This place is great. I can see myself playing eighteen holes this Thursday. Are you going to be around?"

"Maybe. It depends on this deal I'm working on with the guys at Irvine Spectrum. But I should be able to make it. Maybe we can make it a foursome with them."

"Sounds great, Bennie. Go ahead and set it up." Chase didn't play a lot of sports. He liked to shoot baskets in his driveway and loved watching live baseball. But he did take golf seriously, usually playing once or twice a week.

The blonde waitress brought the Newcastles and Bennie ordered the sandwiches. Never one to shy away from an ice-cold beer, Bennie chugged three large gulps. Dabbing his mouth with a cloth napkin in a mockingly sophisticated manner, he said, "Can you believe the weather those poor schmucks on the East Coast are having? Holy shit, Chase. They're already waist-deep in snow, and it's so cold that the pickpockets are sticking their hands in strangers' pockets just to keep their hands warm."

"It's not so bad," Chase retorted. "I like the snow. I don't care for the freezing cold and the wind, but I love a good snowstorm."

"Well, better them than us." Bennie took a few more gulps from his beer and smiled. Leaning back in his chair, he looked at Chase with one eye open and said, "Now, tell me all about Susan. She's *so* hot, Chase! She's really filled out. Remember in high school how skinny she was? Do you think she's had implants?"

"Easy, turbo," Chase replied as he sat straight up and finished his Newcastle. "This is just a first date, that's all. I have reservations at Ti Amo in Laguna Beach, then we'll go see Fred's band at the Marine Room Tavern. Maybe a walk on the beach, too, if it's not too cold."

"Going from the penthouse to the outhouse, Chase? Ti Amo is fancy schmancy. But the Marine Room Tavern? Well, what can I say?" Bennie chuckled, motioning to the blonde waitress for two more Newcastles.

"It's not that bad, Bennie. It's a great place to hang out and have a few cold beers. The people are a good mix, and the bands are great."

"Whatever. Hey, maybe I should tag along in the background—you know, incognito. I can give you an honest assessment of Susan that you may not see right away."

Chase laughed. "There's no such thing as incognito with you, Bennie. No thanks, 'Mom.' I'll be okay."

Chapter 8
Rendezvous

BACK IN BUILDING 6 at the Massachusetts Institute of Technology, in a rarely used storage room that was part of Professor Fischer's labs, a brief corona of orange-and-yellow light appeared. A body miraculously stepped out of it and into existence. Out of nowhere. Out of nothing. The assassin's body simply appeared in a millisecond, standing erect, her sword strapped to her back.

Barely containing his enthusiasm, Nicky quickly ran around to the other side of the table he was standing behind and up to the figure. Glancing at his watch, he said, "Great time, honey. Just over twenty-eight minutes. How'd it go? How do you feel? Mission accomplished?" Taking the black suitcase from her right hand, he gently laid it on the table as if he were putting a newborn child down to sleep. He then picked up the silver suitcase that was used to bring her back and laid it beside the black suitcase.

Pulling off her black hood and mask, she spoke with an excited smile, her entire face lighting up, accentuating her sea-green eyes, nearly perfect white teeth, high cheek bones, deep tan, and beautiful blonde hair cascading down past her shoulders. Mesmerized by her exquisite beauty, Nicky watched her movements unfold in slow motion.

"That was fantastic, Nicky. It's the experience of a lifetime. I'll never get over the feeling of being in one place one moment, then instantly being in another place the next. It's hard to explain, but I felt a sensation of euphoria and elation. I honestly felt what seemed like an awareness of bliss that awaits us on the other side. It was almost as if I had passed through an angelic host along the way. But it's great to be back, Nicky," she said, her eyes still beaming with excitement. "And yes, mission accomplished."

Nicky, a scientist by nature, was not a religious man. He knew his accomplice wasn't religious either. However, he paused for a moment to think about the sensations and feelings that she was communicating to him, and he made a mental note to follow up on what she might experience in future trips through wormholes.

"I'm so glad you're back," he said with genuine concern. Circling around her while looking her over, he noticed a number of items that made the journey back with her. Incriminating items such as strands of brown carpet that lay on the floor by her feet where the wormhole opened up. Dust particles were on her shoulders. And, of course, there was the senator's blood on her sword. Nicky carefully picked up the carpet threads with tweezers, placed them into an envelope, and put the envelope in the inside pocket of his jacket. He then began dusting off her shoulders with the palms of his hands.

"You have everything you left with. Sword, two knives, and all the items of your clothing. Very good." Nicky spread his arms out, breaking into an enormous, triumphant smile. "I'm so proud of you. I couldn't be more pleased right now. Were you able to send off the e-mail?"

"I sure did. Right before I came back. She should be there right now, picking up the transporter suitcase."

Nicky couldn't be happier. This was even easier than he had anticipated.

"I need to clean my sword right away, Nicky. And we need to dispose of these clothes." Taking off her two-handed Ronin sword that hung over her shoulder, she walked over to the deep, shop-style sink and ran hot water. "You should have seen his face when he looked up from his desk and saw me standing in the doorway with my sword drawn," she continued, running hot water over the steel blade while looking over her right shoulder, an effervescent smile stretching from ear to ear.

"He didn't know what to think. O'Connor kept a .38 under his desk that I removed and placed in one of his secretary's desk drawers. Of course, that was the first thing he reached for. The look on his face when he noticed it wasn't there was even more priceless than the first one!"

Nicky was laughing now. "How long did you have to wait for him to arrive?"

"Only about twenty-five minutes. After that, it only took a few minutes to complete the mission and then transport myself back here."

"It was a huge risk," Nicky acknowledged. "But knowing that he was coming in early this week was most helpful. By the way, we owe Khyati a steak dinner for hacking into his network and supplying us with that information. And the snowstorm couldn't have come at a better time. This town is basically shut down and will be for a few more days."

Taking off all items of her *shinobi shozoku* and placing them gently, almost ceremoniously, in a laundry bag, she put on clean clothes, including a new cashmere sweater Nicky bought her to celebrate the occasion. "Khyati's a Hindu, Nicky. She won't eat a steak."

"Oh yeah. Right. We'll take her out for a salad. Anyway, you look terrific, babe. That pink sweater makes you look so hot."

"I'm wondering if you bought this more for your benefit than mine," she said, looking directly into Nicky's eyes, placing one hand on her hip in a most seductive manner.

"Guilty as charged," Nicky said with a boyish grin while reaching out and delicately holding her hands. "Now let's get out of here and find someplace to have breakfast. I'm starving. Jimmy's Grill never closes. Let's go before we're snowed in."

"Jimmy's Grill? Sweetie, my stomach is growling, too, but that's not doing anything for me at the moment, lover boy."

Standing on her tiptoes, she reached up and wrapped her arms tightly around Nicky's neck, pressing her authentic, non-enhanced breasts firmly against his chest. She had no need for anything artificial on her finely-tuned, athletic, twenty-three-year-old body.

"Why don't you give me a little celebration jiggy, *then* we'll talk about breakfast." She was only five-four and Nicky stood at six-two.

Breakthrough

Running her hands all over his dark-blue turtle neck sweater and down to something more easily accessible, she grabbed both sides of Nicky's buttocks and gave them a tight squeeze, causing him to jump.

"Okay, just a quickie, though. It's not a good idea for us to stay here," Nicky easily relented. "Jimmy's Grill can wait."

Chapter 9
Breakfast at Jimmy's

INSIDE THE SAFE HAVEN of Jimmy's Grill, Nicky and his accomplice, Staci Bevere, were the only patrons in the restaurant. He picked at his veggie-cheese omelet. "How can a little thing like you eat so much food? Country-fried steak *and* eggs *and* toast *and* a large stack of pancakes? I mean, eventually, all this junk food is going to catch up with you."

"Do you want to race me across the parking lot?" she challenged, looking up from her three plates of food with a hint of assurance that he would not accept.

"No. You'll beat me. But this is today, and tomorrow is right around the corner. You have to think ahead and plan accordingly."

"Not to worry, Nicky. The day I eat a salad is the day you'll find me in an old folk's home," she said, stuffing another forkful of pancakes and blueberry syrup in her mouth. After pausing briefly to chew her food, she continued, "How old do you think she is, Nicky?"

"Her hair looks natural. No gray roots. She has strong, shapely legs from years of waiting tables and possibly dancing in her younger years. Her breasts still look somewhat firm. But her face and her voice seem aged. Too much partying at low-rent bars, I bet. I'd say she's in her early forties, but she looks more like she's fifty-five."

"Twenty dollars says she's fifty-five."

"You're on, and as usual, you'll lose."

"The law of statistics is working in my favor, Nicky. You'll see."

Looking around the deserted diner and at the lone waitress who snapped her gum loudly while staring out the window at the accumulating snow, Nicky felt comfortable enough to talk about upcoming events.

"I'm excited about the next phase of our project," he said, leaning in while lowering his voice. "This storm has been a blessing for what we needed to do today. But our next mark will be a little more difficult."

Swishing the last remaining forkful of pancakes around in the blueberry syrup on her plate, Staci smiled with anticipation. "I'm sure you'll work out the details, Nicky. You're smart and careful. As long as her receiver suitcase is operable, you can leave the rest up to me," she said as she wolfed down the last of her pancakes.

"I'm just not sure if we should do it at her lab or at her home. They both carry substantial risks. There will be people at both locations that we'll have to work around."

"I'd prefer to do it at her home."

"I think the better option is at her lab. Thanks to Khyati, we know her house is always full of people. Her husband quit his job and is always home. Her son and daughter usually have their friends over after school. Then there's the housekeeper and the three barking dogs," Nicky said, now cupping his chin in his right hand, elbow on the table.

"Globalized Dynamics has sophisticated security," she retorted. "Either way, it's going to be a difficult task. Maybe we can catch her somewhere between home and work? This time of year it's dark when she's coming and going to her job. Perhaps we can find an opportunity then."

"Maybe. But I really need you to bring back that receiver suitcase. We know she keeps it with her at all times. Take out Dr. Newcombe and bring back the receiver suitcase. That's all you have to do."

"What about the security at Globalized Dynamics? What about the cameras and the guards?"

"You would be fully clothed in your *shinobi shozoku*."

"But the cameras will be able to tell I'm a female, Caucasian, how tall I am, and how much I weigh." Staci stirred her straw in her glass of Coke. She was mimicking Nicky with her chin cupped in her right palm, her elbow resting on the table. "This is the only way I see it happening. We have to know when she's in her office alone. That's it, Nicky. I can't be running around a lab full of people with a sword, chasing a screaming woman."

Nicky paused for a few moments and sighed. "I don't know how I can accomplish that. Maybe you can infiltrate the lab, kill Dr. Newcombe, and then run to the office and ..." Nicky's voice trailed off. "That's a stupid idea. OK, we'll just have to find a way to know when she's in her office alone. Let me think about it, sweetheart. We'll work out the logistics and bring you back safely, I promise. Rosie should be here soon. Finish up and let's head out to the truck."

"Are you sure you don't want some of my hash browns, Nicky?"

"I'm sure. That would be like eating French fries. They're just sliced and diced potatoes cooked in grease. No, thank you."

"Suit yourself. Aren't you going to finish your omelet? I think I see a few more veggies in there," she said in a playful, mocking manner.

"I'm not even sure this is real cheese," Nicky said, still picking at his omelet with his fork.

"Do you think Rosie will come peaceably, Nicky? I don't believe that she'll get into the truck with us."

"I doubt it. She's no dummy. She's seen a lot of things in her life, and I'm sure she just wants to give us the suitcase, take her money, and walk away."

"I anticipate she'll be packing one, maybe two guns. An automatic pistol for sure."

"It sounds simple enough. She hands me the suitcase, I give her the $100,000, and when she reaches her hand out to take the sack of money, you reach over to my window and shoot her. Use the .22 and shoot her in the eye. Then we'll throw her in the back of the cab and dispose of the body in the usual way. No mess, no fuss, no muss."

The pretty, young, blonde graduate student from MIT finished her Coke with a loud slurp through her straw, loud enough for the waitress to hear, who then walked over to the table and, looking at Staci's empty plates asked, "You want dessert too, sweetie?"

"I'd like to have a slice of blueberry pie, but we need to get going."

Breakthrough

Since she had introduced herself when she sat Nicky and his lady friend at their booth, Nicky started the conversation with their waitress that would decide the outcome of his friendly little wager with his lady friend. "Gladys, is this restaurant going to stay open all day?"

"Honey, we never close. And how the hell am I going to drive home in this mess? My car is half buried in snowdrifts. I've been here all night, and I'll be here all day, because I doubt anyone will make it into work today to relieve me. It's just gonna be me and a cook. I don't expect many customers, so I plan to drink lots of coffee and finish a couple of paperbacks I brought with me."

"Can you tell me something, Gladys?" Nicky asked sweetly and in a respectful manner, pulling out a roll of cash from his pocket and laying a couple of twenties on the table. "Could you please tell me how old you are?"

Gladys, still popping her gum, locked her eyes on the roll of cash and responded, "Honey, I'm the same age as Jack Benny."

"You're thirty-nine, Gladys? Thirty-nine is what Jack Benny told people he was on his thirty-ninth birthday—and again on the next forty-one birthdays after that." Nicky pulled another twenty from his roll and laid it on the table. "How old are you *really*, Gladys?"

"Honey, I'm forty-two, going on forty-three next month."

Nicky stared directly into Staci's eyes and smiled.

Not to be outdone, Staci pulled her wallet from her purse and laid another twenty on the table. "Gladys," she asked, "can you show us your driver's license, please? You'll pardon my skepticism, but I'd like to verify your claim."

Staring at eighty dollars more than she expected to earn on the day shift, Gladys replied, "Sweetie, I'll be back in thirty seconds." She ran to the other end of the cooking station, made a sharp left, and disappeared down a hall past a hanging sign saying Restrooms and Telephones.

"I assume the employee entrance to the backroom is down that hall," Nicky said.

"Well, duhhh," came the reply.

"Double or nothing?"

"No," she said as she accepted defeat, dropping her chin again into her right palm with her right elbow resting on the table.

Twenty seconds later, Gladys bolted out from the same hallway waving her driver's license.

"Read it and weep, sweetie," Gladys shouted, still only halfway to their booth and looking directly at Staci. "Your honey won the bet."

"One more question, Gladys. Did you ever dance, and if so, where?" Nicky asked, still holding out his roll of cash.

"I danced at bars. You know, biker bars and stuff."

Nicky laid two more twenties on the table before Gladys could hand him the bill. "Thanks, Gladys. Hope you have a nice day."

"You too, hon! Thanks for the tip." Gladys grabbed the money with one swipe of her hand and walked away, leaving the dirty dishes on the table.

Nicky stood up with a big smile on his face, walking toward the front door. "Knowledge of human behavior once again triumphs over statistical analysis."

"I don't know how you do it, Nicky, but for a physics geek, you sure do have a gift for predicting behavioral traits in people."

Stepping out the front door and directly into a blast of freezing cold wind, Nicky led the way, forging a path through the drifting snow to the parking lot in the back. Running to Nicky's four-wheel-drive Ford truck, they passed by a lone car in the parking lot, a dented and rusted 1988 Ford Taurus half buried in a snowdrift.

"That must be Gladys's car," shouted Nicky through the wind. "Like Gladys, her car has seen better days." He could hear Staci laughing out loud through the blustering wind.

Chapter 10
Rosie

ANGELINA CABRERRA WAS AN IMMIGRANT from Colombia and proud to be in the United States. She had left a life of poverty, murder, and a small town run by a drug cartel. At seventeen, she had made her way to the United States the old-fashioned way. She stole enough money to pay "coyotes" to smuggle her across numerous borders and finally into San Diego, where she still had enough remaining money to obtain a stolen Social Security number and other forms of personal identification. Within fifteen minutes, Angelina Cabrerra became Rosie Contreras. Working menial jobs at hotels and restaurants and as a nanny, Rosie migrated across the country before winding up in Boston.

Rosie worked hard. She rarely called in sick and was never late for work. But at thirty-three, Rosie believed she needed to make that one big hit, that one big score, which would put her ahead of the game. She was also very beautiful. Unfortunately, her good looks never translated into that big break she so desperately wanted.

Rosie never made more than twenty dollars an hour and at that rate, she had little to send back to her family in the small mountainside town of La Barinas just outside of Cali. Living in the United States was expensive. Most of her earnings went for taxes, rent, food, utilities, and a reliable car. Whatever was left, which wasn't much, was split between going out and having a good time with her friends and supporting her family in Columbia.

But just last week, Rosie's big day finally arrived. She was approached by a pretty, young, blonde woman with a proposition for that "one big score" that would allow her to pay off her bills, send money to her family, and clear a significant amount of cash. Working at the State House on Beacon Hill did not pay much and the people did not treat her nearly as nice as her employers had in other cities.

Rosie accepted the proposition. All she had to do was place a little black suitcase in the senator's side office where he took his naps, and open it in the middle of the floor in the early hours of the morning while she was picking up the trash. Then, she had to pick up a similar silver suitcase as soon as she was text-messaged. Sure, the sight of the senator lying on the floor, missing his forearm with his head twisted halfway around his body was gruesome. But Rosie had seen much worse in Colombia. And in San Diego, Kansas City, Chicago, and Buffalo. Much, much worse.

Rosie trudged through snowdrifts and braced against brutal winds gusting to more than 100 mph whipping snow in her face. Her legs and back ached as she lifted her right leg and then her left out of two feet of wet snow, repeating the process over and over. The windswept snow blasted against her face with a sting that turned her skin red. The temperature was well below freezing. The windchill factor was below zero. In fact, it was so cold that no one cared what the temperature truly was. But the parking lot for Jimmy's Grill's was less than a mile from the State House, and she would make it there. Rosie was one tough lady. Yet it was days like this when her small hometown in Colombia didn't seem so bad after all.

Approaching the yellow-and-red sign for Jimmy's Grill that began to emerge out of the swirling wind and snow, Rosie gripped her Browning Hi-Power 9mm in her right hand. There were thirteen rounds in the clip and one in the chamber. Rosie also had a Smith & Wesson model 1006 10 mm loaded with a nine-round single-column magazine in her left coat pocket for backup. She thought this would be plenty of protection against "Blondie" and whoever else she might have to take down, if necessary. Rosie wasn't naïve. She knew people don't just hand over large amounts of money without there being some risk involved. But she also didn't want any trouble. She just wanted to trade the suitcase for the cash, retrace her steps to the West Coast, and disappear with another false identity.

Rosie took off her gloves so that she could get a better grip on her two pieces of protection. She held the two handguns flat against her body, pointing down at a 145-degree angle. She also wore an extra-large coat, having cut the stitching at the bottom inside corners of the pockets so she could quickly aim her guns and shoot without having to pull her hands out of her pockets. This had worked for Rosie on a few occasions in the past. She had practiced this maneuver thousands of times in front of the mirror over the years. After all, a young, single, and pretty immigrant girl all alone in this world needed to be able to protect herself.

Taking a deep breath, she walked around to the back parking lot. Rosie didn't see the four-door, black Ford Super-Duty four-wheel-drive truck through the snow until she was about fifty feet away. Approaching the driver's door, she stopped and smiled at Nicky. She released the Smith & Wesson handgun, took her left hand out of the coat pocket, reached into the large handbag strung over her right shoulder, and pulled the silver suitcase out by its handle with her left hand, holding it up for Nicky to see.

Staci immediately understood what was happening. Rosie was carrying handguns in both pockets. In this freezing cold, that could be the only reason she was not wearing gloves. Per Nicky's instructions, she made a point to notice if she was right- or left-handed when they met initially. She knew that in her right hand, Rosie held a gun in her coat pocket.

Nicky reached out the driver's window and took the small silver suitcase, opened it and quickly inspected the contents. With a return smile, he handed Rosie a small, brown paper sack with $100,000 in twenty stacks of fifty crisp, one-hundred-dollar bills. Staci waited for Rosie to open the sack and glance at the contents. Rosie obliged, and with blinding speed, Staci raised the Glock 22 with both hands. In an instant, a well-placed bullet entered Rosie's left eye, ricocheting inside her head like a pinball, and finally coming to rest in her parietal lobe.

Rosie stood for a few seconds before dropping to the ground in a lifeless heap. Somehow, she managed to fire off three rounds—the first in response to the Glock 22 appearing seemingly out of nowhere, and two more as the result of a muscle spasm as her body went into shock a few seconds before her brain flipped the "off" switch on her life.

Staci was so quick with her Glock that Nicky didn't have time to move his head. The sound of the discharge was deafening inside the cab of the truck and temporarily sent Nicky diving for the floor. Then came the three bullets that entered the truck's cab, barely missing Nicky's head as Rosie tried to raise her Browning in defense.

With Rosie still twitching in a three-foot snowdrift, Nicky and his accomplice jumped out of the truck, opened the driver's side back door, and threw Rosie in headfirst on her back. Then Nicky grabbed the sack of cash, jumped back in the truck, and pulled out onto Congress Street, driving toward I-93.

"At least the streets were plowed a few times this morning. Even though there are still a lot of big drifts, we should be able to dispose of Rosie with no problem," he said, shaking his head and rubbing his right ear.

"Do you think anyone heard the shots, Nicky?"

"I wouldn't worry about it. Boston's a ghost town this morning, and the wind is howling loud," he replied, sticking his pinky into his ear, his head still ringing from the sound of the 22 going off next to it.

Staci turned around and looked at Rosie on the floor of the backseat. The black spot where her left eye had been was leaking a little blood. Nicky had taken the necessary preparations to lay a sheet of plastic on the floor and covering the backseat.

"She's dead alright. No mess, no fuss, no muss. And her head is still intact."

"Nice shootin', Tex."

Staci saw a little smoke protruding out of the hole in Rosie's right coat pocket where the three rounds came from. "Now let's see what poor Rosie was carrying for protection."

"Put your gloves on," said a quick-thinking Nicky. "Remember, no fingerprints on anything or anybody."

She twisted around and leaned into the backseat, pulling black rabbit, fur-lined leather gloves out of her coat pockets and putting them on. Reaching down to Rosie's left pocket, she pinched the cuff of the sleeve and lifted up her right hand. The Browning Hi-Power 9mm was still gripped tightly in her fingers. Staci wrestled it free, laying it on the floor in the front seat.

Reaching back again, she pulled Rosie's left hand out from her pocket and found the Smith & Wesson model 1006 and laid it next to the first gun. Giving Rosie a quick pat down, she didn't find any more weapons.

Staci turned around in her seat and looked at Nicky with a broad smile, as if she had just won an Olympic medal. "I didn't even need to lean over to your side. Did you see that Nicky? I drilled her from my side of the truck."

"You're the best," said Nicky, smiling while rubbing her thigh. "Take that freezer bag in the glove compartment, place both guns in there, and slide it under the seat. We'll have the Guu dispose of these later."

Chapter 11
The Detective

The "Beast of the East," as the media affectionately called the storm, was whipping down hard on northern New England, already dropping more than two feet of snow and building snowdrifts at least twice that high, bringing Boston to a virtual standstill. MIT resembled a modern-day ghost town set in one of the most progressive metropolises in the world. There was virtually no traffic on the streets and only a few brave souls dared venture out on foot.

The body of William O'Connor III was found at 6:45 a.m. by Jeffrey Hayden, a constitutional lawyer as well as the assistant executive director of O'Connor's election campaign. Jeffrey, a married man and father of three young children, almost threw up his ham and cheese croissant at the sight of the pale, blood-drained corpse lying on the floor. Running back to the only people he saw in the building, Sam, the security guy, and the new guy whose name Jeffrey had already forgotten, he sprinted past the elevators and ran down the stairs to the first floor. Jumping three or four steps at a time, almost tripping twice, Jeffrey raced down the corridor to the two security guards, managing to spurt out the words through searing lungs that the senator had been brutally murdered.

Breakthrough

Without going up to Sen. O'Connor's office for verification, Sam immediately dialed 911. Looking at Jeffrey's face and demeanor, Sam did not need visual confirmation of the senator's death.

Sam reached the Boston Police Department on nearby Sudbury Street and was connected to Capt. Det. Reginald Cherry of the Bureau of Investigative Services, Homicide Unit. Cherry, a twenty-two-year veteran, was sitting at his desk eating some of the few snacks that were left in the vending machine. He wrongly anticipated that the McDonalds drive-through would be open on the way to work.

"Damn snowstorm," he grumbled aloud as he leaned back in his chair and shook a bag of Fritos into his mouth, washing it down with a Coke. Cherry had promised his wife Lonya that he would lose ten percent of his weight, eat better, and join a gym. Cherry was still a tough guy, one of the toughest on the force. But at forty-four, he did not look anything like his picture on the first day on the job, the same picture that Lonya made him keep in his wallet for inspiration. Cherry stared at the folders of paperwork from his current cases and yelled to anyone who was listening, "I'd better not have to go outside in this freakin' storm today. It's colder than shit out there."

Like clockwork, Cherry's phone rang twenty seconds later. After listening to the voice on the other end, he leapt out of his chair, shouting into the phone, "I'll be there in a few minutes—don't touch anything," with a deep authority that demanded compliance, even over the phone. Running out of his office and down the hall past Officer Rebecca McKinsey as he put on his thick, bronze-colored coat that accentuated the brown tones in his skin and matching gloves, Cherry grabbed the keys to one of the station's four-wheel-drive Ford Explorers. He shouted to McKinsey to call his partner, Sgt. Det. Robert Vasquez, to meet him at the State House.

Seeing the frantic look on Cherry's face as he ran by, Officer McKinsey stood up and yelled, "What's happening at the State House, Cherry?"

Looking over his shoulder while straightening out the collar of his coat, not missing a stride, he yelled back with a booming voice, "There's been a murder. Just get Vasquez over there now!"

Jumping into the dark-blue-and-white Explorer, Cherry sped the short distance through the snow-swept streets to the State House, staying in the center of the streets to avoid the newly formed snowdrifts that were emerging from the curbs. "Good thing the plows are out in force this morning or I'd be jogging to the site," he said out loud. He didn't need to turn on his police lights or siren since the streets were deserted. Pulling up to the front of the State House, Cherry parked along the red-painted curb and ran up to the entrance. Already winded by the time he reached the top of the front steps, Cherry understood Lonya's concern for his health.

Two more of O'Connor's election team members had arrived at the State House, Executive Director Linda Mullins and public relations specialist Rodney Zuckner, were with Sam and Jeffrey Hayden just inside the front door. All were visibly shaken and upset, especially Mullins, who ran up to the scene of the crime after Hayden told her the terrible news. Zuckner had his arm around Mullins' shoulders, trying to comfort her.

Cherry stepped up to the huddled group and introduced himself. "I'm Capt. Det. Cherry from the Boston Police Department. Can someone please tell me what happened here?"

Sam stepped forward and addressed Cherry. "I'm Sam McGowan. I'm the lead security officer here and the one who made the 911 call. These people are part of Sen. O'Connor's advisory team. This is Jeffrey Hayden, Linda Mullins, and Rodney Zuckner," he said, pointing clockwise to the three. "My partner, Erik Davis, is upstairs securing the crime scene, making sure no one enters O'Connor's office."

"Sam, take me to the senator's office, please," said Cherry as he took a few steps into the entryway.

"I can't do that, sir. One of us has to stay here at the security checkpoint and Davis is already upstairs," replied Sam.

"Okay then, Sam, give me a quick rundown on what happened this morning and I'll go up myself."

Sam replied, "Sen. O'Connor arrived early this morning around five o'clock. We spoke for about a minute. You know, small talk. He's a great guy and everyone liked him. The senator went up to his office through the corridor and up the elevator. Then Mr. Hayden arrived just after seven o'clock in the morning and took the same route to the senator's office. A few minutes later, he ran back down the corridor yelling to me that Sen. O'Connor had been murdered."

Breakthrough

"Did you go up to the senator's office, Sam?" asked Cherry.

"No sir, I could tell by the look on Mr. Hayden's face that he was serious. I immediately dialed 911. Then I told Davis to go up to the senator's office and make sure no one entered it. Mrs. Mullins and Mr. Zuckner arrived together just a few minutes after I made the call."

"Did anyone else enter the building or go into the senator's office?"

"Just Mrs. Mullins. As soon as Mrs. Mullins and Mr. Zuckner entered the building, I told them that they would have to wait here and that the senator had been killed. Mrs. Mullins ran past me so quickly I couldn't stop her. She also ran past Davis upstairs and went into the senator's office. Davis brought her back downstairs. Then you arrived." Sam inhaled deeply. He had said all that in one long breath.

"Sam," asked Cherry, "are there any other people in the building? Has anyone left in the past few hours?" Cherry was not sure if the killer had actually left the building and wanted to know what to expect when he went to Sen. O'Connor's office.

"There are maintenance people here and it's possible some of the evening cleaning crew are still here as well. I'll check the log and see who has come and gone overnight and this morning," Sam volunteered.

"I'm going up to the senator's office. My partner, Robert Vasquez, will be here shortly. Sam, have him join me as soon as he arrives. And do not let anyone else enter or leave the building. Now, how do I get to his office?" asked Cherry.

"I'll take you there, Detective. It's right this way," Hayden said, walking down the central corridor and waving to Cherry to follow.

Det. Cherry thought Hayden was as good as anyone to begin questioning about what just happened since he was the first to see the murdered senator.

"When did you arrive here, Mr. Hayden?" asked Cherry.

"Shortly after seven o'clock this morning," he replied.

Cherry look directly into Hayden's eyes as they took the stairs to the second floor and asked, "Why so early, Mr. Hayden? It seems a bit out of the ordinary, especially on a day like today, when the entire city is practically disabled by the storm."

Hayden paused to gather his thoughts, then began to explain his relationship to the state senator. "Now that the senator is dead, I guess it's okay to tell you that he was planning to run for the U.S. Senate this fall. I am the assistant director of his advisory board. Linda Mullins downstairs is the executive director. Mr. Zuckner is our PR specialist. One of the reasons we were meeting today was to decide on a time for Sen. O'Connor to go public with the announcement."

"And you were the first person to find Sen. O'Connor dead in his office?"

"That's right, Detective." Hayden dropped his head as they he spoke, recalling the events of the morning.

Arriving at the top of the stairs, Cherry was already winded. It didn't seem so long ago that he was able to sprint up two flights of stairs without breaking a sweat. "Did you touch the senator's body or anything in his office?" asked Cherry.

"No, Detective, I did not. I approached the office, saw the light on through the sanded glass on the door, knocked twice, and entered. The first room is his secretary's office, and I announced myself as I walked through it and then opened Sen. O'Connor's inner-office door. It was then that I saw the senator lying on the floor and … and … his …" Jeffrey Hayden's voice trailed off as he recalled the initial sight of the murdered senator. Cherry could see that Hayden was disturbed about the murder and that he was visibly shaken.

Eric Davis heard the two approaching and stepped into the hallway. Cherry thought he looked like he was fresh out of high school "This way, guys," the young security officer motioned. "I've never seen anything like this before."

Cherry still did not have all the details of the murder. He wrongly assumed Sen. William O'Connor had been shot. He pictured the senator slumped in a big leather chair with a tiny hole between his eyes and half his head blown off the back of his skull.

Walking through the secretary's office and into O'Connor's office, Cherry saw the corpse. The upper half of the body was exposed and visible from the door and the lower half was hidden behind the desk. He lay in a pool of blood on his left side facing away from the door, but his head was twisted 180 degrees so that his face looked directly at Cherry, eyes wide open. Lying on the left side of the office floor, half of a severed arm was still in the sleeve of the navy-blue blazer. Cherry looked back at the corpse, noting it was missing half of the right arm.

Cherry had seen a great deal of gruesome corpses in his twenty-two years on the force—mob killings, gang killings, murders of passion, suicides, car accidents, and accidental deaths. But this time he was shocked to see the senator lying dead in his office. Cherry wondered if he died like this or if the killer had posed the body.

Quickly gathering his composure, Cherry turned around and looked at Davis and Hayden asking, "Have either of you touched the body or anything else in this office?"

"No sir," they both answered in unison.

"Both of you, please step out into the hallway. I'm securing this area as a crime scene and no one is to enter this office." Cherry spoke into his police radio to Officer McKinsey back at the station. "Listen, McKinsey, Sen. O'Connor has been brutally murdered in his office here on Beacon Hill. I've secured the office. We need a crime scene unit and the ME over here right away. And Rebecca, let's be discreet about this. No sirens."

"Right away, Detective. What happened over there?" she asked with a sense of urgency.

"I'll give you more details later. Right now, I need to take a quick walk-through of the building to see if I can find anything or anyone connected with the murder. Have you gotten ahold of Vasquez yet?"

"He was just leaving for work when I called him a few minutes ago. He said he'll get there as quickly as he can, weather permitting."

"Listen, Rebecca, I also need you to find out Sen. O'Connor's address and send a female officer to his house to break the news to his family. If he lived close enough to the station, maybe you could go over there yourself. You can take one of the Blazers."

"I'm on it, Detective. Let me know if you need anything else."

"Davis," snapped Cherry as he ended the call, "I need you to stand in the hallway at the front of the secretary's door. Do not let anyone into this office, including yourself." Cherry's voice boomed with a level of authority that made the young security officer stand at attention as if he had been in the military for a lifetime.

"Yes sir. You can count on me."

Capt. Det. Reginald Cherry quickly walked the hallways of the State House on the second floor, then made his way to the first, making notes of the elevators, staircases, windows, the back entrance, and fire doors. Working his way back to the front door, Cherry looked outside at the growing intensity of the storm. He could not see the street through the blinding blizzard and fierce winds, nor could he hear the two police cruisers pull up behind his Explorer. But he could make out the sounds of four car doors slamming shut.

"Sam," Cherry said, "the State House is now officially a crime scene. No one is to enter or leave the building until I say so. The police officers will take over controlling the front entrance and O'Connor's office. I need your help to round up any maintenance and cleaning people that may be in the building. Davis, too."

"Yes sir."

Det. Cherry didn't think that Sam had anything to do with the senator's murder, but he would check him out anyway as they made their way through the State House.

"How many cameras are in the building, and where are they positioned? I need to know if all entrances and exits are videotaped as well as Sen. O'Connor's office. We have to be able to identify anyone who could be considered a suspect or suspects."

"Yes sir. I have been here for thirty-eight years. I know the security system inside and out. But I'll be honest with you—hundreds of people enter and exit this building every business day. Someone could have conceivably entered the building yesterday and hid somewhere overnight."

Cherry glared at Sam in astonishment. "Are you kidding me? This is a secured government building. How could something like that happen?"

"We cannot possibly verify that everyone who enters during the day leaves the building, Detective. A person could hide in a number of places: a vacant office, a bathroom stall, a closet. Lots of places."

"Doesn't security sweep the building?"

"We sure do, sir. Davis made several rounds during the night. He's trained to take his time and investigate anything out of the ordinary. Sometimes we have a third security guard on duty at night to help, too. However, the Park Rangers that have been assigned as additional security have not arrived for their shift yet."

Cherry sighed deeply. He wondered if the murderer was already miles away at this point.

"Okay, Sam, let's start with the maintenance and cleaning crews," Cherry said.

"Yes sir. I can check the schedules, sign-in logs, time sheets, and video of all paid employees entering and exiting the building since last evening. We'll find anyone who is still in the building, sir."

Chapter 12
Getting Old

TAKING HIS SECOND SHOWER of the day, Chase wondered about what Bennie said over lunch. Susan had indeed filled out nicely since high school. Maybe she did have implants. But that didn't matter to Chase. He tried to look beyond a woman's external appearances to the character she displayed. Only then did he look at the outward appearance to see if she had the discipline to take good care of her health while applying modest amounts of makeup to enhance whatever God-given beauty she had been graced with.

Chase hadn't seen Susan since high school, but met her at a mutual friend's party in Newport Beach the previous weekend. He knew Susan from as far back as junior high when they shared a few classes together; math class and social studies, if he remembered correctly. He had French class with her in tenth grade and a biology class when they were seniors. He remembered that she was very studious but not too talkative. She was thin but attractive, and she carried herself with a high level of self-confidence that guys found even more attractive. He remembered talking with her a few times, but they were more acquaintances than friends.

Drying off and stepping into his bedroom, Chase looked at himself in the mirror, trying to give himself an honest assessment of his physical, mental, emotional, and spiritual well-being. He recently read in a men's health magazine that men reach their physical peak around twenty-six or twenty-seven: from then on, it was all downhill. It is also the age where many men figure this out and begin to settle down, going out less with the guys, getting married, having children, and taking their careers more seriously. This is where the graph in the article started to taper off, a slow but steady drop from a lifetime of rising and raging hormones to one of decreasing vitality.

Chase, at barely twenty-six years young, sighed as this reality began to settle in for the first time in his life. His body was lean and devoid of excess fat, but he wasn't pumped like a lot of guys at the gym. Chase was built for speed and agility rather than brawn, but he was strong and had endurance. His stomach looked like a washboard and his arms were well-defined, without the lumps and bumps of a bodybuilder. Chase Manhattan stood six-one and weighed 180 pounds. Overall, he, like Susan, had filled out nicely since high school.

Putting on a pair of boxers and khaki cargo shorts, Chase walked over to his 75-gallon saltwater aquarium, opened a bottle of fish food from the stand and fed his fish—a clown fish, two yellow tangs, assorted basslets, dwarf angelfish, and miniature purple lobsters. He bought the setup a few years back from a local pet store, but soon realized how much work the upkeep was on a saltwater tank. So he paid one of the neighbor's boys twenty dollars to do it for him, leaving Chase only the responsibility of feeding them every day. He loved his fish and watched them swim in the glow of the tank's light every night as he fell asleep.

He went downstairs and plopped down on the sofa to watch ESPN highlights. No matter how hard he tried, he could not get that article out of his mind. He thought about settling down and having children. He thought about finding the right woman to domesticate him.

Susan certainly seemed like the right person to spend the rest of his life with. She was pretty, smart, well-respected in the community, and very successful in her career. Chase vaguely knew her parents from a few local charity events and fundraisers that he was involved with over the years, such as Race for the Cure and CHOC, the Children's Hospital of Orange County. He even spent time with her younger brother, Derek, a few years back with a group of guys he golfed with.

Drinking some bottled water, he hoped he hadn't eaten too much at lunch with Bennie. He was feeling a little tired from getting up so early, running, the tai chi, and the lecture. The beer didn't help either.

Chase sighed at the thought of major changes in his life and becoming more responsible the same day he went out with Bennie and ate and drank a little too much.

Just getting up off the sofa, he could feel the fatigue in his legs, something he only recently experienced. He then dressed for his night with Susan, grabbed his keys, and jumped into his Mercedes. As he drove down Blue Bird Canyon Drive to Coast Highway, his mind was racing a mile a minute. He needed these two hours before picking up Susan to think things through.

Driving towards Dana Point, Chase continued to assess his life. He had accomplished more things than most would in a lifetime. He had traveled the world with his parents, earned a graduate degree in physics, and was now teaching at a major university. Looking back, he was very happy with his accomplishments.

But looking forward, he had little vision. Although he wanted to continue his personal and professional development, he just didn't know which direction to move in. Chase had three siblings who he saw a few times a year. They were close in many ways and stayed in touch via e-mail and telephone calls. But he still believed that he was somewhat alone in this world. His brother, Scott, lived with his wife and three children in Phoenix. Debbie, his older sister, had recently left Orange County for the Silicon Valley with her husband and three children to head up a new venture capital firm. His younger, recently-married sister, Theresa, moved to Seattle with her husband. His parents were gone now, and that left Chase as the sole remaining family member in Orange County. He was also the only one who was not married.

Chase had a vacuum in his heart, a deep hole he needed to fill. He didn't like being alone, and when his younger sister moved away last month, he realized for the first time that he needed to make certain life decisions to transition from a free-spirited bachelor to a responsible adult needing to look for that one soul mate with whom he could share his life, dreams, and raise a family.

Yet, he was scared at the prospect of beginning that metamorphosis on his own. He knew he was extremely fortunate to run into Susan again after all these years. She was the "real deal" and Chase was determined not to squander this opportunity. He knew he had to get serious about his life. He *wanted* to make things work with Susan and move forward with her.

Chapter 13
First Date

SUSAN ANDERSON LIVED in Dana Point, which bordered Laguna Beach to the south. Dana Point, a town of about 35,000 people, has one of the few harbors in Orange County, making it a popular destination for surfers, tourists, and locals.

Chase's Hunter 450, named *No Worries*, that he bought new last year was moored in the first of the town's two marinas, even though he only took it out about once a month at the most. It was a small boat compared to the other 2,500 sailboats, fishing boats, and yachts moored at the harbor. He could have afforded a larger boat, but he learned years ago from his father that bigger isn't necessarily better when it comes to boats.

Most who own large vessels do not take them out enough to justify buying them, unless they have money to burn. Chase noticed every time he went out to his boat or walked around the marina that many boats remained moored at the docks. It seemed that the main purpose of most of the boats was for the owners to throw parties while docked at the marina, not for ocean use.

He didn't see the need to buy a boat for hosting parties. In fact, he rarely had more than four or five people at his house for a barbecue or swimming in his pool. His preference was to be invited to other people's houses and boats for parties so *they* could do all of the work—the cooking, catering, and cleanup.

But sailing was still his passion. He had been sailing since he was a youth. His parents owned a number of sailboats when he was growing up. He and his siblings had learned early on how to work together as a team to prepare a sailboat, take it out to sea, and return it safely.

However, the demands of being an associate professor at UC-Irvine were taking their toll on his leisure time. Chase found himself devoting more of his time and energy to his new career than he ever imagined when he was hired last year. But he didn't mind the demands that seemed to grow and multiply weekly. He loved what he was doing with his life now. He had worked very hard to achieve this position. His life now had some structure and stability that provided meaning and purpose, and he was throwing himself headfirst into his new career.

Chase decided to kill the two hours by walking through the marina and looking at the vessels moored there. He could walk up and down the marina looking at the assorted sailboats and fishing boats for hours. He never grew tired of the clever names people gave their boats. There were close to fifty shops and restaurants lining the marina and he could always find a good cup of coffee to take with him on his walks. On an average day at the harbor, he returned for at least one refill, if not two or three.

Chase made his way over to Dana Wharf Sportfishing in Mariners Village at the south end of the marina and talked to the guys who ran the day charters. He checked out the departures times, promising himself he would soon take a day off to enjoy an afternoon of good fishing, clear skies, warm sunshine, cold beer, and a decent cheeseburger. And this time he would actually catch a fish.

Looking at his watch, it was already 6 p.m. He had fifteen minutes to get to Susan's place. Chase finished his coffee while leaning against a fence that divided the sidewalk, stores, and restaurants from the boats moored below and watched the sunset. The sun began its daily descent into the Western horizon before disappearing into a foreign land and giving way to the evening's twilight.

The sunset did not disappoint, as brilliant colors of red emanated from the sun, which quickly turned to pink, and that, in turn, faded to a bright and exuberant yellow as the clouds at different levels of the atmosphere reflected the setting sun's fading light, culminating in a spectacular event of illumination and shadows.

Although Chase wanted to finish watching the sun set, he knew he could not keep a lady waiting. Six fifteen meant just that. He walked briskly to his car, but not so fast that he would break a sweat. He started up his silver Mercedes and drove to the top of the bluffs overlooking the harbor. He had made a dry run the day before so that he knew exactly where Susan lived. The last thing Chase wanted was to get lost and be late looking for her place.

Susan lived just off Golden Lantern Street in a row of town houses that afforded a spectacular view of the harbor one hundred feet below the bluffs. Promptly at six fifteen sharp, he knocked on the door. He was stunned at just how beautiful she truly was! And she smelled delicious, too. She emitted far more God-given natural beauty than any sunset could ever hope to. Susan was dressed in a simple white blouse and stylish blue skirt with low-heeled shoes and a black leather jacket, giving her a mix of good girl/bad girl in her appearance. She wasn't wearing any stockings, but she didn't need to as the skin on her smooth and tanned legs looked like it was spun from deep, rich, shimmering silk.

"You look absolutely beautiful, Susan," Chase said with an ear-to-ear smile that clearly communicated he was glad to see her again.

Susan returned the smile twofold as she stepped toward him. "I'm ready to go. And you're pretty handsome yourself," she added, looking him up and down. "You've really buffed up since high school. I wanted to tell you that Saturday night, but I thought I should wait to say it."

"Um, have you been talking to Bennie Knowles lately?"

"Bennie," Susan said with a snicker. "I haven't spent time with him in months, maybe a year, although I did run into him at a grocery store a while back, and we talked for a few minutes. I think he was trying to pick me up. He kept staring at my breasts. Same old Bennie."

Chase knew he needed to change the subject and the emphasis from Bennie to the evening's agenda. Still standing at her front door he said, "I have reservations at Ti Amo. It's one of my favorite places to eat."

"Mine too, Chase. I'm so excited," she said as she reached out and took his arm while locking her front door with the other. "Our very first date and we already have something in common. Let's go. I'm starved!"

Chase opened the passenger door for Susan. "Nice car, Chase," she said with an appreciative smile, running her hands over the smooth, tan leather seats as she sat down. "I'm really glad that we could get together."

"So am I, Susan. And if I may say so, you have filled out quite nicely, too." Chase closed the passenger door and, unlike Bennie, he managed not to look at her breasts as he said that. The evening had cooled down to sixty-eight degrees. He put the top up on his Mercedes, then headed to Ti Amo.

They drove north on Coast Highway, past the Ritz-Carlton, the St. Regis, and the Montage, three resorts along the coast that Ti Amo catered to along with other tourists and the local regulars. Chase gazed at the sprawling golf course at the St. Regis and thought again of joining Pelican Hill. He asked Susan if she played, and she confirmed that she did in high school, but had not been on a course in more than five years. Chase turned into the parking lot of Ti Amo, pulled up to the valet station, and tossed the keys to one of the high school kids he knew and trusted.

"I'll take good care of your car, Mr. Manhattan," said the tall, lanky 16-year-old surfer.

It was a Tuesday evening, so Chase had made a reservation for 6:30 p.m.—just enough time to get a good seat by the fireplace upstairs and share the romantic ambiance with a very special and very attractive lady. Entering the front door, they met the hostess Elisa.

"Hello, Elisa," Chase said with the freedom that comes from knowing just about everyone on staff at the restaurant.

"Good evening, Mr. Manhattan," she responded, smiling at both of them. "Right this way. I'll see you to your table." Elisa was more than gracious and sophisticated when interacting with the patrons. She turned and moved with a certain fluidity that demanded at least a passing glance from the people waiting at the door who did not have a reservation. She took the two upstairs to their waiting table, making pleasant and small talk along the way.

"Please have a seat. Your waiter will be with you shortly. Enjoy your evening." She turned and walked away, her long, silky, black hair shining brightly in the dim light, mimicking her movements with a delayed reaction that drew careful and cautious glances from most of the men in the immediate area.

Ti Amo is an Italian restaurant with an elegant, yet relaxed atmosphere that was perfect for a relaxed escape from the harsh world outside. It was place where a couple could find authentic Italian food and excellent French wine. From the outside, it didn't look like anything more than a common dinner house. But inside, it resembled a cozy, Italian restaurant where a couple could spend a night in southern Europe without ever leaving Laguna Beach. The restaurant was modeled after an authentic Italian villa, with stone tablet menus, faux and fresco artisan-plastered walls, heavy fabrics, candelabras, and soothing lighting.

Chase made the reservation for the second floor next to the fireplace. He wanted a romantic night they could share and remember for years to come. Susan, however, was thinking more of a night to remember for a lifetime.

She was the first to initiate the dinner conversation. They talked about high school, bringing each other up to date on their lives since they last saw each other ten years earlier. They found out that they had much in common, such as placing an emphasis on education, family, and spiritual matters. Chase found these traits in Susan far more redeeming and desirable than what he saw in most of the previous women he brought here. They were more interested in the latest celebrity red-carpet news and other mindless, trivial matters that Chase only pretended to be interested in.

Although Susan led the conversation at the party the week before, and again tonight, she allowed Chase to order dinner for her. She also let him select the wine. He ordered *Farfalle con Pollo Affumicato* with sun-dried tomatoes in an oven-roasted tomato brandy cream sauce for both of them. He paired the dinner with a bottle of 1998 *Tenuta dell'Ornellaia Bolgheri Ornellaia*, a rare and wonderful wine comprised of several grape varieties, mainly Cabernet Sauvignon, and blended with merlot, Cabernet Franc, and Petit Verdot. Susan loved a man who could pair dinner and wine as wonderfully as Chase could. The evening was off to a terrific start.

The two took their time eating their dinners and drinking the wine. Chase was hungrier than he thought he would be and had no trouble finishing his meal. Susan, for having such a thin waist, made short work of her dinner as well. She even beat Chase by a couple of minutes.

Susan felt they had established a foundation for their relationship. She couldn't have been happier with Chase, the atmosphere of Ti Amo, and the dinner and wine. She decided that it was time to take the conversation to the next level.

"Look, I'll be honest with you, Chase," Susan said gently, wiping her hands with her napkin and placing it back on her right knee. "I don't date anymore just for the sake of dating. I'm not getting any younger, and neither are you, for that matter. I hope you don't mind me being so up front," she said gracefully, yet her words were laced with such boldness that they jump-started something within Chase, an emotional need deep in his heart that cried out to be filled.

"No, no, not at all, Susan." Chase leaned into the table, letting her know he was engaged in the conversation. "I know exactly what you're talking about. I feel the same way."

"That's good, Chase. I'm really glad to hear you say that because I had my doubts up to this point."

"Really? You did? Why would you say that? I mean, we really only recently met."

Susan expected the clueless expression she saw on Chase's face. "That's an easy question to answer. When we arrived here, you tossed your keys to a valet and didn't bother to get a ticket in return. And he called you by name. That tells me that you two know each other quite well."

"Okay ...," Chase said more like a question than a response. "I'm not sure what that means."

"And then you knew the hostess by name. And the waiter."

"Elisa and Antoine. Right ...," Chase said, looking a bit confused.

"Chase, that tells me, or any thinking woman for that matter, that you frequent this establishment often. And my woman's intuition tells me that you most likely have brought quite a few different women here, right? And probably more than just a few." Susan smiled and winked, as if to say "check and mate." She then took a self-congratulatory sip of her wine.

Chase was stumped. It took him more than a few moments to recalibrate. He felt uncomfortable, awkward, and slightly embarrassed. He finally broke the silence with a short laugh and raised his palms up off the table as if to say, "I surrender."

"Okay, I won't lie. You have me pegged on that one. I have brought a number of dates here over the years. Guilty as charged." Chase felt a burden being lifted off of him. He no longer had anything to hide. He didn't have to put on a façade to try to cover up his past.

"That's okay. I appreciate your honesty. What you have done up to this point is really none of my business."

"No, I don't mind. Really. Actually, it's better that we get things out in the open from the start. Relationships are built on trust, and people need to be honest in communicating their expectations. I'm actually glad you brought it up tonight."

"Listen, Chase, I like you. I really do. I felt strongly when we met again after so many years that we could build something together."

"I feel it too, Susan. It's like our meeting again was destiny. It has to be." He was now leaning forward. Just being a foot closer to her gave him a sense of the comfort and security he knew was lacking in his life.

"I hope so, Chase. Last year, I ended a four-year relationship that was not good for me. I hung on because I thought I couldn't do any better. In retrospect, I wasted four years. I just don't want to go through that again. My biological clock is ticking, and I need to get serious about where my life is going."

Although Chase had been thinking along the same lines these past few weeks, the reality of hearing it spoken out loud shook him up. He had mixed feelings. On one hand, he wanted to move forward with a relationship and Susan seemed to be an answer to those silent prayers of his heart. Yet, Chase wasn't sure how to handle change. He was a bit confused by the suddenness of Susan's conversation. But he also knew he had to make changes—regardless of how difficult they may be on him emotionally and mentally.

"We're both adults, Chase," she continued, lifting her glass of wine and emptying it in one seemingly single motion. "We don't have to play boy meets girl, boy loses girl, boy tries to get girl back. No games, okay?" Susan didn't drink often, but she had learned in college how to hold her alcohol while allowing herself room to have fun, displaying her playful and mischievous side at the same time. Chase liked this. He looked at Susan and thought of where they could go together, and his past love life quickly began to slip away. He made no attempt to reach back and try to grab hold of its trailing memories as it disappeared from his sight.

Chase and Susan finished their meal, deciding against ordering any dessert. Their bottle of *Tenuta dell'Ornellaia Bolgheri Ornellaia* finished and a ray of hope emanating from their hearts, Chase paid the bill, leaving Antoine a generous tip, and ending the first part of their first date.

Chapter 14
Marine Room Tavern

CHASE DIDN'T HAVE TO SPEND much time looking for parking in Main Beach since it was still February—off-season for tourists. He found a spot two blocks north from the Marine Room Tavern, and they walked arm-in-arm to keep warm, as the temperature had dropped to the mid-sixties.

They walked up to a row of choppers, all Harleys, representing three generations of riders. The newest Harley crowd consisted of lawyers, doctors, accountants, and heads of companies who, by day, were very successful in the business world. But after hours, they were living a dream they'd longed for since they sat on their first motorcycle. Although the crowd could be extremely loud and raucous, fights were rare at the Marine Room Tavern.

Chase's good friend, Fred Merrill, and his band, The Mulders, were playing classic rock and down and dirty blues, keeping the faithful patrons in the crowded bar happy and ordering drinks all night long. There were no open tables, so Chase ordered two Cadillac margaritas from the bar, and the two enjoyed their drinks standing up while listening to Fred's remakes of classic rock from the late-'70s and early-'80s. One reason The Mulders were so popular was that they could take a classic three-and-a-half-minute song and stretch it out to last ten or more minutes, with numerous guitar solos supplemented by a deep-driving beat from the drummer while the bassist created riff-type rhythms mixed with chords.

Fred played rhythm guitar and sang. He had a custom-made Fender that was painted navy-blue with orange highlights and a large, white Old English *D* just behind the bridge. One commonality that Chase and Fred shared was they were both hardcore Detroit Tigers fans. Chase must have inherited Tigers' DNA from his father, who was born and raised in Detroit, and had passed his love and passion for his team on to Chase.

Chase and Fred had met two years ago when the Tigers were playing the Angels in Anaheim. Fred had seats behind Chase, and they were the only Tiger fans in their section. They hit it off, drank a great deal of beer that night, and found out that they only lived a few miles apart in Laguna Beach.

After twenty minutes, the band took a well-deserved break. Fred set his guitar on its stand, talked over a few things with the other band members, then jumped off the stage and walked straight over to Chase and Susan.

"Chase, glad you could make it." He looked over at Susan. "You must be Susan. Chase hasn't done justice in the way he described you," Fred said in a flirtatious tone with absolutely no shame. Fred was thirty-five, thin, and tanned, and Susan thought he genuinely looked like one of the happiest people she had ever met.

She held her hand out, and Fred shook it. "So you're the famous Fred Merrill. Chase talked about you tonight on the way over here. You guys are really good. And really loud," she added with a smile on her face.

"This is the best bar in all of Orange County. At least I think it is," Fred replied. "Let me get you two another drink. I think I'll have one, too." Fred motioned to Kelli, a fairly new bartender, with three fingers then pointed to Susan's glass. He then held up three fingers again and shouted, "Bring us three tequila shooters, too."

"You don't mess around, do you, Fred?"

"Life's too short, Susan. Why wait for your boat to come in? You have to work hard and take what you want."

Susan deftly slid her arm through Chase's while maintaining eye contact with Fred. "I know what you mean, Fred. If you don't take it, someone else will." She gave Chase a quick squeeze.

The three talked and laughed for a few minutes. Susan felt an immediate bond with Fred. She didn't ask, but her intuition told her he had a serious girlfriend. She hoped they could all get together again soon.

"Alright, here's to you two. You make a great couple." Fred held up his shot glass of tequila, Chase and Susan followed, and they downed their shots.

"Alright, you young kids, I have to get back on stage. Stay a while and have some fun. The Mulders are just getting warmed up. It's a pleasure to meet you, Susan." Fred gave Susan one more playful grin, then gave Chase a tap on his shoulder, letting him know he approved of Susan. With that, he jumped back up on the stage and began tuning his guitar while talking something over with the bass player. The band started up again, this time playing a nasty version of "Whiskey in the Jar" that got the patrons back in the mood for some hard-driving rock and blues.

Chase and Susan found a small piece of real estate on the dance floor and stayed there for a half hour, stopping only for another round of margaritas and tequila shooters. Then it was back to the dance floor, repeating the same pattern a few more times over the course of the night. Last call came at 1:30 a.m., and there was a mad dash for everyone to get their final orders in. This was one bar where few people left early. It was a crowd where everyone stayed as late as they could before heading out onto the sidewalks to look at the Harleys lined along the curb, trading stories of creative bike designs and long rides. Chase and Susan took their time checking out the bikes before finally walking to Chase's car, and by then, it was just past two o'clock in the morning.

On the way back to Susan's place, Chase felt a rumble in his stomach, caused more by the alcohol than by the lapsed time from dinner six hours ago. Susan was hungry, too. So he pulled into a Jack in the Box on Coast Highway and ordered his favorite midnight snack—deep-fried grande tacos. He ordered two for Susan and two for himself, with a couple of Cokes to wash them down. They inhaled their tacos, dropping shreds of lettuce on their laps, and laughed and talked about how much fun they had.

When Chase pulled up in front Susan's town house, it was well past two thirty in the morning, and both looked a far cry from when they started out their evening. The sweat from all their dancing, the margaritas, shooters, and deep-fried tacos all took their toll. Their hair was a mess, and their clothes looked like they had slept in them.

"Look, Chase, I'll make this awkward moment easy on both of us. Let's just call it a night, okay?"

"I had a great time, Susan. I really did."

Susan wasted no time, leaning over to grab Chase's cheeks between the palms of her hands and giving him a semiwet kiss that lasted almost a full minute. "Thanks again, Chase. And don't forget to call me, mister. Do you hear me?" she said smiling as she opened her door and stepped out. "Call me."

Chase watched Susan as she trotted up to her front door and let herself in. Closing the door, she flicked her front porch light a few times and Chase knew that the night was over.

Chapter 15
Helen O'Connor

OFFICER MCKINSEY WAS with Helen O'Connor for almost an hour before Sgt. Det. Robert Vasquez arrived. She broke the news to the senator's wife in a gentle and comforting manner. Mrs. O'Connor was sitting on the living-room sofa, still wearing her nightgown, sobbing. Officer McKinsey held her hands and reminded the new widow that she was a very fortunate woman to have been married to such an honorable and esteemed member of the community and the state of Massachusetts.

McKinsey introduced Helen O'Connor to Vasquez and assured her that he was part of a team that was one of the best in the country at solving crimes such as this. McKinsey had the unpleasant task of explaining the gruesome manner in which her beloved William had been killed. Sixty minutes of sobbing, rocking back and forth, and wailing helped to release some of the hurt and anger that manifested inside of her.

Mrs. O'Connor asked Officer McKinsey to make a pot coffee for the three of them. The town house was still very cold, and she was hungover from the night before.

Det. Vasquez began, "I'm very sorry, Mrs. O'Connor. You must be overwhelmed with grief right now. But I do need to ask you some questions about your husband." Vasquez had a friendly face, one that people trusted. Helen understood that he cared about her and the case. She felt comfortable confiding in him and Officer McKinsey.

Helen was still sitting on her sofa with McKinsey next to her, who was still trying to comfort her and offer her strength and courage. Helen's sobs came further apart now, and after a cup of coffee, she was beginning to regain her composure. "I'm ready, Detective. Please feel free to ask anything you would like."

"Thank you, Mrs. O'Connor." Vasquez had his notepad and pen out, ready to write. "Do you know of anyone who would want harm your husband? Were there any recent or immediate threats that your husband had received?"

Helen continued to wipe her eyes with a tissue. "No, not that I am aware of. My husband was well liked by just about everybody he came in contact with. Even the media was respectful of him."

"Were there any political opponents he had a bad relationship with?"

Helen considered the question while a few more sobs escaped. "No. I really can't imagine any of his Republican opponents or the independents wanting to do this to William."

"What about his own party? Perhaps an incumbent or another person he ran against from the Democratic Party had a motive to kill your husband?"

Helen looked down, considering the question before answering. "I really can't think of any, Detective. Most people who run for the State Senate and lose end up getting other high-ranking political appointments. They are career politicians who would not want to jeopardize their careers by doing something like this."

"Okay." Vasquez was still writing notes as he asked the senator's wife more questions. "Has he ever received any threats before?"

"No, he was never threatened before. If he had been, he would have certainly told me about it. He was very open with me about what he was doing. We were regulars at social events and know a lot of people. There just weren't many people that hated my husband enough to kill him, not in this manner anyway." Helen started crying again, stopping after a few minutes.

Vasquez looked up from his notepad. "Mrs. O'Connor, I know I already asked you, but are you *sure* that no one had it in for your husband?"

"Not many people knew this, Detective, but my husband planned to run for the U.S. Senate this fall. He was meeting with his team of advisors this morning, at the State House, for a strategy session. He was going to go public with the announcement very soon."

Vasquez and McKinsey looked at each other. McKinsey asked the obvious question. "Helen, do you know of anyone who would want to prevent your husband from entering the national political scene?"

She shook her head. "I really can't. William made many friends and few enemies during his career. Maybe someone on his advisory team could better answer that question for you."

Vasquez took a minute to sip his coffee and give the grieving widow time to regroup. McKinsey got up to refill Helen's cup.

Vasquez continued, "Mrs. O'Connor, can you tell me about anybody outside of the political realm who might have reason to harm Mr. O'Connor. Your husband must have made thousands of decisions that affected nearly everybody in the state."

"He did make a few enemies. There were a few people from organized labor who despised him and some of the decisions he made regarding major construction projects in the state."

Vasquez made notes of three high-ranking people from organized labor that Helen knew about who lobbied inside the unions for a candidate to run against William O'Connor III.

"Okay, we'll certainly follow up on these three, Mrs. O'Connor. Now, can you think of anyone else who might have a motive to harm your husband? Did he have any recent altercations with anyone?"

"Well, he did have one instance a few weeks ago at a charity party with a professor from MIT. My husband was cutting off state funding for the professor's projects. William said that his ideas were the fodder of science fiction and were a waste of taxpayers' money. This, of course, caused the professor to fall into trouble with the university, as they stood to lose millions of dollars."

"What was his name?"

"Professor Nicholas Fischer. My husband had ridiculed him at these gatherings on a number of occasions, and Prof. Fischer had embarrassed William by saying he was privy to financial shenanigans that my husband was involved with. He promised to expose him as a corrupt politician. The two have gone back and forth at each other since early last year. Each time they met publicly, the arguments escalated. It was starting to get ugly."

Vasquez continued taking notes. When he got back to his desk, he planned to create a profile of the names the senator's wife gave him and start interviewing these people of interest.

Helen continued to name about a dozen people who had a run-in with her late husband. She told Vasquez she could not imagine any of them would want to kill her husband, but she realized that some of these bad relationships could have run much deeper than she previously thought.

Vasquez wrapped up his questioning, assuring Helen that he would do everything possible to find the people responsible for this wanton act of violence against the senator. She thanked him and showed him to the door. Officer McKinsey stayed behind to support Helen while she made calls to her immediate family and close friends.

Chapter 16
Complications

Although the "Beast of the East" was still hammering New England with powerful winds and snow, Boston and the surrounding cities were doing an almost miraculous job of keeping the streets relatively clear while a few local businesses that steadfastly remained open kept their sidewalks clear. Nicky and Staci were able to walk to a nearby Starbucks just west of the MIT campus in Cambridge. It was now Wednesday evening, the storm was forecasted to end within twenty-four hours, and the events of the day were continuing to escalate, requiring Nicky and his core followers to make decisions that were becoming increasingly difficult.

Nicky looked across the small round table at Staci. "We have a problem. Khyati has been following Dr. Newcombe's e-mails and telephone calls for the past few days. She definitely has plans to sell her suitcase to a third party."

"Do we know who the third party is yet, Nicky?"

Nicky sighed and fidgeted in his chair, holding his hot Chai green tea with both hands. "No, not yet we don't. She can follow the communications, but she has yet to specifically identify who they are. However, when she started peeling off the layers of security from the third party, she found that the messages originated from New York—possibly in Manhattan"

Staci was alarmed as she began to see how easily Nicky's plan could unravel. If an unknown person had a suitcase, he or she could eventually reverse engineer the secrets behind this new breakthrough. But more importantly, if a third party learned that Nicky and Staci had additional suitcases, their lives could be in danger.

"What if it's a terrorist group? What if they find out we have more suitcases? They'll come after us for sure, Nicky."

Nicky reached across the table and held her hands. "We don't believe it's a terrorist group. Khyati thinks the nature of the communications strongly suggests that it's a large, legal entity that is involved."

Staci lowered her head, considering what Nicky said for a few moments, then quickly ran a few scenarios through her mind. After considering the possibilities and outcomes, she looked up at him. "It could be another conglomerate, domestic or foreign. Possibly one of Globalized Dynamics' competitors. But I doubt it. Selling out to a competitor would be too risky, and I doubt Dr. Newcombe is that ignorant. She's greedy, but not dumb."

"I agree," Nicky responded. "I think she wants to sell it to somebody in another industry."

"So let's put those possibilities on the back burner. What does that leave us with?"

Nicky continued, "I think the third party is someone who stands to make millions by brokering a deal, while the global organization would, in turn, make billions of dollars off it. This third party could be an independent middleman or an agent working directly for someone else."

"Okay, so we're looking at New York, specifically Manhattan. That strongly implies that this third party is probably a financial institution—and one of the larger ones."

"It's either a financial institution that operates on a global scale, or possibly a private investment or equity group. We could even be looking at venture capitalists, which would be the worst scenario, because they would sell the suitcase to the highest bidder anywhere in the world, regardless of their intentions. At least with an established firm in Lower Manhattan, we could easily track them. For now, I'm leaning in the direction of the larger banks as the ultimate buyer."

Staci sat back in her chair and took another drink of coffee. She let out a long, slow wisp of air and began tapping her fingers on the table, a nervous habit she had adopted when she learned to play the drums as a child. "That leaves us with two parties we have to deal with, Nicky. Obviously Dr. Newcombe has been able to hide the discovery from her employer until now, but they'll make the connection soon enough. Then we'll have two very large corporations committing large amounts of money and other resources to come after us to retrieve these suitcases."

Staci was letting fear get the better of her. Nicky could see she was concentrating on her breathing techniques, inhaling slowly, holding her breath for ten seconds, then slowly exhaling. But Nicky was unfazed. He viewed this as merely one more obstacle he had to overcome, a challenge to be conquered.

"We need to decide where to retrieve Dr. Newcombe's suitcase. The question is, do we go to her office or to her home? We know that she carries it with her when she leaves work. It rarely leaves her sight. We could try to retrieve it during her drive home."

Staci quickly responded, "We have no experience in running someone off the road, or hijacking, or kidnapping, for that matter. And we'd be out in the open. There would be too many witnesses."

Nicky sighed again, taking another sip of his tea. "We'll just have to be prepared to send you at a moment's notice, regardless if she's at work or at home. Personally, I think you'll have to do it in her office. Dr. Newcombe must be fascinated with the suitcase because she opens it several times a day. My guess is that she'll open it at least one more time, as if to say one final good-bye."

Staci slowed her racing mind and considered Nicky's words. They made sense to her. He understood human behavior, and he was usually right when predicting events, more so than she was using statistical measurements in her deductions.

"Why don't we send Christopher and Mina to Connecticut now? If you send me through a wormhole, the only way to get back will be for me to get a ride. If Dr. Newcombe doesn't open the suitcase and you don't send me, then Christopher and Mina will have to take the suitcase by force."

Nicky sighed between sips of his tea. "I don't trust those two. They're brilliant scientists who are committed to the cause. However, they're not experienced in the dirtier side of this business. But we don't really have anything else going on right now. And time is of the essence."

"So send them to New Haven right now. It's only a two-hour drive as long as the freeways are clear of ice and snow. I'll be ready to go at a moment's notice. Like you said, Dr. Newcombe will probably open the suitcase once more for a final look, then you can send me over to her. Christopher and Mina can drive me back to Cambridge with the suitcase."

Nicky acquiesced to Staci's plan. He would send two individuals from his group of followers, Christopher Thompson and Mina Nguyen, fellow graduate students in physics and chemistry at MIT, to wait at a prearranged area a short distance from Globalized Dynamics' laboratories in New Haven. They would wait for Staci to kill Gloria Newcombe and retrieve the receiver suitcase, then drive her back to Cambridge.

Chapter 17
Greedy Gloria

GLORIA NEWCOMBE WAS hours away from retirement. She was nervous and scared, but she was also anxious to get the day over with. She saw the news on television the day before that Sen. O'Connor, her partner's nemesis and the one who would shortly shut things down on her cohort's end, was brutally slain in his office. Initial details of the murder were sketchy, but it didn't take a stroke of genius for her to conclude that a wormhole was created to get somebody in his office and kill him, then create a new path for the killer to make a clean escape. Gloria could read the writing on the wall. She fully understood that she needed to roll her dice and expedite the sale of her suitcase before the end of the day.

Gloria arrived at work 5:30 that morning so she could tie up a few loose ends, close out this chapter of her life, and begin a new one. The transfer would happen at 10:00 a.m. She would hand off the suitcase to a Mr. Romano, a businessman with contacts in high places she only recently met. He, in turn, would give the order to have $10 million transferred into a series of Swiss bank accounts. Gloria's husband, Brad, had resigned his job as a global wealth consultant in Manhattan a month earlier, and had spent the past few weeks organizing the details of their impending new lives, including the Swiss deposits, down to the minutest detail.

Gloria and Brad were ready to leave at a moment's notice. Gloria was already feigning a bad cold, and planned to use that as an excuse to leave work early. Then, she planned to call and tell her manager she needed a week off to rest. She would do the same for her two children at their school, giving the Newcombes plenty of time to make their getaway before anyone noticed that they were missing.

Brad prepared their escape route via car to Miami. The plan was to drive straight through and be there the following afternoon, where they would sail from Miami to Costa Rica, then fly under false identities to London, on to Athens, and finally to a small island just off the shores of Greece. Their two children, ages fifteen and seventeen, looked forward to moving from the cold Connecticut landscape to the Mediterranean, where the climate was sunny and warm year-round. Gloria could care less about the family dogs. Brad would poison them just before they left so they would neither suffer from lack of food and water, nor bark and howl to draw attention to their house.

Gloria had to acknowledge that her good friend of more than thirty years was a very clever and talented man. He did most of the work on the breakthrough of wormholes. She was skeptical, to say the least, when he first approached her ten years ago regarding the possibilities of the practical use of stabilized wormholes.

But Gloria was able to convince her managers at Globalized Dynamics' Infrastructure Unit to invest in the project and allow her to oversee it. It wasn't a large investment, at least when compared to other projects she was in charge of during her twenty years with the organization. Prof. Nicholas Fischer secured additional state funding, which helped him to obtain his manager's approval to move forward on his projects that included looking for a breakthrough in wormholes.

Nobody honestly believed that Fischer would ever follow through on his vision. After all, a breakthrough in wormholes was only one project among scores of other projects that he headed up over the years at MIT, and it took a backseat to higher profile projects in the eyes of his supporters.

One of the most significant accomplishments Fischer accomplished was developing uranium and plutonium power-pack batteries. He knew how to identify, open, and stabilize wormholes ten years earlier. That was the easy part. The time-consuming part was gathering sufficient sources of energy to open a wormhole. Each battery pack consisted of a single kiloton of fissionable uranium plutonium kept in separate compartments in the upper portion of the suitcases. He developed a triggering device that was activated by typing in a code into the keyboard in the lower portion of the suitcase.

The uranium batteries were similar in strength to the latent power contained in nuclear suitcase bombs produced by the United States and the Soviet Union in the 1970s and early-1980s. Without a compact source powerful enough to open a wormhole, the project would remain nothing more than fuel for science fiction stories.

Fischer benefited from being in the right place at the right time. MIT had the second-largest university-based nuclear research reactor in the country, second only to the University of Missouri in Columbia, Mo. With help from his colleague and good friend Prof. William Decker, the associate director overseeing projects with outside collaborators such as the U.S. Department of Energy and other global corporations, he was able to obtain enough uranium to build eight batteries for the three transporter suitcases and the three receiver suitcases. Gloria could only speculate as to how he was able to obtain the plutonium. In retrospect, she thought she should have done a better job auditing exactly where the quarterly installments were being allocated by her good friend, Nicholas.

Gloria found this out after the fact, and almost shut down Globalized Dynamics' involvement in the project until Fischer proved to her he could send small objects such as paper clips and thumbtacks from his office to hers. That kept the project alive and both scientists made a pact to continue the research in total secrecy until they could send a human being safely through a wormhole.

Once they were sure they could successfully send people safely through wormholes, the two brilliant scientists would dispose of the nuclear batteries, and in theory, announce their discovery to Globalized Dynamics, MIT, and the rest of the world and become two of the most famous people in the history of science. Nicholas and Gloria did not want to enjoy their new fame while spending the rest of their lives in prison for possessing and using enriched uranium illegally siphoned out of MIT's nuclear research program and purchasing it from other "silent" sources.

But as the time approached to tell the world of their breakthrough, Gloria's greed overcame the fame and recognition that she originally believed would satisfy her—and that would have easily satisfied Nicholas. But not Gloria. Not anymore. She earned only $120,000 a year for her amazing talents and expertise in physics, and she was certain that Nicholas would gain most of the recognition, while her employer would reap billions of dollars from the breakthrough. She contemplated what benefits she would end up with. A nice bonus at the end of the year, her name mentioned in a few articles on Globalized Dynamics' Web site, and a handful of congratulatory handshakes. After that, she feared she would soon be forgotten, overshadowed by the media's attention to Nicholas, MIT, and Globalized Dynamics.

Sitting behind her desk in her small, nondescript office, Gloria decided to take one last look at the contents of the black suitcase on her lap. She took a deep breath as she unlatched the top and slowly opened the top compartment. Although she cared far more about the money than the recognition of making this amazing breakthrough with dear old Nicholas, she still felt a sense of satisfaction regarding her contributions to this once-in-a-lifetime accomplishment. She could at least take pride in knowing that she was a partner in one of the greatest scientific breakthroughs in the history of humankind.

Gloria stared at the keyboard on the bottom part of the suitcase. Then she gently ran her fingers across the black felt lining inside of the top of the suitcase that housed the small nuclear power-pack battery. The battery was the source of the energy used to open up a wormhole and enlarge it for a few seconds so that physical objects or even a human could pass through. Opening a wormhole required a tremendous amount energy. The nuclear batteries could only be used six times before being depleted of energy and necessitating their disposal. Two batteries had already been used up when Nicholas Fischer sent her small office supplies. Six batteries remained. The battery pack in the suitcase she held had never been used.

What Gloria didn't know was that Nicholas had already sent a human being through a wormhole. Himself. He crossed over from his office to one of his labs twice in the previous week. Nicholas kept this last stage of trials to himself. He would eventually tell Gloria about his success. But he was concerned that she would leak the final breakthrough before he had a chance to dispose of the uranium and plutonium batteries. Like Gloria, he did not want to spend the rest of his life behind bars.

Gloria also didn't know that Nicholas planted an electronic device that could tell him when each suitcase was opened and closed. Had she known this, and known that a small group of people at MIT were monitoring each suitcase around the clock, she never would have opened it.

Chapter 18
Globalized Dynamics

Gloria stared in horror as an orange-and-yellow corona began to visualize two feet in front of her. She was not expecting a wormhole to appear. Nicholas had not told her that he was conducting any tests. She jumped back into her chair and dropped the black suitcase on the floor in front of her at the same moment the assassin appeared inside the corona four feet off the floor. The mysterious figure simply appeared out of nowhere and fell right on top of Gloria, sending them both sprawling out of her chair and onto the floor.

Gloria was in shock that a human was able to traverse a wormhole and appear in her office, especially one dressed in a black ninja outfit with a sword strapped to her back. But she was smart enough to let her fight or flight responses take over. She immediately decided on flight, reached down to pick up the suitcase, closed it, and ran out her office door, arms flailing in the air and screaming as loud as she could to anyone within hearing distance.

"You'll never take this suitcase from me. Tell Nicholas its *mine*," she yelled in a panicked shout as she ran into the adjoining laboratory.

"It belongs to Nicky, and I'll pry it from your dead fingers if I have to," Staci shouted back through the open door.

The assassin jumped up off the floor and ran out after Gloria. The terrified scientist knew she was no match for someone dressed like an assassin, so she ran as fast as she could and made as much noise as possible. She screamed and used the suitcase and her free arm to swing at every piece of equipment she could reach, knocking over, breaking, and smashing monitors, microscopes, Bunsen burners, test tubes, chairs, stainless steel utensils, and dozens of other small- to medium-sized items in the lab.

It was still very early in the morning, and the assassin did not anticipate too many bystanders. That was the good news. The bad news was, there were two armed security guards working in the building, and they could hear the commotion even though they were more than one hundred feet away in another room.

One of Gloria's colleagues, Dr. Randolph Ostrovsky, was in early to work on an unrelated project. He heard the commotion from an adjoining lab and ran through a connecting door to see what the disturbance was. Gloria ran past him, still breaking everything in sight, before he could try to reach out and stop her.

Ostrovsky yelled out to her as she ran by, "Gloria, what's the matter? Has there been an accident? Should I call the police?"

"Stop her Richard," she yelled as loud as she could, her voice echoing through the otherwise silent laboratory. "Whatever you do, stop her *now*."

"Stop who?" he replied, shrugging his shoulders as he watched Gloria disappear around a corner.

He then turned around to see the figure in black a few steps behind him. Without breaking stride, the assassin pulled out her twenty-six-inch, single-edged, black Ronin sword. She had selected this particular weapon for quick movements as she knew she would be operating in tight quarters. She stopped suddenly to set her feet and use her remaining momentum to gracefully deliver a slamming stab to the unfortunate man's chest. The last thing Ostrovsky heard was the dull cracking of his ribs before his knees gave way beneath his 185-pound frame. He toppled over onto the floor, a lifeless body in an array of shattered glass amidst scattered and broken lab equipment.

Gloria had gained an additional ten steps on the assassin and was heading toward an exit door forty feet in front of her with her employee badge in her free hand, still screaming as loud as she could and knocking anything onto the floor within her reach. Staci knew Gloria would run for an exit. She rolled the corpse over with her right foot, but did not see his employee badge around his neck, and she didn't have time to search him to find it. If Gloria got through the exit door and let it close behind her, the assassin would be locked inside the laboratory and lose Gloria and the suitcase for good.

Staci rounded the corner and stopped in the middle of the hallway. She reached down and pulled out one of the three seven-inch throwing knives that were in the sheath tied to her right thigh. Planting her left foot in front of her right foot while simultaneously shifting her weight on it, she hurled the knife with her right arm in a slightly upward trajectory at the six-foot-tall female professor. The black metal knife struck her in the upper back just to the right of her spine. The initial wound did not kill her, but it momentarily stunned her, dropping her to her knees and causing near-blackness in her mind as an array of varying colors flashed before her eyes.

Before Gloria could regain her balance and stand up, the assassin was upon her and struck Gloria with her sword between the fourth and fifth ribs, puncturing her heart, mercifully ending the professor's life without any further suffering. In seemingly the same movement, Staci reached down and grabbed the black suitcase with her left hand. She pulled the sword out of Gloria's side and put it back in its sheath, picked up the professor's badge that she dropped on the floor, and started to run toward the exit door. Just then, a bullet fired from a model SW990L pistol screamed past her left ear and shattered glass a few feet from her.

The assassin rolled to her right behind a metal table that was secured to the floor. She didn't see who fired the shot at her head, but she could clearly hear the footsteps of two people walking slowly and methodically toward her. She worked her way back into the adjoining laboratory and through a maze of tables and desks, trying to make as little noise as possible while crawling on all fours over the broken glass and other smashed objects scattered across the cement floor. Gloria Newcombe was haunting her from the dead with the scores of objects she had broken and shattered in her terrified run.

The two armed security guards fanned out, one taking the western wall and the other taking the central corridor of the laboratory. The jarhead shouted at his partner, his tone confident and sure, "Just like we practiced. You cover the right side, and I'll take the center and the left. Just follow my lead"

His partner replied with much less certainty, "Okay, but remember, I've never fired a gun at anyone before."

"It's real easy,' he replied with a sly grin. "If it moves, shoot it."

The assassin was forced to backtrack away from the exit door. She moved deeper into the interior of the laboratory, back toward Gloria's office, which offered no escape. She had to hold her ground and take out the guards one at a time. She was pinned down behind a row of a dozen metal tables that could possibly stop or alter the path of a bullet. She at least had this going for her.

She picked up a broken piece of a mirror from the floor and held it an inch beyond the bottom of the table hidden in the shadows of the fluorescent lights above. Then she saw the two security guards. The one in the center of the corridor had a short-cropped haircut, broad shoulders, and a thin waist. His jaw line was rigid, and he held his semiautomatic handgun with both hands like he had entered the world with it. He obviously had a military background and was a force to be reckoned with. He was a jarhead who had just finished his tour in Iraq and found a job in security. The second guard was soft and pudgy, and held his revolver like it was the first time he had ever seen a gun.

"I order you to stand up now with your hands over your head," commanded a deep and authoritative voice. The words echoed through the silent, dimly lit the laboratory. "I'm not messing around with you. I will shoot you dead if you don't immediately show yourself."

She tried to maneuver her way over to the soft and pudgy guard—he was the easier target. But she could not do it without crossing the jarhead's line of sight. Whether she wanted to or not, she had to take him out first. She could hear the measured footsteps of the jarhead, his boots softly crushing the broken pieces of glass beneath his shoes as he slowly advanced. She could also hear the off-beat breathing of the second security guard. She knew he was scared and wished that she could take him out first. It would make her immediate job so much easier if she could take his gun from him and use it on the jarhead.

The jarhead shouted again, his commands leaving no room for misinterpretation. "This is it. No more warnings. I will shoot you if you do not surrender immediately."

The assassin pulled out a black cloth bandana from a pocket on her left hip and wrapped one end around her left hand and palm. She first needed to control the jarhead's right hand that held the gun. She did not want him to be able to pull his arm back and give him extra room and time to fire off additional rounds. Second, she needed to clear her body from the path of the one bullet that he surely would be able to fire before she could disarm him. Third, she would need to control him physically and take him out quickly. He was too big to get into a wrestling match with, especially with a second armed security guard close by.

She needed to keep his body close to her. She didn't want to kick or punch him more than once—that would only knock him back and give him a few extra feet to maneuver a possible second gun in position to shoot her. Additionally, that would only enrage him. One of her strengths was using constant motion in close proximity to confuse an adversary. If she could stay on the offensive and make him react to her without pausing and breaking her momentum, she was confident that she could take him out.

She had the advantage of knowing exactly where he was. The floor was littered with broken glass, and she could hear each crunch of his footsteps. He was careful, methodical, and confident. The jarhead had conducted hundreds of house-to-house searches in Iraq, and he was a professional at this maneuver. He wished he could say the same about his partner who was across the room and a few steps behind.

The assassin laid her sword down beside her and gathered up a handful of small pieces of broken glass off the floor with her right hand and waited in a crouched position. When the jarhead was almost upon the assassin, he shifted his arms to the left to clear the immediate table closest to him. As soon as he started to turn to his right, she threw a hail of small broken glass fragments directly into his eyes. Instinctively, he turned back and fired off a round in the same area the glass flew up from. But the assassin had waited for his sweeping arc to pass her by and she struck, wrapping the open end of the bandana around his right hand and his gun, pulled him into her, and delivered a crushing kick to his lower rib cage that shattered three ribs and caused his knees to buckle.

He swung his left arm in a hook and thrust it in a downward motion. He was sure to connect somewhere on her body and knock her off balance—except she was expecting that particular move and diverted the blow in front of her with her forearm, using his momentum to make him shift his weight on his right foot and alter his balance. She reached down and grabbed her second seven-inch knife with her free hand and drove it deep into his side just below his floating rib. The handle on the knife was thinner than the blade and was big enough only for her hand to grasp. Once the knife penetrated the inside of his abdomen and disappeared, the skin closed over the handle so he could not pull it out. The sharp pain wracked his body and he began to shake violently, but the jarhead managed to remain standing erect.

Although Staci firmly had his hand and gun wrapped up in the other end of the bandana as well as driving the knife deep into his side, the jarhead still managed to drive his left knee into her abdomen and sent her sprawling onto her back with him falling on top of her. He still could not open his eyes, and blood was streaming out of both of them. He tried to head butt her, but she was able to slide a foot to her left side and his forehead slammed against the cement floor. A third and fourth shot ricocheted off the cement. The gun was flush against her left side, and she could feel the heat from the barrel through her cloth outfit.

The jarhead shouted out to his partner, "Shoot her, you idiot! Shoot her now!"

His partner was still aiming his gun at her, but she was using the jarhead effectively as a shield. He was shaking and stuttered, "I ... I can't. She's ... I might hit you."

The jarhead tried to stand up and push the assassin off him to give his partner a clear shot. But his partner was new and nervous and pulled his trigger three times. The assassin still had her free hand clenched onto the jarhead's shirt and pulled him back on top of her. Two of the three bullets struck the jarhead in the back; the third ricocheted off the floor and ended up on the other side of the room.

His body went limp on top of her, and she saw that the second security guard was shaking uncontrollably and unable to steady his aim as he fired off two more rounds. Staci rolled out from underneath the jarhead, pulled out her third throwing knife and—while on her knees—hurled the seven-inch projectile as hard as she could. The knife split his sternum in two, right down the middle, lodging itself deep in the center of his chest. He stood motionless, looking down in shock at his mortal wound. Slowly, he raised his head to look at the black figure in front of him holding his partner's gun. The assassin fired one round cleanly between his eyes.

She searched the three bodies for car keys, finding two sets, one on the jarhead and one on Gloria. She bent over and grabbed the suitcase, then ran to the exit door, rubbing Gloria's employee badge against the detector pad beside the exit door. She let herself out two sets of security doors and down a staircase that led to the parking lot. One car and three trucks were parked there. She held up the two sets of keys and pressed the alarm buttons on the key fobs. A Lincoln Navigator and a two-door Ford F15 truck beeped loudly through the dark and frigid morning. She opted for Gloria's Navigator. Jumping in, Staci set the suitcase on the passenger seat, started the car, and headed to the freeway, undressing out of her *shinobi shozoku* and putting on the spare clothes she had in a thin knapsack strapped to her back.

The next town was seven exits up the freeway, where she pulled off and located the predetermined Jimmy's Grill that was the drop-off point for the vehicle she stole to make her getaway. She parked in the back parking lot and tucked her sword underneath the long, thick jacket she was putting on, then criss-crossed her way through half a mile of meaningless and forgotten streets and stores before meeting Christopher and Mina in front of an abandoned furniture warehouse. The usual two-hour drive took almost four hours because of the ice-covered freeways. But Christopher and Mina brought the assassin and the black receiver suitcase safely home to Nicky, who was already planning to move forward with the next phase of his plan—that would forever change the world and every inhabitant in it within the next seven days.

PART TWO

Chapter 19
A Body Is Found

PRESSURE WAS MOUNTING for Det. Cherry to bring in whoever was responsible for the murder of Sen. O'Connor. It had only been twenty-four hours since the brutal killing at Boston's historic State House, but the governor, the police commissioner, the media, and the public were demanding answers. The media was relentless, asking how one of the state's most beloved sons could be murdered in the sanctity of his office while no substantial leads had developed. News of the grizzly details were posted on the Internet as ham radio buffs had listened in on police scanners and picked up the initial details of the murdered state senator. Det. Cherry changed that by putting a moratorium on any and all information on the crime being discussed on police radios.

Sitting at his desk at 6:00 in the morning with piles of files leading him nowhere, Cherry was no further along in his investigation than he had been the day before. He desperately needed three things. First, he needed to know where the e-mails originated from that the crime scene unit found on the senator's computer. Second, he needed to locate Rosie Contreras. She was the last employee working the night shift before the senator was murdered who he and Vasquez had not spoken with. Further complicating the investigation, Rosie had not shown up as scheduled to work the night shift following the murder. This raised red flags with Cherry, and he wondered if he would ever have

Breakthrough

the chance to interview her. Finally, he needed to finish interviewing the list of known enemies that Helen O'Connor had given to Vasquez. The blizzard had practically stopped the investigation in its tracks, and although the snowplows were doing an impressive job keeping the roads cleared, the storm and the persistent winds continued to drop new snow and blow large drifts back onto the streets.

Cherry's first break came with his first call of the day five minutes after arriving at the station. It was one of the technicians from the crime scene unit who had the task of identifying the source of the fifty e-mails with the bizarre wineskin messages.

"Detective Cherry, this is Jimmy Nielson down at the lab. We spoke yesterday at Sen. O'Connor's office."

"Talk to me, Jimmy. I need some good news, and I need it *now*," Cherry demanded, sitting up ramrod straight in his chair with anticipation that Jimmy had something for him.

"Better than good, Detective. I have *great* news. We know who the e-mails came from. This person opened up an account with Yahoo! and part of the package was a bundle of free e-mail accounts. All fifty e-mails were traced to this single account."

"Great!" Cherry was smiling for the first time in 24 hours. "What else do you have for me?"

"This Yahoo! account was created with a VISA credit card that was opened and then quickly cancelled. The only purchase was the Yahoo! account. The identity to open the VISA account was stolen, but we were still able to trace the original transaction via the IP address back to a local resident, a Prof. Nicholas Fischer at MIT."

"Fischer? Sen. O'Connor's wife identified an individual named Fischer as someone who might want to harm her husband. Hold on a minute, Jimmy." Cherry pulled out his department-issued Blackberry and scrolled through the notes that Vasquez e-mailed him. Cherry located his notes on Fischer and hit the speaker phone.

"Fischer. Prof. Nicholas Fischer from MIT. Mrs. O'Connor told us there was definitely some bad blood between these two. O'Connor threatened to cut off state funding for some of Fischer's projects because he thought they were far-fetched ideas and a waste of time and money. O'Connor also publicly humiliated him at a few social gatherings and charity fundraisers during the past couple of years."

Jimmy Nielson responded, "I don't know anything about that, Detective. But I do know the Yahoo! account that the e-mails originated from were opened by Fischer. I'd like to have some time with his computers and laptops. I'll be able to confirm exactly which computer the e-mails originated from."

"I should be able to arrange that for you within a day or two. Thanks, Jimmie. I'll be in touch with you soon. Keep me posted on anything new." Cherry ended the conversation and called his partner, Robert Vasquez, who was in his kitchen with his wife and one-year-old son. Putting on his coat and hat, he recognized Cherry's name on his caller ID as the call came in.

"Reggie, I'm just heading out the door now. What's up this early in the morning?"

"Listen, we just got a break, Robert. The technicians have identified a Prof. Nicholas Fischer from MIT who sent the e-mails to Senator O'Connor."

"Fischer ... I remember the name from yesterday. He was one of a dozen known persons of interest the senator's wife identified. He's on my list of people to interview today."

"Then you have his address?"

"Yes. I have it right here in my Blackberry."

"Good. Give it to me and meet me there."

Vasquez had planned an itinerary of local people of interest, starting with political enemies and organized crime, then fanning out to cover the rest of the list. Nicholas Fischer lived in Dorchester and was No. 9 on the list. He gave Cherry the address. "I'll be there in about thirty minutes. This storm is seriously slowing down traffic, but I'll get there as fast as I can."

Cherry hung up and pressed the call forwarding option on his phone to direct calls to his cell phone. He grabbed his coat and hat and raced down the hall toward the front door. Passing McKinsey, he shouted, "Rebecca, we have a break. I'm meeting Vasquez in Dorchester to interview one of the people of interest Mrs. O'Connor identified as someone who might have reason to harm her husband."

"At six in the morning? In this storm?"

Breakthrough

"One of the technicians from CSU identified him as the one who sent those nutty e-mails to O'Connor yesterday," his voice boomed as he jogged past her.

Running out the front door of the Sudbury Police Station and past the media vans in front of the station, Det. Cherry jumped into one the department's Ford Explorers, sped out onto Sudbury Street, and drove toward Professor Fischer's home in Dorchester.

Cherry's second break came right on the heels of the first as his cell phone rang. "Second call of the day this early? Hmm, must be good," he said out loud as he answered his cell phone. "Cherry here."

"Detective Cherry? This is Officer Phil Hampton from the Roxbury station. We've just identified a murder victim who I think you've been looking for."

Cherry knew it was Rosie Contreras. He had been around long enough to know that when a person of interest cannot be located and misses work, they were usually a suspect or they were dead. "Who is she?" *She* rolled out of his mouth before he could stop himself.

"Rosie Contreras. She was found dead about twenty minutes ago in Jamaica Plain with a bullet through her left eye."

"Are you sure her name is Rosie Contreras?"

"We didn't find a purse or a driver's license, but she did have her employee badge from the State House with her name and photo around her neck."

Cherry took a deep breath. "What can you tell me so far?"

"Some kids found her this morning in Egleston Square. They were playing in the snow when they came across a pair of legs sticking out of a snowbank made by the plows. Looks like Rosie died along the curb and a plow pushed her up on the sidewalk in a six-foot pile of snow. The kids dug the frozen corpse out, and that's when they told their parents. One of the mothers called 911."

Cherry winced when he heard the details and his smile departed. "Were you able to recover the bullet or the shell?"

"The bullet is still in her head, Detective. Small-caliber weapon, no doubt."

In spite of himself, Cherry smiled for the second time. He knew this was going to be a great day for him. "Phil, how quickly can you guys wrap up your investigation and get the body to the morgue? I need the medical examiner to dig that bullet out and get it over to ballistics this morning."

"Considering that one of our state senators was murdered, we can finish here probably within the hour. I'll call the ME and have him waiting at the morgue ready to perform the autopsy."

"Good. Thanks again, Phil. And keep me posted on everything that happens."

Cherry ended the call then dialed McKinsey and told her to coordinate Hampton, the ME, and ballistics. Rebecca McKinsey was a more-than-competent police officer who everyone trusted and regarded highly. Cherry entrusted her to carry out the most important tasks that he needed on countless cases. She had a better network than most officers in Boston did. He was confident ballistics would have the bullet by the time he and Vasquez were finished talking to Fischer.

Chapter 20
Professor Fischer's House

CAPT. DET. REGINALD CHERRY arrived first at Nicholas Fischer's house. *This is a very nice neighborhood for a college professor to live in*, he thought to himself as he pulled up to the curb. The house was a colonial-style two-story brick house with hunter-green shutters and white fascia trim. Three rectangular bedroom windows protruded from the second story. It looked like the all-American house in an all-American neighborhood. Cherry momentarily wondered how a cold-blooded murderer could live in such an idyllic house. But Cherry had seen this before: a clean-cut, respected citizen turns out to be a psychotic killer.

The detective saw there were lights on and activity in the living room. Someone looked out at him through the plantation shutters. He took a deep breath, grabbed his notepad, and started up the walkway to the front door. Before he reached the porch, a middle-aged woman in a cream-colored bathrobe and fuzzy blue slippers opened the door. She held her robe together at the waist with her left hand as if this would ward off the frigid cold and protect her from the swirling wind that greeted her.

"What's the matter, Officer?" she asked with a shiver in her voice. "Is everything okay?"

"Good morning, ma'am. My name is Capt. Det. Reginald Cherry of the Boston Police Department. Is Mr. Fischer up yet? May I speak to him?" he asked in his most pleasant voice.

"You just missed my husband, Detective. He left for work ten minutes ago. What's wrong? Why are you here?"

Cherry didn't want to upset Fischer's wife. She already looked disturbed just seeing him on her front step this early in the morning.

Cherry replied with his standard response. "Oh, it's really nothing. Just some routine questions that we have for him, ma'am."

"Routine questions?" she repeated with a crinkled face of disbelief. "Do I look stupid to you? Its 6:30 in the morning, and there's a blizzard outside. What do you mean *routine* questions?" The professor's wife looked severely hungover to Cherry. She had yet to brush her short-matted, blonde hair or put any on makeup, and the wind revealed gray roots at her scalp. "What specifically is this about?" she demanded.

"Nothing very important. I'll try to catch him at the campus, Mrs. Fischer. Thank you and have a nice day." He tipped his hat and started to turn away. Cherry did not hear the front door close, and he could feel her glare burning through the back of his hat as he walked briskly back to his SUV.

The detective climbed into the Explorer and backed out of Professor Fischer's neighborhood. He called Vasquez, who was probably in the vicinity. "Robert, I just came from his house. His wife said he left for work ten minutes ago. Where are you now?"

"I'm about halfway there, Reggie. This storm's really slowing me down."

"Meet me back at the station. Pick me up there and we'll go to his lab on campus together. I want to get there before he has a chance to settle in and ask him if he will consent to us searching his office and lab. I want to do that this morning, rather than spending the day finding a judge to sign a search warrant when most are probably at home snugly tucked away on a day like today."

Chapter 21
Professor Fischer's Office

DOUBLING BACK TO THE STATION to meet his partner, then onto the MIT campus in Cambridge with Vasquez, Cherry called the solicitous Police Commissioner Linda Fontana, who had been all over Cherry the previous twenty-four hours regarding the case. She even called him in the middle of the night twice while he was making love to his wife, Lonya. The Cherrys did not appreciate the late-night calls, but they understood that Fontana had the governor breathing down her neck about the investigation.

Fontana was a prudent and sagacious woman who was both stubborn and belligerent when she wanted something. She didn't walk away with many lasting relationships when she accepted a promotion. As a police commissioner, she was tenacious but fair, and Cherry respected her, even liked her, as she made her way to the top with hard work and a savvy understanding of how the political machine worked. The cameras also loved Fontana, and she loved the cameras. It was an amicable relationship that helped launch her through the ranks of police officer, detective, superintendent, and finally, commissioner. Linda Fontana was an icon in the eyes of the good people of Boston as she had solved some of the highest-profile cases in the city's history and made them stick through the judicial process. Cherry updated her on the two breaks in the case and assured her he would keep her abreast of any further developments.

"Listen to me, Reginald," she said in a crisp tone. "I like you. I think you're an outstanding detective. But trust me, you'd better not screw this up. I have the governor all over my ass on this one. He's calling me far more than I'm calling you, so consider yourself fortunate."

"I'm on top of this. Trust me, Linda. We've shortened the list of people of interest significantly in the past hour. We're on our way to talk to someone right now that I think is involved." Cherry could call the police commissioner by her first name privately as the two had worked their way through the ranks for the past twenty years and had spent considerable time working cases together. But in public, Cherry was smart enough to call her Commissioner Fontana.

"Reginald, I don't need to remind you of the gravity of this case. You keep me updated on everything. Do you hear me? *Everything!* I don't want a protracted investigation that the media will expound on during news and talk shows all day long. I have other things going on right now beyond just being the commissioner, and you'd better not mess this up. If I so much as—" And with that Cherry ended the call. He knew this was not the smartest thing to do to the commissioner, but he had only two hours of sleep and only half a cup of coffee.

"I could feel her bad attitude through the air waves, and I didn't even hear what she said. She was so hot I can turn off this heater," Vasquez said, looking over at Cherry and laughing out loud. "Man, is she wound up tight or what?"

Cherry just shook his head and told himself that he would deal with any repercussions of hanging up on her later.

Vasquez was a thorough detective who rarely missed a detail. He printed out an itinerary and individual maps of both the homes and offices of each person of interest they were to follow up on. He even had their home, cell, and work numbers. Cherry had recommended Vasquez for his partner when he was promoted to captain detective after his senior partner had retired three years earlier. Cherry worked with a number of talented detectives, but none had the research abilities and attention to the minutest of details that he had seen in Robert Vasquez. Cherry would take the latter two traits any day and mentor the young detective into his own image.

Vasquez had to look at his printout of MIT only once before driving immediately to Building 6, known also as Eastman Laboratories. He parked in the front, ignoring the parking structure. The detectives trudged through the snow to the front entrance. The door was locked, but they could see one set of footprints recently dug deeply into the nearly two feet of fresh snow that had fallen since the sidewalks were cleared the day before.

Vasquez pulled out his cell phone and called Nicholas Fischer's cell number.

"Prof. Fischer," Nicholas answered confidently, as if he were expecting the call.

"Prof. Fischer, this is Sgt. Det. Robert Vasquez with the Boston Police Department. My partner and I are at the front door of Building 6. We'd like to have a few words with you, sir."

Fischer looked at his cell phone for a moment, wondering if the police were really at the front door, or if this was a prank call from his students who planned to play a trick on him the moment he opened the door. "I'm sorry—you said you're with the Boston Police Department?"

"Yes sir. Please open the front door. We need to speak with you. This is an urgent matter, Prof. Fischer."

Fischer was skeptical, but slowly made his way to the first floor and to the front door. His wife had called him a few minutes ago to tell him someone who claimed to be a detective came to their house looking for him. But clever students in the past had tried to pull pranks on him dressed as police officers and even nuns. He fell for the latter, so he dismissed his wife's phone call as another prank by clever students using the snowstorm as part of their ruse.

Once Fischer was in the hall leading to the front of the building, he saw the two detectives in uniform with Vasquez holding his badge up to the side window for the professor to see. His pace quickened, and his mind started to race. He wondered if something happened to one of his three children. Unlocking the door, he let the two detectives into the lobby.

"What is it, Detectives? Is everything okay with my family?"

"Yes," Cherry responded. "They're fine. I'm Capt. Det. Reginald Cherry of the Boston Police Department." He extended his large, muscular hand and gently shook Fischer's hand. "This is my partner, Sgt. Det. Robert Vasquez." Vasquez merely nodded, keeping his hands at his side.

"What can I do for you, Detectives?" he asked nervously, looking back and forth at the two. Fischer never had a run-in with the law in his life, and the sight of the two detectives in front of him was intimidating. Various scenes began running through his mind as to what would prompt their coming to him at his place of employment, especially so early in the morning.

"Can we go into your office and talk there?" Cherry asked in a good-natured manner.

"Ah … sure, of course. Please follow me," Fischer motioned with his right arm and walked back to his office. The halls were empty as were the rooms that lined both sides of the corridor. The three walked in deafening silence as they meandered through Building 6 and up the elevator to the third floor.

Cherry broke the silence as they entered the elevator. "What exactly is it you teach here, Prof. Fischer?"

"I am a professor of applied physics. I try to make clear our understanding of the nature of matter and energy and the dynamics of the cosmos, while keeping an open mind to what we think exists but cannot yet prove or understand."

The professor opened the door to his office and led the two detectives in. "This is my humble abode. Please take a seat." The only chairs available were two burnt-orange plastic chairs that looked like relics from the early-1970s when Fischer was in college.

"We'll stand, thank you," came Cherry's reply.

"Suit yourself. What is it that you want from me?" Professor Fischer asked as he turned to face the detectives, leaning against the front of his desk, his hands grasping the edge.

Cherry took the initiative. "I'll get right to the point. We'd like to ask you some questions regarding Sen. O'Connor's death yesterday."

Prof. Fischer's eyes opened wide. "Sen. O'Connor? Yes, I heard that he was killed in his office yesterday." He thought to himself for a few moments, looked up, and continued. "I'm not sure what it is that you want from me."

"Did you know Sen. O'Connor?" Cherry asked directly.

"Well ... yes, I did." Fischer hesitated as he answered, as he was sure the detectives were aware of his sour relationship with the state senator.

"Can you please expound, Prof. Fischer?" Cherry's face was no longer engaging, and now was in skeptical-detective mode. Professor Fischer read this right away. But his nervousness began to ebb as he assumed this visit from the two detectives was merely a formality and he was merely a person of interest among scores of other people of interest. He did think it strange, however, to have the detectives show up at his house at 6:30 in the morning, then come directly to his office. Now he wasn't sure what to think.

"It's true that we were not friends," he began. "And that is an understatement to say the least." He continued leaning back on his desk while maintaining direct eye contact with Cherry. "You could say that we were enemies who opposed each other."

Cherry was scrolling through his notes on his Blackberry. "Helen O'Connor, the late senator's wife, claimed that he threatened to cut off state funding to your department and that he had insulted you publicly in numerous social settings." Cherry looked back at Fischer, staring him in the eyes without blinking. Vasquez backed him up with an unblinking stare of his own.

"God rest the senator's soul," Fischer replied. "It's true that I disdained the man. But surely one cannot go through life without making enemies. And I am quite sure that O'Connor made his fair share of them over the years."

"Right now, we are specifically interested in *you*," Vasquez interrupted. "Prof. Fischer, would you please tell us where you were and what specifically you were doing yesterday morning about this time?"

"I drove here about the same time to beat the storm."

"Can you prove that you were here at that time?" Cherry probed.

"Well, I was probably the only one here, although there could have been another professor working. The security to the building is average at best. All that is required is a key to get into the building and a second key to get into my office."

"Did anyone see you enter the building?"

"Hmm, no, I do not think so. The storm was very strong, and I doubt there was anyone else here. I didn't see anyone on the streets except for the city snowplows and a few cars."

"Why did you come into work yesterday, especially so early in the morning and in the face of a blinding blizzard?" Cherry asked, scribbling notes in his notepad. Vasquez was doing the same.

"Well, sirs, I'm working on numerous projects, and I'm under tremendous time constraints to finish them," he answered.

"Did you log onto your computer or make any telephone calls that would determine you were here in your office at that time?"

Fischer was not pleased with the way the conversation was heading. But he knew that he was at work yesterday at this time and was adamant in his rebuttals.

"No, I didn't log onto my computer or call anyone," he replied with a sharpness in his tone. "I had a number of projects to attend to in addition to lecture notes and student papers I had to work on. I was here, in my office, and in my labs."

Cherry sighed, then took a small step forward due to the limited space in the office. "Prof. Fischer, I'll get right to the point."

"Please do," replied the professor with a note of defiance, crossing his arms on his chest, still leaning against the front of his desk.

"We've traced fifty e-mails from O'Connor's computer at the State House that he received yesterday morning." Cherry paused for dramatic effect. "And all fifty e-mails originated from you, Prof. Fischer. Our technicians with the crime scene unit confirmed this. The e-mails came from a Yahoo! account that you opened."

Professor Fischer laughed out loud. "That's preposterous. I've never sent that bloated piece-of-shit windbag politician an e-mail. What are you talking about?"

"Prof. Fischer, this is serious. We have proof that these e-mails of a suspicious nature originated from a Yahoo! account you opened, and they were sent to Sen. O'Connor just before he was murdered," Cherry said in a very deep, authoritative voice. "And Mrs. O'Connor has identified you as one of the most likely people to seek retribution against her husband."

The two detectives continued to stare at the professor. Fischer was starting to feel cornered, agitated, and defensive, a role that he wasn't used to and didn't appreciate. "Detectives, I'm afraid I don't know what you are talking about. I was here working in my office and my labs yesterday morning. This much is certain." He unfolded his arms and stretched them out wide, as if to say that he had nothing to hide from the two detectives.

"Are you positive you do not know of anyone who can confirm you were here at that time?"

Professor Fischer took a few moments to consider the question one more time. He shuffled his feet and replied, "No. Due to the storm, I didn't notice anybody in the building until after 10:00 a.m., when I began to see a few students show up, thinking there were going to be classes."

Cherry did not want to spend time using interrogation techniques. He wanted to look at the office and labs to see if he could find anything that would link Fischer to the murder.

"Professor, I am going to ask that you consent to a search of your office and your labs. I encourage you to comply, or I'll have to ask a judge to issue a search warrant of the place. I strongly suggest that you cooperate with me right now."

Nicholas Fischer was speechless. He could not believe what he was hearing. On one hand, he knew he had not done anything wrong. However, he also knew that a state senator was murdered and the Boston Police Department would want to aggressively follow up on any lead, regardless how inconsequential it might be. He surmised that the police were conducting similar searches across Boston at numerous locations, and that they were simply doing their job by interviewing him. Fischer reluctantly complied.

Cherry was grateful the professor had agreed. Being short of sleep and coffee, he didn't have the fortitude to deal with a difficult personality.

"Do you own any guns, Prof. Fischer?"

The professor paused for a moment, then replied, "Well, yes. Yes, I do."

"What kind of guns do you own?" Cherry's eyes glinted with obvious interest, and Vasquez was writing down notes as fast as he could.

"I have three handguns, one here in my office and two at home. They're strictly for protection, though. I rarely use them except for occasional target practice a few times a year."

"What type of handguns are they?"

"I have a Glock .22 that I keep here in my office. And I have a .38 and a Smith and Wesson revolver in my bedroom at home."

Cherry was now standing just a few inches from Fischer. "Professor, I would like to see the gun in your office right now, please."

Fischer sighed, then shrugged his shoulders. He thought the two detectives were merely putting on a performance, and once the interview was over, he would never see them again.

"It's right here in my drawer." He walked around to the other side of his desk and opened the bottom drawer on the right side.

Cherry and Vasquez followed the professor as he retrieved the black, stainless steel Glock .22 by the tip of the muzzle. He handed it to Cherry, who held the bottom of the grip between his thumb and forefinger. Then he lifted the handgun up to his nose and smelled the muzzle.

"This gun has been fired recently, Professor. Have you fired it in the past few days?"

Fischer's heart skipped a beat, and he swallowed hard. "That's impossible. I haven't fired it in a couple of months. That's the truth, Detectives."

Cherry placed the Glock back in the drawer. Although he suspected a connection between the Glock and the murder of Rosie Contreras, he would have to wait for the ME to retrieve the bullet from Rosie's head before he could confiscate the handgun. But he had a gut feeling from years of experience that ballistics would make a positive match between the gun and bullet.

Vasquez took a step forward and summarized the conversation. "The senator had let you know that he would soon cut off state funding for your projects, you publicly threatened to end his career, you cannot prove you were in your office at the time of the murder, and you have a recently fired handgun in your desk drawer. In our eyes, that gives you a motive, opportunity, and a weapon."

Fischer felt like a boxer being pummeled by his opponent, but held his ground and rebutted, "Detectives, although I did plan to expose him for underhanded things such as misappropriation of funds that I had knowledge of, I can assure you I never had any intention of murdering the senator."

Cherry felt that he and Vasquez had gathered enough preliminary information to take the investigation to the next level by examining the recently fired Glock. He glared at Fischer.

"Listen to me closely, Professor. I don't want you to touch this gun. In fact, I want you to go to one of your labs and stay out of this office. Do you understand me?"

Fischer's emotions pinged back and forth from anger to fear. He hadn't punched anyone since he was in elementary school. But he truly hated Det. Cherry at this moment and wanted to do nothing more than to hit him in his face.

"Fine, Detective," he said through clenched teeth. "I'll go to one of my labs. But let me assure you, you're picking a fight with the wrong man. I'm innocent of anything you might be attempting to connect me with. And I have enough discretionary income to buy an attorney who will make sure you're pushing a pencil until retirement." He looked over to the younger Vasquez, who looked unfazed by his threats. "And I'll end *your* career before it even begins. I promise you that."

Stepping out into the hall, Cherry watched as Fischer locked up his office and walked down the hallway to one of his labs. "Remember, Professor, if you go back into your office, you'll be obstructing a police investigation. Trust me, you *don't* want to do that with me."

The two detectives walked back out to the Explorer. The strong winds had already built twelve-inch snowdrifts on the passenger side of the SUV. Climbing in, Cherry turned the Explorer around and headed back to the Sudbury station on the east side of the Charles River. Vasquez was busy transferring his written notes into his Blackberry and sending them to his partner.

Cherry glanced over at Vasquez, then returned his attention to dodging snowdrifts forming in the middle of the streets. "Robert, I want you to interview the union guys this morning. They live and work close enough that you should be able to drive to them all. I'm going back to the station to make some phone calls and follow up with a few people."

Chapter 22
Ballistics

IT WAS JUST AFTER TEN O'CLOCK in the morning and ballistics now had the bullet that State Chief Medical Examiner Andrew Phillips took out of the gelatinized brain of Rosie Contreras. He confirmed that it was a .22-caliber soft shell bullet that had pinged back and forth inside Rosie's skull and killed her. Michael Dayton, a high-ranking ballistics officer in Boston's Forensics Division, determined the type of bullet used. Cherry gave Dayton his cell number and told him to call the moment he knew the type of bullet that killed Rosie.

Cherry was now back behind his desk at the Sudbury Street office, returning a multitude of calls and finally finishing that second cup of coffee that had eluded him earlier in the morning. He was grateful for Officer McKenzie's assistance. She helped keep things organized during his very busy and hectic days. While calling the commissioner to give her an update on his visit to Prof. Fischer's office at MIT, his cell phone rang. Only a few people called him on this number, and he had a good feeling this was Michael Dayton.

"Commissioner, I have another call coming in, and I think it's Michael Dayton with ballistics."

"Take the call, Reginald, and keep me posted on all developments. I have confidence you can get to the bottom of this. Remember, if you solve this case quickly, I will make sure that you are rewarded handsomely for it. But trust me, Reginald, if you fail …" Her voice trailed off.

"I certainly will." Cherry hung up the desk phone and picked up his cell phone. "Cherry here."

"Reggie, it's me, Michael Dayton at ballistics."

Cherry was already standing up. "Talk to me, Michael. What do you have?" The smile returned to Cherry's face for the third time today, a record in recent memory.

Dayton held up the clear plastic baggie containing the projectile, focusing on it with his left eye closed. "It's a .22 soft shell. It bounced around inside her skull a few times. It's pretty well squashed and fragmented, but I can clearly read the inscription on the base of the shell."

"That was fast." Cherry looked at his watch. It wasn't even lunch yet and he already had the case moving forward on the fast track. Cherry was on a roll, and he felt that the day would bring more breaks in the case.

"We're short-staffed because of the storm, but we were easily able to identify the type of bullet. There was no problem with this one."

"Don't go anywhere, Michael. I may have the gun that fired that bullet," Cherry shouted into the phone as he stood up from his chair.

"That was fast," Michael echoed Cherry's statement back to him.

Cherry slammed the phone down and ran down the hall and out the front door, venturing back out into the storm for the third time in two days. "I'm on my way back to see Prof. Fischer," he yelled over his shoulder to Officer McKinsey. "Have Vasquez meet me there right away. He should be local. He's out interviewing people of interest."

"I'll call him right now," she confirmed as she watched Cherry rush out the door.

Chapter 23
Developments

DET. CHERRY WAS THE FIRST one to reach Eastman Laboratories. The front door to the building was locked, just as it was earlier in the morning. "Shit," Cherry yelled out loud. "I should have written down Fischer's cell number." Sighing deeply, he called Vasquez, and remembered again why he requested him to be his partner.

"Reggie, where are you? Are you with Fischer?"

"I'm at Eastman Laboratories freezing my ass off. The door's locked, and I need you to call him."

"I'm only a short way away. Hang tight. I want to go in there with you. Did ballistics call you?"

"They sure did. It's a .22 soft shell alright. I need to get Fischer's gun over to Dayton right away."

"I'm on Massachusetts Avenue right now crossing Memorial Drive. I'll be there in less than two minutes."

Although Cherry's coat gave him some protection against the wind and the biting cold, his pants, shoes, and hat did not. Hands in his pockets, he jumped up and down a few times to try to keep warm. Three minutes later, Vasquez pulled up to the front of Building 6. He jumped out of the Explorer, his long legs sprinting through the snow to the front door in less than ten seconds. Cell phone in hand, he was already talking to Fischer and asking him to once again unlock the front door and let them in.

Ending the call, he looked over at Cherry and said, "I can't remember it being this cold. Fischer better get his butt out here right away."

"I see him now," Cherry said, peering through the glass in the door. "He sure is taking his sweet-ass time."

Fischer opened the door and let Detectives Cherry and Vasquez in. He didn't like that they returned in just a few short hours. He knew this couldn't be good for him.

"What is it, Detectives? What can I do for you now?" he asked, trying to sound as confident as an innocent man could under the circumstances.

Cherry stepped forward. "Prof. Fischer, I need to confiscate your Glock .22."

Fischer was beside himself now. "You need my gun? For what reason, Detective? I had nothing to do with Sen. O'Connor's death. And from what I heard, he was hacked to death, not shot." Fischer was no longer able to maintain himself. His heartbeat raced and Cherry could see a few veins protruding out of his forehead and neck.

"Prof. Fischer, there's been a development in the case, and I need your Glock .22 right now. I need to take it to ballistics to see if it matches a bullet used in a related crime."

Prof. Fischer stared at the detectives for a few moments. Cherry gave him his best *do it now or else* glare. Fischer thought better of being difficult and led the two detectives down the hallway back to his office.

Upon reaching the door, Cherry said, "I'll retrieve the gun myself. Is it still in your desk drawer?"

"Yes, it is," came the dejected reply. Fischer looked like he was in a state of shock. Desperation and fear began to envelop him.

Cherry pulled out a clear plastic evidence bag from his coat pocket, picked up the Glock .22 from the side drawer in Fischer's desk with two fingers by the muzzle, and placed it in the brown bag. Then he took a pen from his shirt pocket and filled in the pertinent information on a designated white strip on the side of the bag.

"I can't believe you're actually coming into my office and taking my gun. I'm calling my attorney right now," Fischer protested in a tone that contained a hint of arrogance. "I can't believe you're actually trying to connect me with O'Connor's death. I swear to you that I didn't have anything to do with it."

Cherry breathed in deeply, expanding his chest and sucking in his stomach in such a way that would quickly intimidate most people. He was not a bad cop. But this was a method he used when a person of interest became agitated and possibly unpredictable.

"You may certainly call your attorney, Professor. But whatever you do, I strongly suggest you remain cooperative. Believe me, I can get a court order to search this place in a heartbeat if I need to." Cherry thought for a moment and continued, "Actually, I am going to ask you to lock up your office and labs and leave the building until further notice. I would like you to go home and stay there until I call you." He stared at Fischer, not blinking, until the professor relented and agreed.

"Okay, I'll leave. I'll go home. I'll go home and call my attorney. You want to play hardball, Detectives, go ahead. I can play hardball, too. You'll see," Fischer responded, looking the two up and down in disgust. Vasquez thought he might spit on them, but fortunately for the professor's own sake, he didn't.

"We'll see you out the door Prof. Fischer. I'll call you later this afternoon." Fischer locked up his office and labs, and the three men left the building. Fischer headed home, and the two detectives drove to the crime laboratory to drop off Fischer's gun, expecting they would find a match to the bullet that killed Rosie Contreras.

Cherry called Michael Dayton. He was grateful that Dayton was one of the best in the business, and that he was fast.

"Michael, it's me, Cherry, again."

"Do you have the gun, Reginald?"

"I have it with me, and I'm on my way over to you right now. It's a Glock .22. I'll see you in about twenty minutes."

"We're ready for you, Cherry."

"Great. And thanks again for the speedy service."

Cherry had one more call to make while on his way to the Ballistics Lab at One Schroeder Plaza on Tremont Street. He called McKinsey. Before she could say, "Hello," Cherry started talking.

"McKinsey, listen. I just left Fischer's office. I have his Glock .22, and I'm taking it over to Dayton in ballistics right now. I just sent

Fischer home and told him to stay there until I contact him. I need you to park an officer in front of his house."

"Are you placing him under arrest?"

"No, not yet, anyway. But I want to keep an eye on him just the same."

"Okay. I'll send someone over there right now."

"I also need you to get a crime scene unit over to Fischer's office and labs as he consented to a search. We don't need to tape off the entire building, but I want to make sure no one enters the building until the unit has finished going over the place. We'll also go to his house later today."

Cherry and Vasquez drove to Jimmy's Grill since it was close to the station and Fischer's office at MIT. Cherry knew this would be one of the busiest days of his life, and if he and Vasquez didn't eat something now, they might not have a chance to eat until tomorrow. He also wanted to give the crime scene unit time to set up and get started before going back and seeing what they were able to come up with. Finally, Cherry needed to call the Commissioner Fontana and give her an update on his progress.

Chapter 24
The Crime Scene Unit

THE SUPERVISOR OF THE CRIME SCENE UNIT was Lauren Brackenhurst, a savvy investigator with a degree in forensic science and twelve years of experience in some of the highest-profile cases in Boston. She was one of the best at identifying, collecting, preserving, and evaluating evidence at a crime scene. Lauren was scrupulous and thorough and had a reputation for writing and maintaining detailed reports that held up in court better than anyone in her field. Her team consisted of two former detectives and three technicians who solved countless cases. They were also the same crime scene unit that performed the investigation at Sen. O'Connor's office a day earlier.

Detectives Cherry and Vasquez arrived outside the door of one of Fischer's labs a few minutes after 1:00 p.m. "Hello, Lauren. It's good to see you again," Cherry said with a big smile.

Lauren was squatting down looking at something on the floor. She recognized the voice before she turned around. "Well, hello there, Det. Cherry. I'd come over and shake your hand, but you understand …," she said, looking at him over her left shoulder.

Cherry looked around the lab, which wasn't that big to begin with. The six people and their tools of the trade made the room look even smaller. "How are things going in here?"

Standing up with a clear evidence bag in her hand, she replied, "Most interesting, to say the least." She wore a slanted grin that she used when she wanted to tacitly communicate she found something of significance.

"Tell me something good."

"We found some blood in the shop sink over there against the wall." She pointed to her right. "There are splattered drops along the sides of the sink walls. Although it's dry, it looks relatively fresh, maybe a day or two old."

"How can you conclude that without any tests?"

"This sink doesn't look like it's been used for months. There's dust accumulated on the sides but not the bottom of the basin where water had recently been run. No dust on the bottom."

"Now that's interesting for sure."

"It looks like someone tried to wash blood down the sink, but didn't do a very good job."

Cherry shifted his weight from his left side to his right. He wanted to say what was on his mind, that he was confident the blood belonged to either Sen. O'Connor or Rosie Contreras. But he didn't want to taint the investigation in any way. Besides, he was sure that Brackenhurst and her team had the same idea.

"Is there anything else of interest?"

"There certainly is. But concluding on the previous conversation, the blood in the sink was well worth our time here today. We'll be able to conclude if it's human blood and what type it is as soon as we get back to the lab."

"What's in the baggie?" Cherry pointed at the evidence bag she held in her right hand as she stood up and faced him.

"These are some brown fibers we found on the floor by the sink. They look like carpet fibers." She held the bag up and looked at the fibers as she was speaking. "I don't recall seeing any brown carpet anywhere in the building. They definitely look out of place here on the cement floor." She looked at Cherry and winked.

Cherry thought back to the patch of carpet in the senator's little sleeping room off of his office that had a noticeably absent section of fiber laid out in a circular shape. All five rooms in the late senator's office had dark brown carpet. Cherry smiled again. He was glad he took the time to eat, because this day was getting busier by the minute.

Chapter 25
Back to Dr. Fischer's House

THE NOR'EASTER WAS DROPPING the last of its snow over Boston and the surrounding states during the late afternoon. More than four feet fell in less than seventy-two hours and drifts more than ten feet high were common throughout the area. Snowplows were working around the clock in a desperate attempt to keep the main arteries of downtown Boston and the surrounding cities clear. The winds were forecasted to continue for at least two to three days, promising the city more grief from the storm even after the snow stopped falling.

Detective Cherry was back at his desk discussing Prof. Fischer with Detective Vasquez and McKinsey when he received the call he was waiting for at 2:00 p.m. Michael Dayton confirmed that Fischer's Glock .22 had indeed fired the bullet that killed Rosie Contreras. Cherry had suspected as much. He hung up and gave Vasquez that *let's go and get him* look.

McKinsey was memorizing the backside of Cherry. That was mainly all she saw of him as he ran down the corridor one more time from his office to the front door, dragging Vasquez in tow.

"One more thing," Cherry said to her, looking over his right shoulder.

McKinsey looked up at Cherry and smiled with confidence telling Cherry that he could place the fate of the free world in her hands. "Call

Breakthrough

Capt. Hampton at Roxbury. I need to bring Fischer over there for questioning. I don't want the media circus outside filming us bringing in Fischer for questioning."

"I'll call him right now."

"You're the best, McKinsey. Vasquez and I are off to Fischer's house now. I'm going to bring him in for questioning. We'll be at the Roxbury station in less than an hour." McKinsey was already on her way back to her desk and waved at Cherry and Vasquez as she picked up her phone.

Vasquez drove and Cherry rode in the passenger seat. It took half an hour to reach Fischer's home. Vasquez pulled up behind the running undercover patrol car parked in front of the professor's house. Sgt. Jayson Phinney stepped out of his car, and Vasquez reached him first.

"How's it going, Phinney? Anything happen here today?"

"Someone in a suit and carrying a briefcase pulled up and parked in the driveway just a few minutes after I arrived. Fischer let him in the house. He's still in there," Phinney said, pointing to the black Lincoln Navigator in the driveway, then at the house.

"He must be his attorney," Cherry said. "Thanks, Phinney. Stay here in case we need you."

"Okay," Phinney replied and sat back down in his car, engine still running and the heater blasting away.

"Let's go talk to Fischer and see who his attorney is," Cherry said to his partner.

Cherry and Vasquez could see a gap in the plantation shutters and Cherry rightly assumed that Mrs. Fischer was peering at them as they approached the front door. Just before the two Boston detectives stepped on the porch, the front door opened and Nicholas Fischer along with another man stood at the threshold meeting them with confidence.

"Hello, Prof. Fischer," Cherry started, looking first at the professor, then at the man in a fashionable olive-green suit and brown Sanyo Newport Balmacaan coat standing next to him, then back at the professor. "I need you to come downtown with me for questioning."

"Fine, Detective, I will come with you," he said in a calm and self-assured manner. "Please allow me to introduce to you my attorney,

Jacob Buerling. He will be accompanying us." The high-profile attorney nodded to the two detectives.

Cherry and Vasquez both recognized Buerling from previous trials. He was well known in the Boston area as a very good lawyer with a reputable reputation. He looked average on the surface, standing five feet ten, weighing 165 pounds, forty-four-years old, and balding. He'd look great in a tan, if he would ever venture out from his office or the courtroom long enough to see the sun.

But he was shrewd and was one of the most detail-oriented attorneys in the city. He was known for being prepared and exploiting any weakness in the plaintiff's case. He rarely took on the sleazy cases, and mainly represented clients who had a decent reputation. Buerling also recognized Cherry and Vasquez as he had made it a habit to sit in the audience on at least a couple cases that all detectives in Boston and the surrounding cities were involved with.

"That's fine, Prof. Fischer." Cherry looked at Jacob Buerling, "You can follow behind us. We really need to go now."

Mrs. Fischer's head popped out from behind her husband and his attorney. "My husband didn't do anything, Detective. He wouldn't do a thing to harm another human being. Do you hear me? He hasn't done anything wrong."

Cherry noticed that she was dressed professionally, had put on makeup, and brushed her hair. The gray roots were also gone. She looked a world apart from when he first met her at six thirty that morning.

"Thank you, Mrs. Fischer. I appreciate the insight. Prof. Fischer, are you ready to go, sir?"

"I am. But I would like to ride with my attorney, if you don't mind. After all, you are not arresting me, correct?"

Cherry didn't have to consider the question as he did not think Buerling would try to make a break for it. "That's fine. Mr. Buerling, just stay behind us and follow me."

Buerling nodded a second time, and they each walked to their respective SUVs. Fischer looked back at his wife to assure her everything was going to be okay. "Don't worry, honey, I'll be back before you know it."

Driving out of Dorchester, Cherry asked Vasquez about Mrs. Fischer. "What's the story with her? She was like a totally different person just now than when I saw her this morning."

Vasquez didn't have to look at his notes—he had memorized the profiles and details about each of the twelve persons of interest and their immediate families and their backgrounds.

"Mrs. Elaine Ann Fischer. Maiden name Brown. She's fifty-four-years old and born and raised in Boston. She has a masters of art from Boston College, is a successful art dealer, and is very active in the community. She has also been in rehab three times for alcohol. But all in all, she's a stand-up citizen. She's never been in trouble with the law. Never owed back taxes. She has only been married to Nicholas Fischer. They were married when they were both in graduate school during summer break."

"What about the children?"

Vasquez checked his rearview mirror to make sure Buerling made it through the yellow light that he probably should have stopped at. They were right behind him.

"They have three. The oldest, Denise Fischer, age twenty-six, followed in her mother's footsteps as a graduate student in theater and dance at BC. She is currently in New York starting a career in Broadway musicals and plays. She's talented and has already landed a few meaningful parts in a number of plays."

"Interesting. Who else?"

"Nicholas, Jr., is twenty-four. He's a graduate student following in his father's footsteps at MIT in physics, specifically high-energy, advanced nuclear physics, and string theory. He works with his father part-time and is a teaching assistant for Fischer."

"Now that's *very* interesting," Cherry said as he was making notes in his Blackberry.

"Finally, there's little Cindy Fischer, age twenty-one. She's in her second year of undergraduate school at UConn. She took a couple years off between high school and college to party and got arrested twice for public drunkenness and once on marijuana charges. Her major is fine arts."

"I think once we're finished questioning Fischer, we should have a talk with his son, Nicholas, Jr." Cherry looked over his shoulder to confirm Buerling and Fischer were still behind them.

Cherry sat back in his seat and called Capt. Phil Hampton at the Roxbury station. Cherry knew Hampton well as they had worked a number of cases together over the past twenty years.

"Phil, this is Cherry from the Sudbury station."

"Hello, Cherry. How's the investigation going? Believe me, the guys here feel for you. I bet Fontana's all up and down your ass right now."

Cherry laughed and immediately became more relaxed. "It's stressful, no doubt about that. Listen, Phil, I'm on my way over with a person of interest."

"Right. A Prof. Fischer from MIT. McKinsey called and gave me the details. You can use the Green Room."

Cherry understood what Bradley meant by Green Room. When Cherry first joined the BPD as a patrol officer, he worked with Phil Bradley for a few years. They used an interrogation room painted green on the ceiling, all four walls, and the floor when they were sure that they had the right suspect. The lack of colors gave off a deficiency of perception, a sensation of sensory deprivation, that seemed to help break down a suspect's will over the course of the interrogation.

Chapter 26
An Arrest Is Made

CAPT. DET. REGINALD CHERRY was able to avoid the media vans at the Sudbury station by taking Jacob Buerling and Professor Nicholas Fischer to the Roxbury station. Once inside the Green Room, Cherry, along with Sgt. Det. Robert Vasquez, Capt. Phil Hampton, and two interrogation specialists, subjected Nicholas Fischer to intense questioning about the murders of William S. O'Connor, III, and Rosie Contreras. Buerling was somewhat cooperative, but had his client decline to answer a number of questions that dealt with his personal relationship with the late senator.

Then came the call that Cherry was waiting for. It was Lauren Brackenhurst from the Boston Crime Scene Unit. She was able to expedite results for two items of interest that she and her team discovered in Professor Fischer's labs. Cherry saw her name on his caller ID and stepped out of the Green Room to take the call.

"Hello, Det. Cherry," she said in a happy and professional tone that Cherry wished the commissioner demonstrated. Lauren was a professional and placed the integrity of her work above and beyond the pressure of the job and the pressure that the higher-ups at the police department tried to place upon her.

Commissioner Fontana, however, displayed few of these traits over the years. That's how she rose to her current position. To make matters worse, she was now a politician, positioning herself for the next rung on her professional ladder. It was no secret that she wanted to run for mayor of Boston, and she had made it clear to Det. Cherry that he had better solve this case quickly. The last thing she wanted was the national media pressure that came with an unsolved case of this magnitude.

Cherry shuddered, thinking about having to call Fontana with each initial phase of progress. Receiving a call from Lauren brought a sense of calm to the storm raging outside the station and inside the department. Cherry needed that moment of tranquility. A fifth smile came upon his face, and the record kept climbing.

Terminating the conversation, he opened the door and looked directly at Buerling, then beckoned him with his head toward the door. Buerling politely and calmly excused himself to his client and stepped out into the hall with Cherry along with Vasquez and Hampton. As a lifelong physicist and a researcher whose insatiable passion was to find answers to the unknown, Prof. Fischer hated the silence and the uncertainty that followed an event and before the explanation that followed.

The door closed automatically behind the men, then Buerling and Cherry both faced each other, staring into one another's eyes as if they both understood that Cherry's phone call was about to tip the scales in his favor. Nevertheless, Buerling stood at attention, exuding a veneer of confidence, both feet planted symmetrically about a foot apart with his right hand cusped over his left hand and his arms hanging freely in front of him. His head was tilted slightly back as he peered out of half-opened eyes. He had maintained this same pose while they were both standing on Fischer's front porch. Cherry always wondered if people who stood this way were subconsciously trying to hide something.

"Yes, Detective," Buerling said, more like a question than a statement.

Cherry breathed deeply as he usually did when he had something of importance to say. This was a crutch that he leaned on. His wife pointed this out to him on numerous occasions and offered a few solutions that he could use in place of the deep sigh. One of these days he would listen to her advice. But for now, he was content to use his crutch. He was comfortable with it and even relied on it to give bad news when necessary. At least he gave up the shuffling of his feet when he sighed years ago as part of this ritual. Lonya made sure of that.

"That call I just took was from Lauren Brackenhurst." Buerling's eyes, eyelids, and facial expression never changed. Neither did his breathing. He was good. The man could stare for minutes without blinking. Cherry knew that he had one of the best stone-cold poker faces in the business.

Again, Cherry breathed in deeply again and exhaled. "Brackenhurst's team was able to expedite the testing and analysis of two particular items of interest to this case." There was still no change in movement from Buerling. If Cherry didn't know better, he would have thought he was talking to a wax figure.

"First, the blood they found in the sink at Dr. Fischer's lab has been positively identified as human blood, type B positive, the same blood type as O'Connor's. It will still be about five days or so before we expedite the results of the DNA, though." There was still not even the slightest twitch from Buerling. Cherry thought that this was his attempt to try to stay in control of a situation when he knew that he clearly wasn't.

"The second item of interest is the fibers that they found on Prof. Fischer's laboratory floor. These have been matched to the carpet that is in the senator's office. Even the dust particles and dirt on those particular fibers and on O'Connor's shoes and clothes are a match."

Cherry left those statements floating in the air and stared back at Buerling, determined to let him blink first. Buerling broke the silence after about twenty seconds. "Detective, I understand that this is one of the most important cases in Boston's history, but how can you be sure that Brackenhurst's team can safely conclude these results in such a short period of time?"

Never breaking eye contact, Cherry smiled, first through the right side of his mouth, then the left. He worked with Lauren enough times that he could trust her when she called him with results.

"Mr. Buerling, due to the nature of this case, the crime scene unit and the supporting personnel at the lab have put everything else on hold the past two days. Everything. All members have dedicated themselves solely to this investigation, specifically to these two items. The blood in the sink and the brown carpet fibers. Then there are the fifty e-mails that originated from Prof. Fischer and were sent to Sen. O'Connor an hour before his murder."

"So far, this is all circumstantial evidence, Detective," Jacob Buerling interjected, still wearing his stone-cold poker face.

Cherry continued, "I also have to consider him as a prime suspect in the murder of Rosie Contreras too. She was an employee of the State House who worked the night shift. She was the one to clean O'Connor's office an hour before he arrived at work. Ballistics was able to match the .22 bullet that killed her to your client's handgun he kept at his office. His prints and his prints only are on the gun, and it was recently fired."

"So what now, Det. Cherry? Are you going to arrest my client for the murder of Sen. William O'Connor?" Buerling finally let go of his hands and shifted his weight onto his right foot

"I have to. For his murder, and for the murder of Rosie Contreras."

Buerling rubbed his chin for a few moments as he looked down at the floor. Finally he looked up at Cherry and said, "Let me talk to him first. As you can see, he's beside himself right now. Let me tell him."

"That's fine. Do it now. We need to get moving on this. We have to have him processed and begin documenting the case."

Jacob Buerling paused a few more moments as he thought deeply about his client's guilt or innocence in this matter. His forehead was wrought with deep wrinkles as he squeezed his eyes shut and rubbed the back of his neck. "You know, Detective," he said, finally opening his eyes, "I know the circumstances surrounding O'Connor's death and my client—"

"And Rosie Contreras' death too," Cherry interjected.

"Yes, yes, and Rosie Contreras. Please forgive me. But this just doesn't make sense. I honestly find it very difficult to believe that my client was involved in any way in these two terrible deaths. I'm sure that you have heard this all before, but I just can't picture Nicholas Fischer committing these murders. A number of items just don't seem to add up."

"Unfortunately, Mr. Buerling, I see this happen all too often. An all-American person who is an upstanding citizen goes on a killing spree and commits horrible acts. It happens too often."

Buerling looked away and continued rubbing the back of his neck. After half a minute he looked back at Cherry and met his eyes. "Okay, I'm ready. Let's go, Detective."

Cherry led the way and opened the door to the Green Room and Buerling entered. Fischer stood up, eyes wide open with a mixture of anticipation and fear. Buerling slowly walked over to him and put his right arm over his shoulders.

"Listen, Nick, I'm sorry. But the detective here is going to arrest you and press formal charges against you for the murder of Sen. William O'Connor, III." Buerling paused for a moment and continued. "You are also the lead suspect in the murder of Rosie Contreras."

Dr. Fischer's heart sank to a depth he did not know was possible. He had never been arrested before. He had never had a run-in with the law. Not even when he did wild and crazy things as a youth. Yet now, he was being formally charged with the murder of a state senator in a case that quickly gained national media attention. The strength in his knees gave out as he sank to the floor, barely catching himself with his forearm on the edge of the table. His attorney quickly grabbed him in a bear hug around the chest, picked him up, and sat him in his chair.

"No, no, this can't be happening to me." His voice quivered as he began to shake violently. Just this morning, Fischer was on the verge of announcing a major discovery that would place his name among some of the greatest scientists and thinkers of the ages. Now he was about to have his name placed with some of the most deviant criminals of his time. He had been convinced that the media attention regarding his new discovery would make him a household name. Now he was to become infamous.

Fischer stood up and grabbed his attorney by the lapels of his jacket and pulled him in tight. With clenched teeth, he shouted, "Help me, Jacob! Get me out of this mess."

Cherry motioned into the two-way mirror and four police officers rushed into the Green Room. They separated Fischer from his attorney and handcuffed his hands behind his back. By this time, Fischer was sobbing uncontrollably. He resisted for a few seconds, dropping to the floor in a futile protest, but the four officers quickly picked him up by his arms and his legs and carried him out of the Green Room.

Chapter 27
It Doesn't Add Up

LIKE VIRTUALLY EVERYONE ELSE in the country, Chase Manhattan was following the story of the murdered Massachusetts State Senator William S. O'Connor III and Rosie Contreras on television and on the Internet. The story already had the makings of a Hollywood epic, and the media was doing its best to sensationalize the story. Linda Fontana, the Boston Police Commissioner, already announced at a press conference that Prof. Nicholas Fischer of MIT had been arrested for the two murders. The media performed its due diligence and uncovered the bad blood between O'Connor and Fischer. There was even speculation on a love triangle gone awry. The increasingly wild theories and conjecture added fuel to the already-growing national story. The tabloid television shows milked the story for all it was worth and really stoked the public's fascination with the case.

Chase knew who Prof. Fischer was. As a physicist, Chase had read dozens of Fischer's articles over the years, even citing him numerous times in his dissertation as a student at UC-Irvine. Chase quickly started asking himself questions and making connections about the events that mesmerized the nation. He understood there were dozens of brilliant scientists and theoreticians worldwide who devoted their lives to discovering breakthroughs in wormholes. As an MIT professor and partner to some of the top global companies such as Globalized

Dynamics, Fischer was on the fast track and an odds-on favorite to find a breakthrough in this life-changing technology.

Chase had studied the personal and professional lives of about twenty of these men and women, including Fischer, and he had a very good understanding of their character, integrity, and ethics. He wondered how Fischer could end up murdering these two people. It just didn't make sense as he tried to separate fact from fiction in the articles he read and the news stories he watched.

The media already had learned that O'Connor was attacked with a sword in his office and was severely beaten, and that one of his limbs, most likely an arm, was cleanly severed from his body. They also reported that the weapon had not been recovered. Reporters produced a profile of Rosie Contreras from interviews with coworkers and neighbors. Although they uncovered sordid details about Rosie's past (that the background check did not turn up when she applied for work at the State House two years ago), the investigative reporters seriously doubted that Contreras had the ability to inflict this kind of physical damage on the state senator.

Chase asked his good friend, Fred Merrill, to gather as much information as possible on O'Connor, Rosie Contreras, and Nicholas Fischer. He also asked Fred to go as deeply as he felt comfortable in uncovering any information about the murders and the arrest from the Boston Police Department that was not being disclosed to the public.

Fred confirmed that a sword was used but was never recovered, and the police were baffled as to how a sword could be smuggled into and out of the State House. They thoroughly searched the oldest building on Beacon Hill three times and found no such weapon. Video security showed Rosie entering and exiting the building for the previous month and up to the time of the murder, and all she carried in and out with her was a shoulder-strapped handbag.

She had to empty the contents on her way into the building when beginning her shift, but she didn't need to when exiting. Although the police noticed that Rosie began to carry the medium-sized aluminum suitcase in her bag, the security officers only asked her to open it up the first three days she carried it. The security officers confirmed in their report that she only carried a few cosmetics and other personal hygiene items. After that, they never asked her to open it again. The police were certain that she could not conceal a sword in the handbag she had with her that morning.

Using sophisticated data mining and relational software, Fred also discovered an associate of Fischer's, Dr. Gloria Newcombe, was one of the people murdered in the highly publicized killings at Globalized Dynamics. So far, the media had not made the connection between Fischer and Newcombe, and he did not think the detectives in Boston had. At least, not yet.

Sitting in his home office on a Sunday afternoon, Chase leaned back in his chair, closed his eyes, and let his mind run wild. He imagined that it was possible—far-fetched, perhaps, but entirely possible—that Prof. Fischer had done the impossible. Maybe the man had achieved a breakthrough in wormholes and was actually able to enter the state senator's office, kill him, and make his escape. No witnesses, no problems.

But there were problems with this theory. Chase knew that it would take a separate mechanism to open each end of the wormhole. It would take two people to make this happen, one on each end. That's where the State House employee Rosie Contreras entered the picture. She was his accomplice, and he killed her to cover his tracks.

But the holes in this scenario were obvious. Why would Prof. Fischer keep the gun used to kill an accomplice? He didn't seem like the kind of guy who, at fifty-four-years old, could cause that much injury on a man ten years younger and in much better shape. Chase narrowed his eyes, focused on imaginative alternative solutions, then opened them after a few minutes. The answer was obvious. What if someone else stole the ability to open wormholes, kill the two State House employees, and frame the professor? This was entirely feasible. He had to admit it sounded crazy, but he couldn't get the idea out of his mind that a breakthrough in wormholes had actually been discovered and used as the primary vehicle in the murder. The thought consumed his mind for two days as he locked himself in his house and considered the possibilities.

Fred Merrill, who provided Chase with the room key and the combination to the floor safe at the Wynn Hotel in Las Vegas, identified Fischer's attorney Jacob Buerling, and provided his telephone numbers, including his private cell phone. Fred was great at what he did—one of the best in the business. Chase thought to himself that he would not want a guy like Fred trying to hunt him down. Once again, Chase had talked a reluctant Fred Merrill into briefly coming out of retirement just one more time.

Chase picked the phone up off his desk and dialed the professor's attorney's phone using the number written on the yellow Post-it note he slapped against his PC monitor. Buerling and a staff of seven assistants and dozens of boxes of white legal-sized files were packed into a conference room on the forty-fourth floor of his office suite in downtown Boston when his cell phone rang. He picked up on the third ring.

"Jacob Buerling here. Who is this?" he asked in a menacing voice.

Chase realized that he must have seen a name on his caller ID that he did not recognize. "Mr. Buerling, my name is Prof. Chase Manhattan, and I believe that I can offer you and your client, Prof. Fischer, some invaluable help with your case."

Jacob was quick to respond. "You have ten seconds to impress me before I hang up, Prof. Manhattan." The high-profile attorney stopped for a moment and stared at his cell phone. "Chase Manhattan," he mumbled to himself. "What kind of name is that?"

"Listen to me, Mr. Buerling. I know that your client was framed. I'm a professor of physics—just like your client. I understand that he must have been on the verge of an important breakthrough. I believe that someone else must have committed the murders and framed Prof. Fischer."

Buerling snickered into the phone, "That's it, Mr. Manhattan? That's all you have for me?"

"Mr. Buerling, please let me come to Boston to speak with you and Prof. Fischer. I think he's hiding something that he can't tell you about. I think I know what it is, but I can't talk about it over the phone."

Buerling suspected as much from his first meeting with Fischer the previous Wednesday afternoon. But he was unsuccessful in breaking through his client's wall of stone that surrounded his innermost secrets. Making matters more complicated: the murder of one of his client's partners, Gloria Newcombe. Globalized Dynamics was exercising extreme discretion in gathering and disclosing the details of what happened late last week in New Haven. They released a generic report to the public that a disgruntled employee shot up the place, killed four employees, and escaped without a trace. They then immediately proceeded to bury the story with the release of a breakthrough of their own with their Green Revolution initiatives, along with an announcement of a generous increase in their stock dividends that shifted the media's attention away from the four murders.

Jacob was able to gather enough information from his personal network to conclude that a professional assassin was responsible for the four murders, and that this person entered the building without a trace. His contacts ascertained that the assassin was female, and that she left the building with a black, medium-size metal suitcase that contained something worth killing four people over. Buerling's team was clearly days if not weeks ahead of the Boston Police Department in uncovering the link to the murdered state senator and Dr. Newcombe.

Adding to his migraine headache that day, Buerling received a call two hours earlier from Det. Cherry that the evidence sample of blood in Fischer's sink in his lab was a definite match to O'Connor. The DNA match was 99.7989 percent conclusive. Jacob Buerling understood he was up against the wall and had few reasonable options for moving forward with his defense.

He rubbed his forehead, then said the words that Chase thought he had little to no chance of hearing. "Okay, Mr. Manhattan, I'm passing my cell phone on to a Miss Dekker. She is one of my assistants who will perform a background check on you. If you are who you claim to be, I will allow you to speak with my client and me."

Buerling handed his phone to Angela Dekker, a law student and intern from Boston College. Chase e-mailed her the information she requested. Within twenty-four hours, Angela Dekker returned Chase's phone call and confirmed that Buerling had agreed to meet.

Chapter 28
Flight to Boston

FLIGHT 942 TOUCHED DOWN at Logan International Airport at 7:48 a.m. Chase was glad he found a first-class seat at the last moment and enjoyed a good night's sleep on the red-eye flight. He had a lot of work to do and not much time to do it in.

Chase knew that he was taking a huge risk. He couldn't be certain Buerling would allow him to see Prof. Fischer. Buerling told Chase he would do a background check to confirm that Chase was really who he claimed to be. Although he checked out, there was still no guarantee that Buerling would follow through on the agreement. Chase understood that high-profile attorneys changed direction at a moment's notice without any notification to those they deemed insignificant.

Chase only had a carry-on, and he was able to make his way immediately to the shuttle bus that took him to the Taj Boston Hotel on the corner of Arlington and Newbury streets, where he unpacked his suitcase and took a long, hot shower. He chose the Taj Boston because of its cherished tradition and classic style. The hotel had a traditional design with a certain old-world charm that newer hotels lacked. His suite even had a working wood-burning fireplace, complete with a fireplace butler. This was a necessity for a Southern Californian traveling to Boston in the dead of winter.

Chase stayed here once a few years ago and appreciated the art and antiques on display. He also had a sweeping view of the Public Garden and could look out on the ice skaters who braved the cold. Chase shivered at the thought. The hotel was also close to the theater district, although he was not counting on having time to see a play. The professor embraced change and was fascinated by the new Mediterranean-style hotels and resorts in south Orange County, but he also had a deep appreciation of the way things were, a time gone by that existed only in memories of the elderly, history books, museums, and a few choice hotels.

Chase took the elevator downstairs to eat the sumptuous breakfast that he knew he could not get on the plane, even in first class. He needed to start the day right if he were to accomplish what he had set out to do. Chase ate here previously and appreciated dining under the cobalt-blue and crystal chandeliers. New England possessed an old-world charm that was difficult to find in Orange County.

He ordered his favorite breakfast: one egg, two egg whites, spinach, *pico de gallo*, cheddar cheese, and parmesan cheese with a side of fresh fruit. And coffee, of course. Chase drank three cups, half-regular mixed with half-decaffeinated. Normally, he started the day off with a cup within minutes of waking up. But this day, he waited until he was settled into his hotel room, had a hot shower, and sat down waiting for his healthy breakfast. Now he was ready to meet the challenges that lay ahead of him. First up was Jacob Buerling.

Chase paid for his meal and left a generous tip. His philosophy was you never know when you will get the same waitress again and need exceptional service. He knew he would be back for a Mediterranean-style meal for dinner. Well pleased with the food and service, he walked back through the lobby and took the elevator back to his suite on the 15th floor. Sitting at his desk, he dialed Buerling's personal cell phone. Chase knew that Buerling was a very busy man. He was relying on Buerling recognizing his name on his caller ID.

Buerling picked up on the first ring. "Buerling here."

"Mr. Buerling, good morning. This is Chase Manhattan. I'm calling you from the Taj Boston. How are you today?"

"Let's skip the pleasantries, Prof. Manhattan. I'm a very busy man. You have traveled a long way to talk to my client. It's Prof. Fischer who you wish to speak with, not me. Am I correct?"

Chase knew he needed to get to the point. Why waste Buerling's time and risk having him discontinue the conversation "Yes. That's correct, Mr. Buerling. Can I see him today?"

Buerling thought briefly before answering. "Let's be certain about this, Prof. Manhattan. The only reason I am allowing you to speak with my client is because I am quickly exhausting my resources. I have run your background check, and you seem to be who you say you are. If you can add any insight into this matter, then you will be most helpful. If not, then you will be wasting valuable time for me and my staff."

Chase walked a thin line. He knew that what he was acting on was suppositions and assumptions. But he also knew that he would only have one chance to talk to Prof. Fischer and he needed to speak with him as soon as possible, regardless of the consequences.

"Thank you, Mr. Buerling. You won't regret this."

"If I am to regret this, Prof. Manhattan, rest assured, you will do the same. Do I make myself clear?"

"Yes sir," answered Chase in a respectful tone, all the while trying to suppress the disdain he was quickly forming for this prick of an attorney.

"Prof. Fischer is being held at the Suffolk County Jail on Nashua Street. Meet me there at 2:00 this afternoon on the front steps. You have thirty minutes to impress me. Do you understand?" Jacob Buerling wasn't thrilled about allowing someone from the West Coast see his client, so he thought he would make Chase suffer by making him wait outside the station for him in the freezing cold winter of New England.

"Yes, I do. And thank you again, Mr. Buerling. I'll be wearing—"

"I know what you look like, Prof. Manhattan. Trust me, I have performed a more than thorough background check on you. Two o'clock sharp on the front steps." And with that, Jacob Buerling ended the call.

Chapter 29
Suffolk County Jail

CHASE STEPPED OUT of the Taj Boston, hailed the first cab he saw, and made his way to the Suffolk County Jail on Nashua Street. He wanted to arrive early—but not so early that he froze in the 12-degree weather (that didn't even factor in the windchill index).

Wearing only his dark brown leather jacket and a cotton sweater, Chase wasn't dressed for a winter storm in New England. He didn't even have anything to keep his head or neck warm. He couldn't remember the last time he saw his breath before today. To keep warm, Chase paced back and forth in front of the station and occasionally jumped in place. He didn't want to chance going inside the station to warm himself as Buerling seemed like the type of prick who would walk away if Chase wasn't on the front steps when he showed up.

At 2:00 p.m. sharp, Buerling opened the front door of the Suffolk County Jail from the inside. He chuckled at the sight of Chase with his red ears, rosy cheeks, and scarlet-colored nose, underdressed for the weather and doing his best to keep his blood from freezing in his veins.

"Prof. Manhattan," Buerling exclaimed as he stepped out of the lobby and extended his right hand to Chase. "It's a pleasure to meet you," he said with a deviant smirk.

Chase wasn't happy with Buerling telling him to meet him on the front steps while he was warm and comfortable inside the building. But Chase had virtually no leverage, so he reached out with a strained smile and shook the attorney's hand. "Thank you for seeing me today," Chase said through chattering teeth. *Remind me to punch you in the face later*, he thought to himself.

Buerling led Chase through the metal detectors and escorted him through a series of doors and halls until they arrived at the room where Nicholas Fischer was waiting. Two sheriffs were stationed by the door in the hallway, one on either side. They searched Chase again, a little more thoroughly than he thought was necessary. Chase wasn't sure how much privacy he would have with the professor, and seeing the sheriffs on the outside of the door wasn't a good sign.

In his bright orange jumpsuit and sitting in a chair at a table, Prof. Nicholas Fischer looked like he was recovering from a long drinking binge. Although he had showered and shaved a few hours earlier, he looked weak, depressed, and defeated. Chase easily discerned an aura of malaise and melancholy emanating from the professor. He looked very pale, and was in an abysmal state, as if he were suddenly transported from a world of tranquility and peace to an unknown universe filled with fear and uncertainty.

Buerling introduced Chase to Fischer, who merely nodded, keeping his handcuffed wrists and hands clenched together on the table and not offering a handshake. Chase sat down opposite Prof. Fischer while Buerling stood to the side, occupying his favorite position: his hands folded in front of him, head tilted slightly back, and gazing out at Chase through half-closed eyes.

"I have taken the liberty of explaining to Prof. Fischer who you are, your background, and why you are here to see him," Buerling said, displaying as little facial expression as possible.

"Prof. Fischer, first allow me to thank you for seeing me," Chase said with sincerity. Fischer was apathetic and struggled to make eye contact with him. He labored just to keep his head up.

"I'll get right to the point, Professor. I've been following the events of this case very closely."

"So has the rest of the nation, thanks to the media attention this case has been receiving," Fischer snarled sarcastically.

"I believe that there's much more to this story than what the media has been telling us, Prof. Fischer. As a physicist myself, I can clearly see that there is something much deeper below the surface than anyone is aware of, and that you are letting on to."

Fischer looked at Chase through one eye, hands still clenched together on the table. To date, nobody had attempted to make contact with him and dig below the surface of common knowledge. But Chase had at least managed to pique the professor's attention with his cross-country flight. "Oh, and what makes you say that, Prof. Manhattan?"

Chase clasped his hands together and leaned into the table. "Most people think that you killed or had Sen. O'Connor killed to stop him from halting funding to your department and to your projects." Fischer looked intently at Chase. Buerling noticed this was the most emotion his client displayed since his arrest.

"But I believe your work was already completed. You didn't need any additional funding at this point. So why kill the senator? It doesn't make any sense." Fischer continued to stare, and Chase wasn't sure if he had made a connection with the professor or if he would lunge across the table at him in a violent fit of rage.

Chase continued, "Your partner from Globalized Dynamics, Dr. Gloria Newcombe, was also recently killed at her place of employment. The one commonality is that nobody understands how the killer was able to enter the buildings without being noticed. In the events that transpired at the State House, the killer actually left the building without a trace."

Fischer continued to glare at Chase. To his knowledge, the media had not yet made the connection between the murders of O'Connor and Newcombe, and he was amazed that this stranger at the other end of the table knew this.

"As a professor and a physicist myself, I think I can see what was going on here." Chase held eye contact with his counterpart, giving him an *I know what you did last summer* look.

After almost a minute of contemplating and fidgeting while alternating stares up at the ceiling and down at the floor, Fischer looked up at his attorney. "Jacob, would you excuse us, please? I would like a few words with Prof. Manhattan—alone."

Breakthrough

Buerling finally broke from his unblinking poker face. He stepped forward and with a slim, crooked smile said, "Nicky, as your counsel, I think it's prudent that I stay and listen to what Prof. Manhattan has to say." Chase disliked Buerling even more. He despised phony smiles and false pretenses.

Fischer raised his right hand before his attorney could say anything else but not breaking eye contact with Chase. "It's okay, Jacob. We should only be a few minutes. Thank you."

Buerling looked at the two people in front of him—first at his client, then at Chase, and finally back to Fischer. "Okay, Nicky. I'll be right outside the door. But use wisdom and good judgment. This case is difficult enough as it is." Jacob Buerling then stepped outside of the room.

Fischer leaned back in his chair, his shackled hands still folded on the table. He was even beginning to form a slight smile. "So tell me, Prof. Manhattan, why should I allow you to help me? I don't even know you."

Chase countered, "Tell me, who from the scientific community has offered to help you? I'm the first visitor outside of your family who you've had contact with. Is that correct?"

Fischer lowered his head and nodded.

"Who from your network of friends and associates has offered to help you?"

Fischer shook his head but said nothing.

"Prof. Fischer, I see what's going on. Your field of expertise is the same as mine. I also delved into Dr. Newcombe's articles that she wrote over the years, and she had the same vision as you. I can see that you have made a breakthrough in something, and I think I know what that something is."

Fischer looked up at Chase. "Why don't you just come right out and say it, Prof. Manhattan?"

Chase leaned in closer. "You discovered a breakthrough in Einstein-Rosen Bridges. You and Dr. Newcombe discovered how to transport people and things from one place to another. Someone must have found out about your breakthrough, stolen the technology from you, and used it to kill Sen. O'Connor and Dr. Newcombe. They then framed you for O'Connor's murder."

A glimmer of hope surfaced on Nicholas's face as he slowly sat up in his chair. He formed a quick, crafty grin, then let out a loud, boisterous laugh that echoed inside the room. Chase hoped that Buerling wouldn't hear it and return. Fischer took three deep breaths and began to regain his composure. Chase noticed a shade of color came back into his face.

"Okay, Chase, I'm the criminal court system. I'm my attorney. I've been told what you just said. Do you think that would make a good defense?" He laughed some more until tears streamed down his cheeks.

Chase reached across the table and gently grabbed Fischer's left wrist with his right hand. "I understand your problem. I've been theorizing the same material, searching for the same breakthrough, although with much less success, and my peers and students have been laughing at me."

At this point, Fischer was able to gather his composure and was now in an engaging mood. He also leaned into the table. "Tell me, Chase, what would you do in my situation? Would you have the police confiscate the technology that could back up my story?"

"No, I wouldn't do that. I've already thought that through. Breakthroughs like this could be used to further and advance mankind, or they could be used for personal agendas that are not in mankind's best interests."

Fischer leaned back, his face regaining more color. He was smiling again and nodding his head, as if he were lecturing and a student just made an important connection.

"That's right. Instead of transporting goods and people for honest and ethical reasons, the wrong people could transport dangerous material."

Chase continued the thread. "Illegal drugs could be transported across borders, for example."

Fischer formed an even larger smile. "Large sums of money could be stolen from a bank vault. In and out without a trace."

"A terrorist could appear in the Oval Office and blow everybody up."

"A nuclear device could be delivered to the ten largest cities in North America and detonated on the same day. The list goes on and on."

Chase leaned back in his chair and sighed deeply. Fischer stared at him for about a minute before speaking again. "What else, Chase? What other disasters could this breakthrough do to harm mankind?"

"I've thought about that, too," Chase replied. "I've been considering the ramifications of this for years. My parents were Catholics, charismatic Catholics, who believed that the spiritual and physical worlds could interact. An example comes to mind: Jacob's Ladder in the book of Genesis, where there was an actual, physical location here on earth where angels descended from heaven."

"But one doesn't need to be a Christian to believe in the convergence of the spiritual world, the metaphysical world, and our world. Isn't that correct, Chase?"

"Yes, that's true. Most civilizations from the dawn of mankind have believed that there is a spiritual world that is actually more real than our physical world."

Fischer allowed those words to float in the air for a few moments before continuing. "What if someone took a journey through a wormhole and brought something back with them—something that they wouldn't be aware of with their five senses, yet something that is very much alive and ultimately unleashed on an unsuspecting world?"

Chase squinted in disbelief, then took a few moments to reflect on the professor's last statement. "I remember when I finally graduated with my Ph.D. I thought that I was so smart. I thought I would discover all kinds of amazing answers to things that have plagued mankind for millennia. But I approached them in the physical realm. I remember sitting with my father and discussing this with him shortly after I finished school."

"What did your father have to add to the conversation? I'm confident he had a perception of reality that was quite different than yours."

Chase nodded. "He did. He reminded me that our physical world is not so concrete after all. For example, the distance between an atom's nucleus and its electrons is vast, not to mention the distance between atoms themselves. An electron can orbit as much as 100,000 times the diameter of its respective atom's nucleus. This, of course, means that solids such as these chairs we're sitting on are, in reality, made up of more space than matter."

"That's correct, Chase. It is the energy given off by the negatively charged electrons being attracted to the pull of the positively charged protons in the nucleus of the atom that causes the structural integrity we perceive when we see and touch solid objects."

"And then there's dark matter," Chase continued, wasting no time escalating the conversation to a higher level. "According to the theory, our universe is missing most of its mass. In an indirect manner, we know it's out there, but we cannot measure it directly. Theoretically, this is where the spiritual world could exist. A sort of parallel universe that is actually more real than our physical world."

"Okay, Chase, what if a spirit, a spiritual hitchhiker, if you will, who was less than friendly, decided to latch onto a person who was traveling through a wormhole? Do you think that would be possible?"

Chase considered the question, then replied, "I'm not sure, Professor. If a person is transported immediately from point A to point B, how can a spirit latch on and enter our world at the other end?"

Fischer was beaming. He was excited that someone else not only understood these matters, but actually believed that they could indeed be realistic. "Listen to me, Chase. May I call you Chase? We do not really have any idea what else is out there, but there is no reason to believe that we are the only intelligent beings in the universe. That would be arrogant and asinine. There is no reason to believe that whatever else is out there will necessarily have to obey the same laws of physics that we do." Fischer stared and smiled at Chase as his student considered the matter.

"The Bible does say that a day is like 1,000 years, and that 1,000 years are as a day to God. Although we may experience almost instantaneous transportation through a wormhole, time may not behave at all like we think it should within the wormhole."

Fischer looked like a new man, one who had just been released from a prison. In a sense, he was. He could now share his secrets with someone else who could comprehend what he was involved with for the past ten years. His colleagues could understand the physical aspects, and he knew peers who could understand the metaphysical aspect, but

Chase was the first who he felt had a balanced grasp on both sides of the subject.

"Chase, oh, and you can call me Nick. In fact, call me Nicky. All my friends do. Chase, I need your help."

Chase leaned back into the table. "That's what I flew all the way across the country for, Nicky. Just tell me what you need."

"You obviously understand what I have been up to. There are currently six suitcases for opening and closing wormholes, and all have been successfully tested. Three are for sending and three are for receiving. They work. They actually can transport a human being from point A to point B." Then Fischer's demeanor dropped. He sighed deeply. "The problem is that they have fallen into the wrong hands."

"And you want me to locate and retrieve the six suitcases?"

"Yes. I need you to retrieve all six suitcases and destroy them."

Chase immediately grew suspicious and wondered why Fischer would ask him to locate and destroy the six suitcases. "Nicky, why don't you have someone else do this for you? You have a son that works with you, correct? Why not ask him?"

Sitting back up in his chair and leaning into Chase, Fischer dropped his bombshell.

"Isn't it apparent yet, Chase? The only other person who could specifically know what I was doing, outside of the recently deceased Dr. Newcombe, would be my son, Nicholas."

Chase let the reality of the statement set in, then replied with astonishment. "Do you mean that you believe your *son* was the one who murdered those people?"

"He may not have been the actual killer, but he certainly played a major role. He planned everything. I'm pretty his group of friends that he runs with are also involved and helping him with the murders. He made sure that the murders were carried out. And, sadly, he framed *me* for the murders."

Chase stared intensely at Fischer. Although he flew across the county to meet the professor on the premise he believed Fischer was somehow innocent of the murders, Chase was still a bit hesitant to move forward with the professor's plan of retrieving the suitcases.

Fischer perceived Chase's tentativeness and responded, "Chase, if there's any doubt in your heart, then you've *got* to believe me when I say that I *never* killed any of those people. Although it's true the late senator and I disdained each other, I merely wanted to derail his political career by exposing inappropriate actions he indulged in. I swear to you I never had any intention or involvement in murdering him."

Chase stood up and shook his head. "I don't know what to say, Nicky."

Fischer stood as well. Shackled at the ankles, he shuffled over to Chase at the other side of the table. "Just say that you will find the suitcases and destroy them."

Chase had been faced with a similar decision when he agreed to retrieve the stolen flash drive a few weeks earlier in Las Vegas. He was not a person who normally broke into a place with the intention of taking items that did not belong to him, *especially items that would be of special interest to police investigating the murder of a state senator.* But he also understood that breakthrough technologies in the wrong hands could harm countless innocent lives. In a utilitarian sense, Chase knew that the moral worth of his actions and the contribution to the greater good of mankind outweighed the ethical dilemma of breaking the law. Considering the potential consequences of Prof. Fischer's son's future actions, he felt a moral obligation to stop further murders, and that the end would certainly justify the means.

"I guess I can do that." Chase and Nicky were now standing a few feet apart, looking deeply into each other's eyes as if they were at the pinnacle of the largest negotiating session in the history of humankind. "But there is still one more question that you have yet to address."

"Indeed, there is, Chase," an ardent Fischer replied, forming a full ear-to-ear smile. "You wish to know the source of the power the suitcases use to open the wormholes."

Chase continued to stare at the professor. He fully understood what Fischer had accomplished. "Either you have harnessed the power of antimatter, or you're using nuclear material."

Nicky stepped back, still grinning. "Guilty as charged, Chase. There are only six enriched uranium and plutonium batteries left out of eight that I originally built. My son, Nicholas, must have found at least two of them, one to send an assassin into the State House and a second to transport the assassin back. I believe that this is where Rosie Contreras—the murdered State House employee—enters the picture.

Breakthrough

She must have been used to bring a receiver suitcase into the State House and get the transporter out. She was killed shortly after that. A third battery was in the suitcase that Dr. Newcombe kept with her. She had a receiver suitcase. I sent her small office supplies over the past couple of weeks—staplers and paper clips and such. We used up two of the batteries in this manner. Again, Chase, these really do work."

Chase was skeptical. "How can these battery packs have the energy to open and close wormholes? Wouldn't an almost infinite amount of power be necessary to accomplish this?"

Fischer chuckled. "Chase, we are not traveling through time, nor are we traveling from our universe to another universe. We are not even traveling to another world within our own Milky Way. That would require energy from black holes or a gravitational pull that is beyond our means. Chase, all we are doing is opening and closing wormholes on a far smaller scale here on planet Earth. Consider this: a 3,000-mile wormhole from Boston to Los Angeles would require the smallest fraction of the energy needed to open a wormhole from our galaxy to a distant galaxy. Although a one-kiloton battery on both ends of a wormhole may seem extreme to us, this isn't even a minute fraction of the energy needed to travel to another galaxy. A 3,000-mile journey through a wormhole is not unreachable. Certainly a crosstown journey, like the one my son used to murder Sen. O'Connor, is possible."

Chase knew that he needed to carry out Fischer's request to retrieve and destroy the suitcases and the batteries. The suitcases would be easy. The batteries would take considerable planning. He would need help.

"I suggest you start at my offices. The police have finished their investigations there and my son has been working in the labs. I suspect he has four of the suitcases and the six batteries stored somewhere on or off campus. But there are still two more suitcases that are in one of my labs. I have them hidden in the bottom of an old oak cabinet. You can't miss it as it is unique to everything else in the lab. There's twelve inches between the base of the cabinet and the floor where I have a transporter and a receiver suitcase hidden. You can start with those."

"But how do I get in there?"

"I'll make arrangements with Nicholas through Jacob. My son probably still doesn't realize I know he's responsible for these recent events, so we still have the elements of discretion and surprise on our side. Jacob will tell him you are an associate of mine from out of town picking up a few small but expensive items that I borrowed from you. Just make it look good and pick up something that looks innocent enough, but expensive. However, it will be up to you as to how you retrieve the two suitcases. I suggest you send Jacob a text message to call Nicky a few minutes after you enter the building to have him retrieve some documents from my office that relate to my case. That should provide a distraction for you to work in the lab."

Chase took a deep breath and shifted his head side to side. "Okay, Nicky, I'll do it. I'll retrieve the suitcases for you, and then I'll find a way to destroy them."

"Thank you, Chase." Nicholas Fischer appeared relieved and hopeful. "I know I can count on you. Remember, these two suitcases in the oak cabinet do not have batteries in them, so transporting them in public should not be a problem. Once opened, they look like a geeky scientist's suitcase with a keyboard and not much more. They look innocent enough."

Chase was reluctant. He eyed Fischer and asked, "Are you sure, Nicky? I mean, these suitcases don't sound like your average laptops that one would take through an airport security checkpoint."

"Don't worry. I've taken them through numerous checkpoints without any problems. In fact, I took one through a TSA checkpoint here at Logan and flew to La Guardia and then back again. It drew the scrutiny of the TSA security, but they eventually let me through with no problem."

Fischer and Chase talked for another ten minutes, the elder professor enlightening the younger on other pieces of the wormhole puzzle, possible unforeseen risks, and implications that could benefit or harm humankind, depending on who possessed the suitcases and the batteries that he developed.

Finally the door opened, and two sheriffs walked in and escorted Prof. Fischer back to his isolated cell. Buerling peeked into the room, glared at Chase, and gave him a firm gesture with his middle finger then quickly left. Chase stood alone in silence for a few minutes to gather his thoughts and showed himself out.

Chapter 30
MIT

IT WAS NOW ALMOST FIVE O'CLOCK in the afternoon when the cab carrying Chase crossed the Charles River on the Harvard Bridge. It made a right turn onto Memorial Drive before turning left into the 168-acre Massachusetts Institute of Technology campus. MIT is one of the most prestigious schools in the nation, having produced 27 Nobel Prize winners and 37 Rhodes Scholars. Chase had been here once before on a previous trip to Boston when he was on vacation in New York. He took a day to drive up to Boston, explore the city, and spend an afternoon touring the campus. The college stretched out along a 1-mile path parallel to the Charles River in Cambridge. Looking across to Back Bay, Chase could see downtown Boston and its skyline from an impressive viewpoint. Although the chill factor was well below zero and he was woefully underdressed for the frigid air, Chase was mesmerized by the Boston skyline. It was a beautiful sight to see with the sun setting behind him and the lights from some of Boston's tallest skyscrapers reflecting off the surface of the Charles River.

MIT was going undergoing its third revitalization plan in its esteemed history as 10 new major construction programs transformed the campus once again. In Chase's eyes, the progressive yet inconsistent architecture such as the Stata Center for Computer, Information, and Intelligence Sciences at first resembled an adult version of Toontown in Disneyland. But he soon realized that there was continuity in the complex as the buildings were interconnected, a feature that was appreciated on bitterly cold days—like this one.

The cab stopped in front of Building 1 at 33 Mass. Ave. The Physics Department was spread across 13 different buildings and interconnected by sunlit walkways. Chase would have to meander through five buildings before reaching Eastman Laboratories.

He learned in his previous visit here that everything on campus is identified by numbers. The courses, the students—even the professors—are all assigned numbers. The buildings, even though they have names, are identified by numbers. The uninitiated can easily become disoriented trying to find their way around the campus. Chase once made the mistake of following a corridor with a large number 1 painted on it, thinking this would lead to Building 1, but the number 1 he saw merely identified the floor he was on and Chase ended up becoming more lost than he already was.

To make matters worse, in many sections of the campus, the buildings are not laid out in numerical order—or any kind of order for that matter. While wandering the corridors, Chase noticed Building 50 is situated between buildings 14, 18, 54, and 62. However, the buildings that ended in the number 6 were all connected, but in typical MIT fashion, not in numerical order. Chase had stubbornly tried to figure out the maze of corridors himself without asking for help.

Fortunately for him, some of the campus building numbers contained a letter with their number that helped give him a sense of direction. The buildings with a W told him that he was west of Mass. Ave. An N meant you were north of Vasser Street, and an E meant that you were east of Ames Street. There were no buildings identified with an S, as that would place him in the Charles River.

Despite the freezing cold, Chase slowly strolled into Building 1, taking a few moments to try to get a feel for the campus once again. He walked past a few people bundled up in parkas and scarves, walking briskly up and down the sidewalk. He thought about the warm, balmy weather he left the night before and hoped he could reschedule a flight out of Boston later that evening to return to the warmth and safety of Orange County.

Jacob Buerling set up a meeting between Chase and Nicholas Fischer, Jr. Chase was to meet him inside Building 1, otherwise known as Pierce Laboratory. Once he was inside the doors immediately facing Mass. Ave., a tall, thin, young man with short, dark brown curly hair and elongated facial features briskly walked up to him. He had a warm and welcoming smile, almost charming. His right arm was extended while he was still 10 steps away, and he quickly and enthusiastically covered the distance in a matter of a few seconds.

"You must be Professor Manhattan. Welcome to Cambridge. I'm Nicholas Fischer, Jr. Please call me Nicky," he said with a little more enthusiasm than Chase had anticipated. Nicky was dressed in black jeans, a thin, dark blue turtleneck sweater, and black tennis shoes. Chase noticed he was dressed as if he had been inside the warm building all day and would probably be here well into the evening. Chase immediately despised the man the moment he set eyes on him and wanted nothing more than to retrieve the two suitcases and get out as fast as he could. He hoped that Buerling would not be in a meeting or doing something that would distract him from calling Nicky.

Chase held out his hand and shook Nicky's while forcing a smile. "Thank you for seeing me on such short notice, Nicky. I really appreciate it."

"It's always a pleasure to meet one of my father's associates. I understand you're here to retrieve a few items that you lent to him?"

"That's right. I should be able to fit them into a banker's box, if you have one that I could use."

"I'm sure I do. I'll take you up to the labs right now."

Nicky led Chase through the interconnected buildings 1, 3, 10, 4, and finally into Building 6. Chase tried to avoid engaging in conversation with Nicky and was glad that Nicky was carrying on a monologue. He acted almost as a tour guide, pointing out areas of interest as they walked through the buildings and telling Chase about a few historical facts, famous alumni, and some of the breakthrough projects MIT was currently involved with. Nicky then began talking about himself and some of his projects. Chase noted he neglected to mention anything about his father's breakthrough in wormholes or anything concerning his father, Nicky, Sr.

Chase immediately saw that Fischer's son was nothing at all like his father. He was self-absorbed, and Chase was convinced he was delusional and driven by a nervous energy mixed with a touch of madness. He showed no signs of sorrow or remorse that he was responsible for the recent string of murders and then topping it off, framing his own father for them. But Chase played along, feigning interest in what Nicky was saying, occasionally nodding his head and looking around as if he were a fascinated tourist experiencing the place for the first time.

They entered Eastman Laboratories, took the elevator up to the third floor, and walked down two hallways to one of three labs that the elder Fischer shared with his son. Two labs were open to other students and staff. But only Nicholas, Sr., and Nicholas, Jr., had access to a small third lab, the same lab that junior used to send Staci through a wormhole to kill Sen. O'Connor. Nicky was still talking while he unlocked the door and let Chase in. The lab was fairly small. Chase estimated it was about 700 square feet. There was nothing unique that would distinguish this lab from any other lab. It was filled with the standard stainless steel tables, filing and storage cabinets, and about a dozen computers and monitors.

Once inside, Nicky finally stopped talking and looked at Chase as if he were expecting an ovation from his long-winded discussion about the campus and some of the projects that were currently taking place in the physics and chemistry departments at Eastman Laboratories. By now, Chase was completely repulsed by Nicky, Jr. For at least a few seconds, the pleasant thought passed through his mind about reaching out and punching this smug and obnoxious man in the face, and junior would never have known what hit him. He could literally knock the hell out of him, and no witnesses were around. Instead, Chase mustered up all the inner strength he had and restrained himself from acting on his impulses. He gracefully thanked Nicky again for meeting him on such a short notice. His hands still in the pockets of his leather jacket, Chase hit the send button on his cell phone that sent the prewritten message to Buerling notifying him to call Nicky immediately.

Chase looked around the laboratory and started to list a few items Fischer told him would be here, pointing to them as he called them out. Then Nicky's cell phone rang. It was Buerling. Nicky politely excused himself and took a few steps away from his guest to take the call. Chase looked around the lab and spotted the old oak cabinet the professor described. It was about 20 feet from him against a wall. He remained standing just inside the door of the lab and waited for Buerling to carry out his job.

Two minutes later, Nicky ended his call and faced Chase. "Prof. Manhattan, please excuse me for a few minutes. I need to go to my father's office and take care of some business. I'll be right back. Please feel free to take a look around for your items."

Once Nicky stepped out the door, Chase ran over to the cabinet, bent down, opened the two doors on the front, and quickly emptied the bottom shelf of its contents. Lacking proper tools and the time to remove the floorboard like he had been instructed by the professor, he then smashed his left palm into the floorboard and made a hole in it that he used to pry off the thin boards lining the bottom of the cabinet. Chase stared for a few moments at the silver and black suitcases that lay side by side on the cold, gray concrete floor. His heart began to race as he picked up first the silver transporter suitcase with his right hand and then the black receiver suitcase with his left. In his two hands, he held one of the deepest and most sought-after secrets of the universe.

Chase felt both elation and terror at the same time. His blood raced through his veins, bringing an extreme sense of euphoria. In his hands, he held the keys that could unlock one of the most wonderful and significant eras in the history of humankind. He also understood that he held the breakthrough that could destroy modern civilization and possibly send his world back to the dark ages. It was a mind-boggling thought. Carefully, he set the suitcases down on the floor and tossed the boxes, the files, and the splintered pieces of wood back into the cabinet, closed the doors, and retrieved the two suitcases again.

There was no time to waste. He walked out of the lab and into the hallway as fast as he could while trying not to look like he was up to something out of the ordinary. Fortunately, at this hour, the building was mostly empty. Fischer had given Chase a verbal layout of his office and the labs. Since the office was farther down the hall, Chase knew he could make it back to the elevator without having to pass Nicky on his way out.

Instead, he opted for the stairs. He did not want to chance Nicky walking the halls looking for him while he stood waiting for the elevator to slowly make its way up to the third floor for his escape. Chase cleared four to five stairs at a time. He held a suitcase in each hand so he wasn't able to steady himself using the guard rails. But he was more focused than he probably had ever been in his life. His adrenaline was pumping. He felt like he could almost fly down to the first floor with his eyes closed.

At the bottom of the stairwell, Chase slowed his pace to a fast walk and made his way back to Building I and out the front door to his waiting cab at the curb. He jumped in the backseat and told the driver to take him to the Taj Boston as fast as he could. The yellow and orange taxi made a three-point turn and sped back over the Charles River and into Boston.

Back in Cambridge on Mass. Ave., Jacob Buerling sat in his black Lincoln Navigator two blocks north from where the cab sped away with Chase and the two suitcases. He set his binoculars down on the passenger seat, picked up a yellow legal pad of paper, and noted the events that had just transpired and the time. Then he took a sip of his coffee and cursed under his breath, wondering what this slimeball from Southern California was really doing. He had originally humored the senior Fischer and Chase only because he saw that his case was quickly going nowhere and he seriously needed a break.

But now his client pulled some type of shenanigans and was withholding vital information. He was certain that an illegal activity just occurred inside Eastman Laboratories. He thought back to the information he received from one of his contacts regarding a suitcase stolen from Globalized Dynamics' New Haven laboratories that was worth killing Fischer's partner, Gloria Newcombe, one of their top scientists, and three other employees.

Buerling had no idea what was inside the two suitcases that Chase walked out of the building with. But he would find out. He always did. He had been in this business a long time, and he had a lot of money, a network of contacts across the country, and a prideful mean streak that would not allow anybody to make a fool out of him.

Chapter 31
Missing Treasure

NICHOLAS FISCHER, JR., finished gathering the documents Jacob Buerling asked him to put together. He failed to grasp the importance of these files, but followed through anyway so he would not display negative behavior that might attract unwanted attention as the investigation of his father proceeded.

Nicky reveled in his meticulous planning and cunning and his excellent play-acting abilities that fooled everybody, including the two detectives who questioned him about his father regarding the recent string of murders. Fortunately, he was in the presence of his mother during the time of questioning, and the direction of the questions fell mostly upon her. For all Nicky cared, his father could rot in jail. He didn't plan on ever visiting him again. Ever. Instead, Nicky would move forward with his plan to change the world in ways not seen since the Renaissance, the Industrial Revolution, or the Information Age. He had more important things to occupy his attention these days, like being the master architect who would usher in global changes. The world was waiting at his fingertips.

He walked back into the lab where he had left Chase a few minutes earlier, with an empty banker's box in one hand and a manila folder holding the documents that Buerling requested in the other. His heart skipped a beat when he saw the room empty. He immediately grew suspicious that his guest, a professor of physics, would take sensitive and expensive equipment out of the lab in his arms and not in the protection of a box. A professor would not normally do something like that.

Nicky dropped the empty banker's box and the manila file on the floor and very quickly walked through the lab looking for anything amiss. Junior was obsessive-compulsive when it came to order. He had a place for everything and kept everything in its place. Nicky ran from table to table, opening then closing every drawer. If anything was missing, or if Chase had searched for something, he would immediately know: the items in the drawer would be out of the precise order he had arranged them.

Nicky circled around the back wall of the lab, made his way to the front, and opened every drawer in the cabinets, then quickly closed them and moved on to the next cabinet. He also examined each desk drawer. Then he approached the old oak cabinet and immediately saw a few small pieces of splintered wood on the cement floor. He jerked open the two front doors. Inside, boxes, files, and splintered pieces of the floorboard were strewn haphazardly. Bewildered, he dropped to his knees and hurled the contents out across the floor. Suddenly he froze as he stared at what appeared to be a hiding place between the bottom of the cabinet and the gray cement floor, a hiding place just big enough to house the remaining two missing suitcases he had been desperately searching for.

Stunned, Nicky slowly stood up. He was beside himself. His head was a swirling storm of emotions ranging from rage to terror. His father clearly understood what had been taking place behind the scenes the past few days, and he had now taken the offensive from behind bars. Nicky had underestimated his father. The last time Nicky visited him in jail, he was with his mother, and the senior Fischer was a rambling mess who struggled to put a noun and a verb together. But now he obviously had a plan. He was organized and had competent people working with him to turn the situation to his favor.

Cursing silently, Nicky ran down the hallway and descended the same stairwell that Chase had taken a few minutes earlier. He pulled out his cell phone and called Buerling. The high-profile attorney saw the name on his caller ID. He was wondering what role his client's son was playing in this. He decided to let Nicky take the lead and monitor where he would go with it.

"Jacob Buerling here," he said calmly as he answered the call now on the other side of the Charles River and driving back to his office in downtown Boston.

Nicky was breathing erratically, but composed enough to converse. "Mr. Buerling, can you explain what's going on here?"

"I'm not sure I understand what you're talking about, Nicky," he replied.

"You send over this professor named Chase Manhattan who you tell me is an associate of my father. Then, once he is inside the lab, you call me to my father's office to retrieve some documents."

Buerling knew the two suitcases Chase walked out with from the Eastman Laboratories were stolen, and Nicholas Fischer, Sr., had used him to provide the distraction. He was convinced that whatever was transpiring with the senior Fischer and Chase Manhattan, the younger Fischer was not privy to.

"Nicky, I was merely following through with your father's request to assist Prof. Manhattan on retrieving some personal items he loaned your father, and to have you retrieve some files I need for his case. That is all," he assured him in a monotone.

Nicky was not sure what to think at the moment. He was confused by the events that had just unfolded. But he knew he had to bring those suitcases back, and to accomplish that, he had to locate Chase Manhattan. He burst out of the stairwell on the first floor and ran toward Building 1, where he first met Chase, feverishly looking around the near-empty lobby, then sprinting to the front door. "I need to speak with Prof. Manhattan. Where does he live? Do you have his phone number?"

Buerling heard the urgency in his voice. He knew that he could have Nicky, Jr., do his work for him. He wouldn't need to go through expensive channels to uncover what exactly was transpiring behind his back.

"Is something wrong, Nicky? Is everything okay?" he asked, sounding genuinely concerned.

"No, um … yes. Yes … everything is okay. He left while I went back to my father's office when I was on the phone with you. I think he may have taken a few items that I was using for a very important project. I just need to verify what he took from the lab, that's all."

Buerling was skilled at reading and interpreting what existed below the surface of a conversation, and he could hear the lie in Nicky's stammering voice. He was convinced that the contents in the suitcases would answer the most important questions he had about his case. He also understood that there was something else at stake that transcended the defense of Prof. Nicholas Fischer. Buerling knew that whatever Chase took from the laboratory was of such monumental importance that he began to place the well-being of his client on the back burner and gave the secret of the suitcases his No. 1 priority. He decided to give Chase's address to Nicky and then monitor events in the days to come through one of his channels.

"Sure, Nicky. Prof. Manhattan lives in Laguna Beach, Calif. It's in Orange County, south of Los Angeles. He's a professor at the University of California in Irvine."

Nicky was now standing at the front door and looking out onto the near-deserted Mass. Ave. He pulled out a small notepad he kept in his pocket and scribbled down the information, but stopped as soon as he heard Buerling utter the word *California*. Trying to catch his breath, he asked, "California? I don't understand, Mr. Buerling. Why is somebody from California here at my labs?"

Jacob noticed the words *my labs* that Nicky subconsciously used. He was beginning to have less respect for him. "You will have to ask your father about that. Are you sure everything is okay, Nicky? Is there anything I can do to help?" he asked with a smirk on his face and a false hint of compassion that was second nature to him. "Please let me know if I can do anything else for you."

"No. No, I'm okay, Mr. Buerling. Thanks for your help. I have to go now. Please tell my father I said hello when you see him again."

Chapter 32
The Plan

NICKY DIALED HIS GOOD FRIEND and one of the people in his inner circle, Khyati Dasmunsi, who, he knew, would be home from class by now. Khyati was born and raised in Mumbai, India, spoke fluent English, and retained little of her Indian accent. Her parents had sent her to MIT when she was eighteen to study computer science. Like Staci, she was a nerd at heart, but lacked the extreme physical looks and physical abilities that Staci possessed. However, Khyati more than made up for these deficiencies in the way that she carried herself and by her self-confidence and proper upbringing that translated into a particular sexiness. She was pretty and took care of herself in a simple manner that most men found attractive. On the surface, she seemed shy and even timid, but those she allowed in her inner circle of friends came to know her as fun-loving, quick-witted, and a clever practical jokester.

Khyati had worked as a professional hacker for some of the most sophisticated security system companies in the country. She started as a designer for computer and network systems, but her managers soon realized her talent for finding gaps in her coworkers' work. Originally, she was a white-hat hacker who went to great lengths to identify and exploit gaps in existing systems that were already sold and in use, then she had the solutions in place and ready to go.

In a relatively short time, Khyati's expertise became in high demand as she was employed to try to break into security and network systems in the private and corporate world. Soon, the federal government approached her, employing her services to find holes in some of their most sensitive security systems. Khyati did not come cheap. She could basically name her price. That's why she could afford the house by herself.

But the security business was a game of cat-and-mouse, where the good guys and the bad guys were in a constant struggle to devise new ways to outwit each other. Khyati transitioned into the shady world of working as a grey hacker, where she used illegal black-hat techniques to satisfy her employer's needs, such as spying on some very bad people without a search warrant. These acts may not have been malicious in nature, but they were illegal acts, and crimes had been committed.

Khyati quickly grew bored, and the thrill of being a black-hat hacker, or a cracker, soon became the outlet of her creativity and curiosity. In the past year, she had found herself taking fewer honest jobs and more assignments that crossed the gray line into the black-hat realm.

She picked up on the first ring.

"Khyati," Nicky said before she could say hello, "I … I need you to find out everything you can about a Chase Manhattan in Laguna Beach, Calif. He's … he's a professor at the University of California at Irvine."

Khyati sat at her kitchen table finishing a plate of chicken tikka masala. "I can do that, Nicky. Do you need this information right away? You sound frantic."

Nicky always prided himself on maintaining his self-control under pressure. But he was clearly shaken by the day's events in the laboratory. He didn't realize that he was stammering, a problem he thought he conquered in junior high school.

"Listen, Khyati, my father and his attorney just arranged for a man named Prof. Chase Manhattan to visit the laboratory on campus. Long story short, he managed to walk away with the two missing suitcases that we've been looking for."

Khyati abruptly stopped eating her dinner and quickly stood up from her chair. She carried the paper plate with her half-eaten meal and the plastic silverware to the trash can, and then walked toward the basement. "Chase Manhattan? What kind of name is that? Anyway, he should be easy to profile. Give me a few hours and I'll have it for you."

"I'll be at your place shortly. I'll also need a false identity in order to fly a certain someone out to California and bring back the two suitcases. She'll need a driver's license and a couple of credit cards. I'll have her get a haircut on the way over and pick up some black or brown hair dye."

"We can easily do that. I'm walking down the basement stairs now. I'll see you when you get here."

Nicky ended that call, hit the preprogrammed number for Staci at her apartment, and explained the chain of events to her. She closed her textbooks on robust statistics and nonparametric methods and drove to a salon halfway to Khyati's house. Thirty minutes later, she emerged without her blonde ponytail that she kept for the past fifteen years—and *with* a flirtatious, shoulder-length angled bob haircut. She saw a picture of Eva Longoria sporting the style on the cover of an entertainment magazine at the salon and thought that would be a good choice for this particular assignment. She stopped at a beauty supply store two blocks away and bought black hair dye. Ten minutes later, she pulled up to Khyati's house. Nicky's truck was already there. She walked up the driveway to the side door and knocked. Nicky sprinted up the basement stairs in a few seconds and let her in.

"Wow! You look great, sweetie. That's a terrific look for you," he said.

"Men, you're all alike," she said, turning around and modeling the back of her new hair style. "I know what you're thinking."

"No, really, I like it. It's time you lost the ponytail anyway."

At the bottom of the stairs, she stopped to look in a small mirror on the wall and run her fingers through her hair. "Well, maybe I just need a few days to get used to it."

Nicky ran his hands over her shoulders and kissed her on the neck. "I like it a lot. I can't tell you how much better you look with it."

She smiled at him in the mirror. "Well, then, if you like it so much, you can help me dye it black." She handed him a plastic bag with the dye, a plastic smock, and some plastic gloves. "Okay, let's get busy."

By 10:00 p.m., Khyati had the profile she needed on Chase. She called a friend who worked at the Massachusetts Registry of Motor Vehicles and e-mailed him the picture of a smiling young lady sporting a new jet-black hair style. She also started profiling her friend's new identity. Staci Bevere had just been transformed into Cathy Bennett of Concord, N.H. This was an identity she had created a few months earlier, complete with credit cards, ATM debit cards, and more than $24,000 spread out over three bank accounts. Khyati like to be prepared for these occasions when they arose. Cathy Bennett stared in the mirror, looking at her left and right profiles and modeling various poses and facial expressions while Nicky sat on a chair staring at her and fantasizing lustful thoughts about his girlfriend's new look.

Meanwhile, Chase changed his return flight and checked out of the Taj Boston, finding a seat in business class on the last flight out of Logan to Orange County. Getting the two suitcases through TSA was not easy, as they attracted the scrutiny of the security team as soon as they traveled through the X-ray machine. But after the X-raying, probing, and checking for any explosive residues were completed, Chase was able to board the plane with both suitcases as carry-ons, although he had to pay extra for one.

He had no idea what to do once he was back in Orange County. He would take the suitcases home and worry about it then. He was too anxious to sleep at this moment. Chase was running a number of wormhole scenarios through his head that Prof. Fischer spoke to him about earlier in the day. He thought about how to stabilize them so that they would not collapse while someone was traversing them. Finally, about an hour into the flight, an exhausted Chase Manhattan collapsed in his seat and nodded off for the rest of the flight back to the safety of the West Coast.

Back in Cambridge, Nicholas Fischer, Jr., Staci Bevere, and Khyati Dasmunsi were still awake, drawing up plans to fly the assassin to the West Coast and retrieve the suitcases. Time was of the essence. They needed to bring them back as soon as possible so that they could move on to the second phase of their operation. Nicky was very close to building a suitcase that could send *and* receive a traveler. The only real challenge left: decoding the secret of how to stabilize wormholes so that they would not collapse on the person traveling through them. Once he had this information, he could develop a two-way suitcase and send someone through a wormhole along with a second suitcase so they could send themselves back. He would no longer need a second person to set up a receiver suitcase—like he had needed Rosie Contreras to do in the State House.

The logistics for this trip were demanding, especially with a very small time frame to work with. But Nicky had an ace up his sleeve. There were three graduate students at the University of California at Santa Barbara who were friends of his and were actively part of his new vision for the world that Nicky had fashioned during the past two years. They met at a symposium in San Francisco the year before regarding the latest and greatest advancements in applied physics. They quickly learned that they had the same interests, the same disdain for the current state of the world, and the same vision for the immediate future that could replace the current failures caused by inefficient governments, large, greedy global conglomerates, and even larger banking institutions.

The UC, Santa Barbara students claimed to have had connections to a sophisticated, competent, organized, and very vicious group of people who were skilled in the dirty work that people like Nicky did not have the ability to perform himself. Nicky slowly leaked information regarding the possible breakthrough in wormholes and different plans of how they could use this discovery to change the world. The three UC, Santa Barbara physics students were more than a little excited about being a part of Nicky's venture. They were dedicated followers of Nicky and his vision. They had thrown their lot in with his group, which consisted of five adherents from MIT and a handful of other graduate students networked in Germany and Belgium.

Nicky made the call. He needed somebody to coordinate transportation, a hotel, a geographic overview of the Southland, and a ham sandwich for Staci. The cost was high. It would take Nicky a full day to wire the $100,000 broken down into 11 smaller increments, the same money that had lured Rosie Contreras to plant the receiver suitcase in the State House and smuggle the transporter suitcase out.

But the effort and the cash would be a small price to pay in order for Nicky to get his plan back on track. He would retrieve the two suitcases and kill the only witness who was privy to what had transpired in Boston the previous week. Nicky had accepted Chase Manhattan's challenge as to who would control this life-changing breakthrough. He considered the odds. He was the home team. He still had four suitcases and the six nuclear-powered battery packs. He believed he still maintained the momentum. He had the network of graduate students. He possessed the vision, and he was about to buy himself the services of a crime syndicate for a few days in Southern California who would give him the support necessary to clean things up on the West Coast, leaving no loose ends. He liked his odds very much. Nicky rolled the dice. He was ready to go.

Chapter 33
Sensei Masakata

DRIVING A RED AND WHITE DUCATI Desmosedici RR from Los Angeles north on the coastal highway to Santa Barbara was a dream come true for Staci Bevere. Leaving one of the worst snowstorms in recent memory for sunny days in the mid-seventies was the source of revitalization she desperately needed. With the three-hour time change working in her favor, her flight arrived at just past ten o'clock in the morning. The 100-mile drive north on Highway 1 snaked its way through some of the most beautiful and expensive real estate in Southern California.

When the crime syndicate responded that it had arranged transportation, along with a hotel and additional supporting personnel in Orange County for the next four days, she wasn't expecting a motorcycle in one of the parking structures at Los Angeles International Airport. But she wasn't complaining. Growing up with three brothers, she became a very experienced rider, especially off-road. The key was hidden between the seat and the gas tank, and Staci wasted no time making her way north on Century Boulevard and onto Coast Highway. She had no luggage as the syndicate had prepared fresh changes of clothing waiting for her at her hotel room in Orange County, along with any toiletries that she would need. All she brought with her was the knapsack on her back containing the clothes she flew in and the leathers she was now wearing.

Staci's destination was a Spanish-style villa north of Santa Barbara on the seaward side of Highway 101. A half mile separated the anonymous villa from the highway, and 300 feet of rocky bluffs separated the villa from the Pacific Ocean. The ringleader of the syndicate, Sensei Masakata, rarely accepted visitors, especially strangers. But Staci came highly recommended, and a large sum of cash was delivered to him the day before from an unknown source on the East Coast.

It was easy to miss the dirt-road entrance to the villa. Most drove right by without noticing or giving it a second thought even if they did see it. The entrance gate divided two pale pink, nondescript, fifteen-foot-high cracked stucco-covered walls that spread out over the 320-acre confine. Staci pulled up to the call box, took off her helmet, and pushed the black speaker phone button, then uttered the Japanese words, *Ai suru*, which translated means, "to love."

Sensei Masakata demanded his students display love and passion for the martial arts regardless of the style or form they practiced. To Sensei Masakata, martial arts were more than an art form or a way of life. They were a religion that superseded other relational affinities, and he compelled his disciples to train on a level that was far removed from the neighborhood martial arts studios that dotted the American landscape.

The sensei had seen too many American students who lacked love and passion for martial arts. They were more interested in the recognition of a black belt rather than earning the honor through discipline, time, and hard work under the tutelage of a master. He placed much of the blame on American instructors who lacked the passion themselves, people who advanced their students to the next level whether they were ready or not.

The gate opened, and Staci slowly made her way up the half-mile dirt path that led up to the villa where she would prepare for her task. The scrub, dirt, and rocks that dominated the scenery quickly gave way to a beautifully landscaped yard with terraced gardens of plants and flowers, many of which she had never seen before. The villa looked small at first glance. The scent of salt greeted her nostrils and she knew that the ocean had to be on the other side of the estate. She correctly deduced that what she saw was merely the entrance and the rest of the villa descended down the slope at least two or three levels and stopped at the edge of a cliff hundreds of feet above the shoreline.

She suspected there was probably no beach at the bottom of the bluffs, just a sheer wall of rock ascending almost straight up out of the water to the base of the villa. The place was more like a fortress rather than another multimillion dollar home lining the seashore. She expected the place to be at least 10,000 square feet and staffed by about a dozen servants and bodyguards. Although the exterior was distinctively Mediterranean, she understood that, in typical Japanese fashion, the outside of the building gave no hint as to what was inside.

Pulling up to the front door, she lowered her kickstand, climbed off the Ducati, and stretched. She expected to be met by at least two bodyguards, but instead, she was greeted by a gentle cool ocean breeze that came down from the northwest and swept around the north side of the villa's rounded walls. She took a few minutes to relax from her ride and attempt to distinguish the different scents given off by the flowering plants in the terraced gardens. Although she did not recognize all of the aromas, Staci was able to separate and identify twelve distinctive fragrances.

She was sure that there would be at least a few tests awaiting her. Nothing like what Black Mamba endured from Pai Mei in the *Kill Bill* movies. She only had three hours here. But the fact that she was to enter the villa without escort told her that there were tests to pass. Smell was the first test. Clearly there were four more waiting.

Staci walked up the three steps to the front door, took off her black leather boots, and let herself in. The foyer was dark except for a dimly lit path of small candles that extended forward twelve paces and immediately led down twelve steps to a second level. Staci slowly walked across the travertine tile to allow her eyes time to adjust from the bright sunlight to the barely lit indoors. Inwardly, she chided herself as she was fairly certain that she passed the first test but failed the second. Had the situation demanded, she would not be able to use her sight to defend herself in the dimly lit entryway.

The third test, she was certain, was to identify who or what was in the shadows to her left and her right on the second level. Controlling her breathing, slowly stepping forward through the candlelit path, and recalibrating her senses from temporary confusion, Staci could faintly make out the sounds of breathing from three different sources, two on the left and one on the right. She was now two out of three.

The path wound to the right, down a hall with two shoji doors on either side, and down another set of twelve stairs where the candles finally stopped. Looking forward, she saw by the fading light from the candles that the hallway had three shoji screen dividers on either side. Staci proceeded forward with cautious steps, feeling each screen with the palms of her hands. Only one door, the middle door on her right, had a slight variation in temperature that would be noticeable to a trained and disciplined student of Eastern martial arts. At least that's what Staci concluded. She deduced that there was activity of some kind in this room and entered it.

The room was barely lit by four candles in the four corners. In the center was a traditional Japanese rectangular *kotatsu* table with three indigo porcelain cups of green tea that sat upon three woven straw tatami placemats and three matching coasters. Beneath the center of the table, a heater barely raised the temperature of the room and, consequently, the door, and yet, Staci was able to discern the slight change in the temperature.

She immediately understood that she had to select the favorable tea—that is, the Japanese tea—over two close competitors. Sitting down in a <u>seiza</u> position and facing the door with her back to the far wall, she sampled all three teas. They were all very warm and she thought that they must have been just poured within the past two to three minutes.

Staci took her time smelling and sipping each cup of tea through her lips, allowing the liquid to gently wash over her tongue and teeth and making a slight hissing sound, pausing for thirty seconds between each sip. She gave herself five minutes to make her decision as to which was the authentic Japanese tea. The four candles in the corners were made of herbs and lacked any chemicals. As she slowly savored the tea, she inhaled deeply the faint, delicate aroma of the burning candles. Staci correctly deduced that the herbs in the candles were grown in Japan and would complement and enhance the Japanese green tea. Halfway through the three cups, she knew which tea was the Japanese tea. She realized that two of the teas were grown somewhere other than Japan, probably China and India. The taste of the tea on the left, however, was enhanced by the aromas of the candles and, thus, she was able to identify the proper tea.

There had been four tests requiring extraordinary use of each of the physical senses. Staci was three for four. *Not bad*, she thought, *after a cross-country, red-eye flight and a two-hour motorcycle ride, but probably not good enough for the master teacher.* She stood up from her *seiza* position, walked out of the room, and proceeded to the end of the hallway, to the seventh and last shoji door where the hallway ended.

She opened it and entered a classical Japanese room, forty-by-forty feet, with tatami mats lining the floor and a single shoji lamp centered on the ceiling. On the left and right sides of the room, elegant sliding shoji double doors made with opaque rice paper allowed diffused light to seep through, giving off a soft amber color and allowing a soothing effect to emanate across the room. The far wall was divided by a single-planed red cedar tree trunk. On the left was a tokonoma, featuring a black-and-white silk hanging scroll, and on the right, a *chigaidana* sparsely furnished with Japanese artifacts and small paintings.

Sensei Masakata sat at the *kotatsu* table with his back to Staci. To the uninitiated, this might seem a bit odd. But the guest of honor sits at the seat farthest from the door with the tokonoma behind him. This was a good sign. Staci felt far more confident than she had before entering the room a few moments ago. She slowly and gracefully walked to the far side of the table and sat in the traditional *seiza* position for Japanese women. She briefly looked at the teacher as she sat down. He was older than she imagined but had a vibrancy and energy that made him look twenty years younger.

The table sat on a deep, royal-blue futon with a red-and-black embroidered silk covering resting on the surface. On the table: a simple lunch in dark green bowls with pink lotus blossoms. The dishes included noodles, dried seaweed, and pickled vegetables. In the center of the table was an antique black-and-white glazed porcelain serving bottle of slightly warm sake.

She bowed her head and humbly said, *itadakimasu*, which translated means "I gratefully receive." The teacher was the first to act, picking up the dish of noodles, placing a healthy portion on his plate, and passing the dish to Staci. She only took half the amount which raised an eyebrow from the teacher. "I cannot perform business on a full stomach," she said in a most humble tone. The teacher grunted, helped himself to the dry seaweed and pickled vegetables, and passed the simple dishes to Staci. Sensei Masakata looked up at Staci with one eye as she feigned pleasure at eating the pickled vegetables. She doubted her performance fooled the teacher.

After finishing her meal, Staci placed her dishes back in the same places they were when she first sat down at the table and set her chopsticks back on the chopstick holder. She bowed her head again and said, *gochisosama*, which translated is a simple show of gratitude for the meal just eaten.

The teacher finally spoke in Japanese to Staci. "Tell me, how many different flowers did you smell while standing at the front of the villa?"

"Twelve, Teacher. Some I recognized and some were new to me for the first time," she responded in her best Japanese.

"There were fifteen in all," he frowned. "But twelve is the best to date. Nobody else has been able to smell more than eight distinct scents. You passed the first test, but only on a graded curve." Staci nodded her head.

"But you failed miserably in the second test. I could have easily killed you as soon as you closed the front door."

"I should have covered one eye for a couple of minutes before entering so at least one of them would have been accustomed to the dark."

"How many people were on the second level?"

"Three," Staci said confidently. "Two on the left and one on the right."

"Hmmm," the teacher growled in a low tone. "I'll have to have a word with my three bodyguards later. How did you know which door to enter on the third level?"

"I could feel a slight variation in temperature on the middle door on the right. The variation was caused by the heater under the *kotatsu* and the presence of the person pouring the tea."

Sensei Masakata paused for about thirty seconds, then asked, "Which tea was the Japanese tea?"

"The cup on the left. I was having difficulty distinguishing a difference between the three teas, but the herbs in the Japanese candles gave me the hint that I needed."

"There is nothing wrong with using one sense to aid a second sense in making a distinction." He smiled slightly for the first time.

"Very good. Even though you failed the vision test, you were able to use your other senses to pass the other four."

"And my final test, Master?"

"Your Japanese is good but not great. We'll stay with English for the remainder of the day. Yes, you passed that test as well. But only because I grade on a curve for Americans."

"Am I ready to proceed, Teacher?"

"Not yet," his tone and face expressed anger. "You have a problem many Americans have. You take drugs and use alcohol for recreational purposes and as a crutch when you are emotionally unstable. You need a clear head if you wish to proceed to the next level. You also take foolish chances and make bad decisions when you conduct business. You need to keep things simple and filter out these distractions or they can become the root of defeat or even death for you."

Staci looked with mouth agape. She did not know how the teacher would possibly know this other than he was gifted in the ability to see into the inner soul and spirit of people.

"And you also smoke cigarettes. You are weak in this area and must stop. Immediately. Before we go any further." He slammed his fist on the table for emphasis, stood up, and walked out the door.

Chapter 34
Ham Sandwich

Two of Sensei Masakata's female assistants led Staci away to a quiet room where she bathed, changed her clothes, and meditated for an hour. At 3:30 in the afternoon, Staci had more business to conduct. Her ham sandwich was being prepared.

Someone else was also meditating and preparing himself for the inevitable. How he ended up in this situation did not concern him at the moment. He only wanted to get through this particular day of trials and tribulation and leave this terrible place forever.

His name was Michael Vitter, twenty-two years young from Thousand Oaks. Only yesterday, he was employed as a salesman for a successful door and window company. He had a girlfriend he wanted to marry. Just three nights earlier, he went out to dinner with his parents and younger sister. Now he sat in a lotus position in a room that he had never been in before, eyes closed for the past hour, and wearing a white tae kwon do uniform with loose fitting white pants, a traditional white V-neck pullover top with a black collar, and a black belt tied around his waist. He took off his black cotton shoes and elected to go barefoot. He was the ham sandwich, a term used by Staci to designate a young, male martial arts expert who was a warm-up fight for her official business that would soon follow. Staci could have used any term for this warm-up, but ham sandwiches were her favorite food, and on a whim, this is the term she decided to use to designate her victim.

The previous night, Michael had been at a bar drinking a few too many apple martinis. He met two young and beautiful Asian girls who came on to him quickly. Michael was a strapping, good-looking young man and this was nothing new to him. However, he was about to make a big mistake for someone who already had a girlfriend whom he wanted to marry. The three of them went to the home of one of the Asian girls. He had a couple more drinks, and the next thing he knew, he woke up in this strange place in a room that was clearly used for fighting. Fighting to the death. He had to wonder if he had been watched and targeted since he was a black belt in tae kwon do and someone had appropriately dressed him for this occasion.

The room was eighty-by-eighty feet, large enough to comfortably move around in. The walls were made of cinderblocks painted a soothing amber color, and thin blue mats lined the floor. The lighting was subtle but bright enough so one could clearly see his opponent and the assortment of weapons on the wall. The only door was centered on the northern wall.

Lining the walls were tools of the trade. There were swords of diverse origins on all four walls: black and gold tapestry samurai swords, straight-blade ninja swords, and kung fu broad swords. Hardwood staffs, rattan *escrima* sticks, batons, *tonfas*, and nunchakus were displayed, as well as a wide assortment of *kamas*, *sais*, knives, ninja throwing spikes, and throwing stars. There were fighting fans, too. Unfortunately for Michael, there were no guns. That would have simplified things greatly. He thought this was similar to the movie *Thunderdome,* where two men enter but only one man leaves. There was one adjoining bathroom for him to use but escape was not possible as the walls were also cinderblocks and the ceiling was too high to reach.

Sensei Masakata and his assistant Ueshiba Funakoshi studied Michael for twenty minutes through a small one-way mirror at the southwest corner of the room. From here, they could watch the action from every angle. So far, there wasn't much to see as Michael sat and continued meditating in a lotus position as he had much of the day.

Sensei Masakata initiated the normal wager with his assistant. "I believe the girl, although lacking in judgment and wisdom, will prevail."

"I will gladly wager on the tall male," he replied to his master with a confident smile. "You are correct in that she lacks wisdom. She will lose within the first three minutes."

Sensei Masakata looked sternly at Ueshiba. "You talk about lacking wisdom, and yet you wager on the one who so foolishly ended up here?"

Ueshiba paused for a moment, then looked down at the floor while his master laughed out loud. "You will lose, but I do think that the tall male will prove to be a most worthy adversary."

The master's two female assistants, the ones who drugged Michael and brought him here in the wee hours of the morning, escorted Staci to the door of the fighting room, then stepped away. Staci took a deep breath, opened the door, and entered. The door closed and was immediately followed by a loud clicking noise as it locked behind her. The two young Asian women joined the master and his assistant, standing on their toes behind them and looking over their shoulders through the mirror. They both cast their lots for Staci.

Michael was as prepared as he possibly could be, considering the circumstances. He was ready for whoever came through that door. He opened his eyes to meet his opponent. Even though his head was prepared, his heart was not when he saw a girl, a most beautiful girl at that, standing twenty feet in front of him. She was wearing a traditional black kung fu uniform with white trim, a white collar, white cuffs, traditional loop and knot closures, and black cotton-soled shoes. Staci stood in front of Michael, feet spread a foot apart and arms down to her side, and bowed.

Michael could not believe this was happening. But his survival instincts quickly took over as he stood up and bowed. If he had to kill a girl to get out of here alive, then so be it. If she wanted combat, he would bring her a war. He gracefully returned the bow, his eyes never leaving Staci's, then assumed a traditional parallel stance with his feet a shoulder's width apart and loosely held fists just below and slightly in front of his naval.

Breakthrough

Staci began to circle her opponent in a counter clockwise direction and quickly attacked in an effort to keep him off balance. She stepped into him and delivered a series of spinning kicks at his knees while mixing in a volley of punches to his ribs. Like a boxer who uses jabs early in a fight to get a feel for his opponent, Staci wanted to first test his reflexes and try to anticipate how he would react.

Michael stood his ground, thwarted the initial attack with graceful footwork and a few blocks with his forearms, and responded with a barrage of fast and powerful front, side, and roundhouse kicks, concluding an axe kick intended for her head that, if connected as intended, would have surely knocked her unconscious, if not killed her. They backed away from each other, both satisfied that they had not only survived the initial sparring, but believing that they had identified some of their respective opponent's strengths and weaknesses.

Michael stood almost a foot taller than Staci, but he struggled with fighting people significantly shorter than himself. One of his previous instructors was about Staci's height, and Michael's higher center of balance proved to be a liability as he tried to keep up with the shorter and quicker strikes from a crouched position. To counter this weakness, he planned to use his height and employ his leg power and greater reach to disable the female assassin from a distance rather than allow her to step into him and strike at his knees and midsection.

Michael did not want Staci to exploit this weakness, so he was determined to take the offensive and end the fight quickly. He directed two front snap kicks that Staci blocked with her wrists. He then faked a low-high roundhouse kick and instead, delivered a jumping reverse side kick. Staci deftly avoided the strikes or blocked them with her wrists and forearms. She quickly confirmed his weakness when he didn't step into her and try to mix in close range elbow strikes with his knuckle punches. He was doing his best to keep as much distance between them as possible.

Taking the offensive, Staci struck with two spinning kicks directed at Michael's knees. She then landed her first punch to his abdomen with such force that he staggered backwards three steps. Staci wanted to send him a message and let him know that she knew his weakness and that would be the area where she was going to attack. She immediately stepped into him again, delivered a front kick to the exact same spot where her previous punch had landed, followed by a crescent kick that just missed his chin. Then she executed a series of kicks directed at his midsection and landed punches to both his left and right ribs. He tried to block the strikes, but Staci was quicker than just about anyone he had ever fought, and she grabbed his arm and hit him in his face with a back-fist punch.

Michael pulled his arm back and countered with a front-rising kick. Staci anticipated it and grabbed his fully extended leg between her left arm and her side, and delivered three rising punches from a bow stance to his upper stomach in an attempt to knock the wind out of him. But Michael was lean and had worked hard on developing his abdominal muscles over the past ten years, so Staci's punches had little effect other than inflicting a stinging sensation on the surface of his skin.

Michael knew he was in no position to put up a reasonable defense against his smaller and much-quicker opponent at close range, so he pulled his leg back, turned around, and ran to the back of the wall, pulling down a *sankaku yari* spear and hurling it at Staci.

"You can go to hell, and I'll gladly send you there now," Michael boasted as the spear left his hand.

Staci stopped midstride, just barely sidestepping the projectile. "I'm a scientist. I don't believe in hell," she replied.

Michael was not as skilled with throwing weapons as he should have been at this level of his craft. Although his black belt demanded skill in knives, swords, and other martial arts weapons, he mainly focused on kicking techniques and hand-to-hand combat. He thought the odds of ever having to use weapons in a life-or-death situation were slim. Besides, as a six-foot three-inch gifted athlete who excelled in athletics and martial arts, Michael had always simply overpowered anyone who threatened him with his speed, power, and agility. Looking back on some of his teachers' advice over the years, he should have heeded their wisdom and spent far more time attacking with and defending against the wide array of weapons that now surrounded him.

He grabbed two throwing spikes with each hand and threw them almost point-blank at her chest. Staci ducked under them and leaped forward in one movement, delivering a solid kick to his left side in the same area where she earlier landed a punch and a kick. Michael stepped to his right to give himself some room to maneuver as he was too close to a corner. He grabbed a second spear off the wall and stepped backward to the center of the room.

To counter the spear, Staci picked out two 18-inch black iron *sais* with aged dark brown, leather-wrapped handles. The *sai* originated in Okinawa and Southwest Asia and originally was designed to plant vegetables and rice seeds. A traditional *sai* resembles a trident with a central dagger extending out 15–24 inches and a smaller prong on either side that could be used as wrist guards or to thrust, stab, block, and even throw at an opponent. Properly used, they are very efficient in blocking, trapping, or breaking a stick, club, staff, or a spear. Normally, a third *sai* was used for throwing at an opponent, but since Staci had no means of carrying another one on her uniform, she settled for using two. Unlike Michael, Staci had spent countless late nights perfecting her use of weapons over the past ten years. Armed with a *sai* in each hand, she matched Michael footstep for footstep as they circled each other in the center of the killing room.

Michael's graceful footwork was one of his physical gifts. He took the offensive, using choreographed footwork from one of his demonstrations while earning his black belt. He skillfully handed off the 12-foot spear from hand to hand and gracefully yet violently spun the spear in a circular motion, a red ribbon tied to the end spinning and designed to confuse the opponent. In stride with his front, side, and roundhouse kicks, Michael mixed in jabbing motions and thrusts of his spear from both his left and right side that were difficult for Staci to distinguish the tip of the spear from the spinning of the red ribbon. Staci had six elements to track that came at her quickly and violently: two feet, two hands, a spear, and that damned confusing red ribbon that made it look like the tip of the spear was a couple inches away from where it really was.

Michael's strategy was working. He held Staci at bay a few feet in front of him and had her on the retreat. He continued with his frontal assault, mixing jabs, thrusts, and an assortment of kicks and confused Staci with spin moves and quick footwork.

Staci had no choice but to try to avoid his thrusts while allowing Michael to waste precious energy and tire himself out. She even slowed her movements to trap him into excessive thrusting and expending more of his energy. The risk was high for Staci, and Michael managed to tear her outfit three times, nearly piercing her stomach and chest.

But her strategy worked to her advantage. Michael began to tire and she discerned that his thrusts grew a bit slower and carried less energy than his original assault. She decided to take advantage of the moment and stood still, the insides of her feet touching each other, bowing her head, eyes closed, and hands to her side still holding the *sais*. Michael wasn't sure what to make of her move. He didn't know what to make of the past twelve hours, only that the three women he just met had meant nothing but trouble for him.

But he wasn't about to pass up this opportunity to end this madness. It was all or nothing. One thrust of his spear and he would either kill his opponent or he would leave himself wide open for a retaliatory death blow at the hands of this beautiful young girl with short, jet-black hair. He planted his left foot in front of his right, and with every ounce of his being, lunged forward, faked left, and thrust right. Staci opened her eyes just in time to see the tip of the spear, the red ribbon forced straight back due to the forward motion of the thrust, and rolled underneath the stab. She stood up in a bow stance and blocked the spear with both weapons, moving her attacker's weapon to her left while simultaneously bringing the two *sais* back around to strike him in a forward motion, delivering a mortal wound to his abdomen.

Chapter 35
A Close Call

Kneeling down and bending forward while holding the wound to his stomach, Michael knew he was going to die. But he was determined to take someone with him. He understood that his female opponent would not be the one. She was far too skilled, and she had anticipated most of his moves. There was only one thing left for him at this stage of the contest.

Standing up before weakness and dizziness overpowered his remaining physical strength and faltering will, Michael picked up the javelin that lay on the floor a few feet to his right that he previously threw at his opponent. He slowly walked in an arc around Staci, placing her between him and the one-way mirror he was sure somebody was standing behind. They were only fifteen feet away from the mirrored window, and Michael was confident that he would not leave this world alone.

This was one move that Staci did not anticipate, and she readied herself for the attack. But instead of thrusting the javelin at her, Michael planted his feet, reached back, and with blinding speed and unrestrained power, heaved the wooden projectile as hard as he could at the one-way mirror in the corner of the room. Staci ducked beneath the spear as Michael knew she would. Sensei Masakata and Ueshiba Funakoshi were alert enough to step out of the way of the missile, but one of the two Asian women who brought Michael here was distractedly talking to her partner. Neither girl saw the javelin coming. It broke through the mirror with a high rate of velocity and plunged into the side of Akiko Miyazaki's head, pinning her to the wall three feet to her right.

Her partner, Miyuki Tanaka, was sure that Akiko was alive for at least half a minute. Her eyes never closed and her lips looked as if she were trying to formulate words that could not quite escape her mouth. Her arms and legs were limp, but her fingers were twitching as the javelin was embedded in a stud in the wall and held the flaccid body, preventing it from falling to the floor.

Masakata and Funakoshi reacted quickly. They tried to pull the javelin out of the wall, but the projectile was buried deep within the stud. Funakoshi thrust his palm into the space between Akiko's head and the wall and shattered the spear in half. Masakata grabbed the still-twitching body and laid it on the floor with the projectile still protruding three-quarters of the way out the right side of her head. Miyuki was beside herself, screaming uncontrollably and stomping her feet in no particular rhythm. Funakoshi grabbed her and held her down while Masakata stepped back to look in on the action in the fighting room, careful not to let another missile take him out of this world before his appointed time.

Staci was momentarily stunned, and Michael took advantage of the confusion on both sides of the wall. He pulled out three ninja stars that he had tucked away in his sleeve earlier in the morning and threw them in rapid succession at Staci's chest, forcing her to move in the direction opposite of four black *kamas* that were on the near wall. She barely avoided the stars streaking past her at over 100 miles an hour, and Michael sprinted as fast as he could to grab weapons that he could use to throw at her. Then he would grab a sword and bring the attack to her so quickly that he stood a good chance of killing her. He felt the winds of fortune had quickly changed in his favor.

But Staci was too fast, and they arrived at the wall at the same time. Michael grabbed two sickle-shaped *kamas* and Staci pulled off a wushu whip chain for both defense and offense. She circled to her left and began spinning the eight thin rods connected end to end by small metal rings with a metal dart on the end in an attempt to keep Michael against the wall. This was a risky move because he was close enough to grab new weapons. But it enabled her to keep him from running off, and she could close in on him and deliver the final strike that would end the battle.

Michael knew he had made a mistake in his selections of weapons. Although he was highly skilled at using *kamas*, part of their effectiveness is using the light in the room to reflect at different angles off the shiny silver surface of the stainless steel blades to confuse the opponent as the user went through his routine, twisting his arms and wrists at different angles to add to the confusion. With little light in the room, he lost this potential advantage. Even with his ability to handle, spin, thrust, and mix in kicks and punches, he could not use the flashing reflections of light off the moving *kamas* to confound his opponent.

Staci had the advantage because the wushu whip chain had four long, thin strips of yellow and red cloth tied close to the ends of the chain one inch apart, making a dizzying optical illusion similar to the red cloth at the end of the spear that Michael used. She seemed to dance as she spun and moved as if she were performing a gymnastic floor exercise. She was clearly skilled in this weapon, spinning the wushu whip so fast that to Michael, it looked like a helicopter blade, blending into one perfectly symmetrical silver circle. The red and yellow bands on the outer edges blended into orange and the whip made a sound like a rushing wind.

Losing blood and growing weaker by the moment, Michael felt he had only one option left. He thrust the *kama* from his left hand directly into the spinning chain and quickly pulled his hand back. The effect was like slamming a metal pipe in a spoked wheel moving at more than 100 miles an hour. The chain jerked itself out of Staci's hand, and Michael quickly jumped toward her, spinning the second *kama* and slashing at her head and neck. He had practiced with much heavier *kamas*, and that practice strengthened his hands and wrists so that he was much more adept at handling the weapon.

He, now, spun and sliced his lone *kama* through the air. Staci gave him time to expend more energy and lose more blood until finally he began to slow down and stumble. She performed three reverse summersaults to the wall behind her, grabbed three throwing spikes, planted her feet firmly, and with three quick throws, sent them directly into his left rib cage, the second entering between the fifth and sixth ribs and piercing his heart. Michael died instantly, his lifeless body falling forward to the floor before he had a chance to grasp his second wound.

Chapter 36
The Blessing

SENSEI MASAKATA LEANED OVER the stone balcony of the Mediterranean-style garden patio and slowly breathed in the cool Pacific air carrying the mixed smells of the indigenous fauna and sea salt from the ocean. The breeze blew his shoulder-length silver hair behind his head. Staci stood next to him, silent, waiting for the master to speak.

Three hundred feet below the alfresco patio, they watched as Ueshiba Funakoshi and three men lifted two body bags onto a 38-foot blue and white Sea Ray Sundancer Cruiser fishing boat. Funakoshi had lost the bet with his master, and the loser had to clean up the mess in the killing room and dispose of the bodies at sea. Staci was not a religious person, but she found herself saying a silent prayer for the souls of Michael Vitter and Akiko Miyazaki. Staci felt they died honorably, and for the first time in her life, she had an epiphany: that somebody deserved a better fate on the other side.

"They will receive a proper blessing for their souls when they are laid to rest at sea," the master said.

Staci bowed her head and stared at the tile floor of the patio. "I feel bad about Akiko. She was an innocent casualty in this battle."

Sensei Masakata stared at her. "Do not be concerned about Akiko. She understood the risks of working for me. She should have been paying attention to what was happening with you rather than talking

Breakthrough

to Miyuki. She paid the ultimate price for allowing distractions into her surroundings."

Staci looked back at the master and asked a question she never previously considered. "Master, will you bless me before I leave? I feel so alone and lost out here, and my journey is perilous and filled with unforeseen danger. I do not have time to meditate or consider the ramifications of what I am about to do."

Sensei Masakata smiled at Staci, like a father would to a daughter who asked for blessings upon her life that would allow her to advance into the next stage of womanhood. "Yes, yes, I will bless you." He closed his eyes and placed both hands upon her head. Staci fell to her knees and held her hands out to her sides, palms facing skyward.

"May the gentle winds of peace blow through your spirit, soul, and body and calm the torrents of your heart. May clarity of vision replace the smokescreens that the demons have blown in your face to confuse and distract you. May you find clearly lit paths that allow you to see far down the roads you are to travel, with lanterns at your feet for those paths so dark that you cannot see more than a few footsteps ahead of you."

He lifted his hands from Staci's head and she stood up. She genuinely felt as if something had been deeply imparted within the very fibers of her spirit, soul, and body. She felt stronger and more aware of her surroundings and the importance of her mission. "Thank you, Master, for all that you have done for me today. I feel that I have learned more in just a few hours here than many years with other masters I have been with."

"Go in peace, and may your paths be smooth and straight," he said with a fatherly smile that pierced her heart. He then turned and walked back into the villa without uttering another word. Miyuki appeared from the same set of french doors Masakata disappeared through and solemnly guided Staci back to the quiet room where she had bathed, changed her clothes, and meditated earlier in the afternoon. Miyuki waited for her to change into the clothes she arrived in and guided her back to the front door where she put on her black leather boots. Staci looked over her right shoulder and took one last look at the pink Spanish-styled villa, then she started the red and white Ducati Desmosedici RR and left for her journey to Orange County, far more at peace with herself, memorizing, believing, and soaking in every prophetic word that Sensei Masakata had spoken over her.

Chapter 37
Trip to Orange County

RUSH HOUR IS BRUTAL in Ventura, Los Angeles, and Orange Counties, and it can begin as early as 2:00 in the afternoon and last until well after 7:00 p.m. And that's if there *aren't* any accidents or construction projects. But it's legal to ride a motorcycle between the lanes in California, and Staci made the 150-mile trek from Santa Barbara to south Orange County in just under three hours in the stop-and-go traffic. The ride was refreshing after her encounter with Michael earlier in the afternoon, and she needed the time to clear her head and prepare herself for the task that lay ahead.

She took the 101 Freeway from Santa Barbara to Sherman Oaks north of Los Angeles, then merged onto the 405 South and rode through Los Angeles and Long Beach and finally into Orange County. She exited the 405 at the Bristol Street exit in Costa Mesa and passed the South Coast Plaza Mall on her way to the Westin Hotel, where she was staying. She desperately wanted to spend a day shopping at the mall, considered one of the largest upscale malls on the West Coast. But that would have to wait until her next visit to the Southland. She needed to stay out of public places as much as possible in case she was caught on surveillance cameras that could help to identify her.

Self-parking at the Westin was somewhat inconvenient—it was in a separate structure one block away. But she didn't want to use valet parking. The less attention she received, the better, and Staci wasn't convinced that a young kid would know how to handle a motorcycle like this one. She parked on the fifth floor of the garage and took the stairs to the ground level so she could stretch her legs after the long ride.

The sun sank below the western horizon and the night life was beginning to wake from its daytime slumber. Staci took the scenic route to the hotel as she was attracted to the lights and people converging on the Orange County Performing Arts Center where the San Francisco Symphony was playing. However, she kept her distance and watched the people dressed up in their eloquent clothing for a few minutes. Then she strolled to the hotel to soak in a Jacuzzi and rest and recover from her plane ride and her fight.

Chapter 38
A Chance Encounter

It was six o'clock in the morning and Staci was already pulling out of the parking structure on her way to Laguna Beach. Thanks to Khyati and her hacking into every electronic communication Chase had made in the past few months, they were able to construct a typical Saturday morning in the life of Chase Manhattan.

The temperature was chilly, so Staci was dressed in her leathers to stay warm for the 20-minute ride to Laguna Beach. She had an extra set of clothes in her knapsack to wear when she was at the beach. She might be a bit cold once she changed, but the sun would be up shortly, and she was convinced that Chase would not be able to resist striking up a conversation with her when he saw her in her workout outfit.

She took the 405 Freeway south to Laguna Canyon Road, then rode through the canyon and into downtown Laguna Beach. She parked the Ducati one block north of Main Beach and changed into her outfit in a putrid public restroom. The smell was disgusting. *People sure can be pigs*, she thought to herself, careful to watch where she placed her feet while changing. Her leather pants and boots barely fit in her knapsack. Although the sun now peeked over the canyon walls, it was still only 57 degrees, so she decided to leave her leather jacket on.

Staci walked across Coast Highway to the local Starbucks. She could smell the aroma of coffee brewing 100 yards away, and it was very refreshing, especially compared to the public restroom she just walked out of. A hot grande coffee with cream was just what she needed to help her warm up and wake up.

It was now just a little past six thirty, so she had a few minutes to walk south a couple of blocks and look through the windows of the quaint art galleries and family-owned boutiques that graced the street. After a few minutes of window-shopping and allowing the caffeine from her coffee to revitalize her body and mind, she crossed the street to the beachside and passed a couple of open restaurants. Staci needed to eat, but thought she would first try to entice Chase to take her out for breakfast.

She walked over to the boardwalk on Main Beach, and then jumped a couple feet down to the sandy beach. Staci loved to walk on the sand. It was too cold to take off her aerobic shoes and stroll barefoot, so she left them on. She made her way south along the edge of the shore and walked briskly, looking at the few joggers and strollers already out and about on the beach. Up ahead about a quarter mile, she could see what looked like a group of six people gathering together and stretching on the packed portion of the sand where the tide had been just a few hours ago. The figures in the distance had to be the Chinese tourists performing tai chi that Khyati identified.

Staci smiled in anticipation, figuring that at any moment, one of the joggers passing her on the sand would be her mark. The man who stole one-third of Nicky's suitcases and brought them with him 3,000 miles away from their home and their rightful owners.

Approaching the Chinese tourists, Staci counted eight male joggers who fit the description of Chase, at least from the backside as they ran past her. One of them would stop for about twenty minutes to join in on his way back, and she would be there waiting for him, ready to spring a trap that countless men over the millennia had fallen for all too easily.

She reached the Asian tourists and smiled as they finished their warm-up stretches. The group consisted of three couples in their mid- to-late-forties. Two of the women smiled back, and Staci took off her jacket, laid it down in the sand, and did a few stretches of her own. She wore a red Daytona racerback tank top with a black sporty side-stripe that was appropriate for working out, yet revealed more than enough of her breasts to entice a man, especially when bending forward. She also wore black ramble pants and a new pair of white New Balance aerobic shoes. The temperature was inching its way up to 60 degrees, but Staci was still cold. She did a few more stretches but needed to jump in place and shake to keep from shivering. At least there wasn't a marine layer in February, so the sun shone brightly and immediately added some welcome warmth to the crisp morning air.

One of the men, about forty-five years old with a receding black hairline, led the group. He stood with his back to the Pacific and faced the rocky bluffs that were landscaped with multimillion-dollar homes. The rest of the group, including Staci, formed a line facing him looking out over the calm blue ocean.

Staci quickly recognized these movements as the Yang short form that emphasized breathing techniques, stability, and precision. Because of their age, she thought they might be performing the Wu style that focuses on smaller, more compact movements. But all six looked to be in tremendous shape, even though they were quickly approaching fifty.

Two of the joggers who passed Staci were now on their way back. The first one looked like he did not even notice the group, or her, for that matter, and ran right by as if they weren't even there. The second jogger looked over and smiled at Staci, but kept going. She knew he wasn't Chase. He was too old, and his hair was straight.

The leader was transitioning from the brush-knee-and-twist-step movement to play guitar when she saw *him* jogging toward her. He wore matching gray sweatpants and sweater, stood about six feet one, was thin, and had brown, wavy hair, a bit on the pasty side. Staci had seen a picture of Chase on the UC-Irvine faculty Web page, but in person, he was better looking than she imagined.

Chase noticed the new girl in the group. He noticed her when he jogged past her ten minutes earlier. She was even better looking from the front than she was from the back. He slowed down about fifty yards ahead of the group to give himself time to catch his breath. He didn't want to look winded in front of this beautiful girl when he joined in.

Chase walked up to the group, stopped about twenty feet away, and did a few quick stretches. Then he joined the group while they were performing the single-whip movement and took his place in line next to the newcomer.

"You look cold. Why aren't you wearing a sweater?" Chase smiled and asked in a whisper as he leaned slightly into her.

"I do have my jacket," she replied with the brightest smile and whitest set of near-perfect teeth that Chase had ever seen. She looked over at her jacket off to the right of them on the sand. "I didn't expect to run into this group, and when I saw them, I thought I would join in for a few minutes."

"They've been here for a couple of weeks now. I often run here and stop by for about twenty minutes."

Staci could see that Chase was already infatuated. She had seen that look before. She recognized that tone of voice. She remembered the glazed look in the eyes. *Hmm, this is going to be easier than I had anticipated.* The leader of the group led them in separating right foot and separating left foot.

"You look like you have been doing this for a while. You're really good." Staci actually meant this. Chase *was* really good. He had practiced tai chi since he was eight years old. He and his siblings practiced for weeks at a time when their parents took them along on missionary trips but left them back at a hotel or a house they were staying in while they went out and did the work of the Lord.

"I confess—I've been doing this for a while. I love tai chi. It's a great way to stretch, relax, and get a great workout. You look like you've been doing this for a while yourself," Chase added, keeping his tone hushed and trying not to disturb the group. He thought she looked incredible while going through the movements. She was every bit as fluid as anyone else he had ever seen, and he thought that she had the grace and agility of a dancer or an acrobat.

But she also looked uncomfortable and underdressed for the crisp morning breeze coming in off the ocean. "You look really cold. Why don't we leave and go get something to eat for breakfast? There's a terrific restaurant on Main Beach where we can eat and watch these guys from the balcony."

"That sounds like the best of both worlds. Okay, you talked me into it, mister." She smiled with that award-winning smile that seemed to raise her cheekbones even higher. Her hazel-blue eyes, thanks to tinted contact lenses, were soft and sultry, and her jet-black hair looked so soft that Chase fantasized running his fingers through it. All of these features contrasted with her tan that was a little darker than what most people had this time of year in Southern California.

Chase bent down, picked up her black leather jacket, and held it up for her to put her arms into the sleeves. "Chivalry is still alive and well, I see. Thank you."

Chase could now talk out loud as they left the group of Chinese tourists. "My name's Chase. Chase Manhattan."

"Chase Manhattan? That's a unique name," she said, walking beside him and looking up at him.

"My mom named me. She said she liked the way it sounded when she said it."

"My name is Cathy Bennett," she said, briefly stopping to shake Chase's hand.

They continued with small talk as they walked along the edge of the sand recently exposed by the receding tide to the boardwalk and made their way to the C'est La Vie Restaurant. "You'll really like this place," Chase promised. "They have a great breakfast and even better coffee."

Chapter 39
C'est La Vie

C'est La Vie is a French restaurant and bakery that serves spectacular French cuisine in an elegant, yet comfortable, atmosphere. The hostess recognized Chase as she greeted him and his new friend at the front door. "Good morning, Mr. Manhattan," she said with a smile. "Welcome. Are you going to sit on the balcony again today?"

"Yes, we will. Thanks."

The hostess led them through the restaurant. The smell of the kitchen's bakery overwhelmed their olfactory senses and immediately triggered a spontaneous rumbling in Staci's stomach. They went upstairs to the small deck, where the hostess sat them at a table with a heat lamp that opened up to a spectacular ocean view overlooking Main Beach and the sparkling Pacific Ocean.

"What a view. This place is really nice. Thanks for inviting me to breakfast with you," Staci said with the one of the most engaging and energetic smiles Chase had ever seen.

"I usually eat breakfast here a couple of days a week. I like to come down to the beach early and get in a morning run two or three days a week."

"And tai chi," Staci added, looking at Chase with her big beautiful eyes.

A waiter in a white shirt and black bow tie brought them coffee, water, and menus. "Actually, that's a group of tourists who have been here a couple of weeks and I've been joining them when I see them. But I do like to do tai chi on my own at home, too." Chase offered Staci cream for her coffee, and then poured some into his own.

"You're good, Chase," she said, raising her cup to her mouth. "Hmmm, you are so right. This is *great* coffee."

"Thanks. I've been practicing since I was eight."

"Eight? That's pretty young. You don't see too many American kids involved in tai chi at that age," she remarked, looking at her menu and taking another sip of her brew.

"My parents were missionaries. They took me and my siblings on many of their trips while I was growing up. We went to China, Tibet, Cambodia, Japan, Mongolia, lots of places. During that time, we all had a lot of exposure to tai chi and various forms of the martial arts."

Staci already had more information on Chase than Khyati had been able to gather. She set her cup down and smiled. "Wow. That's really cool, Chase. Martial arts, too? What forms did you learn?"

"Well, in China, Tibet, and Mongolia, I learned kung fu, mainly the Shaolin form."

Stacy noted that Chase would be adept at kicking and probably use a broader stance in combat. "That's so exciting," she said with a feigned smile as she took another drink of her coffee. "What else did you learn?"

Chase falsely assumed that Staci was developing an affinity with him. While he believed she displayed an affable nature, she was more interested in extracting as much information from him as she could to simplify her job of retrieving the transporter and receiver suitcases and eliminating him.

Chase continued to offer information, in the false sense that Staci was actually interested in him as a human being. "My parents also took us to Japan and Okinawa where we learned karate." Staci made more mental notes of the weapons that Chase might be skilled in using, such as staffs and *saises*. She appreciated hand-to-hand combat with an opponent skilled at using these implements of war, shorter weapons that forced opponents to stand closer together.

"What about yourself? You looked like you've been doing tai chi for a long time."

Staci replied, "I have been. I do tai chi at the gym along with yoga. I have some instructional DVDs at home that I use, too."

The waiter returned to their table. He looked at Staci and asked, "Are you ready to order, ma'am?"

She glanced back and forth over the menu. "It all looks so good."

"Don't be shy," Chase encouraged her. "Order whatever you want."

Staci sat up straight. "Okay. I'll have the ham and cheese omelet and a stack of blueberry pancakes," she said in a perky manner, still feigning the same smile that looked natural and genuine. "And a glass of orange juice, too."

Chase was impressed that a girl her size could put away that much food, but he wasn't sure how to express it, so he decided that he'd better not try.

"I'll have the roasted vegetable and fontina cheese omelet. And a glass of orange juice, too."

Staci remembered this item from the menu and shuddered inside. The thought of eggplant, zucchini, and peppers in her breakfast was just too gross for her to fathom.

Chase and Staci continued their small talk for a few minutes. Chase tried not to come on too strong once he realized he was quickly becoming infatuated. Staci tried to gather a more detailed profile of the man she knew she would probably have to kill later that day.

She paused and looked out over the Pacific. "This must provide a wonderful view of the sunset up here." Chase noticed that she said this like a tourist would—a tourist who would soon be going back to whatever state she came from and never see the deep blue Pacific Ocean again. He thought this was as good of time as any to find out a little about her background.

"So, Cathy, do you live here in Orange County?"

Staci quickly realized that she might have just given away a clue that she was not from Southern California and needed to get her story back on track. "I'm from Santa Barbara—born and raised," she said looking at Chase. "I'm down here for a few days by myself to, you know, to get away from it all. At least for a long weekend. I go back home Monday."

"Are you staying with friends? Family?"

"I'm staying at Vacation Village. I stay there when I come down here, which isn't very often. Maybe twice a year or so."

The waiter brought their food, a welcome interruption for Staci. He placed their omelets and orange juice in front of them and Staci's pancakes in the middle of the table. "Will there be anything else?" he asked.

The hungry eaters shook their heads, their mouths already full with bites of their respective omelets.

Ten minutes later, breakfast was over. Chase decided it was now or never. "What are you doing tonight, Cathy? There's a terrific Italian restaurant close by. We could go out for a nice dinner. Then we could balance the night out by going to a not-so-great bar that's only a few blocks from here. A good friend of mine plays guitar in the band that'll be there tonight."

Staci knew that she needed to get things done. Conduct business. Get in and get out. She didn't have time to play hard to get.

"I'd really like that, Chase," she said in a humble manner, wiping her hands with the white cloth napkin. "This girl could certainly use a break."

"Great. Should I pick you up at 7:00 p.m., Vacation Village?"

"Yes, that's right," Staci said, remembering that's what she told Chase. "Let me give you my cell number." She pulled the pen from the waiter's folder, wrote down her number on a napkin, and handed it to Chase with an innocent smile that could melt an iceberg.

"This is really your number, right?"

"She tilted her head and gave Chase a goofy look. "Of course, it is, silly. I may be out and about shopping today so call me on my cell if you want. I'll be ready to go at seven o'clock sharp. Just stop by the lobby and I'll be there."

Chase stood up and walked with Staci downstairs and back through the restaurant. "I love the smell of freshly baked bread in the morning. It reminds me of my childhood and my mom baking bread or croissants before we went to church," she said wistfully.

"I guess I've grown accustomed to the smell since I come here so often. I actually didn't notice it until you mentioned it," Chase replied.

Staci made yet one more mental note that Chase's senses had dulled over the years. She doubted that he was as sharp and attuned to his environment now as he probably once was. She hoped that his martial arts skills had deteriorated over the years as well.

"Thanks again for breakfast, Chase," she said as they walked out onto the sidewalk and headed south one block, then crossed the street. "It's nice to meet, well, a nice guy. There are so many creepy men that hit on me. You're a breath of fresh air," she said in an assuring manner that made Chase falsely feel confident in himself and his ability to appeal to her.

"It's been my pleasure, Cathy. I'll walk you to your car."

She pointed to the red and white Ducati. "I'm parked right over there."

"That's yours?" he asked in astonishment.

"Actually, it's my daddy's. But he lets me ride it."

Chase shook his head. "Honestly, if I had a daughter that looked like you, I would never let her ride a bike like this."

"You're sweet. I like that." Staci caught herself as she really meant what she just said. *A Freudian slip maybe*, she thought to herself. On the ride back to the Westin Hotel in Costa Mesa, she would have to hit the rewind button, search her heart, and think about what she just said.

They walked up to the bike and Staci unhooked her black helmet, swung her right leg over the seat, sat down, and held the helmet on her lap. Chase just stood there with his hands on his hips, looking at a sight that he had never imagined in his wildest dreams. One of the most beautiful women he had ever laid eyes on sitting on a $50,000 Ducati. And he was taking her out tonight.

"Thanks again for breakfast, Chase," she said, extending her right hand out. "I really do look forward to tonight."

Chase shook her hand. Just her touch was enough to send him to a place he had never been before. "Seven o'clock at the Vacation Village lobby. I'll be there," he confirmed.

Stacy spun her knapsack over her shoulder, took out her leather gloves, and pulled them tight over her fingers and hands. She put her helmet on and started up the Ducati. Chase thought she was an angel sent to him from heaven.

She backpedaled the bike to the center of the street, smiled and waved, then made a U-turn and headed south on Coast Highway. It was the opposite direction she needed to take to get back to Laguna Canyon Road and on to Costa Mesa. But the Vacation Village was a few blocks to the south and she didn't want to give Chase any reason for doubts.

Chase crossed Coast Highway and walked the block and a half to his car. His mind wandered back to Susan and the time they spent together a few nights before. He really liked Susan a lot. He thought he could love her. Maybe he was *already* in love with her. He knew that he needed to settle down with a girl like her—someone who had her priorities aligned and knew which direction she wanted to go. But the other night with her at Ti Amo was too much and too fast for him. The thought of settling down was a paramount shift that he wasn't sure he was ready for, even if he knew that's exactly what he needed in his life.

Chase couldn't get Susan out of his mind. His conscience told him that she was the right path for him. And in his mind, he agreed that Susan would be the best woman for him to plan a future with. But he rationalized that he would have to transition into this role. There was no reason for him to jump right into this. What harm could there be in one more date?

Chapter 40
Phone Calls

STACI LAY STOMACH-DOWN on her bed watching the QVC network, her legs bent at the knees and her feet in the air and crossed, her shoulder-length black hair hugging her neck. She had a paperback book lying open in front of her and she was smoking a cigarette. If she couldn't shop at South Coast Plaza, she could at least look at things to buy on television. Bored after an hour of imaginary shopping, she called Nicky on her cell phone.

"Hi, baby doll," answered the friendly voice from the other side of the country.

"Hey, sweetie. It's me. I miss you bunches," she said with a tone of laughter mixed with sorrow.

"I sure do miss you, too. How are things going on the left coast? Are you doing okay?" It was noon on the East Coast and Nicky was at his off-campus home making a sandwich and warming up a bowl of homemade vegetable soup.

"It's lunchtime. Are you eating your vegetable soup like a good boy?" she asked teasingly.

"Laugh all you want. But I plan to live to be 103."

"Because I'm no fool," Staci sang, ending one of Nicky's favorite lines he had memorized as a small child from a children's story.

Nicky sat down at his dining room table with his soup and sandwich. "How's progress? Were you able to meet with our mark?"

Staci didn't like the way that Nicky dehumanized people. But she also believed that they had a mission, a quest to fulfill which would involve sacrificing human lives—for the greater good of mankind. Since receiving the blessing from Sensei Masakata the day before, Staci now felt a sense of ordination, an anointing from a Higher Source who predestined this very moment in time for her to join the battle of good versus evil that must be brought to its finality at all costs for the good of mankind. She justified the inevitable collateral damage as a necessary evil that they must endure in order to carry out their destiny.

"I did, Nicky. We met for breakfast. He's taking me out for dinner tonight. I'm sure I'll have no problem in seducing him to take me to his place."

"That's my girl. I knew you could do it."

Staci was disturbed that Nicky didn't sound jealous at the thought of her going over to another man's house and the probability that certain inappropriate acts would be committed. But she also understood that sacrifices were required if they were to fulfill their quest. The important matter at hand was to retrieve the suitcases and eliminate Chase from the picture.

"Don't you worry, Nicky. I'm on top of things." She was assuring herself as much as Nicky. "I'll call you tonight when I have the suitcases, okay, sweetie?"

"Okay. I may be asleep, but definitely call me regardless of the time. I love you, my little princess."

Staci loved to hear Nicky say this to her, just like her father used to call her his little princess, but stopped when she reached junior high. It was mainly her fault—she told him to stop calling her that because it embarrassed her. But deep down, she missed the confidence and boost to her self-esteem hearing that she was special to someone important in her life.

"I will, Nicky. I need to take a nap now. I've got a big night ahead of me, and I don't want jet lag interfering with my ability to perform my job." Staci was already yawning just talking about sleep.

Shortly after she ended her call, Bennie called Chase from his office in Irvine. Chase was sitting in his office at home going over baseball box scores from Spring Training on the Internet. "Hi, Bennie. Good to hear from you."

"Chase, what's going this weekend? Are you up for doing anything, or are you doing something with Susan?"

"Um ... no," Chase said with a hint of regret. "I'm not going to be with Susan tonight."

Bennie did his exaggerated long look at his phone, and then placed it back to his ear. "Chase, why not? Susan is the best thing that ever happened to you."

The tone in Bennie's voice made it clear that he did not approve of Chase's plans for the night, whatever they were. "Listen, Bennie," Chase said, his mood quickly changing to one of enthusiasm, "I met this girl this morning on the beach. Bennie, she's great. I met her doing tai chi by Main Beach. She understands that part of me. And—"

"Whoa. Easy turbo. Listen to me. *Susan* is the girl that you need to be involved with, not some little bimbo you just met."

"Bimbo? You've never even seen her before." Chase was becoming defensive with Bennie, but Bennie's long suit was cutting through the smokescreens and getting to the root of the situation. This was a trait that Chase was still developing.

"Listen to me, Chase. I know bimbo when I see one. Or even *hear* about one over the phone. It's a gift." Chase tried not to laugh but couldn't refrain himself.

"Anyway, there's nothing to worry about. I like Susan a lot. Maybe even love her. But she wants too much too soon, Bennie. I'm not sure that I can do that."

"That's *exactly* what you need, Chase. Right now, you're on the road to nowhere. You need a girl like Susan who has her head screwed on straight."

Chase knew Bennie was right. But maybe one more fling was all he needed—just *one* more night to sow his remaining wild oats before entering that new era of his life where he would begin to build his future with Susan and never look back.

"Look, it's a harmless date. We're going out to Ti Amo for dinner tonight, then it's off to the Marine Room Tavern."

"Going from the penthouse to the outhouse, huh, Chase? Don't tell me that Fred guy is playing again tonight."

"He is. Fred's an alright guy, Bennie. You just don't know him very well yet."

"Whatever." Bennie rolled his eyes. "Since I'm your best friend and I'm sold that Susan is the girl for you, I'm going to be at Ti Amo tonight, too. I want to see what this new girl looks like."

"No, no, no. No way, Bennie. I don't want you ruining this."

"I promise I won't come over to your table. You won't even know I'm there. I know you like a table on the second floor by the fireplace, so I'll get a table on the other side of the room. I'll be, you know ..., incognito."

"Incognito is not your strength, Bennie. Who are you going to be with?"

"I don't know yet. But I'll find somebody. No worries in that department. You know me, Chase. I know bimbos, right?"

Chapter 41
The Pickup

STACI ARRIVED AT VACATION VILLAGE at 6:40 p.m. After parking the Ducati on the street around the corner from the hotel, she walked into the lobby, which was much smaller than she had pictured it in her mind on her way to Laguna Beach, and began to look at tourist brochures that were positioned a few feet inside the door. The young clerk behind the front desk made eye contact with her before she had a chance to open the front door.

"Can I help you, Miss?" he asked, leaning into the counter and ogling her. Staci looked at him and forced a smile. She thought he was barely old enough to drive, and was probably just an annoying teenager that would keep pestering her.

"No, thanks," she replied, picking out a tourist brochure at random from a slatwall kiosk literature stand and sat down in one of the chairs. "I'm just waiting for a friend who's staying here. I'm a bit early, but he'll be here shortly."

"I can call the room and let him know you're here," he volunteered, making steady eye contact that Staci found increasingly creepy.

She pulled her cell phone out of her purse so the attendant could see it. "I have a cell phone," she said in a tone that said, "Leave me the hell alone, you little jerk." The attendant got the message, turned around, and began typing something into the computer.

Within a few minutes, Chase pulled up to the Vacation Village entrance in his Mercedes-Benz SLK350 hardtop convertible. He left the top on as the afternoon heat gave way to the coolness of the February evening. Staci quickly jumped up out of her chair and opened the front door when she saw the car pull up. She hoped this was Chase—the creepy hotel attendant continued to sneak peeks at her.

Chase put the car in park, walked around to the other side, and opened the passenger door. He gave her a smile that was warm and inviting. "Chase," she said, looking far better than he could have possibly imagined, "get me out of here before I smack the hotel clerk."

Chase laughed out loud while closing the door, getting his own sneak peek of her beautifully sculpted tan legs as she sat herself down into the brown leather seat. The first thing Staci did was to sniff for cigarette smoke, hoping that Chase was a smoker, but no such luck. There was not even a hint of cigarette smoke. Chase got in the car, closed his door, and drove out onto Coast Highway heading south toward Ti Amo. "You look great tonight, Cathy. I hope you're hungry. I have reservations at a terrific Italian restaurant just down Coast Highway a little way."

"That sounds great, Chase," she said with that face and smile that could make her a million dollars on Madison Avenue. "I love Italian food." The sun was quickly sinking over the Pacific with deep orange, pink, and purple hues that broke out across a deepening blue horizon. Being from the East Coast, Staci had never seen such a gorgeous sunset like this before, and wanted nothing more than to stop and stroll down the beach and forever etch the memory in her mind. But she knew better than to give away hints that she was not from Santa Barbara.

"Another beautiful sunset on another beautiful day," she said with a sigh, looking out the passenger window. "I just can't get enough of them, although I know that there will be another one tomorrow."

Chase felt an immediate connection, because he felt the same way about sunsets. Not many people he met appreciated them as much as he did, so he felt an immediate bond, something that he thought he could begin to build a relationship on.

"I bet sunsets are spectacular in Santa Barbara. That's a real pretty town. I've driven through it quite a few times over the years."

"We live a couple of miles inland, but Daddy would take us to the beach and we'd have campfires together as a family," she said, now looking at Chase. "Those were some of the best memories I had as a child."

"Mine, too. My parents would take us to Aliso Creek Beach, which is just a few miles ahead of us. There are fire pits there and we'd make s'mores and roast hot dogs." Chase was enjoying the conversation, and he liked the direction it was taking. Family and sunsets. Those are ultimately what mattered most to him.

"So, do your parents live in the area?"

Chase was prepared for this question, but he let out a little sigh and paused for a moment anyway. "Both of my parents are gone now. They died a few years ago on a missionary trip to Rwanda." He knew her reaction would be one of shock and mixed emotion, so he said it in a way that was comforting.

Staci donned a look of horror on her face for a brief moment. "Oh, I'm so sorry, Chase. I didn't mean to …"

Chase placed his right hand on her knee for a moment, squeezed, then put it back on the steering wheel. "It's okay. The question was bound to come up tonight. Better sooner than later." Chase took the occasion to explain a little more about his youth and his personal life.

"I was actually born in Detroit, Michigan, but raised in Orange County, California. My family moved to Newport Beach when I was six. My parents were Catholic missionaries who traveled the world starting small churches, building schools and medical centers, and generally helping to make the world a little bit of a better place. They were also explorers and archeologists. Both held doctorates in archeology, my father with Columbia University in New York City and my mother from Yale. Some would say that my parents used their careers in archeology to support and further their missionary work around the world. Others would argue that they used their missionary journeys as a free ticket to explore the last vestiges of bygone worlds and cultures, while looting artifacts and selling them on the open market and on the black market. In retrospect, I guess they used one to support the other."

Staci was stunned. She remained silent while Chase told her his story. He turned on his right blinker and pulled into the Ti Amo parking lot. A valet met him and Chase got out of the car and handed him the keys. A second valet immediately appeared on the passenger side and opened the door for Staci.

She noticed that the first valet did not give Chase a ticket when he turned over the key. *He must be a regular here*, she thought. She grew more certain that Chase was one of the area's more desirable and eligible bachelors and that he probably brought quite a number of dates here over the years. The valets, she figured, knew him, but were probably being discreet and did not greet him by calling out his name.

Successful men, she knew from experience, grew careless over time. They become too comfortable with their surroundings and the luxuries that they enjoy. This was yet one more advantage in her favor that she could exploit later in the evening when she would retrieve the suitcases and kill Chase.

Chapter 42
Ti Amo

THE HOSTESS SEATED CHASE AND STACI at a table close to the fireplace. Chase took her black leather jacket with one hand while pulling her chair out with the other. Staci was dressed a little lightly for the occasion, and the warmth generated from the fire was welcomed.

"This place is great, Chase," she said, sweeping her head from left to right and looking around. "It really feels like we are in Italy."

"Have you ever been to Italy?"

"Twice, once in the fourth grade and once on the seventh grade. My parents took us there for vacations." Staci couldn't believe she had mentioned her parents as she felt she had brought up a sore subject for the second time in ten minutes.

Chase caught on and quickly soothed over the uncomfortable moment. "My parents took us there when we were kids as well. I was in the ninth grade. We spent most of our time in Rome and Florence. Since my parents were both archeologists as well as Catholic missionaries, we had to visit the Vatican as well."

"Did you get to meet the pope?" Staci asked jokingly.

"Actually, we did. My father arranged for us, as a family, to meet Pope John Paul II for a few minutes."

Staci was stunned. Her jaw dropped and her eyes opened wide in astonishment. "You're kidding me, right?"

Chase laughed. "I kid you not. We all got to meet John Paul. Every one of us shook his hand too. In my study at home, I have a picture of us with him."

Staci was dumbfounded. Coming from a family of influence, she had met many famous and influential people. But nothing she had experienced had come close to a personal meeting with the pope. "How did your father arrange a meeting with the pope? You don't just walk up to the Vatican and say, 'I'd like to meet the pope.'"

Chase looked up in the air for a few moments as his mouth slowly opened to speak. He wanted to word this right. "I'm not sure how he arranged the meeting. But I'm assuming he wrote a check, a very large check, to the Church as a gift. My brother and sisters and I guess it was probably a cool million dollars."

A young, slightly built waiter brought water and menus to the table. "Good evening," he said, smiling first at Staci and then at Chase. My name is Antoine, and I will be serving you tonight. I trust your table next to the fireplace is satisfactory?" he asked.

"Yes," Staci said with the biggest of smiles that seemed to add to the warmth of the fireplace. "This place is very nice. Thank you."

"Can I get you something to drink?" Antoine asked, looking in the direction of Staci.

Staci thought that Antoine knew Chase as a regular, but like the valet, he was being discreet. *Men,* she thought, *they are all in on something together. They're always looking out for each other.*

Just as Antoine walked away from the table, Chase saw Elisa seat Bennie and his date a few tables to the left of where he sat. He tried not to make eye contact as he certainly did not want Bennie coming over, introducing himself, and striking up a conversation. However, Chase appreciated that Bennie was there to look out for his best interests and did not mind that he was there.

Yet, just as Bennie was looking out for Chase, Chase felt a dual obligation to reciprocate the favor. Chase noticed his date was young and very pretty. She had Hispanic or Mediterranean features, and was well-endowed. She possessed a typical profile for one of Bennie's dates.

Bennie liked to meet girls who were young professionals, usually in banking or finance. That's where he could find girls who were just

Breakthrough

getting started in a career and had a good head on their shoulders. Bennie was into brokering big-time commercial property deals and knew a lot of people in the banking and financial businesses in south Orange County.

The evening progressed, Antoine brought Chase and Staci their meals, and the two enjoyed small talk, a few glasses of wine, and a lot of laughs. Chase was famished and set his table manners aside as he ate his meal faster than he ever had at Ti Amo. Staci picked through her meal and left her plate half-finished. Chase could see Bennie and his date look over their way numerous times throughout the evening, but he avoided direct eye contact. He wanted to focus his attention on Staci, and only Staci. The more they talked, the more infatuated with her Chase became. Staci picked up on this from the time the first met at the beach, and she allowed the evening to take its natural course and develop.

"So, what's up next, Chase? You said you had a friend in a band playing nearby tonight?"

Every time Staci would shift gears on a subject, she would smile, sit erect, and allow her breasts to stand at attention, but in a nonchalant and unassuming manner. Chase was smitten alright.

"That's right. Fred Merrill. He plays in a band at the Marine Room Tavern by Main Beach. Are you ready for some live entertainment?"

"You bet I am. This girl needs to stretch her legs and kick back with a margarita." Staci was leaning into the table with her chin in her right palm, elbow on the table, and staring at Chase with those big, baby-blue and hazel eyes of hers. Her smile was contagious and full of confidence. Chase saw mischief and innocence intertwined in her smile, and it turned him on more than anything else about her. He noticed again how perfect her teeth were, and how the whiteness contrasted against her tanned skin and the color of her eyes.

"So am I." Chase pulled his wallet from the side pocket of his jacket and removed his American Express card. He looked over at Antoine and held up his card.

"Chase, at least let me leave the tip. This must be costing you a small fortune tonight." Staci pulled out a rolled up fifty-dollar bill from her jacket pocket—the same fifty-dollar bill that she took as a souvenir from William O'Connor's office at the Massachusetts State House. It was the bill the late senator's wife gave him on that fateful morning and that he had dropped on his desk when Staci appeared in his doorway dressed in her black *shinobi shozoku* with her sword drawn. She rolled the note back and forth across her fingers similar to a poker player who rolls a chip across his fingers when he contemplates his next move.

Chase learned a long time ago never to argue with a girl who wants to leave a tip. This gesture shows that she wants a participative role in the evening, and that denying her the opportunity to leave the tip would be counterproductive to developing their relationship.

"Sure. You can leave the tip," he said. "The meals tonight though are not as expensive as you might think. I think they were about thirty dollars each. And the wine we drank was only a little over one hundred dollars."

Staci continued to roll the fifty-dollar bill back and forth over her fingers. She unrolled and re-rolled it over and over again as she stared at him with her large, expressive eyes, her chin still resting in her right palm.

"I like you, Chase. You don't mind me saying that, do you?"

"No, not at all." Chase leaned into the table. "I knew I had to stop and talk to you the moment I saw you at the beach this morning," he confessed, his eyes set fast upon Staci and staring deep into what he believed was the soul of an angelic being.

Antoine returned with Chase's American Express card and laid it on the table. "Thanks, you two. Enjoy the rest of your evening and come see us again."

The two finished up their night on the town at the Marine Room Tavern and had a few margaritas. The Mulders were playing, and Fred took a few minutes during their break to talk to Chase and meet his new friend. Fred was polite and cordial, but he let Chase know through a number of glares that he did not approve of him being with anyone other than Susan Anderson.

Staci insisted that Chase stop at Vacation Village on their way back to his place to pick up her motorcycle. It was on their way back to his house. She told him she would be up in the morning before he would be, and that she would probably want to leave, although she assured him that they would be on for lunch.

Breakthrough

At the hotel, Staci walked through the front entrance and out the back door, then made her way over to the side street where she parked the Ducati. She had a small, thin, black knapsack tied to the seat so that she could place the suitcases in them when she left his house. Ready, she pulled around to the front and followed Chase back onto Coast Highway.

Chapter 43
Chase's House

CHASE LED THE WAY up Blue Bird Canyon Drive and through two side streets before making a right into his driveway. Staci noticed the trees in the front yard blocked most of the house from the neighbors on the other side of the street. This was advantageous in the event that there was any noise or cries for help from Chase when she killed him.

Chase pressed the garage door opener on his visor as he pulled up into his curved driveway and into the three-car garage, then parked on the left side closest to the kitchen door. Staci pulled up behind him, but stopped short of the garage before turning the Ducati around and shutting it off so that the bike was facing towards the street. She got off the motorcycle, strapped her helmet to the side, and walked into the garage to meet Chase.

The moon was full, and Chase could clearly see the shapely figure of Staci walking up to the front of the garage. He paused as he put his keys back into his pocket after unlocking the side door to watch her slowly approach, one leg seductively stepping in front of the other, her shirt purposely unbuttoned to reveal more cleavage than she showed him earlier that morning on the beach and at the restaurant. She looked beyond beautiful to him right now, especially after a few glasses of wine and three Cadillac margaritas. Her mouth was open, and he could make out the outline of her tongue slowly circling the inner circle of her lips. He wondered if they would even make it inside the house.

Staci approached him and stopped only when they were toe to toe. Aggressively, she grabbed his belt with both hands and pulled him sharply and deeply into her. Looking at him with her big, baby-bluish hazel eyes, she puckered her lips and slowly let out an inebriated breath of air that she ran over his neck, down over his exposed chest, and back up his neck that finally ended deep inside his right ear. Chase was now beside himself and could not afford to waste any time on foreplay that would reduce his time in bed. Chase always considered himself an above-average lover, but he knew his limitations and a girl like Staci could cause him to fizzle earlier than he would like to.

He kissed her gently but firmly, running his lips and tongue over her ear lobes, down her neck, across her cleavage, and back up to her lips. She responded, sticking her tongue inside his mouth and playfully tugging at his lips with her teeth. Time was up. Chase could wait no longer. He reached out with his left hand, hit the garage door button to close it and swooped her up. She was light, but he could feel the tight, muscular thighs and buttocks as he carried her through the kitchen and dining room and then the living room, and up the stairs. He was a man with a purpose.

Chase didn't bother to turn on any lights on the way up to the master bedroom. The bright moonlight shining through the windows gave plenty of definition to the contour of his house and its furnishings. They continued to kiss and fondle each other up the stairs, down the hall past a Jack-and-Jill dual bedroom and bathroom, and into his master bedroom. Staci climbed out of his arms and quickly began to undress herself. In seconds, her clothes lay in a heap on the floor as she stepped out of her pants and underwear that were crumpled down around her ankles and jumped into his bed. Chase was right behind her, his clothes tossed aside and scattered across the carpeted floor.

They made love passionately from the start. Chase's 75-gallon saltwater tank gave off an aura of light that allowed their shadows to accentuate their passion. A small pool of sweat formed between Staci's firm breasts. Chase tried to pace himself, as he did not want to erupt before she had a chance to be satisfied.

After a few minutes, Chase whispered in her left ear with a smile, "Why don't you get on top now? I want to make sure that you get what you deserve before …"

"Say no more, lover boy," his erotic lover replied. Chase got off and rolled over onto his back. Staci quickly mounted herself on top of him, and in less than two minutes, she experienced one of the best orgasms ever in her life. Much more powerful and longer lasting than what she had ever experienced with her selfish boyfriend, Nicky.

Chase looked up at her ample breasts bouncing up and down in the moonlight and her head tilted back. He could see beads of sweat dripping down her ears onto her shoulders as she let out a muffled scream that lasted what seemed an eternity for both. He was glad that she was able to pleasure herself, as he had already spent himself a minute earlier and could not take any more.

Staci collapsed in a heap on his chest, heaving fast and deeply. Chase welcomed her with his arms and mixed in gentle caresses with hugs and massaged her shoulders. After a few minutes, she rolled over to the other side of the bed. She reached out and cupped his left hand with her right. Both lovers caught their breath and lay there for a few minutes in silence. He looked up at the ceiling and she gazed at the fish tank on the far wall near the master bedroom door.

She saw the fish swim in a graceful, carefree manner that matched her current demeanor. All of the weekend's stresses were gone like vapor in the wind. She felt more serene and at peace than she had in months, maybe years. She wanted to enjoy a few more minutes of this before she had to forsake pleasure and return to business.

Staci looked over at Chase with a soft and gentle smile. He smiled back and squeezed her hand. "I have to admit, Cathy, that was the best I ever had. No lie. I can't explain it, but you absolutely brought out the best in me.

Staci continued to smile and look deeply into his hazel eyes. She squeezed his hand for a few moments, then said, "Save your breath, lover boy. I'm going outside to smoke a cigarette. Maybe two. You stay right here and gather your strength. You're going to need it. When I come back, we're going to take it nice and slow and make the evening last forever. You've got twenty minutes."

Breakthrough

She climbed out of bed and pulled the comforter over Chase as the night was really starting to cool off. He watched the outline of her body move across the bedroom floor, her hands up and pulling her hair back over her head, her buttocks gracefully shifting from left to right and the slight outline of her breasts that peaked from either side of her chest.

Staci walked over to a laundry basket sitting on a large off-white sofa chair in the corner of the bedroom by the fish tank that contained Chase's clean underwear, socks, T-shirts, and tank tops. She pulled out a pair of white boxers with thin blue pinstripes and slowly slipped them up over her waist. He watched her every movement in the light from the moon and the fish tank. Staci suspected Chase wore boxers, and she was glad for two reasons. First, she would look and feel ridiculous wearing tightie whities. And guys who wore tightie whities were invariably assholes. Nicky wore tightie whities, and at the moment, she compared her tryst with Chase and boxer shorts to Nicky and his tightie whities. For the record, Staci was far more impressed with Chase than Nicky.

Twenty minutes to get ready. No problem, Chase thought. Staci pulled out a white tank top, turned around, and walked back toward the bed while slowly pulling it over her head. The shirt fit snuggly and hugged the curves of her body, leaving little for Chase's imagination.

"Twenty minutes," she said, licking her index finger and running it over the foot of the bed as she walked by toward the door and disappeared into the hallway.

Chapter 44
Valley of Indecision

Staci walked downstairs, looking at the pictures on the wall. In the dim light, she could make out what appeared to be an extended family picture with Chase's parents standing up in the middle, five other adults who were undoubtedly his three siblings and two spouses, and four small children. She assumed the group would be larger today with more grandchildren and this picture must have been taken a few years ago. Since it was prominently centered in the middle of the rest of the pictures, she guessed it was the last group photo of the family.

Continuing to the bottom of the stairs, she looked over the living room and the dining room. To the right, a small hallway led to two other rooms, and then made a right turn. The house had a circular traffic pattern with a big bonus room between the kitchen and whatever was beyond the hall that turned right. She knew that his study must be one of the two doors she was looking at. No doubt, that's where the suitcases were hidden.

On her left, in the living room, she saw a dimmer switch on the wall and turned it slowly clockwise between her index and middle knuckles, careful not to leave any of her fingerprints on the switch. The entire first floor, like the staircase and the upstairs, was covered in a plush light tan carpet. The walls were a slightly darker tan, with thick, bright white trim identical to the baseboards and six-panel doors. The first floor was modern and sparsely furnished, with a plenty of room for people to move around. She thought Chase had yet to experience a woman's touch in the house and liked to entertain guests at parties. She correctly deduced that he had a pool and one hell of a barbecue setup in the backyard.

Staci walked over to the stereo, pulled out a Norah Jones CD from the rack, and played it. Not too loudly—just loud enough to cover any sounds she might make. Then she opened up the front door as if she were stepping out for a cigarette.

Walking down the hall to Chase's study, she took a brief look at the pictures on the walls. She stopped in astonishment at the family picture taken with Pope John Paul II. There they were—all six of the Manhattans with the pope. She quickly identified Chase among the siblings. He must have been about twelve or thirteen at most. She remembered at Ti Amo Chase said he was in the ninth grade when they went to Italy. That meant that Chase was ahead of the curve academically if he was that young in the picture as a freshman in high school. She realized Chase wasn't just a guy with good looks, culture, and having a great taste in fine wine. He was also very intelligent.

Thanks to Khyati's superior hacking skills, Staci already knew that Chase purchased a fireproof floor safe and had it installed a couple of days ago. She also had the combination as Chase, with a false sense of security, thought it was safe to record it on a Word document. His firewall and security system were no match for the talents of MIT's own Khyati Dasmunsi.

In less than three minutes, she accomplished the first half of her mission. The suitcases were relatively small and light since they lacked the battery packs. She quickly walked out of the study and out the front door to the waiting red and white Ducati Desmosedici RR sitting idly in the driveway. She untied the thin black twine that she used to tie the knapsack to the seat and pulled out a pack of Marlboro Lights containing her last two cigarettes and a small lighter. Then she placed the thin black twine and the suitcases in the knapsack and hid it in the small shrubs that lined the driveway.

Staci was thankful for the trees that concealed her movements from the neighbors across the street and on either side of the house. Chase's bedroom windows faced the back of the house, so, as long as he was still in bed waiting for her, she would be all alone in front of the house. Although she hadn't had time to look out his bay-view window from upstairs, she was sure that it faced the ocean.

Staci lit the first cigarette. It was starting to get really chilly outside, but she needed a smoke. She needed to make a decision that was much harder than she realized on her drive to Laguna Beach a few hours earlier. She wondered if she should just get on her bike and leave with the suitcases, her mission only half accomplished, or if she should go back inside and finish her assignment.

Staci had several major reservations at this point. She really liked Chase. She felt deeply that he was a good guy who wasn't just out for himself in this world. This was a rarity among people who seemed to have everything going for them at that age. She was beginning to like him even more than Nicky, and she only knew him one day. Staci sucked down another puff and blew out a large cloud of smoke that was intensified in size and shape by the coolness of the evening air and the brilliance of the full moon's near orbit on a cloudless night. She looked up at the bright evening orb giving off its luminescence that allowed her to see so clearly in the dark.

She finished her first cigarette, put it out on the driveway, and placed it into her knapsack. She was still undecided about the second half of her assignment. She pulled out the second cigarette, lit it, and began pacing back and forth in front of the house. She thought of how Chase treated her to an elegant dinner and a bottle of fine French wine, then balanced the night out with margaritas at a local bar. She really had a great time.

She contrasted the night's events with her last date with Nicky at Jimmy's Grill. Sure, the storm prevented them from going somewhere nicer, but Nicky could have taken her out for a big juicy steak once the weather broke. After all, she did risk her life by allowing herself to be transported to the State House when there had not been proper testing to see if it were truly safe for a human to be sent through a wormhole, even though the journey was only about a mile long. She was the one who killed a beloved state senator, and all she got out of it was a pink sweater, a quick jump that did nothing for her, and a lousy meal at Jimmy's served by a washed-up waitress with a bad attitude.

But ultimately, she understood that the world would quickly change, and that it would never be the same again. Nicky and his dedicated followers were determined that this breakthrough would not fall into the wrong hands. Not to the military or to a political group. Not to a terrorist group. And certainly not to corporations who would use it for their own greedy gain rather than to benefit those who needed it the most. Nicky had a vision for the future of the world, and Staci, along with a number of other gifted graduate students at MIT and a few other select campuses around the country and the world, had bought into it.

She lowered her head and sighed, then put out her second cigarette and placed it in the knapsack. Next, she took out a piece of gum and placed the empty wrapper along with the empty box of cigarettes and the lighter back in the side pocket. Finally, she took out a pair of thin, black leather gloves, put them on, and headed back into the house. She had made up her mind. She understood that Chase must die. He knew too much. She knew that he had spoken to Nicky Sr., stole both a transporter and a receiver suitcase from Nicky, and realized that this breakthrough was now a reality. He had to die—and he had to die right now.

She fidgeted at the thought, then stopped just outside of the door. Closing her eyes and taking three deep breaths, she closed her heart and cleared her head. She thought back on the words the master had spoken over her, quickly shed off distractions, and entered a state of homeostasis where she could block out everything except for the immediate task at hand.

Walking into the house, Staci quietly shut the door and took a look around the place. She was still undecided on how she would kill Chase. She strolled into the kitchen to get a glass of water to help clear her head before going back upstairs.

In the kitchen, she turned on the light. Chase seemed to have dimmer switches throughout the house. This was good. Staci wanted to keep any attention to what she was doing to a bare minimum. She first walked to the refrigerator to see what Chase might have in there. Opening the door, the refrigerator light gave view to a most horrific sight—numerous bowls and Tupperware containers full of fresh fruits and vegetables, and a loaf of what appeared to be nine-grain bread.

"Yuck," she said softly. "How can people eat this crap? There's no pie or cake or anything good in here." Noticing a bowl of red grapes, she popped a few in her mouth and decided that they weren't that bad. In fact, they were actually pretty good, almost as tasty as blueberries. She noted to herself that she would have to pick some up at the grocery store when she arrived back in Cambridge.

Turning to the cupboard, she took a glass, turned on the water purifier at the sink, filled the glass to the top, and took a long, slow drink. From the left corner of her eye, she spotted a block set of chef's knives on the counter. She finished the water and set the glass back in the cupboard.

Staci stepped to the left and in front of the twenty-three-piece Wusthof set of chef's knives. Her eyes immediately focused on the eight-inch chef's knife, and she quickly pulled it out. She held it up and spun it around in her hand, then threw it up in the air over her head and snatched it hard by the handle on its way back down. It had a good weight and balance to it. Sturdy, too. And sharp. Very, *very* sharp. The knife felt good in her hand, and it quickly became an extension of her. It was now a part of her and she could control it with her will just as she could control any mechanical movement of her hands.

Staci really liked Chase. He deserved to die quickly, with little pain. She decided she would go upstairs, slowly and seductively walk up to him with the knife behind her back, leap upon him suddenly, plunge the chef's knife deep into his heart, and kill him instantly. She didn't want him to die slowly, or even know what hit him. She felt she owed him that for being a great guy, and for giving her a fun night out on the town, and for all that great sex.

Chapter 45
Fight for Life

STACI WALKED BACK across the carpeted floor through the living room and dining room, Norah Jones still singing softly and seductively through the speakers. She was focused and shed off all distractions, even her new heartfelt attraction toward Chase. She climbed the stairs, careful not to look at any of the pictures on the wall, especially the family picture of Chase and his loved ones. With her deep guilt about what she was about to do to their son, she did not want to make eye contact with Mr. and Mrs. Manhattan.

At the top of the stairs, she took one more deep breath, then mentally set her breathing on cruise control consisting of evenly paced deep breathing. Passing the Jack-and-Jill bedrooms, she entered the last door at the end of the hall. She still wore the thin black gloves, and she had the eight-inch chef's knife in her right hand behind her back. Her left hand was behind her back, too, so she looked somewhat symmetrical and not too suspicious.

"Hey, sweetie," Chase smiled, still lying in bed with the comforter pulled up just over his waist, his hands folded behind his head. He felt the nip of the evening coolness, too, and had gotten up out of bed to put on a pair of boxer shorts and a UC-Irvine tank top. He also placed two pairs of socks on the floor next to the bed to wear when they were both ready to go to sleep.

Staci only had about eight steps to reach the bed. The chef's knife still in hand, she smiled and whispered, "Are you ready for me, big guy? Well, are you?"

At that moment, Chase was in another world that he felt was created solely for him. They were the only two people who existed, and everything else around them was created for the sole purpose of enhancing their night together. An earthquake could slide his house off its concrete foundation and Chase would not be shaken.

"I'm ready," he said with more confidence than he ever felt in his life. "I'm ready, right here and now."

Staci was four steps away. She took another step. Then one more. Chase looked her deeply in the eyes, and at the moment, nothing else really mattered. He started to fold back the comforter with his left hand to welcome her back to his own little universe when she suddenly sprung toward him like a tiger pouncing upon its prey, a feat that she had practiced hundreds of times.

With blinding speed, the stainless steel chef's knife made its appearance from behind her back as her feet left the carpet. If it wasn't for the glimmer of a moon ray from the bay window reflecting off the metal blade, Chase never would have seen it coming. Instinct and reflex overcame trust and confidence, and Chase rolled to his right directly into his attacker, his left hand making an outward arching sweeping motion that deflected her right wrist into the far left side of the bed, where the knife buried itself deep in the mattress. He continued his roll underneath Staci's lunging body, out of the bed, and onto the floor.

Staci recovered from her failed assassination attempt and was on her feet on the other side of the bed in a few seconds, chef's knife in hand once again, and in an attack position.

"What the *hell* are you doing, Cathy?" Chase screamed, breathing heavier and more deeply than he had twenty minutes ago.

"I'm so very sorry to have to do this, Chase," she said, circling around the foot of the bed and walking steadily toward him. She held the deadly blade firmly in her right hand. "I truly am. But I have to do what I have to do and carry out my mission."

"Mission? *What* mission?" he demanded, stepping back slowly but deliberately, trying to buy himself a few seconds to recalibrate his five senses, assess the sudden change of events, and react accordingly.

Staci did not want to waste any breath, energy, or time on conversation. She quickened her pace and was upon him in a moment, slashing the knife at his neck and forcing him to backpedal and nearly lose his balance. Although Chase had no idea why his new girlfriend was trying to kill him, his mind quickly made the connection to the MIT campus in Cambridge, Nicky Jr., and the two suitcases he brought back to Orange County.

Staci did not want Chase to escape into the hall, so she quickly circled around between him and the door and then slowly backed Chase up to the far wall where there were no tables or drawers that could contain a gun. The closet was across the room and the master bathroom door was at least twenty feet away. Chase realized he made a mistake by allowing Staci to stand between him and the door to the hallway. But the twenty seconds of silence was all he needed to partially regain his composure and construct an offense.

He stepped into Staci and struck with a reverse kick directed at her head that barely missed its target and followed with a series of alternating left and right front snap kicks. Staci reached over to the nightstand and grabbed two lead crystal water glasses and threw them at Chase. She threw the coasters and two glass candleholders at him, too. He sidestepped the glasses and coasters and ducked under the candleholders, then heard the sound of glass shattering behind him and water pouring out onto the floor. He momentarily swung his head around to see his seventy-five-gallon saltwater aquarium spilling its contents of water and fish onto his bedroom carpet.

Now his emotions shifted into high gear. He was far angrier than he could ever remember. This psychotic bitch had manipulated her way into his life, tried to kill him, and now broke the one thing that brought peace and serenity to his otherwise lonely life. Strike three and you're out. *That* was strike three. He was no longer scared of this sociopath. He wanted nothing more than to kick this bitch's ass all the way back to Cambridge.

Chase stepped around the side of the bed until he was three feet from Staci, who waited in a catlike stance with her body weight on her back leg and the right foot in front of her, ready for a counterattack. Using his right arm, Chase led with a punch and Staci grabbed his wrist and used his momentum to shove it off to the side. She countered with three rapid snap kicks with her right foot to his stomach, neck, and head before bringing her foot back down to rest on the floor.

Chase recovered quickly and struck with an inside crescent kick followed by a roundhouse kick, the latter hitting Staci on the left side of her head. He was astounded she was held her ground *and* held onto the knife. Any average martial arts student would have dropped the knife and crumpled to the floor after being kicked in the side of the head. At that point, he recognized that he was not fighting any average person. Standing before him was a professional assassin, one who was skilled, experienced, and disciplined enough to withstand the pain of a roundhouse kick to the side of the head and ready herself for another attack.

Jumping into Chase, Staci thrust the knife at his chest and midsection, then slashed side-to-side at his neck. He sidestepped the attack and grabbed her bicep and forearm with both hands, flipping her over in midair. He attempted to drive her head hard onto the floor, but Staci used her momentum and turned the flip into a backwards somersault, breaking free of Chase's grip at the same time. She planted her hands on the carpet and went into a backflip, landing on her feet in the doorway in a fighting stance, still holding the knife in her hand.

Chase was determined to stay on the offensive and not allow her to dictate the pace of the fight. He charged Staci with a barrage of kicks and rising punches from his waist, driving her out of his bedroom door and down the hallway to the edge of the staircase. He then tried to do something unexpected and knock her feet out from underneath her by falling to his left side and swinging his right leg in a whipping motion. Staci not only jumped to avoid the sweep, but she lunged through the air over Chase, rolling into a somersault as she hit the floor. In virtually the same motion, she stood and landed a kick directly to Chase's sternum as he stood to face her.

The force of the blow knocked him backward to the edge of the staircase and onto his back. Staci lunged and landed on top of him, the knife still gripped tightly in her right hand. He looked up into her mussed and sweat-laden jet-black hair that stuck to her cheeks and forehead. It was a far cry from the smooth and silky bob that bounced off her shoulders an hour ago. Her breathing was rapid and deep, but quickly turned erratic. Her eyes bulged and her lips began to quiver. Her skin started to drain its natural color and sweat had caused her black mascara to run down her cheeks. She was focused—yet disoriented. To Chase, she looked as if she were possessed. He knew she was starting to unravel because she understood he could beat her.

Yet, no matter how hard Chase tried, he could not force her to drop the knife. Staci drew her arm back and tried to drive the knife deep into his chest. He blocked the forward thrust, using his left palm to redirect the stab to the side just enough to miss, and taking advantage of her momentum, drove his right knee directly into her stomach. Staci tumbled forward over Chase headfirst down the stairs. He hoped that would buy him a few seconds to regroup and stage another offensive.

But Staci was too quick, and she grabbed him by the back of the neck and pulled him down the stairs with her. They tumbled over the top of each other down half the flight of stairs, Chase still holding her right wrist with his left hand, keeping the knife at bay.

They stopped at the midway point of the staircase with Chase at the lower step. Standing up, he used his leverage to pick her up and slam her into the wall, her head hitting the family photo that she avoided looking at earlier. The glass shattered and the impact made a large hole in the drywall and sent half of the pictures flying in all directions. Chase let out a yell, then threw her over the railing onto the living room carpet below. She landed with a loud thud that told him she landed squarely on her back.

He took a few brief seconds to clear his head and take a deep breath. When he looked over the banister to assess her condition, to his amazement, she was already back on her feet, lucid and alert, ready to carry the fight back to him. He couldn't believe she recovered so quickly and took the offensive to him once again.

Staci sprinted to the bottom of the stairs and leaped up to the fifth step. Chase had no choice but to place his left hand onto the railing and leap over onto the living room floor. Staci turned around and jumped back to the bottom of the stairs and slowly stepped towards Chase, the eight-inch knife still in her right hand like an unwelcome appendage.

Staci was breathing hard. She took a moment to use her free hand to wipe the sweat from her forehead and to run her fingers through her hair, pulling it to the back of her head. "I tried to make this easy on you, Chase. I tried to make this quick and easy. But now you've made me do this the hard way. Why don't you just give it up right now and I'll make it painless for you?"

Chase wasn't afraid. He knew he was fortunate to be alive. He should have been lying in his bed, a corpse with a knife sticking out of him, waiting for someone to notice him missing. But he wasn't about to lie down and die. Not in his own house. Not at this bitch's hand.

Chase didn't flinch. He stared her down for a few moments, taking advantage of the break to catch his breath. "You're messing with the wrong guy. You've made the biggest mistake of your life by coming in here and attempting to kill me in my house."

His living room and dining room were sparsely furnished, but there were a few items that Chase saw that he could use as weapons. To his left, beneath the staircase, was a small oval side table that held a clear, crystal, ten-inch bud vase along with five decorative black onyx oval stones. He picked up the stones and threw them hard at her in rapid succession. The fourth stone bounced off the left side of her forehead. It wasn't a clean hit, but it made a nice *thud* sound upon impact, and Chase knew that it must have hurt. The vase quickly followed, and Staci barely managed to duck to the left to avoid its trajectory before it shattered into dozens of pieces against the front door. Chase then grabbed the table by one of its legs and threw *that* too. Staci blocked it with her left forearm, and it bounced harmlessly off the wall behind her.

Chase had to get the knife out of her hand. Stepping out into the center of the living room, he stood silently with his clenched fists to his side, issuing a silent challenge to meet him there and fight him hand-to-hand. Staci accepted his challenge and tossed the knife a few inches over his head and onto the dining room carpet behind him. The two fighters faced each other, each barefoot and dressed only in boxer shorts and tank tops, sweat dripping down their heads and necks and soaking the upper portions of their shirts and shorts. The living room and dining room were not separated by a wall, and offered four hundred square feet of room to maneuver and fight.

Staci took two steps forward and launched a powerful lunge kick at Chase's chest. He dropped to the floor and rolled under the kick, stood back up in a left forward stance, and delivered a volley of punches mixed with front snap and push kicks. Chase preferred the snap kicks as they offered many variations and combinations that could be improvised upon and used to overwhelm an opponent who was inexperienced or unprepared.

But Staci was experienced and prepared. She quickly spun and either blocked or avoided each individual strike while countering with a flip kick that was meant to be a diversionary kick to the groin to get Chase to lower his guard. It worked just as she hoped, and she delivered a second roundhouse kick that landed hard on the left side of his jaw, knocking out an upper molar and sending it flying out of his mouth and across the room.

Chase reeled a few steps and Staci shuffled into him and directed another roundhouse kick to his head. He squatted to duck underneath it, but Staci grabbed his head as he began to stand back up. She used his momentum to throw Chase onto the dining table, breaking it in half. Stunned, Chase barely rolled out of the way just in time to avoid having his head stomped. He reached around at the same time her right foot slammed into the floor between the broken table pieces and grabbed her ankle, pulling it up and out and dropping her to the floor on her back. Chase was back on his feet and attacked her with kicks and knee drops while she rolled back and forth on her left and right sides. He was able to connect three times to her back and left shoulder before she regained a fighting stance on her feet.

Chase turned and jumped up onto the sofa behind him in the center of the living room. He stepped onto the top, forcing it over onto its back and making Staci trip over it as she pursued him, causing the cushions to scatter across the carpet. He grabbed an empty coffee cup from an end table and threw that at her, barely missing her head.

Among the broken glass and splintered wood strewn over the carpet, Staci saw a letter opener among the items that were on top of Chase's dining-room table. She grabbed it with her right hand and jumped into Chase, faking a thrust into his chest, then faking a kick to his groin, and finally thrusting the letter opener directly at his heart. Chase could do nothing but swing his left arm directly into the path of the letter opener and catching the brunt of the thrust with his left shoulder.

The letter opener lay buried three inches deep in his muscles and tissues. Despite the initial shock and the excruciating pain, he was able to disarm Staci by pulling his arm back to himself with the letter opener still stuck into his shoulder. He pulled the letter opener out and hurled it at Staci's chest as she took a few steps backward. She shifted to her left, barely avoiding the projectile.

Thinking back to numerous experiences in Southeast Asia where he subjected himself to trials and tribulations of pain and suffering that would land a sensei in prison in the United States, Chase had learned to how to manage pain that would render most people inoperable and useless. In less than a second, he regained control and balance of his five senses and sprinted back into the dining room, where he tried to pick up the chef's knife Staci threw there a few minutes earlier. But she saw what he was doing, and managed to get there first and grabbed it with her right hand. He grabbed a dining chair next to the busted and broken table and snapped off two legs. The sharp splintered ends made resourceful weapons.

"So you want to play rough, do you, Chase?" Staci said, breathing heavily and again wiping the sweat off her forehead with her free hand." You should have just given up back in the living room and made it easy on yourself." She followed suit by shattering a second chair with her left foot and picking up a splintered leg with her free hand. Chase threw the remains of his broken chair at her, then picked up a second chair and threw that at her too. The second chair hit Staci in the left shin and foot and caused her to reach down and make sure nothing was broken.

The two then traded stabs and swings with the broken table legs, moving back and forth between the dining room and the living room. Staci managed to knock the table leg out of Chase's right hand with kick to his forearm. He shifted the other chair leg from his left to his right hand. Staci still had the chef's knife in her right hand, stepped into Chase, and took a few slashes at him. The action was fast and furious, and Chase did not notice that her second slash actually sliced across his stomach and cut a half-inch gash horizontally across his abdomen. Blood immediately began to ooze out and stain his light green tank top, but he didn't notice it as the fight for survival overwhelmed the pain and bleeding inflicted from her slash.

The fight continued for a few more minutes when Chase finally landed a left kick into Staci's right hand that caused the knife to fly across the room and land next to the broken dining-room table. She stood in the middle, the knife a mere ten feet from her and Chase about five feet from her. Hesitating a moment, Staci looked at Chase and the blood leaking from his stomach and left shoulder, then to the knife, then back at Chase. Instead of trying to finish him off with her hands, she opted to lunge for the knife.

That was when Chase found a clear path to the wall behind him, the wall where he had a 9mm Glock hidden behind the drywall just below the stairwell. At the same time Staci jumped for the knife, Chase spun around on his left heel and took five large strides toward the wall, plunged his two fists through the drywall, and pulled out the already-loaded semi-automatic. He planted his left foot, and with the gun in his right hand, spun around to aim directly at the center of Staci's chest.

But Staci saw what Chase was doing. She grabbed a sofa cushion off the floor and ducked under the ensuing five shots with a series of somersaults that vaulted her toward the far wall of the dining room. She held the pillow to her face and jumped out of the window and into the shrubs and wood chips in the front yard. Her momentum carried her forward as she rolled twice, jumped up onto her feet, and sprinted toward the waiting red and white speed demon parked in the driveway, keys in the ignition. Wasting no time, she grabbed the knapsack with the suitcases she previously hid in the shrubs, threw them over her right shoulder, started the Ducati up, and shot off down the driveway and back toward Coast Highway as fast as the curved streets physically allowed her to.

Inside, Chase's ears were ringing with the echoing roar of the five shots he just fired, but his other senses were on high alert. He raced to the front door, threw it open, and ran out into his driveway with eight bullets still left in the clip. But all he could hear was the sound of the Ducati screaming through the canyon as his assailant, his date, his lover, the girl a mere hour earlier he thought was the possible love of his life, was making her getaway—in his underwear and tank top and nothing else.

PART THREE

Chapter 46
911

Looking around his living room and dining room, Chase couldn't believe the amount of damage inflicted on his house in just minutes. It looked as if a small war had broken out. Shattered glass was strewn across the carpet, holes pocked the walls, furniture was toppled over, pictures were knocked off the stair wall, and splintered pieces of wood from what was left of his dining-room table and chairs were scattered everywhere. "I'm glad I opted for the carpet rather than listening to the interior designer who wanted travertine in here," Chase said aloud as he considered the consequences of fighting on a hard rather than soft floor.

He stumbled a bit as he walked to the kitchen looking for a phone. Chase thought he was fortunate that the fight didn't proceed in here or he would surely be dead. He stood with his hands on his hips and looked around at the knives, pots and pans, plates, silverware, and other cooking utensils in the kitchen. He gazed at the set of Wusthof chef's knives on the granite countertop conspicuously missing the eight-inch butcher's knife, inhaled deeply, exhaled, and considered himself extremely fortunate that he was still alive. Then, looking down at the floor, he saw where the carpet ended at the door and the travertine tile began. "Yeah, this could have ended in a bad way for sure," he said, shaking his head.

Chase opened a drawer, pulled out a box of tea bags, opened the individual cellophane packets, placed two in a bowl, and soaked them in cool water. Then he gently placed them in his left upper jaw where his molar had been kicked out. He walked across the kitchen to the cupboards where he kept the Advil. Still shaking slightly while opening the bottle, he poured four tablets into his hand and popped them in his mouth. Stepping over to the sink, he turned on the water, cupped his hands, and drank from the running faucet. He then went into the adjoining laundry room, found a recently washed bath towel, and wrapped it around his abdomen where Staci had sliced through a half inch of his skin.

Chase picked up the phone and started to dial 911. Catching himself as clarity started replacing shock, he asked himself what exactly he would say. *Ah ... hello, a girl just kicked my ass, destroyed my house, and almost killed me.* Then he thought of the suitcases that were in his recently installed floor safe in his study. Tossing the phone on the counter, Chase ran back through the dining room and the living room to the study, careful not to step on any of the broken glass with his bare feet. Once inside, he set the Glock 9mm on top of his desk.

At first glance, he didn't notice anything out of the ordinary. Like the kitchen, the study was spared any damage. Opening the walk-in closet door, Chase looked down at the shoe boxes that once covered the floor safe and were now tossed aside. His heart sank deeply into his chest and he realized that he was out of breath. Shock was setting back in, replacing the clarity in his mind.

Kneeling down, he spun the dial of the safe to the left, right, then left again. Opening the lid, he saw the cash, watches, and other valuables. Everything was there—everything except the black and silver suitcases. Chase stood as a blanket of confusion overwhelmed him. He felt lightheaded as he stepped out of the closet and placed his right hand firmly on the side of his desk to balance himself. Nausea began to set in his lower bowels.

Chase knew that he needed to catch this girl. Clearly he had stumbled upon something bigger than anything that he could have imagined when he first talked to Prof. Fischer a few days ago. The suitcases were obviously worth killing over. If he didn't act quickly and retrieve them, he intuitively knew that many innocent people would die. He picked up the phone on his desk and dialed 911. His pride evaporated. He needed medical attention, and he needed to have the police catch this girl and return the suitcases.

"911. What's your emergency?" said a pleasant female voice.

Still trying to gather his thoughts, Chase just blurted it out. "I was robbed and almost killed inside my house. And I need medical attention." Chase shifted his weight, cleared a spot on his desk with his left hand, and sat down.

"Are you alright, sir?"

"I think so. I think I have some cracked ribs and I had a tooth knocked out. I have a few cuts, but nothing life-threatening."

"Are you alone now, sir? Is there anybody else in the house?"

"I'm alone. The girl ..." Chase's voice trailed off.

"A girl, sir?"

"Yes," Chase sighed. "Her name is Cathy Bennett. She attacked me with one of my kitchen knives. She almost killed me. She stole something out of my safe and then took off on a Ducati motorcycle speeding toward Coast Highway, and is now heading north through the canyon on the 133." Chase was now adding to the conversation with exaggerated hand movements with his right arm.

"When did this happen?"

"Just a few minutes ago. Listen, if you send somebody after her, you can probably still catch her."

"Are you also bleeding, sir? You said you need medical attention."

Chase looked down at the towel wrapped around his torso. "Yes, I'm bleeding, but not very much now. Listen, you need to dispatch someone after this girl. She should be easy to find. She's speeding like a bat out of hell on a red Ducati motorcycle through the canyon and she's barefoot. She's only wearing a pair of my boxer shorts and one of my tank tops.

"I see. And what is your name, sir?"

"Chase Manhattan."

"Your name is Chase Manhattan? And a girl robbed you and almost killed you, then sped away on a motorcycle in your underwear." Suddenly the lady on the other end sounded like a completely different person. Her voice became lower, monotonal, and downright cold. Chase knew that she didn't believe him.

"Listen to me. This really happened. And my name really is Chase Manhattan. You can trace this call. I'm not trying to be funny. I need you to dispatch someone to look for this girl. Her name is—"

"Cathy Bennett. *Right.* You already told me that." Chase noticed that she was no longer calling him "sir."

"Okay. I'll dispatch someone right now. We should have a sheriff's officer in that vicinity. Stay on the phone. I'll also get someone over to your house. A police officer will be there shortly, Mr. ... ah ... Manhattan."

Chapter 47
Wild Police Chase

THE SOUND OF THE DUCATI Desmosedici RR screamed and echoed through the canyon as Staci sped north on Laguna Canyon Road, weaving around cars coming into and going out of Laguna Beach. Traffic was light, but at her speed, she needed to dodge cars about every five seconds. The temperature had cooled from a balmy seventy-five degrees that afternoon to cool fifty-nine degrees, and it was still dropping.

Staci's helmet was a MOMO Fighter helmet with a Mot HS810 Bluetooth headset. Slowing down to reduce the noise of the bike, she made the call for help with a preprogrammed telephone number entered by Sensei Masakata. An anonymous person on the other end immediately picked up the phone on the first ring. "This is Jeb."

"Jeb, listen. I need your help. I picked up what I needed to but failed to drop the mark. I need to be picked up *fast*."

"Where exactly are you now, Miss Bevere?" The voice was deep and loud with a sense of urgency.

"I'm heading north through the canyon. I remember there's a toll road a few miles ahead."

"Listen to me. When you approach the toll road, you will see a street named El Toro. Make a right on that. After about a mile, turn right on Aliso Creek Road. I will guide you to a place where we can pick you up."

"Got it. And let's make this quick. I'm wearing only boxer shorts and a tank top, and I'm freezing my ass off right now."

"Will do. And don't hang up, Miss Bevere. Stay with me. Everything will be just fine."

"Thanks a million, Jeb."

"No worries."

After a few minutes of speeding through the weaving canyon at twice the posted speed limit, Staci saw the sign for the toll road. "The toll road is up ahead," she said. "Make a right on El Toro, correct?"

"That's correct. Then another right on Aliso Creek Road about a mile up the street."

Slowing down to ten miles an hour to make the sharp right turn on El Toro, Staci spotted a sheriff's black-and-white Crown Victoria approaching the intersection. The gold sheriff's emblem on the driver's side door shone brightly in her headlight. All she could do was smile and wink at the sheriff, who rolled down his window and stared at her with his mouth wide open.

Doing the speed limit, she hoped that he would think she was just another nutty Southern Californian and that this was nothing out of the ordinary. No such luck. He made a quick U-turn and turned his red and blue lights on.

Controlling her breathing and her rapidly rising heart rate, she shouted into the helmet phone, "We have trouble, Jeb. A sheriff's car is barreling up on me with his lights flashing."

"Lose him! Lose him right now! I just heard over the scanner that they're looking for you. There are more units driving to the area right now."

Tightening her grip on the throttle, she shifted into fourth gear and immediately put distance between her and the sheriff's car.

Picking up his radio, Sheriff Ronald Lee shouted, "I have her right in front of me. She just turned off the 133 and is speeding up El Toro Road. And, sure as shit, she's wearing nothing but boxer shorts and a tank top."

Another sheriff's car appeared over the top of the hill in front of Staci, driving toward her with his lights flashing. Staci had no choice.

To avoid the oncoming sheriff, she entered the southbound San Joaquin Hills Toll Road entrance. She veered to the right onto the onramp and approached the toll booth at seventy-five mph. The onramp split into two lanes, the left lane for vehicles with pre-paid transponders and the right for drivers who needed change to enter. A sign said, *Toll, One Dollar. Violations, Eighty-Five Dollars.* She was confident she could reach back into her knapsack, grab four quarters, and throw them into the basket as she raced by, but decided against it. Nicky had preached against greed, carelessness, and arrogance more times than she could count. A loud buzzer—almost like what you'd hear at a hockey rink—sounded as she screamed past the toll booth at one hundred mph.

With both sheriff cars behind her in full pursuit, Staci opened up the bike to 120 mph. She was beyond cold now. Her hands were so numb she was having trouble holding the throttle. But she maintained her breathing and her focus. Both sheriff cars were a half a mile behind her. She opened up the throttle even more.

"Jeb, I've got two of them on me now. Where do I go from here?"

"Listen to me. Turn around now! I'm following the action on the police scanner, and they're sending more sheriffs up ahead to block the toll road. They're also sending a chopper your way, too. Turn around and get off the exit you just got on."

Staci slowed the Ducati to forty-five mph and drove onto the gravel emergency lane. A grassy median separated the northbound and southbound lanes. It was just 200 yards of real estate that she had to cross, an immediate dip in terrain of about forty feet with a slope of thirty degrees, and the ground was still soft and full of large pools of water from the recent rains. She could use this to her advantage if she performed the maneuver right.

Staci slowed down enough to flip a U-turn, spinning her rear wheel and making a wall of smoke across the three lanes of pavement. She opened up the throttle and drove north, still on the southbound lanes and heading straight at the two sheriff's cars that were fast approaching. Staci drove on the center line that separated the first two lanes, heading straight for the two cruisers at more than 120 mph.

Sheriff Lee had seen this maneuver before and held his ground. A few years ago, the same scenario played out on Laguna Canyon Road. A biker on a customized Harley-Davidson chopper tried to outrun him when Lee attempted to pull him over for not wearing a helmet. The biker sped off with Lee in pursuit half a mile behind. Seeing a second sheriff coming at him with lights flashing, the biker flipped a U-turn and drove directly at Lee, hoping he would be the one to swerve. But at the last second, it was the biker who blinked, drove off the canyon road, and ended up wrapped around a one-hundred-year-old oak tree. *Checkmate*, Lee reminisced and smiled. Sheriff Lee yelled into the radio to the much-younger deputy sheriff next to him, "Listen to me, Michelson. Whatever you do, *don't* move. Let the young lady in underwear make the first move."

But Matthew Michelson had only been on the job for less than a year and didn't have the intestinal fortitude that Lee had developed over his twenty years on the force. The rookie deputy swerved at the last second to avoid colliding with the young lady on the Ducati and almost lost control of his cruiser in the process, but was able to straighten it out after nearly spinning onto the wet, grassy median.

Staci bought herself an additional sixty seconds and looked for a dry spot in the median, as the recent rains had partially flooded the grassy median. The full moon gave off enough light that she could look for a slim, flat path that was at least partially dry that would increase her chances of crossing the median. Less than a mile ahead, Staci saw what she was looking for, a small strip of ground that rose up between two very large pools of water. She quickly assessed the angle, slope of the median, the distance to the level ground, and the speed of the bike, and calculated that she needed to slow down to thirty mph to have the best chance of successfully making this maneuver. Staci slowed the bike down from 140 mph to the desired speed, then veered off to the right onto the gravel, onto the wet grass, down the thirty-degree dip, and across the small patch of grass that she anticipated would be the driest section of the median.

The two sheriffs spun around and followed her onto the soft, grassy strip, spreading out into a pincher formation. Sheriff Lee came up on her left side and the rookie deputy sheriff was on her right. She saw the headlights follow her onto the wet grassy median as they first rose, then dropped out of sight from her rearview mirrors as they hit the dip. Just as she expected, they drove onto the median as fast as they could to try and close the distance between them. They must have been doing at least seventy mph. She could hear the crunch of the front ends of their cruisers as they became momentarily airborne, then hit the ground as the grade quickly dropped forty feet over the first one hundred twenty feet of the median.

Staci reached the bridge of ground that divided the two ponds of rain water. It was soft and muddy as she expected, and all she had to do was keep control of the bike and her momentum would theoretically get her safely across to the southbound lanes. Her rear tire started to wobble to the left and right as she crossed, but she was able to use her feet to keep control. Mud covered her from helmet to toe and the bike slowed down to fifteen mph. A large glob of foul-smelling mud made its way under her visor and splattered across her face. Using her left hand, she reached up and wiped the mud from her eyes and face while letting out a loud, "yuck!" She had no choice but to rip the visor off as her attempts to wipe it clean only smeared the gooey glob around and made her vision worse. She tossed it over her shoulder, sure that her fingerprints were not on the muddied visor since she was wearing gloves.

The embankment to the other side of the toll road rose slowly—less then ten feet—and Staci was barely able to make it to the graveled shoulder before her rear tire found the traction it needed to grip the ground and give the bike speed. Opening up the throttle on the northbound lanes, she exited at El Toro Road and saw the two sheriff cruisers regain their momentum and also enter the southbound lanes. "Are you still with me, Jeb?" she finally shouted into her helmet phone. "I'm back on the southbound lanes and bought myself about another minute of distance between us."

"I'm still here. Nice maneuver. Now turn right on Aliso Creek Road. About two miles up you will see a Carl's Jr. Restaurant on the right."

"Carl's Jr. Got it."

"The sign looks like—"

"The sign has a yellow star on a red background. I know. I've already eaten at one twice since I've been here."

"Just past Carl's Jr. is a side street that leads into an industrial area. Pull in there. We'll be parked about one hundred feet up on the right side."

"Turn the heater on, would you, Jeb? I'm so cold right now I can hardly grip the bike."

"It's on. Hang in there, Miss Bevere. I'll talk you through this."

Turning right on Aliso Creek Road, she again opened up the muddied bike. At just past midnight, there was no traffic passing through this sleepy residential neighborhood of Aliso Viejo. Green lights were her friend and she made it to her rendezvous in just one minute.

"I'm pulling in, Jeb. Where are you?"

"I see you. Look to your right." Jeb flashed his parking lights for a brief moment. "Pull around to the driver's side of the back of the truck and shut it off."

Two tall and well-built hulks dressed in dark pants and black leather jackets stepped out of the doors and to the back of the truck. Staci drove up to them and stopped. Jeb's partner steadied the bike while he took her gently by the right elbow, helped her off the bike, and escorted her to the driver's door. "Please sit down in the middle of the seat, Miss Bevere. I'll be right back." Staci pulled off her backpack with the two suitcases, reached into the backseat, and gently set it on the floor.

Jeb walked over to his partner and, with one easy movement, they picked up the $50,000 red and white Ducati Desmosedici RR and unceremoniously dumped it in the back of the truck. Quickly they pulled a black plastic tarp over it and tied it to the bed of the truck.

"Let's go!" Jeb shouted to his partner, and they both climbed back into the cab. They could hear the wailing sirens approaching and pulled the truck into the Carl's Jr. parking lot from the side entrance. There they watched two sheriff's cruisers with crushed grill plates race up Aliso Creek Road. They could hear more sirens to the north.

After about a minute of listening to the scanner and convinced that they were looking for Staci a couple of miles away, Jeb pulled out of the parking lot onto Aliso Creek Road and started to work his way to the 405 Freeway. Looking over at Staci, he asked, "Why don't you put your hands up against the heating vents? They'll warm up faster. We'll have you back at your hotel in about twenty minutes."

"Thanks again, Jeb," she managed to say through chattering teeth. "The heat feels great." Looking up, she finally noticed that Jeb was nothing at all like she pictured he would be when he talked her through the high-speed chase. She also didn't notice that her eyes were wide open and her mouth agape.

"What's the matter, Miss Bevere?" he asked with a smirk on his face.

"Nothing. It's just that ..."

"I'm black. It's okay. I know I talk like a white person. I get this look often when people meet me for the first time after only hearing my voice. And my name is Jeb. That really throws them off. Please allow me to introduce my partner, Vincent. Vincent, Miss Bevere."

"Nice to meet you," said the young white male, doing his best to cover his Brooklyn accent and placing his leather jacket over her shoulders. "If you don't mind me saying so, you look like you're in pretty bad shape right now," Vincent continued with a deviant grin and a tone that communicated approval, as if getting oneself into a knock-down, drag-out fight and surviving offered acceptance into his exclusive club. Staci noticed Vincent had one of the strongest jaw lines she had ever seen on a man. She discerned that together, his voice, smile, and eyes carried a particular level of demented intensity that bordered on the insane.

She observed Jeb and Vincent played very convincing roles of polar opposites, similar to the good-cop-bad-cop routine. Jeb was the leader, exuding an educated and professional calmness, and Vincent, a street-smart pit bull. Very simply, Jeb would do things the easy way, and Vincent would do things the hard way. Together, they were two of the scariest people she had ever seen. But Staci felt secure sitting between the two behemoths, safe knowing that Jeb and Vincent worked directly for Sensei Masakata.

Since moving from Miami to Cambridge, she had only seen her father two or three times a year during the holidays or occasionally during the summer break when he returned briefly to his home between long international business trips. She missed her papa, and as his only daughter, she yearned for the special relationship they had developed and shared together over the first eighteen years of her life.

However, the master had unexpectedly helped to fill this fatherly void in her heart. She had no intentions of bonding with this stranger on her flight out to the West Coast, yet their meeting the day before had suddenly produced a relationship that mirrored a father-daughter connection. She now felt a sense of belonging and wondered if what she considered family should now be extended beyond generational DNA or if her new emotional connection was merely a temporary soul tie. Perhaps, she thought, she was in a vulnerable place emotionally, being alone 3,000 miles from home. So many events had transpired the past 36 hours that she needed time to sort through everything.

Until then, she would hold fast to the blessing Sensei Masakata spoke over her the day before. She reiterated his blessing in her heart, word for word, holding fast to their meaning. She found courage to continue forward with her role in Nicky's vision, even though she failed to kill Chase.

Finally taking a moment to assess herself, Staci looked over her outward features starting with her legs, torso, arms, and then her face in the rearview mirror. She thought she looked like she had a starring role in *Dawn of the Dead*. There was little color in her face except for the smeared mud and her hair was matted and soaked with water and muck.

She was a far cry from her drop-dead gorgeous self from a mere hour ago. Already, her face was swelling up in numerous places. Her left eye was beginning to close shut and the ruptured blood vessels beneath her skin were producing bruises in ghastly dark purple hues. Her top lip was swollen but not bleeding. Her feet ached as she had to make her escape barefoot while running through shrubs and across gravel in Chase's front yard on her way to her Ducati.

She then went through an inventory of her inner body starting at her head and working her way down to her feet. There were no internal injuries that she could notice. There were no broken bones either. She thought she might have a mild concussion. Her abs throbbed from the kick Chase delivered that knocked her halfway downstairs.

"Is there anything we can do for you right now?" Jeb asked with genuine concern.

Taking a moment to gather her thoughts, she asked, "Do either of you guys have a cigarette? I could sure use a smoke right about now."

"We don't smoke," Jeb replied. "It's a bad habit. You have to take care of your body. It's a temple that you live in, and ultimately, it's not your own."

Her mouth fidgeting, Staci stretched and looked in the rearview mirror again. With clarity setting in as she began to warm up, she thought she looked twice as bad as she did a few moments ago.

"Well, I am hungry. In fact, I'm starved. I hardly ate since breakfast this morning. Let's find a drive-through on the way back to the hotel."

"I think we should get you back to the hotel and have someone look at you. I've already called Dr. Paschke to meet us there. She'll give you the medical attention that you need."

"Dr. Paschke? Who's Dr. Paschke?"

"We took the precaution to have one of our doctors give you an examination just in case ..." Jeb looked Staci over from head to toe and smirked again.

Still gathering herself together, she thought of her fight with Chase. He had beaten her up far worse than she realized. "Yeah, but you should have seen the other guy," she quipped with a smile.

Jeb and Vince both let out a deep laugh. "Good comeback. Classic," Vince said with another laugh.

Jeb drove back to El Toro Road to reach the freeway in an arching way to avoid the action taking place a few short miles from them. Once he was satisfied they were far enough from the activity, Jeb said, "There's an In-N-Out Burger up here. If the line's not too long, we'll go through the drive-through."

Entering Laguna Hills Mall from the south, Jeb could see that there were only five cars in the drive-through. "Slow night, Vincent. Only five cars. Are you getting anything?"

"Sure. I haven't eaten here in a while. I'll have the double-double cheeseburger, fries, and a Coke. Hold the sauce."

Pulling up to the microphone, Jeb ordered. "Three double-double cheeseburgers, three fries, and three Cokes. Hold the sauce on one of the burgers."

With his window down, Jeb could now hear the muffled sound of a helicopter in the distance. Turning up his scanner, the three listened to the sheriffs coordinating the search and meticulously laying out the dragnet.

"These guys really want you bad," Jeb said with a smile. He looked at Staci and noticed how small she really was, at least compared to

Vincent and himself. "How can one little girl cause so much trouble? Wait. Never mind. *Women.* You sure do know how to mix things up," he said with another deep laugh—and an underlying sense of humor few people could get away with.

"Please turn it off," Staci said as she looked with fascination through the large window on the drive-through wall that displayed a dozen employees working together in an assembly line putting the meals together.

"I've never seen anything like this before. Nobody else has this large of a window at the drive-through where you can see everything that's going on inside. This place is so cool. Hey, what's that girl doing to the fries?"

"They actually cook the fries in cholesterol-free oil, and then they pat the fries down with a towel to absorb the excess oil," Jeb responded.

"That sounds like something they'd do at a fast-food restaurant in California," Staci said, still amazed at the assembly line features and efficiency the employees displayed.

Pulling up to the window, Jeb handed a twenty-dollar bill to a short, peppy blonde with a ponytail. "Thanks," she said as she handed Jeb the change. Staci noticed how much this young girl looked like her when she was a senior in high school.

"Is this a fun place to work at?" Staci asked her in a bubbly manner, smiling brightly and sticking her head out to see around Jeb.

The girl hesitated when she got a good look at Staci. "Um, yeah, it's … it's a lot of fun. I'm saving money for when I start college next year." She forced out a smile back at Staci.

"That's great," Staci said in an encouraging tone. "I'm in college, too. I'm a graduate student at MIT, and I'm finishing up my degree in applied statistics. I'm sure you'll do great. What's your major going to be?"

The girl had a startled look on her face and quickly closed the drive-through window.

Staci sat back in her seat. "Wow. What's the matter with her?"

Jeb and Vincent laughed. Vincent slanted the rearview mirror so Staci could take another look at herself.

"Oh yeah, I look a mess. No wonder she looked at me like I'm from another planet. I guess I don't look much like a graduate student at MIT, do I?"

Jeb flashed his smirk. "No, you don't. Are you sure you can eat a double-double, Miss Bevere? Your lip is very swollen. You look like you're in a lot of pain, too."

"No problem, Jeb. I'm so hungry I could eat if half my teeth were missing." Staci still stared in the drive-through window, fascinated with the white restaurant with red trim and red-neon tubing. "This looks like a fun place to eat inside. I see the T-shirts on the wall. It looks like there's a lot of the Southern California culture embedded in them. It's like going back in time to *Happy Days* on Nick at Nite."

Looking at Staci in her dirty tank top, Jeb said, "I'd better buy you one. It's warmer than what you're wearing, and a lot better looking, too."

The young girl came back to the window and handed Jeb the food in three white rectangular open cardboard boxes. In turn, he handed two boxes of food to Staci and asked for a T-shirt. She reached under the counter for a plastic-wrapped T-shirt, and he paid for it.

"Thank you, sir. Have a great night, everyone." She looked once more at Staci and quickly closed the drive-through window.

Chapter 48
Bennie and Carol

AFTER PRESSING THE END BUTTON on his phone to terminate his call to the 911 dispatcher, Chase dialed Bennie Knowles. Chase knew Bennie would be awake and hoped he was still in the area. He needed immediate help. Bennie and Chase had always been there for each other over the past fifteen years.

Bennie's cell phone rang, and he saw Chase's number on the screen. He answered on the first ring. "Chase, what's up, buddy? Is your date over so soon with that new hot chick? Cathy is it?" Bennie asked.

"Listen, Bennie, I need your help."

"I knew she was out of your league, Chase. What'd I tell you? I told you so, but you wouldn't listen to me."

"Bennie," Chase sighed, pacing back and forth in front of his desk. "You're not going to believe this, but that girl tried to kill me tonight with one of my own kitchen knives."

"Chase, you can't get out of this one that easily. Come on. You can tell me the truth. Five minutes—max—is all you could handle from her, and then it was over. And out the door she went."

"Bennie, listen to me. She did try to kill me. She was after something that I took while I was in Boston earlier this week."

"You're shitting me, right, Chase?"

"No, Bennie, I'm not. You should see my house," Chase said, walking back into his living room, careful again to avoid stepping on any broken glass. "It looks like a tornado swept through here. She tried to stab me in the heart with an eight-inch chef's knife. We fought our way through the bedroom, head-over-heels down the stairs, and into the living room and dining room."

"Wow!" Bennie exclaimed in shocked disbelief. "Are you alright? Where is she now?"

"I'm okay. She jumped out the dining-room window after I grabbed a gun I had hidden behind the drywall in the living-room wall. I fired off a few shots, but she managed to get away."

"Whoa! Whoa! *Whoa!* You *shot* at her, and she jumped out your window? Chase, what's going on over there?" Bennie was now standing up and grabbing his car keys off the coffee table. "Carol and I are coming over right now."

"Carol? Who's Carol? Never mind. Thanks, Bennie. I really appreciate this. I have to get ready for the police now. I dialed 911 to have them chase down Cathy, and they're sending the police over here as well."

"I'll see you in about twenty minutes, Chase." Bennie ended the call, took his latest girlfriend by the right hand, and pulled her up from the sofa as the cozy blanket they shared dropped to the floor.

"Ohhhh, we were just getting comfortable, schnookums. And *Déjà Vu* was just getting to the good part," the busty brunette said as she stepped into Bennie and ran her fingers through his curly hair.

Bennie grabbed the remote and pointed it at the TV. "I'll hit the pause button. I'm sure Denzel will figure out a way to save the day. Grab your coat, baby, and let's go."

Bennie picked up his jacket lying over the back of one of the dining-room chairs and put it on. Checking to see he still had his wallet in the inner pocket, he grabbed Carol's hand again and they shuffled out the front door, hugging and giggling like two junior high kids out on a first date.

Chapter 49
Crime Scene

CHASE HAD BEEN IN MANY dangerous situations before, but he was always in control to some extent. But not this time. He had been confronted by someone determined to kill him in a premeditated attack, and he had little defense for her attacks. Chase almost lost his life. If he didn't have a gun at his disposal, he knew he would have been killed in his own home.

Chase realized that he was now involved with something far deeper than anything he could have imagined. Whatever was at the root of this was so big, so important, that somebody wanted him dead. Clearly someone from Cambridge came all the way out to Laguna Beach to steal the two suitcases and kill him. All he could think of was that, by the grace of God above, he was still alive. When he first moved into his house a few years ago, he felt a strong urge to conceal a loaded semi-automatic gun behind the drywall. At the time, he didn't have any enemies or any reason to hide a loaded weapon in such a manner. But he was thankful that he listened to that small voice in his head and followed through with it.

Walking upstairs, Chase stopped halfway and looked over the damage to his living and dining rooms. The elevated viewpoint gave him a clearer perspective of what had just taken place a few minutes ago. He looked at the five bullet holes in the wall and the broken window the assassin jumped out and shook his head. The scene below spoke loudly of a lot of violence. It was a gosh-awful mess. He was furious that someone had entered his house, stolen something of his, and tried to murder him in his own bed. He had never hit a woman before, but he wanted a second chance at the psycho who did this to him. He also needed time to sort through his thoughts and decide if this was worth pursuing, or if he should simply count his blessings, walk away, and leave things alone.

Now that he had a second lease on life, Chase was determined to turn things around. He immediately thought of Susan Anderson and how he had really messed things up with her. Straightening things out with Susan had to be his highest priority.

Entering his bedroom and turning on his light, Chase grew even more furious looking over the battle scene here at ground zero. He considered his room his inner sanctuary, a place that was sacred, a place of intimacy where he allowed himself to be exposed. He had opened up his heart to someone who he felt deep down inside that he could build something special and unique with. But what he received in return was betrayal and a violent attempt on his life.

Chase looked down at her clothes lying on the floor in a heap. Right by his feet were her leather jacket, top, pants, shoes, and her undergarments. He wanted to give them a good kick, as if she were somehow still in the center of them. But this was now a crime scene, and he needed to leave her clothing items for the police. Hopefully, they'd yield clues to help identify and find her. He knew that she was not from the Santa Barbara area, that Cathy Bennett was not her name, and that she was certainly not here in south Orange County to *get away from it all* for a few days. She was sent by somebody in Cambridge who wanted the suitcases just as badly as he did, and this person wanted to leave no connection to him. He immediately thought of Nicky Fischer, Jr., and understood that there had to be a connection with him.

Walking over to his broken saltwater fish tank, Chase saw a few fish were still alive on his carpet. He filled his bathroom sink with lukewarm water, walked back into his bedroom, picked the fish up off the floor, and put them in the water. Reaching under the sink, he pulled out a box of Epsom salt. Pouring a little at a time into the sink, he taste-tested the water until he thought there was an adequate mixture of water and salt to keep the fish alive.

Then he pulled the towel off his stomach and looked at the cut across his abdomen in the mirror. He considered himself a blessed man indeed that he was still alive. Kneeling down on one knee, Chase pulled out a bottle of hydrogen peroxide and a roll of gauze. Standing up and closing his eyes tightly, he unscrewed the cap, leaned back, pushed his stomach out, and poured the hydrogen peroxide directly onto the open wound. Taking a few seconds to recover from the burning sensation, he gingerly wrapped the gauze around his torso, favoring his left shoulder. The bleeding wasn't pronounced, but it was still dripping from his wound. Chase wrapped himself a few more times with the roll.

His shoulder wound was not as bad as he feared. The puncture was small but deep. Although there was only a small trickle of blood oozing out of the wound, his shoulder hurt like hell and was beginning to throb. He reached up into his medicine cabinet with his right hand and pulled out a pair of hair trimming scissors and cut a strip of cloth off a towel hanging on a hook on the inside of the door. Wrapping his shoulder tightly, Chase winced as he pulled the strip even tighter and folded the ends underneath.

Entering his bedroom, he pulled out a clean pair of boxer shorts from his dresser and replaced the old pair that was wet with sweat and blood from his fight and his stomach wound. After that, he walked to his closet, pulled down a pair of gray sweatpants with the UCI letters and a green anteater on the side of the right leg and put them on. He then stepped into a pair of tan moccasin-style slippers that his mother had given him on his birthday a few years ago. This was the last gift that he received from her before she died, and he only wore these on special occasions or when he was feeling insecure. And this was certainly one of those nights.

Walking back to his dresser, he pulled out a light green T-shirt and put it on. Looking into the mirror on top of the dresser, first from the front, then from both sides, Chase sighed as he examined his beaten and swelling face.

While contemplating his next move, he saw red and blue lights through his bedroom window as two police cars drove up his street and pulled into his driveway. Chase hoped that they would come discreetly, but he was sure that all of his neighbors were awake now and looking out their windows at his place. At least his house sat back off the street a bit and there were a lot of trees that gave the house some privacy from the nosy onlookers.

Walking back downstairs and across the living room, he opened the front door before the police could knock. "Hey, guys, thanks for getting here so fast. Do you think you could turn off your lights? There's no reason to make all this commotion for my neighbors to see."

"Turn the lights off," the first officer shouted to the rest as he reached the front door.

"Come in," Chase said to the lead officer.

Chase left the door open, turned around, and stepped into his living room. The first officer followed him into the house followed by his partner. "I'm Officer Chappell, and this is Officer Edwards. Officers Martinez and Holston are right behind us. You're Chase Manhattan?" Chappell asked as he looked around the living room and dining room.

"Yes, I am," Chase replied, running his right hand through his hair.

"What exactly happened here, Mr. Manhattan? We were sent out on a domestic violence call, but something obviously happened here tonight that is more than just a lover's quarrel."

The other two officers walked through the open front door. One of them whistled as he surveyed the damage. The last officer looked at the place, then at Chase, and said, "At first glance, I would have said you were responsible for all of this. But looking at your face, I bet it was the girl."

The other three policemen looked directly at Chase and laughed in unison. "Alright, alright," Chappell said as he tried to don a straight face. Chappell looked like a tough guy. He was in his mid-thirties with short-cropped black hair, a barrel chest, and a couple of big guns for arms. He looked like he purposely requested a uniform that was one or two sizes too small just so he could show the world his powerful physique. His thighs were so big they rubbed together as he walked. Chappell took out a notepad and a pen from his front pocket. "From the top, Mr. Manhattan, give us a brief summary of what happened here tonight, then we can fill in the details as we go along, OK?"

"Sure," Chase said. He hesitated a few moments as he mentally recounted the events that led up to the evening, and then began, "I met this girl today. It was this morning at Main Beach. I was jogging when I came upon a group of Asian tourists performing tai chi on the sand. The group had been there for more than a week at about the same time each morning. As I was jogging, I stopped for a while and joined them as I had previously done a few times during the week. Only today, this girl was there. Her name is Cathy Bennett."

Officer Chappell was looking at his notepad while jotting down his notes but looked up when Chase said her name. "Cathy Bennett?"

"That's right. At least, that's what she told me. She was absolutely one of the most beautiful women I have ever seen, so, of course, I stopped to join in."

"What did she look like?"

"Well," Chase said, again running his fingers through his hair, "she's in her early twenties, shoulder-length jet-black hair and about five-four. I'm not good at guessing weight, but she was certainly in great shape. She had a good tan. I'm sure her hair was dyed. It was cut in a short, fashionable hairstyle."

"What color eyes did she have?"

"Blueish-hazel. They were some of the brightest eyes I have ever seen."

"And you struck up a conversation with her?"

"She looked at me and winked while bending over and showing me her cleavage. Normally I wouldn't stare, but she was so beautiful, and she had the greatest smile I have ever seen. So yes, I smiled back and stopped to join in. After a few minutes, we walked away from the group and started talking. She told me she was from Santa Barbara and she was down here for the weekend to get away for a couple of days."

The other three police officers were walking around the living room and the dining room checking the damage. "Did she say where she was staying?"

"Vacation Village on Coast Highway. We stopped for breakfast at C'est La Vie and talked for a while."

"Did you notice anything peculiar about her?"

"She had a healthy appetite for breakfast. She could put away a lot of food for a person her size. At dinner, though, she only picked through her food."

"Probably so she wouldn't have a full stomach. It sounds like a premeditated murder attempt. Alright, then what happened?"

"We exchanged cell phone numbers and I asked her if she would like to go out to eat tonight and hang out. She said yes. She was parked a few blocks from my car, and we went our own separate ways. That was about seven this morning."

"Okay," said Officer Chappell, looking up from his notepad. "Let's get to tonight."

Chase shuffled his feet, and then started toward the stairs. "We went out tonight to a couple of places, then came back here and immediately went upstairs."

A set of headlights came up the driveway and parked. Two car doors opened and closed. All four officers turned to look at the front door that was still open.

"That must be my friend, Bennie Knowles. I called him right before you arrived and asked him to come over."

Bennie and Carol ran into the front door, still holding hands. "Chase, are you alright? What the hell happened here?" Bennie asked, stepping carefully into the living room and looking around.

"Hey, buddy, why don't you and your lady friend just stand over there and don't touch anything," bellowed Chappell, pointing to the only corner of the living room where there was no damage. Looking back over to Chase, he continued, "Let's you, me, and Edwards go upstairs. Martinez, Holston, keep looking around the place down here and take good notes." Looking over to Bennie and Carol, he reiterated with a snarl, "And you two stand right where you are. I don't want you touching anything."

Chase led Chappell and Edwards upstairs to the master bedroom. Officer Chappell said, "This room looks just as bad as the downstairs. Is this where the attack originally took place?"

"That's right. We had sex, and she went downstairs for a cigarette while I stayed up here in bed. She came back about twenty minutes later with a knife from my kitchen. She held it behind her back as she approached me, then lunged at me just as she got to the foot of the bed. That's when it all began. The fight moved out of the bedroom and down the stairs, and continued into the living room and the dining room. That's when I took a few shots at her with my 9mm, and she jumped out of my window and got away."

"Are those her clothes?" Chappell asked, walking over to the pile of discarded items and bending down to get a closer look.

"Yes. I haven't touched them. Hopefully you guys can extract some clues as to exactly who this person is."

Chappell stood up and continued writing in his notepad. Looking at Chase, he said, "Show me the knife and the gun, Mr. Manhattan."

"The knife is in the dining room and the gun is in my study."

Walking back downstairs, Martinez squatted and looked at the knife lying on the dining room floor next to the table. "That's the knife she used on me," Chase said, pointing to the eight-inch chef's knife next to Officer Martinez. "She got it from the kitchen. She was using it in my bedroom, living room, and dining room before I finally knocked it out of her hand. The fight continued back into the living room, where I was able to grab a 9mm I keep hidden in the wall. She tried to run back for the knife and that's when I fired off five rounds. She saw what I was doing, grabbed a pillow from the couch that was lying on the floor, used it to cover her head, and jumped out the window." Chase walked over to the wall where there were five bullet holes in the drywall.

Officer Holston scratched his head and spoke up. "A girl did all of this to your place? And to you? You had to use a gun on her, and she still escaped?" Looking at Martinez, then back at Chase, Chappell shook his head and said, "I just can't picture this. I mean, a girl kicks your ass and destroys your place, and you can't even hit her with a semi-automatic?" Martinez and Holston both started laughing, and Edwards even smiled.

"Knock if off, guys," Bennie yelled at them. "Can't you see he was almost killed here tonight? How about doing your job and finding this psychopath."

"Why don't *you* shut up before I throw you out of here?" yelled Chappell as he glared back at Bennie, his arms stiff, muscles rippling, and veins pulsing out of his neck.

"Let's go to the study," Chase said to Officer Chappell. Chappell and Edwards followed him to the study where he walked to his desk, picked up the Glock, and gave it to Chappell. "I'm registered to own this gun," he added.

Walking over to his closet, he showed the officers his floor safe. "I had these shoe boxes covering the floor safe, but when I checked on the contents before you arrived, I saw they were strewn across the closet floor. Cathy had been able to open the safe and stole something that I need to get back."

"What was taken, Mr. Manhattan?"

"A couple of suitcases that are used for scientific research. It's a smaller piece of a larger technical physics project I'm working on." Chase was technically lying, but he knew that he could not explain the real intrinsic value of the suitcases to the police.

More flashing red lights appeared up the driveway. "That's the ambulance, Mr. Manhattan," Chappell said, clicking his pen closed, folding up his notepad, and putting them both back into his shirt pocket. "Why don't you come back out into the living room so the paramedics can take a look at you? How do you feel right now?"

Chase lifted up his shirt with his right hand and showed Chappell and Edwards the red-stained gauze wrapped around his stomach. "She cut me pretty good on my stomach, but it's only a flesh wound. She didn't penetrate into the muscle or anything." Peeling back his left sleeve, Chase revealed the strip of cloth wrapped around his shoulder. I also have a puncture wound on my shoulder, but it's not that bad either." Chappell noticed that Chase grimaced when he said that.

Both officers' eyes opened as wide as they could. "I'm sorry, Mr. Manhattan. I didn't realize the extent of your injuries. Please, go sit down in the living room."

As the paramedics attended to Chase, Chappell called for a crime scene unit while the other three officers took notes as they continued to look at the damage in the living room and dining room. Bennie and Carol stood near where the five bullet holes punctured the wall. "Can you two please wait outside while we conduct the investigation?" Officer Holston asked, looking at the bullet holes rather than Bennie.

"Don't go too far, Bennie. The paramedics want me to go to Laguna Beach Memorial to get stitches for my stomach and shoulder. I want you to meet me there," Chase said before the two walked outside.

"Sure, Chase. We'll be right outside. Let's go, sweetie," Bennie said to Carol as he reached out and held her hand, leading her outside to the front of the house.

"Mr. Manhattan," Chappell said, "I'm going to have a team come over and dust for prints. She had to have left her prints somewhere. We'll see what else the team can find."

"My housecleaner, Maria, cleaned the place two days ago and no one else has been here. You should be able to get a good set of her prints somewhere. She got into my safe so be sure to have them check the study, too."

"Right now, the paramedics will take you to the hospital and get you stitched up." Chappell reached into his wallet and pulled out one of his cards. "In the meantime, here's my card. Feel free to call me anytime." Chase thanked Chappell and placed the card into the pocket of his sweatpants.

Chapter 50
The Good Doctor

ENTERING THE 405 FREEWAY from El Toro Road, Staci unwrapped her double-double cheeseburger from In-N-Out Burger and pulled off the top bun. She removed the layer of lettuce and tomatoes and dropped them into the cardboard box next to the french fries. The onions came off next.

"That's the only nutritious part of the entire meal, Miss Bevere, and you're throwing them away," Jeb said, looking down at the discarded vegetables.

"Vegetables are not for me. I'm just a burger and fries girl."

"Suit yourself. But you really should incorporate some fresh vegetables into your diet."

"I'll do it tomorrow," Staci promised through a grinning mouthful of In-N-Out Burger's finest cuisine.

Driving north on the 405, Jeb picked up his cell phone and dialed the good doctor. "Hello, Dr. Paschke. We're on the 405 and will be exiting to the hotel in a few minutes."

"Very good," she replied. "I'm in her room right now. Is there anything you need from me at the moment?"

"Yes. Miss Bevere will need a pair of sweatpants and a sweater from her room."

"I'll gather those items for her right now," she said with a pleasant smile that translated through Jeb's cell phone and caused him to smile. "Is there anything else she requires?"

Jeb looked at Staci, already halfway through her double-double cheeseburger and fries. "Do you need anything else other than a pair of sweatpants and a sweater?"

Swallowing her mouthful of food in one big gulp and wiping ketchup off her bottom lip, she replied, "A bottle of Cabernet Sauvignon, please. And something chocolate."

"One bottle of Cabernet Sauvignon. And something chocolate."

"I'll see to it," the good doctor replied.

"Thanks again, Doctor. We'll see you shortly." Jeb ended the call and stared out the driver's window. Driving past the Laguna Canyon Road exit on their way to Costa Mesa, Jeb could see the searchlight of a police chopper piercing the dark sky in search of a young girl in a pair of men's boxer shorts on a red Ducati motorcycle who they would never find.

"Looks like they're still looking for you," Jeb said with a grin.

"What a night," was all Staci could muster, tussling her hair and rubbing her head as she inhaled the remainder of her burger.

"We'll be there by the time you finish your fries."

"Irvine is a very pretty city to drive through at night. I like the Ferris wheel and the outdoor mall we just passed."

"That's Irvine Spectrum. You'd love it there. Unfortunately, you'll not be able to visit because you'll be on a plane back to Boston in a few days. You'll need to stay inside your hotel room until you leave."

Staci continued to look out at the surrounding environs as they approached Orange County Airport. "The office buildings are new and big, but not so big that they block out the sky, unlike Boston and New York."

"No building in Orange County is more than twenty-one stories. I like it that way. A modern metropolis with a booming economy, but not so built-up that the community's personality is swallowed up and lost."

Exiting the freeway at Avenue of the Arts in the South Coast Metro area, Jeb smiled at his beautiful but beat-up passenger. "It certainly has been a pleasure meeting you, Miss Bevere."

"Same here," Vincent said in a sincere manner. "Have a safe flight back."

"Thanks, guys. I really appreciate everything. I would have probably been on my way to jail right now if it hadn't been for you two."

Pulling up to the Westin Hotel, but careful to stay away from the activity at the front entrance, Jeb pulled the truck to a stop. Dr. Paschke was already standing curbside. She stepped up to the passenger window and handed a small gym bag to Vincent. "Here are the clothes you requested. I'll wait for you at the front door," she said to her patient in a kind and soothing, motherly tone. Then she walked away toward the front entrance of the hotel.

Staci quickly put on the sweats. New pain in her shoulders, legs, and lower back—pain that was not there an hour ago—now caused her to grimace as she slid the sweats on over the mud-stained boxer shorts and the sweater over her new In-N-Out T-shirt. Numerous other pains stabbed at her as she donned her clothes.

Vincent opened his door and stepped out of the truck, allowing Staci to step out onto the sidewalk. Turning around, she pulled out her knapsack with the two suitcases and then behind the front seat, then reached for the empty cardboard box of discarded vegetables and used napkins. "Let me throw that away."

"That won't be necessary. I'll take care of it. Have a nice night, Miss Bevere."

Staci took her backpack containing the two suitcases, waved to Jeb and Vincent, and walked with a noticeable limp to Dr. Paschke, who was standing at the front of the lobby door.

"Hello, Staci. Welcome back. You don't look so well," she said, placing her right arm gently around her shoulder and escorting her into the lobby and onto the elevator.

"Thank you for being here for me. I don't feel so well."

"Not to worry. We will have you patched up and ready to go in no time," Paschke assured her with a soft smile.

"I would really enjoy sitting in a Jacuzzi about now," Staci said.

"My dear, my recommendation for you right now is ice packs. Lots and lots of ice packs. And don't worry, I'll be staying with you until your flight leaves. You'll need at least a few days of rest," she said in a comforting manner.

The elevator doors opened on the sixteenth floor, and the two walked slowly down the hall to the fifth door on the right. Placing the key card in the lock, Paschke opened the door for Staci, who walked straight to the sofa and sank deep into its cushions, keeping her knapsack at her feet.

Paschke pulled up a dining-table chair in front of Staci and sat down. She was thirty-six but looked at least five years younger. She was impeccably dressed in a blue and white St. John wool V-neck blazer with a low-cut top on underneath it and blue pants. In fact, she looked like she either just came straight from a boardroom meeting or she was a high-priced call girl. Staci thought she could have been a model at one time.

"I hurt all over," Staci said, still slouched on the sofa and looking up at the doctor. Staci looked tired and very pale.

Reaching down into her black Levenger tote bag, Paschke pulled out a notepad and pen. Leaning forward but keeping her knees together, her feet angled to the left and her ankles crossed, she said, "First, give me a rundown of the fight and all contact that was made, both to you and to him. That includes not only bodily contact such as punches and kicks, but landing on the floor or bouncing off walls as well."

Staci gave Paschke a brief account of the events that happened only a short hour ago.

"Tell me," Paschke asked, "do you think you have any internal injuries?"

"No, I really don't. I'm an expert at protecting my internal organs. I would lose a limb before I would allow someone to damage me internally."

"How about any broken bones?"

"No, no broken bones," Stacie replied, grimacing in pain as she moved her arms and legs in circular motions and bending her joints and her neck.

The doctor stood up, set the pad and pen down on the coffee table, and gently cupped Stacie's head, leaning it gently to the left and to the right. She pulled out a few small pieces of broken glass and fragments of drywall from Staci's matted hair. "You have a number of bruises on your face and your head. Do you think you have a concussion?"

"I don't think so. I think I'll just wake up with a lot of deep bruises and some serious aches and pains. It'll probably be very difficult just to get out of bed in the morning."

There was a knock at the door. "Room service," said the heavily accented voice behind the door.

"I'll get it. It's the wine and chocolate I ordered."

Opening the door, she saw a young Latino man with a name tag of Ricardo standing with a cart draped in a white embroidered cloth. A bottle of Cabernet Sauvignon was on the left of the silver tray and two, one-pound bags of M&Ms, plain and peanut, were on the right.

Ricardo was quick to speak. "The kitchen and the gift shop are closed, so this is the only chocolate I could find. I had to drive to the 7-11 around the corner for them."

"Thank you," Paschke said as she handed Ricardo a twenty-dollar bill for a tip. "I'll take the cart." She maneuvered it in the door and wheeled it into the living room while closing the door behind her.

"It doesn't get any better than this, Staci. You've earned it."

Staci looked up and a smile came over her dreary and pale face as she saw Dr. Paschke pushing the cart toward her. "Can you please open the wine for me? I can hardly open my fingers up," she muttered through her swollen lip as she lifted her hands and looked at her knotted fingers.

"I'll even pour it for you. Once you have a few glasses in you, I will need to lay ice packs pretty much all over your body. I may also have you take an ice bath depending on the extent of the swelling. So drink up. Enjoy. You'll need the entire bottle."

Chapter 51
South Coast Medical Center

Laguna Beach Memorial Hospital was only a ten-minute drive from Chase's house. The night brought in an odd mixture of patients involved in car accidents, domestic assaults, bar fights, freak accidents, and now a black belt martial arts expert who just got his ass kicked by a girl.

Chase stood in front of a table in one of the many rooms in the emergency department. He watched as two teenage girls barely old enough to drive were wheeled past his room with a team of nurses and paramedics frantically attending to them. He overheard the conversations between the nurses hurrying back and forth that the girls were in a car accident on Coast Highway. A drunk driver crossed lanes and hit their car head-on twenty minutes ago. He died at the scene, and these two were desperately clinging to their lives. Chase suddenly stopped thinking about his injuries and said a silent prayer for the badly injured young girls.

He watched as a nurse led a man with blood running down the side of his head into another room. Most of the left side and the front of his shirt were soaked with blood. Chase guessed he was involved in a barroom brawl in downtown Laguna Beach. Quite a few bikers hang out at some of the bars there. This guy probably said one too many things to the wrong guy.

His eyes wandered to a young couple with a crying child about a year and a half old receiving a nebulizer treatment. *Probably childhood asthma*, he thought. His neighbors across the street went through the same thing a couple of months ago with their tot.

The nurse was rolling the final layers of gauze around the waterproof medical patch across his abdomen that protected his stitches. The doctor also gave him a few stitches in his shoulder and placed his left arm in a sling to limit his arm and shoulder movement.

Once the nurse finished with the gauze, she helped Chase put his shirt back on. "There you go. Good as new. How do you feel, Mr. Manhattan?" she asked.

Chase pulled the ball of cotton out of his mouth where the doctor had stitched up his gum where his tooth was knocked out. "Better now. The pain killers are starting to work, but I still hurt all over."

"Chase," Bennie said, "I think you did the right thing by letting me call Susan. She's someone that you don't want to ruin a good thing with. She sounded genuinely concerned."

"I appreciate you stepping in for me, Bennie. You really came through—like you always do. I owe you, buddy."

"I hope you're not mad at me for explaining to Susan what happened tonight. She needs to know the details right from the start. No more fooling around with her, Chase. She's a nice girl, and you have to treat her accordingly."

Bennie's new girlfriend, Carol, was standing at his side and still holding his hand. She didn't speak, but her expression said a thousand words, and Chase could see that she was silently confirming what Bennie had just told him regarding his relationship with Susan.

Chapter 52
Held Over for Observation

CHASE WANTED TO CALL Officer Chappell for any new information from the investigation at his house. *Were they able to find Cathy Bennett? How difficult could that be?* he wondered. *I mean, how many girls drive a red Ducati motorcycle wearing only men's boxer shorts and a tank top late at night through the middle of Laguna Canyon?*

Lying in the hospital room, Chase pulled out Chappell's card and dialed the number on his cell phone. Chappell answered on the second ring. "Officer Chappell here."

"Hello, Officer Chappell, this is Chase Manhattan," he said with a wince of pain from his ribs and shoulder. The right side of his mouth was still numb from the Novocain the doctor had injected.

"Mr. Manhattan, how are you? Are you still at the hospital?" Chase thought he sounded genuinely concerned, not at all like the wise-cracking smart guy he was when he first responded to the 911 call.

"I'm feeling better. The good doctors here have patched me up, but they want me to stay here overnight for observation in case I have a concussion or any internal injuries they were not able to detect. And my lady friend is right here beside me as we speak." Chase said the words "lady friend" with warmth and thanksgiving that caused a radiant smile to appear on Susan's face.

"I know it's only been a few hours, but were you able to come up with anything? Was anyone able to catch her driving through the canyon?"

Officer Chappell sighed deeply. "No. I'm sorry, but they didn't. A sheriff spotted her at the toll road and a chase ensued. An APB was posted and a chopper was even sent out to the area. But she managed to elude them in Aliso Viejo. She just seemed to vanish right in thin air. From what I understand, it was a really wild chase. Everything happened so fast that the sheriff's department just didn't have enough time to properly respond."

Chase lowered his head as the immediate sense of failure to catch her and the tranquilizer both took effect. Susan rubbed Chase's right arm with both of her hands, gently stroking it up and down and massaging his palm and fingers. Then, snapping his head up, he asked, "What about fingerprints? Where you able to lift her prints from my place?"

"The crime scene unit was over about thirty minutes after you left. Your housecleaner, what was her name? She must have done a very thorough job. There were mainly two sets of prints in the house and they are yours and the housecleaner's. They did find a few miscellaneous prints and are following up on them. I'll let you know what they come up with."

"What about her clothes? There has to be something there for you to follow up on."

"They took her clothes away. If there is anything that will give us a positive ID on her, then they'll find it. These guys are really good, Mr. Manhattan. Trust me on that."

There was a hesitation, and then Chappell spoke again. "However, you did say that when she attacked you, she was wearing a set of thin leather gloves. That tells me she was careful not to leave any fingerprints. Before you two went upstairs, do you remember her touching anything in your house?"

Chase took a few moments to collect his thoughts. "Now that you mention it, she didn't touch anything. I opened the door for her, and we only spent a few minutes downstairs." Suddenly, Susan stopped caressing Chase's arm and sat back in her chair, her arms folded.

Chase was ashamed and embarrassed as he gave sordid details to Chappell in the presence of Susan. Slowly regaining his momentum, he continued. "We went upstairs and …" Chase sighed, "I guess the only thing she touched was me." He did not have the courage to look at Susan so Chase focused on the television mounted on the wall in front of him and stared straight ahead through unseeing eyes. The chill in the air was unbearable, and Chase looked down at the blanket that was covering his legs and midsection.

"And at this point, I assume that the nurses have cleaned you up from head to toe."

"Yes, that's correct." Chase felt even more hopeless now realizing how efficiently Cathy had covered her tracks. She was a professional killer who left no evidence of her presence—except her clothes and the destruction in his house. Chase still held out hope that the crime scene unit could turn up something.

Chappell sighed again. "Get some sleep, Mr. Manhattan. I'll call you as soon as I have anything important to tell you. Good night."

The tone in Chappell's voice spoke volumes to Chase. He knew that the trail would probably run cold and the assassin had made her escape. For all he knew, she was already out of California by now. Chase ended the call and placed his phone on the table to his right. He had to look up at Susan, who was only three feet away and staring directly into his eyes, arms still folded.

"Look, Susan," Chase started, "I know that I completely messed everything up with you. I can't even begin to tell you how sorry I am. But I am truly sorry."

"Get some sleep, Chase," Susan said, unfolding her arms and once again caressing his right arm. "I'm going to sleep here with you tonight. I'll ask the nurse to bring me in a blanket and pillow, and I'll sleep on this musty old chair."

"I should be sleeping on the chair, and you should be sleeping in the bed."

"Relax, Chase. We're not married. But you *are* in the doghouse. Make no mistake about that."

Susan stood up, gathered her composure, and started walking toward the door. "I'm going out to the nurse's station," she said. "I want to make sure that they give you the best of care tonight. I'll give you the best of care tomorrow." She smiled a small, brief smile at Chase, and then walked out the door.

Slumber was quickly overtaking him. His head nodded to the right in anticipation of Susan spending the night on that musty old chair. He thought of her being there at his side and once again and counted his blessings for the final time today. Moments later, he saw a blurry slice of light grow wide, then narrow and disappear. He knew that Susan had re-entered his room. Her presence gave him the peace and serenity to voluntarily turn off his own internal light. The blackness of night overtook him, and Chase slept better than he had in months.

Chapter 53
The Day After

THE DIGITAL CLOCK by the side of the bed read 12:09 p.m. Staci could hardly open her eyes, let alone roll over on her side. Yet somehow, she managed to muster the strength to reach over, pick up the clock, and bring it in for a closer look. 12:11 p.m. Breathing slowly and deeply, she felt her head, ribs, shoulders, and lower back throb with pain. She breathed out and rolled onto her back. Then she spread her arms out to both sides and slowly breathed in and out again.

Staci looked around at the unfamiliar surroundings of the bedroom, starting at the white knockdown ceiling and making her way to the white crown molding. Her eyes proceeded down the light gold walls and finally to the glossy white baseboards. It took a few moments to recalibrate her senses. Her thoughts immediately turned to Chase Manhattan. He proved to be a respectable adversary, far more worthy than what she had anticipated. She thought she would be able to simply walk in and walk out with what she wanted: the two suitcases and a dead Chase Manhattan. Perhaps, she pondered, she should have taken a gun into his house. After all, he used one on her.

The thought of respect and honor for her foe quickly disappeared like vapor in the wind as she thought back on the five rounds he fired at her. After all, *he* had been the one to challenge *her* to fight hand-to-hand. The bullets barely missed her. She could—perhaps should—be dead right now, an unidentified Jane Doe lying in a cold morgue 3,000 miles from home.

Struggling to sit up and rest on her elbows, she recounted in order each event of the previous evening starting at Vacation Village, the fight with Chase, the wild police chase, and salvation through Jeb, Vincent, and Dr. Paschke. Staci experienced similar events numerous times over the past few years, but never all in one night. Exhausted just thinking about the happenings of the previous night, she collapsed back down on the bed and took more slow, deep breaths. She needed a few more minutes to decompress before attempting to get up out of bed. And she needed this time to rest and recuperate before her flight back to Boston.

Chapter 54
A Break in the Case

AFTER A SIX-HOUR NAP, Chase sat up in his bed just before five in the afternoon feeling like a new man. He was refreshed with a sense of clarity and well-being about the events that took place over the past week. Despite that, the aches and pains that dominated his body felt worse than they did before Susan tucked him into his own bed earlier that morning.

He looked out of his bedroom door that led out to the hallway and to the staircase. He didn't know if Susan was still in the house, but he hoped she was. It was quiet downstairs, and in his heart, he pictured her taking a nap on the sofa or reading a book in his study.

Standing up a little too quickly, Chase grimaced as his two cracked ribs on his right side sent shearing pain radiating throughout his chest. Not letting that reminder of his fight the night before get the better of him, he stood up straight, flashed a smile of victory, and strolled into the master bathroom. Turning on the light, he stood at attention and looked in the mirror. Again, he counted his blessings as he felt a sense of a new lease on life. Although it was late afternoon and the sun was setting in another magnificent display over the Pacific, Chase felt the dawn of a new day, a new era that was special and unique, one designed specifically for him. Again, he thought of Susan and assured himself that she was close, even if she was not currently in his house.

In his Jacuzzi, he ran water as cold as he could tolerate, filling it halfway. Then he emptied the two large bags of ice Susan had placed in a large cooler that she brought up from the garage. Stepping in first with his left foot and acclimating himself to the cold temperature, he then stepped in with his right foot. Taking a deep breath, he sat on the tub's edge and quickly took the plunge. Lifting his head out of the bitterly cold water, he thought, *What a waste of a Jacuzzi tub*. He wanted nothing more than to soak his entire body in *hot* water right now, but the doctors strongly recommended ice baths for at least the next few days to treat his pronounced black, red, blue, and purple bruises. Shivering, he wondered if it would be cheating if he wore his wet suit.

After five minutes of pure misery, Chase stepped out of the tub and grasped his largest, thickest, warmest bath towel and hurried over to his bureau and closet, quickly dressing in a pair of khaki cargo pants and a blue hooded sweater with the UC-Irvine twill lettering across the chest. Lastly, he put on the thickest pair of socks he could find.

Chase was hungry now. He hadn't eaten since the previous night, and he was ready to devour something really big. He walked out into the hallway and made more noise than he normally would. He hoped Susan was in the house and that she would hear him rustling about upstairs.

As he walked downstairs, he noticed that a few of his family pictures had survived the war and Susan must have hung them back up on the wall. As he approached the bottom of the stairs, he looked over the living room and dining room. All the broken glass was cleaned up. The furniture that was not broken was back in its original place. The dirt from overturned plants had been vacuumed up and the broken furniture was gone.

The kitchen light was on. Chase walked over and peered in. No Susan. Walking back across his living room to his study, he saw that light was on and he allowed his hopes to get up. He stopped at the threshold and stuck his head in with a grin. No Susan there either.

Chase saw that Susan had clearly been in his study and had a few projects underway. Her laptop sat on his desk and was still on. He sat at his chair and hit the enter key to get rid of the screen saver. Susan had been looking through Yahoo! Yellow Pages at local art stores that sold picture frames. She was obviously a family-oriented person and Chase was impressed that she would take the time and effort to fix his family photos and place them back on the wall.

There was also a yellow Post-it note stuck to his monitor: *Bennie called at 4:15 p.m. and would like you to return his call.* Now she was answering his phone rather than letting the answering machine take the calls. Chase liked this, too. He liked it a lot. Susan had courage and a bit of aggressive audacity, and this made a deep impression on him. Pulling off the Post-it note and leaning back in his chair, he noticed that although she didn't sign her name, she took her time to use her best penmanship when writing the message for him. He stared at the note and took in one more trait of the person now the central figure of his life.

But Chase waited to savor the best for last, the subtle and soft scent of Susan's perfume that filled the air. He thought that she must have dabbed a drop here and a drop there in his office. Her scent was faint yet distinct, just enough for Chase to feel she was still there with him.

Even though Susan had not communicated this to him, Chase figured she stepped out to run a few errands and would be back soon. He decided to get started on a few projects of his own. The first thing he wanted to do was call Chappell to get any updates from the last time they spoke at 3:15 a.m. that morning while he was at South Coast Medical Center. Chase leaned forward, pasted the Post-it note on his desk, and keyed Chappell's number into his favorites so that he didn't have to worry about carrying his card around.

"Officer Chappell here," came the voice on the other end after only one ring.

"Hello, Officer Chappell. It's Chase Manhattan again. I'm hoping that your guys came up with something—anything—on this girl."

Chappell sighed long and deep. "Listen to me, Mr. Manhattan. I'll be honest with you. I don't think we're going to get any of her prints. I'm working closely with the Sheriff's Department in Aliso Viejo. They also want this girl real bad, too. Understand that, OK? There were seven sheriff cars and one chopper that were ultimately committed to the chase when she seemed to just vanish like a puff of smoke in the wind."

"I can't believe this," Chase said with a trace of anger. "How can one girl elude so many people?"

"This girl is good. She's obviously a professional. We ran the prints we found at your place in every law enforcement database available. Most have come back and we have zilch. Nothing. Nada. We have your prints. We were able to locate your housecleaner and verify her prints. The few miscellaneous prints in the kitchen have turned up nothing, so at this time, we assume they are prints from friends you have had over. Regardless, our people weren't able to turn up anything of a suspicious nature from them."

"You've seen my house. You've seen what she did to me. There were sheriffs and a chopper involved in the chase. And you're telling me that you've got zilch?" Chase was beside himself and once again pacing back and forth in front of his desk.

"Listen to me, Mr. Manhattan. Believe it or not, these things do happen. People commit violent crimes every day here in Orange County and get away with it." Chappell didn't sound so chummy anymore, and Chase didn't appreciate it. "We'll obviously do what we can, but if we are not able to turn up any leads, then there's not much that we can do, understand?"

Chase's sense of peace and serenity was quickly changing to anger and frustration. He was getting the feeling that the investigation was quickly being funneled down a dead-end street and the authorities would soon focus their resources on other matters.

"OK, Officer Chappell. Thanks. Please call me if anything breaks," Chase said with little emotion in his voice. He wanted to get off the phone and move in another direction himself. He didn't bother to wait for Chappell to say good-bye before he ended the call.

Leaning against his desk, Chase let his right arm hang limp, still holding the phone. Looking over at the Post-it note, his eyes lit up. "Bennie," he said out loud, and selected another of his favorites. His man picked up on the first ring. He was at home, sitting on his sofa with Carol, trying to finish the movie that they started yesterday.

"Chase!" Bennie's shouted after the screen on his cell phone revealed his friend's number. "How are things with you?" he asked, sitting up and almost dropping his cell phone.

"I feel really good, Bennie. I'm at home. Susan was here but stepped out to run some errands."

"You had us really worried last night. The doctors kept finding things wrong with you. How are you feeling?"

"Sore. But I'll be okay. I just need a little time to heal, that's all."

"What's going on with the psycho lady?" Bennie was now standing up. "Did they catch her? I called the Laguna Beach Police Department three times, but they wouldn't tell me anything."

"They weren't any help to me either. I just called Chappell, and it doesn't look like he's going to be able to come up with anything meaningful on her. Looks like she's going to make a clean getaway, whoever she is."

"What do you make of that? How can a girl on a motorcycle wearing only your boxer shorts and tank top manage to elude all those sheriffs and a police helicopter? I mean, it was at night, and there can't be *that* much traffic on the streets at that time."

Chase's emotions dropped from frustrated to despondent. She was a professional. That much he knew. The police looked like they had already exhausted their resources. But he knew that he was onto something that was big and he could not walk away from it. He had to wonder if she used a wormhole to make her escape. Chase knew that the suitcases she retrieved from his floor safe didn't contain any batteries, and there was no way that she could have had one on herself. But he had to leave open the notion that she may have been able to use a wormhole to disappear.

"Bennie, I need a break. I need a break that that the police can't provide. I'm sure that someone in Cambridge sent her out here to kill me, but that really leaves me nowhere closer to finding out who she is."

"Yeah, Chase. Carol and I were talking about that all day." Bennie had his game face on and was speaking in his closing negotiator's voice. "Carol couldn't leave that fact alone, which screwed up my entire weekend, if you know what I mean. Anyway, why would somebody from Cambridge send an assassin clear across the country to kill you? There's something else going on that you're not letting us in on. And by *us*, I mean *Susan*, too."

Chase knew that Bennie would pop this question on him. Bennie was a brilliant salesman and an even better negotiator, and he didn't miss too many details.

"Listen, Bennie, you're a smart guy. Yes, there's more going on here than I have let on. But events have progressed so quickly that I haven't had a chance to keep you in the loop."

"Then you and I need to sit down and get everything out on the table."

"You're right. And I want to. I know that you can help me. I think if we discuss everything that's happened so far, we might be able to find the break that will help us find out who this girl really is."

"Or we may just decide that we should, as you yourself stated last night, count our blessings, drop it, and move on. Like you said many times in the past, you have to know when to run."

Chase sighed. "Maybe you're right. But I just can't get over how she just disappeared. And how is it that she didn't leave any fingerprints on anything? I mean, how can a person go through an entire evening and not leave any fingerprints *anywhere?*"

"Hmmm," Bennie said, pacing back and forth across his living-room floor with one hand on his hip and the other holding his phone to his ear while Carol stared at her newfound boyfriend like she was watching a tennis match.

"Think, Chase. Think of the instances where she touched something that the police did not look at. Like your car! Chase, *what about your car?*"

"No good, Bennie. She made sure not to touch anything. Of course, I opened the car door for her each time she got in and out. She then drove her Ducati to my house."

"What about the restaurant? What about a wine glass or a plate?" Carol watched Bennie who, although he was dressed in sweats and a light blue sweatshirt, looked like a boardroom executive ready to close a big deal.

"Those items would be washed." There was a long pause as the neurons in Chase's brain produced a series of chemical synapses that began to reconstruct a recent memory. As if in slow motion, Chase *saw* Staci rolling a fifty-dollar bill between her fingers, playfully unrolling and rerolling it as her chin rested in her left hand, elbow on the table, and smiling seductively at him.

"That's it, Bennie! The *tip!* She left the tip. I paid for the dinner at Ti Amo last night, and she left a fifty-dollar bill for the tip. I bet her fingerprints are all over that bill!" Chase was excited now. His mood shifted gears to elation as he clenched his left fist and inadvertently sent a sharp pain through his left shoulder that nearly caused him to pass out.

"Bennie," Chase said, quickly gaining his composure. "I need you to pick me up and drive me someplace. I'm still drugged up and shouldn't be behind the wheel right now. Susan left to run a few errands. How quickly can you be over here? I need to see Antoine, my waiter from last night. I hope to God that he hasn't spent that fifty-dollar bill yet."

Looking over at Carol and picking up the remote to select the pause button on *Déjà Vu* for the second time in less than twenty-four hours, Bennie smiled and said to Chase, "We'll be there in twenty minutes," and ended the call.

Chase sat his phone down. He was ready to go. But first, he had one more phone call to make—to his good friend, Fred Merrill. Fred saw Chase's name on his cell phone screen. "Hey, Chase, you Tigers fan, you. What's going on?"

"Fred, is this a good time? Where are you?"

"I'm at Hennessy's with Nancy. What's up?"

"Fred, I need a big, *big* favor from you. Can we meet in an hour or so?"

"Sure. We're going to be here for a while. We just sat down and haven't even ordered yet."

"Great. Fred, keep your evening open, will you? I have something important that I need to talk to you about. I'll stop by with a few friends. So have some beers with your dinner. I'll pick up the tab when I get there."

Chapter 55
Antoine

LAYING THE PHONE DOWN on his desk, Chase scribbled a quick note to Susan. *Susan, I have to take care of something important. Bennie will pick me up. Call me on my cell. Chase.* Chase looked at his note to Susan and compared their penmanship. He also wondered if his message looked too much like a telegram. *Susan has her work cut out for her*, he thought with a smile.

Walking back to his chair and sitting down, Chase typed Ti Amo into Yahoo! Yellow Pages, pulled up the number, and dialed the restaurant. He didn't know if his waiter from the night before, Antoine, would be working. If he wasn't, then he would have to get his personal number from the manager.

"Ti Amo Ristorante," came the soft and sultry female voice picking up the phone.

"Hello. This is Chase Manhattan, and I had dinner there last night with a friend."

"Yes, Chase. I remember. This is Elisa. I seated you and your date." Chase was a regular at Ti Amo, usually visiting at least once a week, and he knew most of the personnel by name.

"Hi, Elisa. How are you tonight?" Chase said in a deeper, slightly seductive voice of his own. He wasn't sure if Elisa would be cooperative so he thought he'd better butter her up a bit. Elisa was beautiful, and she was used to men coming on to her, so Chase hoped that she would be receptive and help him.

"I'm doing great, Chase, thank you. Are you calling to make a reservation for tonight?"

"Actually, Elisa, I need to speak with Antoine, who was our waiter last night. Is he working?"

"Antoine has the evening off. I think he's working on Tuesday, though."

"I really need to talk with him, Elisa. I can't wait until Tuesday. Can you give me his personal number?"

"Unfortunately, I can't do that. You understand …"

"Elisa," Chase interjected, "listen. This is a very important matter. I need to speak with Antoine right away. Tonight. Now." Chase took a deep breath and tried to speak as sexy as he could. "Could you *please* give me Antoine's home number? I really need to speak with him right away bec—"

Elisa interrupted Chase in mid-sentence. "I'm sorry, Chase, but I can not do that. I can not give out an employee's telephone number. Antoine will be here on Tuesday, however."

Chase had no other choice, "Okay, Elisa, can you please call Antoine and have him call me. I need to see him tonight. Right away. I can not stress the urgency of the matter."

"Sure, I can do that. No worries."

Chase gave Elisa his cell and home numbers, thanked her, and ended the call.

The manager of Ti Amo, a tall, slender, beautiful woman of Asian-American descent named Celine Emerson, stood next to Elisa, trying to piece together the gist of the conversation. "Who was that, Elisa?" she asked quizzically.

"That was Chase Manhattan," she replied, taking a moment to let her thoughts clear. "He wants to speak with Antoine. Right away. Tonight."

"Antoine?" Celine asked, taking a step back. "Why would he want to talk to him?"

"I don't know. He just said that it was urgent. He even gave me both his home and cell numbers to give to him."

"That strikes me as odd," Celine said. Mr. Playboy himself. You'd think he'd be calling for your number or mine."

"And listen to this," Elisa interjected. "He tried to talk with a deep voice. I think he was trying to sound sexy."

"Really?" Celine paused, and then took a big gulp of air, her eyes wide open and her right hand covering her mouth. She then burst out in laughter.

"Shhhhhhh," Elisa said in a hushed voice. "Not so loud." Now Elisa was giggling.

"Who would of thought of that one? Not me," Celine said over her shoulder as she turned and walked away, her long black hair swaying side to side. "Wait until I tell the other girls."

"Hey, don't forget to come back with Antoine's number. I did tell Chase that I would call him."

A few minutes later, Chase's phone rang. He was in the kitchen making a turkey and Swiss sandwich. He wondered if Susan was able to find something to eat out of the slim pickings in his refrigerator.

Chase put the phone on speaker. "Chase here."

"Mr. Manhattan. This is Antoine. How are you? The restaurant called and said you wanted to talk to me."

Chase finished spreading a thin layer of mustard on the top slice of bread and put his sandwich together. "Antoine, thanks for calling me back so quickly. I have a big problem, and I hope you can help me out. And you can call me Chase."

"Of course, Chase. Anything for one of my best tippers."

"Last night you waited on me and a friend of mine."

"Oh yes, we were calling her Blackie, because of her jet-black hair. We usually see you coming in with a blondie. Very pretty, Chase. *Very pretty.*"

"She gave you a fifty-dollar bill as a tip. Do you still have that bill?"

"Yes, I do. Today is Sunday, so I haven't gone to the bank yet." Antoine picked up a jar that he threw his tips in after every shift and pulled out the rolled up bill.

"Listen, Antoine, I need to get that back. I'll replace it with another fifty. It's very important that I get that back tonight."

Breakthrough

Antoine was now holding the bill up to the light. "Why is this so important, Chase? It looks like just another fifty-dollar bill to me. There are no phone numbers on it."

"Antoine, please don't touch it! I need to lift her prints off it."

"Ohhh, this is getting *interesting*," Antoine said with a giddy smile. "What's the matter, Chase? Did you lose her number? Yes, she was *very* pretty."

Chase sighed. "I'll level with you, Antoine. She tried to kill me last night, and that fifty-dollar bill is the only thing that has her fingerprints on it. She gave me a false name, so I need to lift her prints off that bill."

Antoine immediately laid the note down on his coffee table. "Chase, this is getting really exciting now."

Julio, Antoine's roommate, sat on the sofa and listened to the conversation. He reached out to pick up the note Antoine laid down.

Antoine lowered the phone and slapped Julio's hand. "No, no, Julio. Don't touch that." Speaking again to Chase, Antoine said, "I'll keep the bill for you to come over and pick up, Chase." Looking down at Julio he added, "If Julio can keep his hands off it. He's been using it all day, if you know what I mean."

Chapter 56
Evidence Bagged

BENNIE AND CAROL picked Chase up in Carol's Toyota Camry and they drove to Antoine's condo in nearby Laguna Niguel. Susan still had not returned, but Chase was sure that she would see his note and call him. It was six thirty in the evening, and the sun had completely set in the Western sky.

Floodlights lit up the mini date palm trees that lined both sides of the entrance to the Las Palisades Condominiums where Antoine lived. This was a gated community, and Antoine had already called the security booth to let them in. Chase gave directions to Carol as they drove through the Mediterranean-style complex. "Antoine lives in a very nice place for a waiter," Chase said with a grin.

"Make your first right, then a right on Del Norte, then a left on Vista Las Palmas. It's the second building on the right, No. 242."

Carol maneuvered through the winding streets and over the speed bumps and parked in a red zone in front of the building. "You can't ever find a decent parking spot in one of these places," she complained.

All three jumped out of the Camry and hurried up the stairs to No. 242. Antoine heard them coming and opened the door before they could knock. "Come in, come in," he gestured excitedly, waving them in with his right hand. Chase noticed that although Antoine looked like he had been up all night, he sure did have a lot of energy.

Looking at Chase's swollen and bruised face and his left arm in a sling, Antoine gasped, "My goodness, Chase, you look terrible. When you said she tried to kill you, I thought maybe she tried to shoot you."

"I'm OK, Antoine, but I really need to catch this psycho, so if you have that fifty, I need to get it."

"I have the bill right here on the table, Chase," he responded, leading the three into the living room.

"Uh … hello," came a sarcastic greeting from someone sitting cross-legged on the sofa.

"Oh, this is my roommate, Julio. Julio, this is everybody," Antoine said with a flip of his right wrist. Julio was frail-looking, barefoot, and wearing a tight pair of white tennis shorts that looked two sizes too small for him and an even tighter red tank top that he tucked into his shorts.

Chase leaned down and looked at the note without giving Julio a further look. "How can you be sure this is the one?"

"Oh, that's easy, Chase," he said. "The note your lady friend left had been rolled up. See, it won't lay flat." Antoine held the fifty at both ends, then let go as the bill rolled back up.

"You're sure about this, Antoine?" Chase asked with a hint of doubt in his voice.

"Oh yes, I'm sure. Most of my tips are left on credit cards anyway. I only received three fifty-dollar bills this weekend, and this is the one that she left. See, here are the other two." Antoine motioned to the other side of the coffee table to two crisp new fifty-dollar bills.

Chase pulled a fifty out of his hooded sweater pocket and gave it to Antoine. "Do you have a baggie that I can put this in? I want to make sure that no more fingerprints get on it."

"Baggies are one thing that we have a lot of. Julio, make yourself useful," Antoine said, clapping his hands twice. "Get up. Get us a baggie." Julio rolled his eyes, stood up, and trotted out to the kitchen and quickly returned with a ziplock baggie.

Chase laid the baggie sideways on the coffee table and scooped the note into it. Looking at Bennie, Chase said, "We're going to get this bitch. I can feel it." Both Bennie and Carol smiled. "This is so cool," Carol said. "This is much better than sitting at home watching movies."

Antoine clasped his hands in delight. "How exciting. This is just like a dinner play I was in once—you know, where the audience participates in a whodunit murder."

Julio sighed. "Your life is so boring, Antoine."

"Just you shut your mouth, Julio," Antoine snapped, then he looked back at Chase. "Chase, please tell me there is something else I can do. Anything is more fun than watching Julio coming down on a Sunday night."

"That's it for now. Thanks, Antoine, you've been a big help." Chase placed the baggie in his pocket and headed for the door with Bennie and Carol. They could hear Antoine and Julio arguing loudly as they closed the door and walked downstairs.

"Man, I could *not* get out of there fast enough," Bennie said, shaking his head.

The three walked swiftly back to Carol's car and got in, Chase taking the backseat. Bennie looked back at Chase and asked, "Where to now, chief? The police? Are you going to call Chappell?"

Chase had already given the issue much thought. "No," he replied. "I'm not. I don't like the way that Chappell has been handling things. When I talked to him this afternoon, he had the attitude that he had done pretty much all that he was going to do. I didn't appreciate that at all." Chase also had reservations about bringing the authorities deeper into the events of this breakthrough.

"What else is there to do? You have to take that bill to the police for prints. This is the key to her identity," Bennie said.

"Actually, I want to be discreet about things right now, Bennie."

"There you go again with your secrets. Listen, Chase," Bennie said, resting his left elbow on the front seat and glaring back at Chase. "You've got to level with us. What the hell is going on?" Bennie had that stern look that changed his harmless chubby face into a nasty negotiator who was used to getting what he was after.

"I will, Bennie. I promise. But first I have to talk to Fred. I'm going to give him this bill to lift her prints."

"Fred?" Bennie's face crinkled up. "You mean the guitar-playing dude from the Marine Room Tavern? Chase, this is getting weirder and weirder."

"Trust me, Bennie. I know what I'm doing. I'll clue you in on everything once we get to Hennessy's. I promise."

"You'd better. I'm holding you to your word. We're your friends, and we're the ones helping you out when you don't really deserve this support. Especially Susan. Not after what you've pulled the past couple of days, amigo."

Chase lowered his head slightly and nodded. "You're right. And thanks again. Trust me, though. This is big. *Really* big."

"I know that, Chase. It's big enough that somebody from the other side of the country wants you dead."

Chapter 57
Coming Clean

DRIVING NORTH ON COAST HIGHWAY back to downtown Laguna Beach, Chase looked out the driver's side window as they passed Ti Amo Ristorante. Less than twenty-four hours earlier, Chase thought that he was having dinner with the girl of his dreams. What a nightmare that turned out to be.

Chase's cell phone rang, immediately bringing him back to the present. "I hope this is Susan," he said with a sense of renewed hope. "Chase here."

"Hi, Chase. I just got back to your place and saw your note. I've been running a few errands for you and—"

Chase interrupted. "Susan, can you meet me at Hennessy's? I'm with Bennie and Carol right now, and we should be there in about ten minutes."

"OK. I picked up some groceries. I'll put them in your refrigerator and see you there. Are you feeling better?"

"I feel great. Much better than I look, trust me," Chase said with a crooked smile, still favoring the left side of his mouth. "And thanks again for all of your help. I don't know where I'd be without you."

"Technically, you're still in the doghouse, but dinner with friends should help get you out. I'm starved. Hennessey's sounds much better than the cold cuts I was going to put together."

"Great. I'll see you shortly. Bye, Susan," Chase said, continuing with his crooked smile and ending the call.

Bennie looked back at Chase. "I hope things work out between you two. She's a nice girl. You're not going to meet anyone better than her."

Chase rubbed his jaw with his right hand. "I'll second that."

Carol found a parking spot a couple of blocks up the street from Hennessey's on Ocean Avenue. Hennessey's Tavern is a cozy establishment in the heart of Laguna Beach's art district a few blocks off the main beach, with the feel of the Irish and English pubs that cater to younger, more affluent customers. The place looked deceptively small from the outside but could seat more than 300 with an outdoor patio near the sidewalk and an upstairs lounge featuring live bands on Friday and Saturday nights. Tonight, a Sunday evening, the place had less than fifty patrons.

As they entered Hennessy's, Chase, Bennie, and Carol saw Fred and Nancy sitting at a round table. Two empty red baskets were all that remained of grilled turkey and avocado sandwiches and fries. They looked happy, and Chase was sure they were on at least their second schooner of beer. Fred had already pulled a second round table to accommodate the additional people.

Fred looked at Chase's face and his left arm in a sling and slowly started to reach out his right hand, but decided to let it fall to his side. "I'd shake your hand, but, hey, it's the only good one you have left. Are you okay? What happened? Did that Cathy girl get you in a fight last night? She did, didn't she? Honestly, Chase, I didn't really care for her. I like Susan much better," he said.

"Fred, you remember Bennie. And this is his friend, Carol."

Fred reached out to shake Bennie's hand. "Hi, Bennie. Hi, Carol," he said with a smile. This is my girlfriend, Nancy Hudgins," he said, turning toward her and smiling even more. Nancy, a young, pretty girl with strawberry blonde hair and ten years Fred's junior smiled and waved. "Hi. Nice to meet you, Bennie and Carol. Nice to see you again, Chase."

Fred, Chase, Bennie, and Carol sat down. Fred signaled the waitress to bring two more pitchers of beer and glasses. "So, Chase, tell me what happened. Was Cathy in the center of all this?"

Chase looked Fred directly in the eyes. "Fred, Cathy tried to kill me last night." Fred's eyes opened wider than they probably ever had in his life. His beer stopped midway to his mouth.

Chase continued. "We went back to my place and made love. We took a break while she went outside to smoke a cigarette. When she returned, she had a chef's knife from my kitchen and she literally tried to slice me up with it."

There was a long pause at the table that provided the perfect timing for the waitress to return with the cold beer. "Here you go, guys. Do you want menus?" she asked, looking at Chase, Bennie, and Carol.

"We'll take four," said Bennie. "We're expecting one more to join us."

Like clockwork, Susan walked in. Chase stood up as did Fred and Bennie. "Hi, Susan. You look great. You're a sight for sore eyes, literally," Chase said as he took her by her hand, pulled her chair out, and sat her down. A round of hellos and final introductions followed. Fred poured three glasses of beer and signaled the waitress to bring a fourth.

"OK, Fred, let me continue."

Fred poured four beers while staring Chase in the eyes without spilling a drop or forming more than a half inch of foam on each beer.

"This psycho must have been a professional killer. I'm sure she's done this before. I was barely able to avoid her initial lunge at me with the chef's knife, and a fight ensued, and we literally tore my place apart. Only after I was able to retrieve a 9mm and fire off five rounds did she jump out a window and escape on a Ducati."

Fred didn't blink once. Neither did Nancy. Chase looked around the table at everybody and continued, using his hands while he talked. "I dialed 911, but she was able to get away without a trace. I spent last night in South Coast Medical Center. I'm lucky to be alive right now." He looked at Susan, and she grabbed his right hand and held it tight.

"That's a quick rundown of what happened in the last twenty-four hours."

"But why would she want to kill you, Chase? Where do you know her from?" Nancy asked. Bennie was listening attentively, looking for any details that had eluded him so far.

Chase sighed as he had to recount the story again in front of Susan. "I actually met her yesterday morning while doing tai chi with a group of tourists on the beach. We struck up a conversation and decided to meet for dinner. We stopped to see Fred's band last night at the Marine Room Tavern, then went back to my place. That's when all hell broke loose."

Bennie finally spoke up. "There's something else going on that you're not telling us. The million-dollar question, Chase: what is it?"

"OK, as you know, Bennie, about a week ago, I flew to Boston to follow up on a cutting-edge breakthrough in the field of physics. It's technical, but I'll make it simple."

Fred looked at Nancy. "Chase teaches physics at UC-Irvine. He's one brainy guy who understands this stuff." Nancy nodded with a smile, but she already knew that she was in over her head in this conversation.

"Remember that state senator and the girl from Boston who were murdered a couple of weeks ago?" The group nodded in unison. "The person who was arrested in the murder, Prof. Nicholas Fischer, is a brilliant and well-known physicist on the cutting edge of some ideas that have been fodder for science fiction for decades. I looked into the story and the arrest and some things just didn't seem right to me. Physics being my long suit, I quickly recognized that there was something lying below the surface of the media's attention. I decided to fly out to Boston to talk with Prof. Fischer. It wasn't easy, but I was able to get into the facility where he was being held."

"OK, so far the story seems innocent enough, but it's getting very interesting," Fred said, leaning into the table.

"At first, he didn't want to talk to me. He seemed scared out of his wits, and not just because he was behind bars for a murder that gained national attention. I took a shot in the dark and told Fischer I thought he was innocent and that the murders and a recent discovery of his were related."

The group at the table was silent and focused on what Chase would say next. "He started to confide in me—probably because no one else, including the detectives investigating the case or his attorney, was able to comprehend what the professor was involved with. I convinced him that I could help him, but that he had to trust me and tell me what was going on."

Bennie spoke up. "*This* is what we've been waiting for, Chase."

Chase looked around the tavern to see if anyone was eavesdropping. The waitress was three tables over serving cold drafts to a group of locals. He leaned into the group and lowered his voice.

"Prof. Fischer confirmed that one of his recent discoveries was indeed used to aid in murdering the senator. But he also was adamant that he played no role in the murder. After talking more with him, I believed he was telling the truth."

"So, do you think that someone else murdered the senator, found out that you were talking to the Prof. Fischer, and then sent that psycho out here to kill you?" Bennie sat back in his chair and took a deep breath, trying to dictate the conversation as he knew Chase wasn't giving them all of the details.

"Wait, there's more."

Bennie chuckled. "Only you, Chase, could get yourself involved in a national conspiracy like this."

Chase looked at Susan who was just as spellbound as the rest of the group. He put his arm around her chair. Everyone was now leaning into the center of the table.

"Fischer asked me to go to his office at MIT and take something. He told me how I could get in. I found the items and then brought them back to California."

"And a few days later, this wacko shows up, flashes her breasts—sorry, Susan," Bennie said, looking at Chase's better half, "and then tries to kill you?"

"That's the gist of it, people," Chase said, looking around at the group.

Fred couldn't believe what he was hearing. "Sooooooo ... um, that's quite a story, Chase." He paused for a few seconds. "But how do we fit in? And what exactly is it that you took from his office?"

Chase was prepared for this question. He knew that he shouldn't reveal to the group just what it was he took. Not at the moment, anyway. He gave his rehearsed response that centered on a positive spin that would help mankind.

"The items I took were two devices—a breakthrough in the field of physics that Fischer claimed could help save countless live. It includes nanotechnology and biotechnology." Chase felt that he was forced to be as vague as possible at this point, but was confident that he could reveal the truth to his friends later.

Everyone in the group had a completely dumfounded look on their face. "Why would that be a bad thing, Chase?" Bennie asked in a restless tone.

"It's not a bad thing, Bennie," Chase responded. "But this is a new breakthrough and it can mean billions of dollars to whoever has it. And it looks like a third party now has this technology."

"Then why did Prof. Fischer get arrested for the murder?" Bennie continued, arms folded and wearing a skeptical look.

"Obviously, somebody framed him."

"Somebody steals this new technology, kills the senator, frames this Fischer guy, and now you're mixed up in all of it and they are trying to kill you?" Bennie sounded like he was mocking Chase.

"As crazy as it all sounds, yes, that's exactly what I think is happening." Chase looked around the table to gauge the reaction of the group. Everyone still looked shell-shocked.

Nancy turned to Fred. "Is this something that we should be mixed up in, Fred? Shouldn't Chase go to the police with this?" she asked apprehensively.

"Yeah, Chase, why not go to the police?" Fred asked directly.

"Actually, he did, Fred." Bennie interrupted the conversation and sat up. "I was there when they came over to Chase's place. The police and the Sheriff's Department both came up with zilch in the help department. The story is farfetched to be sure. They probably did a cursory investigation then decided it was just another wacko conspiracy theory." Bennie stared at Chase more intently than he had all evening.

Chase realized that Bennie was now helping him with his semitruthful explanation of what he brought back from Cambridge rather than digging further for more details in front of the others. "So Chase, where do you go from here?" he said in a merry tone. "Hey, drink up, everybody. Beer's getting warm." Bennie took four huge gulps from his beer. The others, still stunned over Chase's story, took little sips from their glasses.

"Yeah, Chase. Where do you go from here? And why did you ask to meet me tonight?" Fred demanded.

"Because the psycho who tried to kill me last night made a clean getaway without a trace. Except for this." He pulled out the baggie with the fifty-dollar bill in it and laid it on the table directly in front of Fred. "This bill has her fingerprints all over it. And I need you to lift the prints and find out who she is. I need you to find out everything about her that you possibly can."

Fred picked up the baggie and studied the rolled up note. "I don't know, Chase. Why don't you just go back to the police?"

"Because, Fred, this is big. *Really* big. There's something going on that the police won't be able to comprehend."

"But you do?" Fred asked, his voice dripping with skepticism.

"Listen, Fred, I want one shot at this," Chase exclaimed, now in a loud and excited voice. "I want to find out *who* Cathy Bennett really is. I want to find out what's going on with Fischer and why he's been framed for two murders he didn't commit. I want to know—"

"Whoa, whoa, slow down a minute, Chase," Susan finally spoke. "I will quote you your own wisdom that you live your life by, and this is definitely one time that *you have to know when to run*." Susan was gripping Chase's hand very tightly.

Chase softened his tone. "Listen, everyone, I have the ability to get in and get out very quickly. So far, I am the only one who is making the connections in all of this. I can do this. I can sort all this out." Chase had more than a mystery and revenge on his mind. Chase was also a modern-day treasure hunter, and this discovery was the biggest treasure that he could dig up. This is what Chase was born to do. It was inherent in his DNA wiring, passed down from both his father and mother.

"Here we go again. Chase Manhattan off on yet another whirlwind adventure." Bennie was now sitting back in his chair, smiling for the first time at Hennessey's, with his hands folded behind his head. "It's okay, folks," he said after sitting up and holding his hands in front of him like he was trying to slow down a runaway locomotive. "I've been through similar situations with Chase before. As crazy as this story sounds, this is just another day in the life of Chase Manhattan."

"Chase," Susan said, "you can't be serious. Just let it go."

"I can't. I'm already involved. And I really do think that Fischer is innocent, and I think I can help him out."

"No, Chase. You almost got yourself killed. Let it go."

"Listen to Susan," Fred said, sliding the baggie back across the table to Chase. Staring at Chase, Nancy wrapped both arms around Fred's neck and laid her head on his shoulder in a show of support. Bennie had an open smile on his face and sat back in his chair once more, again folding his hands behind his head. Carol looked completely confused and slid her chair closer to Bennie.

Chase sighed. "OK, I can understand your apprehension. But just give me three days, and then I will call it quits. Three days, that's all." Chase slid the baggie back over to Fred.

Fred slid the baggie back to Chase. "No."

Chase slid it back, leaned into Fred, and stared him right in the eyes. "Fred, you know me. I'm *not* a stupid person."

Fred stared back. "I'm beginning to have my doubts." He slid the baggie back.

"Let's take a vote. I say let's help Chase out," Bennie said as he raised his right hand straight up.

"This is stupid. I'm not going to vote," Susan quickly responded, looking around the table at everybody.

"This is getting exciting," Carol said and raised her hand.

Chase raised his. "That's three. One more and I win." He looked directly at Susan. "I need to go back to Boston. You can come with me. You can pull the plug anytime. How about it?"

"I don't know, Chase. This is dangerous."

"Listen, Chase has been doing this sort of thing for years. Hey, I'll come along too. You know, to protect Chase." Bennie stuck out his barrel chest and flexed his arms.

Susan rubbed Chase's knee, looked away for a moment, then looked back at him. "Three days, mister. That's all you have. Then I pull the plug. And I'm tagging along with you."

"That's four against two," Bennie said to Fred, sliding the baggie back over to him.

Fred shuffled in his chair a bit, picked up the baggie, and stared at the note. "I'm officially retired from the business, but I guess one more time won't hurt. What do you think, Nancy? Are you in?"

Nancy shook her hair to the left side of her head and said, "Sure. Why not? I'm bored and need some excitement right about now anyway."

Bennie lifted the remainder of his beer. "A toast. A toast to Chase and to another adventure."

Everyone lifted their glasses. "Bottoms up," said Bennie. All six finished their beers and one by one, starting with Bennie, slammed their empty glasses down on the table.

Chapter 58
Fred to the Rescue

HENNESSEY'S TAVERN ON Ocean Avenue was quiet the following afternoon after the lunch rush was over. The few tourists and locals who were out spent their time strolling along the side streets and the boardwalk of Main Beach, enjoying the balmy seventy-eight-degree weather and cool, briny breeze coming in off the Pacific. The sidewalks were busier than usual for a Monday afternoon in late February. The china-blue sky and deliciously warm sun drew people young and old to one of the most serene and tranquil destinations in south Orange County on yet another perfect day in paradise.

Fred and Nancy had stayed up all night identifying and profiling the real identity of Cathy Bennett. Both were ecstatic at their results and the speed with which they achieved them. They took a brief three-hour nap Monday morning and then called a meeting to discuss the results of their findings.

Chase and Susan arrived for the meeting ten minutes early, only to find Fred, Nancy, Bennie, and Carol already seated on the patio. They sipped cold beers and engaged in a lively conversation. It looked to Chase and Susan that the four had known each for twenty years but hadn't seen each other in ten. That surprised Chase as Bennie and Fred were not necessarily the most compatible people in the world.

Bennie was the first to see Chase and Susan walking up the sidewalk a block to the north and waved to them. Chase could see that he began pouring beer into two empty glasses for them. Susan asked Chase, "I wonder how long they've been here?"

Chase answered suspiciously, "I don't know." But he was pretty sure that Fred had asked Bennie to arrive early to discuss additional information that Chase had not disclosed the evening before. Chase knew Fred was very smart, and his specialty was uncovering truths and facts that other people tried desperately to hide.

Chase and Susan entered the front patio from the sidewalk, and Susan greeted Carol and Nancy with smiles and hugs. Bennie could only fantasize about getting in the middle of that one. He made a mental note and filed the memory away under F for fantasies.

As everyone sat, Chase began the conversation. "Fred, that was fast. I'm very impressed."

Fred reached into his leather tote bag and pulled out three thick manila envelopes and set them on top of the table, one upon the other. Everyone was silent as Fred looked around at the group, smiled, and untied the string to the first envelope.

"Let's get right down to business, everyone. Chase, you're going to be blown away at what Nancy and I have dug up on these people, I kid you not. We know who *Cathy Bennett* is. And we know what Prof. Fischer was working on. We're pretty damn sure who murdered the senator in Massachusetts, and it wasn't Fischer. He didn't have anything to do with it." He smiled an even larger smile at Chase and continued, "And I took the liberty of filling in Bernie and Nancy on the parts that you neglected to mention last night."

Chase swallowed hard. Susan looked at him and said, "I'm glad that *Fred* is being forthright, Chase. Before we leave here today, *everything* has to be out on the table. Do you understand me? *Everything*, or I walk."

Chase looked at Susan, then around the table. Each individual face was staring him in the eyes. He knew this was it and that he could no longer hold back any detail, no matter how bizarre it might sound to them. Or to him.

"I understand. But you have to realize that we are not talking about an average discovery such as the existence of another galaxy or a breakthrough in medicine. This could alter the way we perceive reality *and* our very existence."

Fred interjected. "We understand that now, Chase," he said in a confident tone. "Allow me to open exhibit A." Fred pulled out a series of glossy pictures and laid them out on the table. They were of a beautiful blonde-haired girl at different stages of her life, from winning a state decathlon at the age of sixteen in Orlando, Florida, to four high school pictures, passport pictures, her college ID, and other miscellaneous photos.

Chase's eyes widened as he slowly stood up and shuffled the pictures around the center of the table. "That's *her*, Fred! That's her, but with blonde hair. Yeah, that's definitely her." Chase downed his beer and sat back down. Susan followed suit with her beer. Chase liked a girl who could down a cold beer.

"Her name is …" Fred paused to build the moment with a sense of anticipation, "Staci Bevere. She's twenty-three and a graduate student at MIT. Her specialty is applied statistics. She has an IQ of 135. What else would you expect from someone in this field at MIT?" Fred was still smiling, obviously excited that he was able to profile Staci Bevere so succinctly and so quickly.

Looking around the table, Fred continued. "Staci Bevere was born and raised in a family with a lot of money and influence in Miami. She has three siblings and is the third child with three brothers. Her father comes from a long history of money and is a businessman who traveled much of her life in Europe, Asia, and the Middle East, brokering very large financial deals in everything from banking to transportation. Her mother is a socialite who mainly raised the children and entertained. The kids all went to a private school that costs more per student than most people make in a year." Fred pulled out a recent color picture of her parents that was originally part of a story in a local newspaper on their charitable acts and laid it on top of the glossy pictures of Staci Bevere.

"She's very beautiful, and he's very handsome," Carol said, picking up the picture and handing it to Susan, who nodded in agreement and passed it on to Nancy.

"We have a name for her now. That's great, Fred," Chase said. "What else?" He poured Susan another beer, refilled his glass, and then slid the remaining contents of the pitcher over to Bennie's side of the table.

"Oh, I've only just begun, Chase," Fred said with a grin. "Listen to this. Staci is not only very smart, but she also excelled at sports, too. She was involved with track and field and gymnastics throughout junior high and high school. She was one of the fastest sprinters in the state. She was also a decathlete, placing first through third in various state meets. I don't know if any of you have every tried out for the decathlon when you were in high school, but it takes an exceptional athlete to be good at that. And Staci was one of the best in the state of Florida during high school."

"She's turning out to be one supergirl," quipped Carol, who just finished her beer. Bennie picked up the pitcher, filled up Carol's glass, and topped the others off.

"Oh, our girl is very impressive," said Nancy. "There's more. Much, much more." She looked at Fred and let him continue.

"As good as Staci was at track and field, she excelled even more in gymnastics, a sport that her parents started her in when she was five. She not only went on to win countless medals in state competitions, she was also selected as an alternate in the floor exercise for the U.S. Women's National Team for the Olympics. That's no lie. Here are a few pictures of her in action." Fred laid those pictures on top of the table and everyone shuffled through them.

Chase picked up a picture of Staci receiving a silver medal. The picture had "Gymnix International Tournament, March 17–18, in Montreal, Quebec" written at the bottom in Fred's handwriting. Things started to make sense to Chase now. He didn't feel quite so bad about getting his ass kicked by the girl.

"That would explain why I could throw her off the staircase on her back and she could get right back up and was ready to go," Chase said.

Carol responded, "My parents put me in gymnastics when I was the same age and I was involved until I was fourteen. I must have fallen off the balance beam hundreds of times, and my coaches would yell at me to get right back up there again. I actually got to the point where I could land hard on my back and jump right back into my routine without even thinking about it."

"What happened to her? Why isn't she still competing?" Susan asked Fred.

"Staci tore a ligament in her left knee while competing for the U.S. Women's Junior Olympics in Indianapolis. She didn't blow out her knee, but she did have to take a long time off to heal and rehabilitate it. The knee did heal, but not to the extent that was necessary to compete as an amateur. This was in her senior year of high school. That's when she decided to focus her attention solely on academics."

Chase made a mental note of her left knee, just in case they ever happened to meet again. "That's very impressive, Fred. Nice work. I can't tell you how much I appreciate this," Chase said.

The waitress, a young, thin girl with long, light-brown hair accented with blonde streaks walked over to take their orders. She looked intently at the pictures strewn across the table. Fred, caught up in his presentation, was taken by surprise.

"She's pretty," the waitress quipped. "Are you people talent scouts?"

Bennie was quick to react. "Yes, we are. We'll have six chicken teriyaki sandwiches and two more pitchers of Heineken. Thanks," he said to her in an authoritative yet polite voice that was meant to break off any further discussion. Being a bit short and pudgy and with balding hair, Bennie did not command a lot of respect at first glance. But he more than made up for that by the way he carried himself, which consisted of years of rehearsed techniques that most people quickly bought into. The waitress nodded her head and said, "I'll be right back with the pitchers."

All six leaned into the center of the table in unison as Fred continued. "Okay, Staci ended up going to MIT on a scholarship. Not that she needed one, not with her brains and what her dad makes. But she has been there the last five years. Again, she's a very smart girl, and she has world-class athletic abilities."

"What about martial arts training?" Chase asked. "She's obviously had formal training. There's no doubt about that. I've been around martial arts all my life. I've studied under masters from across the globe since I was seven. This girl is no amateur. She's had to have some training from teachers other than the YWCA."

The others stared at Chase's bruised face when he said this. Bennie knew that Chase was better as a blue belt than most black belts were. He knew that, traveling with his missionary parents throughout his childhood, Chase learned under masters in China, Japan, Nepal, and Hong Kong, among other countries. Bennie was starting to realize just what they were getting themselves into.

"I do have some information regarding this. In her yearbooks, she listed martial arts as one of her interests beginning in the sixth grade. We know her father was an avid hunter and frequently took all four kids hunting and taught them how to shoot rifles and handguns. This was a very competitive family, and it all started with the father. He pushed his kids to be the very best at whatever they did. Most parents only brag about their kid's exploits with bumper stickers. But the Bevere kids, especially Staci, brought home the gold."

"That sounds kind of generic, Fred. Do you have anything solid?" Chase asked.

"Not at this time. But we are looking into her credit card purchases and her checking accounts, too, as well as her father's. I'm sure that we can find a paper trail for her training. But we have established a pattern, Chase. She was once a world-class athlete, and she has martial arts interests. She also has a very high IQ and lots of money at her disposal."

"I'm very impressed," Susan said, with Bennie and Carol nodding their heads in agreement. "You're both good. Very good."

Fred smiled and put his arm around Nancy. "Thanks. But we already know that. We've been doing this sort of thing for years for some of the largest U.S. corporations and some pretty powerful people." Fred scooped up the photos and placed them back in the manila envelope, tying it, and placing it back in his leather bag.

"You have two more envelopes, Fred," said Chase. "What else do you have for us?"

"First, I need a cigarette," he said, reaching in his shirt pocket for his smokes. "Come on, baby, let's go out on the sidewalk for a few minutes. I need a break." Nancy stood up and followed Fred out to the sidewalk, where they disappeared for about ten minutes.

Chapter 59
More Fred

When Fred returned, two new pitchers of ice-cold beer sat on the table and Bennie was filling up six glasses. Sitting Nancy down first, Fred sat and took a few gulps from his beer. "Ahhhhh, that's better. There's nothing like good, cold beer and a good smoke when telling an interesting story."

Bennie noticed that their eyes were a little glazy and wondered just what they had stepped out to smoke.

Fred opened up the second manila envelope and pulled out more documents and photos. "Here are the police reports from a Cap. Det. Reginald Cherry of the Boston Police Department. These documents contain information that has not been released to the public yet."

"How do you have this information, Fred?" Bennie asked sharply.

Fred ignored the question. He was already tiring of Bennie's act, although he did like Carol and wondered what a nice girl like her was doing with a guy like him. He took another sip of his beer.

"I believe Sen. William O'Connor III was killed by a professional assassin. His right arm was sliced off just above the elbow, his neck was broken, his head turned around 180 degrees. What's troubling to the detectives is that there was absolutely no sign of an intruder entering or leaving his office or the State House. More on this later." Fred gave

Chase a glare as if telling him he knew the parts of the story Chase was withholding.

"There was quite a bit of blood splattered around the office floor, yet there wasn't a second set of footprints. According to the police reports, there was definitely a fight. They were careful not to call it a struggle. They concluded that it was a one-sided fight, and the unfortunate senator was on the losing end of it. Anyway, if I may jump ahead of the story a bit, I would have to say that your lady friend, Chase, fits the profile of his killer."

Stunned silence surrounded the table. Fred flashed an exultant smile, and Chase knew he had one more crowning piece of information to deliver. "By the way, we found more than just Staci's prints on the fifty-dollar bill, Chase. Care to guess who else's we found on it?"

After more silence, Nancy answered Fred's question. "Senator O'Connor's. There were about a dozen prints we lifted off the front and back of the bill, and his were one of them."

Bennie finally broke the silence. "How would you two have his fingerprints to match one of the prints on the bill?"

Fred briefly smiled triumphantly at Bennie and winked, then continued. "There's more. Cherry arrested Fischer for the murder. The evidence used to arrest him included a ballistics report matching of Fischer's .22 Glock automatic and the bullet found in Rosie Contreras' head. Rosie worked at the State House where O'Connor was murdered and was on shift when he was killed. This is common knowledge as it was printed in the newspapers."

"Tell us the *un*common knowledge," Bennie said in a bored voice into the air to no one in particular.

Just then the waitress walked up to their tables with six red plastic baskets of chicken teriyaki sandwiches and fries. "I'm so hungry," Fred said.

Nancy giggled a little too much. "So am I."

All six indulged in their lunch baskets, ignoring all table manners, and made quick work of their sandwiches and fries. Fred felt the need to continue even though he was not finished eating. "There were carpet fibers from the senator's office confiscated by the crime scene unit at one of Fischer's labs. This was not in the newspapers, nor was the

Breakthrough

senator's blood being found in a sink in one of his labs. DNA proved the match."

Opening the final manila envelope, Fred looked at Chase and said, "This is where things *really* get interesting." He took the last bite of his sandwich, washed it down with his beer, and exhaled slowly. "In fact, this is where the story gets really freaky. Prof. Fischer was working with a Dr. Gloria Newcombe, who was employed with Globalized Dynamics. She was a big shot in the field of physics and a high roller at Globalized Dynamics." Chase stopped fidgeting in his chair. He soon settled in as he felt a sense of relief that he no longer had to keep any more secrets from the group.

"She really knew her stuff. Prof. Fischer and Dr. Newcombe were working on a joint venture regarding a breakthrough in transportation of very large, heavy equipment that was expensive to ship and expensive to insure. GD was looking for ways to cut costs in this area. Fischer and Newcombe found the breakthrough they were looking for. Chase, I believe this is what you were afraid to tell us. As you said, this is the matter that could alter the way that we perceive reality and our very existence."

Susan looked at Chase and Chase nodded, and then he looked at the rest of the table. "Yes, Fred. This is it. This is the part that I did not think you would understand. It's imperative that I pursue the matter and get to the bottom of it." Chase finished his beer and filled his glass again.

"Dr. Newcombe was killed in her office, along with another scientist and two armed security guards. Security cameras caught a ninja—a female ninja no less—slicing, dicing, and shooting these people. Sound familiar, Chase?"

Chase nodded, and once again thanked the good Lord above that he was still alive. Susan and the rest stared at Chase. "You are *so* lucky to be alive right now, Chase," Nancy said matter-of-factly. Carol shook her head as if she could not believe what was unfolding in front of her.

"The senator's murder, Prof. Fischer's arrest, and the four slain Globalized Dynamics employees are linked by one commonality: a suitcase. A little suitcase that enables people and things to be transported from point A to point B in a flash." Fred paused a few moments to gauge the reaction of Susan. He had already updated Bennie and Carol, although he was not sure if they truly comprehended its significance.

Susan thought for a while, then looked over at Chase, who stared intently at her. "Now do you understand why I did not come right out and tell you this?" he asked. Chase was now facing Susan and cupping both of her hands gently in his.

"I … I don't know, Chase. This all sounds so futuristic. How can you transport things from one place to the next like on TV or in the movies?"

"Susan, listen to me. I have already accepted this reality. It looks like the rest of the group has too. You need to come to the realization that our world as we know it will drastically change very quickly."

"But why do you have to involve yourself further? These people are willing to go to great lengths to kill anyone who stands in their way. For God's sake, Chase, they killed a state senator right in his own office."

"That's why I need to go back to Boston and talk with Prof. Fischer. This technology cannot remain in the hands of the wrong people. I think that I can get to the bottom of everything and hopefully prove Fischer is innocent. I …" Chase looked at each person sitting at the tables individually and realized that this was no longer a solo project. "*We* need to get Prof. Fischer out of jail and retrieve all six of the suitcases."

"I agree with Chase," Fred said to everyone. "Right now, it seems that everything is localized in Boston. The people, the suitcases, the investigation. I think if we come up with a plan and move now, we can do what we need to do. If we wait, our chances of success will greatly diminish."

"Fred, why are you jumping on the bandwagon?" Bennie asked. "I mean, the research you have done is great, but I thought that is the only level of involvement that you were able to commit to."

Fred took a deep breath. "Because things are going to heat up *very* soon. We haven't seen anything yet, people. Greed is an ugly sin, and there are a number of groups already involved who will stop at nothing to get this technology. I think the sooner we can stop this thing, the better."

Breakthrough

"For the greater good of mankind, is that what you're saying is motivating you?"

"Yeah, Bennie, something like that." Fred didn't even look up at him. He pulled out some more photos and documents from the third envelope and handed Chase a picture of Staci and Nicky Junior drinking coffee inside a Starbucks in downtown Cambridge. "Chase, I just received this picture a couple hours ago. This is what prompted me to move quickly and call everybody here."

"That's Prof. Fischer's son, Nicky," Chase said. "He's a student at MIT and worked with his father. He's a real son-of-a-bitch, too, and he's the one responsible for the murders and for framing his father."

Fred continued. "I asked a good friend of mine from Connecticut to drive up to Boston and follow Staci. This was easy since I was able to retrieve her credit and ATM card numbers." Fred and Nancy exchanged glances and winked. "We knew she was in Starbucks. He was able to get over there and take this picture. Surprise, surprise, there's Nicky sitting with her. From what my friend tells me, they looked like they were more than just friends. You know what I mean, Chase?"

Chase was beside himself with a mixture of anger, frustration, emotional distress, and embarrassment. "That scumbag and Staci are behind all of this. That makes sense now. Nicky would have access to everything his father was working on. And he sent Staci through wormholes to kill all those innocent people, and then sent her out here to kill me because I was getting too close to them."

Fred sat back and smiled triumphantly. "We now know *who* the mastermind and the murderer are. Good ol' Nicky certainly did frame his father for the senator's murder. You were right to believe Nicky senior was innocent, Chase. And you are right to believe that you need to go back to Cambridge and stop these two."

"But why not call the police now and let them deal with it?" Susan asked the group. "Why do we need to get involved? Just call the police and *bang bang*, they go in and arrest these two."

"Susan, it's not that simple," Nancy replied. "What are we going to say? 'Officer, we know of two people who can transport each other around the country through wormholes and murder people.' *Sure*, they would take us seriously." She rolled her eyes.

"Finally," Fred said, "there are other groups after this technology. We followed up on some relationships Prof. Fischer had. We already knew about Dr. Newcombe. I sent out some feelers to Globalized Dynamics. After all, two of their top scientists and two armed security guards were killed. I wondered what they were doing."

Fred finished his beer and continued. "Like all Globalized Dynamics employees, Dr. Newcombe signed an Employee Innovation and Proprietary Agreement that outlines her relationship with the company. Basically, this means that any invention made by her, including the project that she was overseeing with Prof. Fischer, is property of Globalized Dynamics, including the suitcases. Make no mistake about it. Globalized Dynamics recognizes that the project she was working on and the masked ninja who mysteriously appeared are connected. They are aggressively trying to find out what happened. They want this technology, too, and they want it now. I don't think they quite understand the breakthrough that Fischer and Newcombe discovered, or that Fischer is even involved at the moment, but they're on the right track, and it's only a matter of time before they make the connection."

"Do you know what actions Globalized Dynamics is taking?" Chase asked.

"Right now, it looks like they're working by themselves. They are definitely trying to be discreet. I don't know if the detectives working the Fischer case and Globalized Dynamics have gotten together yet, but I would not be surprised if one party connects the dots between Dr. Newcombe and the murdered senator and contacts the other soon, if they have not already."

Fred put the photos and documents back in the third manila envelope and all six sat back in their chairs and took deep breaths. No one spoke for a couple of minutes as they tried to assimilate all this information. The silence was broken by their waitress appearing and taking their empty baskets from the table. "Hey, guys, can I get you some more beer?"

"Whew," Bennie sighed. "I don't think so. I think I need to take a walk on the beach." He laid his hand on Carol's knee, and she placed her hand on his.

Breakthrough

"Yeah, let's all take a walk and clear our heads," Chase added, pulling out a credit card and handing it to the waitress.

PART FOUR

Chapter 60
Second Flight to Boston

CHASE WASN'T ABLE TO FIND FOUR, first-class tickets to Boston on a day's notice. He couldn't even find four coach seats, so he had to spring for a chartered private jet. The super, mid-sized Dassault Falcon 50EX jet sat eight people and was the smallest plane available that could reach Boston nonstop. At $38,000 for the three-day round-trip, Chase stopped caring about what this venture was costing him. When Fred and Nancy were finished with what they had to do, the cost would approach $70,000. Susan had taken the liberty of reserving two, five-star hotel rooms and a Ford Excursion, which added to the spiraling costs.

Chase wasn't even thinking of what it would mean if he were the one to walk away with this technology once the dust settled. That was his original intention. But right now, what he wanted most was to confront Nicky and Staci, destroy the suitcases, and, if possible, try to prove Professor Fischer's innocence.

On Monday at 9:07 p.m., Chase, Susan, Bennie, and Carol boarded the private flight to Boston's Logan International Airport. Fred and Nancy remained in Orange County to offer backup for Chase. They already had Nicky's and Staci's ATM and credit card numbers and could trace their points-of-sale in real time. Fred and Nancy didn't come cheap. Chase gave Fred a check for $20,000 as a retainer when he

Breakthrough

first delivered the fifty-dollar bill to him yesterday and promised to pay Fred whatever he thought was fair above and beyond the retainer fee.

Boarding the plane, the four were immediately stunned by the opulence and the sheer luxury of the interior. Two beautiful young flight attendants, who looked like they were dressed for a board meeting, immediately greeted them with wide smiles and matching, near-perfect teeth. The first four seats were arranged in a way that the two seats on both sides of the fuselage were facing each other so that four people could conduct business or simply talk face-to-face. Behind them, two more seats were positioned side by side on either side of the aisle facing forward.

Susan and Carol were awed by the interior as they stepped into the plane and laid their personal bags on the first two cream-colored leather seats as if to say, "The women get the best seats."

"Wow! I've never seen anything like this before," exclaimed Carol, as one of the flight attendants helped her with her two carry-on bags.

"My name is Denise," said the blonde attendant, "and this is Amy," pointing to the tall, lanky brunette with Middle Eastern features.

Bennie stretched, looked at Chase, and said, "Now *this* is living, people. I could get used to this." Bennie's ego soared as he saw himself as a major player who should be flying chartered flights over the first-class flights he had to negotiate for with his manager.

After boarding the Falcon 50, the four quickly settled into the front seats, stretched their legs, and began to unwind from a very busy and hectic day. Fred had so many details to cover and rehearse with them in such a short period of time that they were well past being fatigued and tired. Once in flight, Bennie and Carol ordered apple martinis to help them relax while Chase and Susan each took Dramamine to counter the effects of motion sickness they were both susceptible to. The in-flight service was superb, and the flight was uneventful.

After about an hour, Bennie and Carol moved to the two seats behind them and snuggled underneath a big, warm, blue blanket. Chase and Susan stayed in the forward seats and tried to get as comfortable as they could. Chase ran over some of the details in his mind that Fred had given to him just a few short hours ago while his eyelids simultaneously ceased to stay open. Susan was leaning on his right shoulder, already asleep. Denise draped a blanket over them to keep them warm.

Bennie peeked over at them and saw the two fast asleep. "Awww, aren't they so cute? Maybe I should tuck them in."

Carol was laughing under her breath, already punchy from finishing three apple martinis. "Okay, one more, then that's it. We need to get our rest, Bennie." Bennie motioned to Denise with a smile and raised his empty glass. After the last round, both quickly fell asleep to the gentle hum and rhythm of the jet.

Morning came quickly as the plane crossed over three time zones and caught the sun rising over the Allegheny Mountains in central Pennsylvania. Bennie had forgotten to close his window shade, so he was the first to be woken up as the morning's first rays of sunlight pierced his tightly closed eyelids. Holding his head and running his hand through his mussed-up curly hair, he took one of the packets of Advil he brought with him out of his pocket. He nudged Carol ever so subtly. She inhaled deeply, and then let out a breath of stale alcohol breath in Bennie's face, causing him to flinch and cough.

"Whew, hoo hoo!" he said, standing up, waving a hand in front of his face, causing Carol to wake up from her slumber. Bennie stretched his arms wide and yawned. "Hey, babe, wakey wakey. How are you feeling today?"

Carol sat up, smacked her lips, and stuck out her tongue. "I need a drink of water." Even with her hair a mess and her morning breath smelling bad, Bennie thought she looked hot. She was the kind of girl who seemed to look better the more she dressed down.

The flight attendant was a step ahead of them, and was walking over with two Evian bottled waters and two Waterford crystal glasses. The water brought life to their parched mouths.

Looking out the window, Bennie could see the ground was covered with a white layer of snow. "It sure looks cold out there. I'm shivering just thinking about stepping off the plane."

Chase and Susan began to stir from underneath their blankets, their two heads slowly appearing from the cocoon they had spun the night before.

"Can I get you anything? A glass of water, perhaps?" Denise asked them.

"Water and coffee for both of us," came the reply from Susan, who was still acting out the role of caregiver for Chase and nursing him back to health.

The Falcon 50 landed at 7:41 a.m. at Logan International Airport and ended what was just another routine flight with little turbulence and no delays. As the four were gathering their personal belongings, the pilot and the co-pilot emerged from the cockpit, shook everyone's hand, and thanked them for using their service.

The four sleuthhounds grabbed their carry-ons and prepared themselves for the inevitable. The fuselage door opened, and the frigid six-degree air greeted them in a cruel way as they shivered and walked down the stairs onto the tarmac. "Enjoy your stay in Boston," the blonde flight attendant said as she smiled, waved, and quickly closed the door.

"She said that with a tinge of sarcasm," Bennie grumbled to the group.

Carol and Susan led the way as the four skittered over to the door that led up the stairs to the terminal. Once inside, Bennie was the first to say, "I need to buy a heavy coat. There's no way that I can get by with just my leather jacket and a sweater."

The two girls nodded in agreement. Their stylish ski coats were fine for the Southern California ski slopes, where temperatures could rise above freezing during the day. But Boston in mid-February was a different world altogether, and the four already looked lost and out of place.

"*Brrrrrrr.* This is the first time I have been farther east than Las Vegas," Carol stated. "I can't believe how cold it is. Where's the nearest mall?"

"We should have listened to Fred and bought heavy coats yesterday. Let's drive to the hotel first so we can situate ourselves and drop off our luggage. Then we'll go to a mall and buy some warm coats," Chase suggested.

The four made their way through the airport to the curbside shuttle that brought them to the Hertz Rental Car facility. "I hope they have the engine running and the heater blasting when we get there," Susan said as they huddled together in the shuttle bus.

Chase kept a close eye on their bags, as he did not want to lose any of the equipment that Fred had sent them off with. The laptops contained costly, sensitive equipment and would be difficult to replace. Chase wasn't even sure if what Fred set them up with was completely legal. Surveillance and eavesdropping could be a shady business depending on how aggressive one needed to be. In a day when no information is truly secret and can be gleaned in a very short time, there was still a lot of gray area in what was considered legal and illegal, ethical and unethical.

Once at the Hertz agency, Chase was in and out in less than ten minutes and the four walked towards the parking lot that contained their Excursion. Fortunately for the four Southern Californians, the engine was running and the heater blasting hot air as they climbed in. Their hotel, the Intercontinental Boston, was a five-star hotel located on the waterfront just a few miles from the airport. Susan had reserved two suites on the fourteenth floor that offered sweeping views of the waterfront and the city skyline. Pulling up to the valet parking at the front entrance, Chase traded in his keys for a valet voucher. They stood outside for a few moments and looked in appreciation at the elegant, blue-glass architecture reflecting the waters of Boston Harbor.

"You selected a real winner, Susan," Chase said. "Well done."

Susan squeezed his right hand, grinned, and said, "It better be, for the price I charged on your American Express Card." She led the way into the lobby. Upon settling into their rooms, they immediately set up their laptops and called Fred to let him know they had landed safely. It wasn't long before they registered activity on Nicky's and Staci's credit cards and began scrolling through Nicky's text messages. Thanks to Fred and Nancy, the sleuthhounds knew exactly where the two were, what they were doing, and headed back out the door to confront them.

They would have to move fast. Nicky and Staci were sitting at a Starbucks in Cambridge, and they had a receiver suitcase with them. Nicky was finalizing the details to drop it off to an unknown third party later that morning. Back in Orange County, Nancy was confident that she had cracked Nicky's coded messages. She was sure that Nicky was ready to kill three more people in Manhattan who sat atop the global financial world. Fred correctly concluded that the third party was a mole similar to the role Rosie Contreras played for Nicky at the State

House, someone who had the ability to physically get close to at least one of these powerful moguls of Wall Street.

Although Fred and Nancy had developed an elaborate scheme to retrieve the suitcases over the next two days, Chase didn't have time to implement it. He needed to act now. He knew that he had to do the right thing and try to prevent another murder. He didn't have a plan on how to stop Nicky and Staci. He would have to develop one on the way to the Starbucks.

Chapter 61
Starbucks

Susan pulled the Excursion to a stop in a crosswalk in front of the Starbucks on the corner of Massachusetts Avenue and Prospect Street. The café was situated on a prime corner in Central Square, a lively commercial and business area about a mile northeast of the MIT campus. The four looked into the front window in a futile attempt to make visual contact with Nicky and Staci. The glare from the midmorning sun made it impossible for them to see inside.

A few of the locals gave Susan dirty looks as they had to walk around the Excursion since the length of the SUV completely covered the crosswalk. One man gave her the finger.

Bennie rolled down the rear passenger-side window and yelled at him in a bad East Coast accent, "Hey, where do you think you are, New York or something?"

"Okay, we all know the plan. Let's go," Chase said to the group. Susan made a right onto Prospect Street and pulled over. Chase, Bennie, and Carol all got out onto the sidewalk and Susan would look for a parking spot, park illegally with her flashers on, or drive around the block until all three emerged from the café with the suitcase, and then they would drive back to the hotel.

Bennie and Carol would enter Starbucks first, scope the place out, and find a table close to Nicky and Staci. Adjusting his Red Sox cap, which he had bought at the airport to blend in, Bennie led Carol into the café. It was small with limited seating, but almost all of the customers who came in seemed to be in a hurry, bought their drinks and pastries, and headed back outside into the freezing madness.

Bennie and Carol saw Nicky and Staci right away. They sat at a small, round table with Nicky sitting with his back to the wall on the middle of the Prospect Street side of the building. Staci sat with her back to the people in line waiting to order.

Bennie was discreetly talking to Chase on his cell phone while they took their place in line to order their coffees. There were no open tables, but Bennie was pretty sure a group of chatty college girls sitting to Nicky's left was about ready to leave. Two young gothic-looking guys sat at the table on the other side of Nicky. They had their laptops out, their Grande coffees in hand, and looked like they were there to stay for a while.

After a few minutes in line, Bennie and Carol ordered two Grande half cafs with room for cream. The barista was very nice and poured their coffees. Bennie and Carol walked over to the station and took their time pouring cream in their coffees when, just as Bennie thought, the table of garrulous girls got up and left. Moving quickly to claim the table, Carol sat against the wall next to Nicky, and Bennie followed with two steaming coffees in hand.

Bennie sat down with Staci to his left side and Nicky against the wall. Carol had given Bennie a wink signaling she could see the black leather gym bag sitting on the floor at Nicky's left. They knew Nicky was right-handed, and expected the bag to be to his right. However, the two gothic guys had made Nicky nervous, so he decided to place the bag to his left, next to Carol's feet. Bennie ended his call with "See ya," which was the signal for Chase to enter the café and confront the assassin and her lover.

Wasting no time, Chase immediately walked through the front door. He spotted Bennie, who didn't look up at him but maintained eye contact with Carol as they conversed about the weather. Chase walked straight to the table and stood directly behind Staci, who was taking a sip of her coffee. He glared at Nicky with a look that transcended rage. In fact, his face was turning beet red and veins were beginning to swell in his neck.

Nicky did a double take at Chase. He didn't immediately recognize him as Chase's face was still bruised and swollen and Chase wore a dark navy-blue knit cap pulled over the top of his head.

"What the hell is your problem, pal?"

Turning around, Staci almost choked on the coffee she was swallowing. She did not think Chase had the ability to track her down, let alone show up in a coffee shop and confront her only four days after her attempt to kill him. She was sure she had done a great job of covering her tracks, not leaving any fingerprints at his house and staying away from cameras.

"Chase, what are you doing here?" Staci asked, still sitting down in her chair, too stunned to stand up.

"Surprised to see me, *Staci*?"

Staci swallowed hard. She hadn't forgotten that when she left Chase's house he was still calling her Cathy.

"Well, if it isn't Chase Manhattan," Nicky sneered. "I can't believe my girlfriend actually slept with a piece of trash like you."

"She certainly wasn't complaining, asshole."

"Chase," Staci said in a hushed but firm voice, "you have to be out of your mind coming here."

Chase glared back at Staci, the bruises on his face still prominent and his jaw still swollen where she'd knocked out his tooth. She could tell he was still favoring his left arm where she had stabbed him with the letter opener. Staci still had plenty of deep blue and black bruises as well, but she was able to hide them with makeup.

Chase grabbed an empty chair from the table Bennie and Carol were sitting at and sat down between Nicky and Staci with his back directly to his companions. Chase's right foot was now almost touching Nicky's gym bag. He leaned into the table, veins now protruding so far out of his neck that Staci thought they were about to burst.

"There's *no way* that you're going to get away with this. Do you understand me, Nicky?"

Nicky looked as smug and arrogant as a man possibly could. He felt like a prince who had just usurped the throne of the king, and there was absolutely nothing that anybody in the kingdom could do to stop him.

"Get away with *what*, Chase? What the hell are you talking about?"

"I know what this is all about, you creep. I know what it is that you're so desperately trying to protect. I know that you sent *Staci* out to steal the suitcases and then kill me."

"Steal from you? Are you out of your mind? Are you mad? *You* stole them from *me* first. I was merely retrieving what rightfully belongs to me." Nicky wore a sneer of contempt and utter disgust on his face while talking to Chase.

"Those suitcases belong to your father, and he's the one who sent me over to take them from you."

Nicky chuckled, folded his arms, and leaned back in his chair. "Oh yeah, that's right. You talked to my father. My father—the murderer of one of the most beloved politicians of our state."

One of the gothic guys sitting next to Nicky's table, a short, fat, white guy with pasty-pale skin and a really bad haircut to match leaned over and interrupted. "Hey, man, your dad was the one who whacked that O'Connor guy?"

Chase, Nicky, and Staci all turned their heads and glared at the guy in silence until he slinked back into his chair and re-entered his electronic netherworld.

"So what? What now, Chase? What does that all mean? So you talked with my father. Where is that going to get you?"

Chase was talking through clenched teeth. It was all he could do from lunging across the table and punching Nicky right where he sat.

"I'll tell you what I'm going to do. I'm going to expose you." He turned to Staci and continued. "And I'm going to expose you for killing Senator O'Connor and trying to kill me."

Nicky jumped out of his chair. "And just *how* are you going to do that, Chase? Cathy … errr, Staci, has an alibi. I mean, think about it, you cretin." Nicky was now leaning into Chase and talking in a tone barely above a whisper. It was all Chase could do to refrain from reaching up with his right hand and ripping out his larynx that was moving in and out as he spoke.

"I beam her down to you early in the morning, and then beam her back up to the mother ship when she's finished with you? No intelligent life down there for her to see? Are you going to tell *that* to the authorities?" Nicky was bluffing, correctly concluding Chase had no idea if she flew out to Southern California or was transported using a wormhole.

Chase wasn't deterred by Nicky's overbearing arrogance. He stood up and pressed forward. "I also know that you were the one behind the killing of those four people at Globalized Dynamics in Connecticut last week. Then there's the cleaning lady from the State House too. Remember her, asshole? That's *six* people dead. You tried to make me number seven and failed. That was a big mistake on your part."

"Listen to me, you lousy, stinking sack of white trash. What makes you think you can fly out all the way from California and come in here and threaten me? Do you *know* who you're talking to?"

Nicky was now yelling, and every set of eyes in the café were glued on their table. Bennie and Carol were up close and personal to the confrontation. He tried to sip his coffee in a nonchalant manner while keeping an eye on the black leather gym bag that was twelve inches from Carol's feet.

"Hey, guys, knock it off right now!" Staci interjected. She looked up at Chase and as calmly as she could, said, "Chase, you should really leave right now. Just get back on a plane, go home, and forget that you ever saw either one of us."

Nicky's mouth was still running at full speed, spewing out ramblings of how Chase had made the biggest mistake of his life by tracking them down. He was also pointing his finger into Chase's chest, which was one of the things that Chase hated most. That was strike one. Strike two was when he spread his arms out in a mocking fashion, asking Chase once again what he was going to do about it. Strike three was sticking his face into Chase's face with his mouth still running.

Chase's right fist slammed into Nicky's jaw. Nicky never saw it coming. The next thing Nicky knew, he was reeling backwards, bouncing off the wall behind him at an angle that made him stumble and fall onto the table that the two gothic guys were sitting at and knocking their laptops onto the floor. People sitting at other tables quickly stood up and started backing away, some of them even running out the door.

Staci jumped out of her chair and stood toe-to-toe with Chase.

This was just the distraction that Bennie and Carol needed. Carol used her right foot to slide the black leather gym bag under the table over to Bennie, who bent over, picked it up, and spun around so that his back was to Staci as he headed out the door. Carol was right behind him, as were about a dozen other patrons.

"Get out of here now, Chase. I mean it. Get out, go home, and never come back. Never make contact with Nicky or myself again. Do you understand me?" She was looking Chase dead in the eyes, and Chase stumbled over his thoughts for a few seconds. There was a brief moment of awkward silence.

"What?"

"Your eyes. They're green," Chase said.

"What? What are you talking about? They're green. So what?" Then she remembered that she wore hazel-blue contacts when she was in California.

Chase couldn't believe that he was momentarily caught staring deeply into the eyes of the woman who had only recently tried to kill him. With her blonde hair and green eyes, she was even more incredibly beautiful than she looked in Laguna Beach. Chase quickly recalibrated his bearings. He started to turn towards the door when Nicky stood up, rubbing his jaw with his right hand. "It's okay, folks," he said, looking around the café and holding his hands up in the air. "Just a little lovers' spat, that's all."

He then stepped into Chase. "Listen up, buddy. I know that you're not going away. Fine. Have it your way. But understand this. You've accomplished absolutely nothing by coming all the way out here. I'm going to bury you, Chase. Know that. I'm going to *personally* bury you. Now get the hell out of here while you still can."

Chase had finished the three things that he had set out to do: confront Staci, grab the suitcase, and punch Nicky in the face. Mission accomplished. It was a good day for Chase.

He turned and headed out the door. Once out on the sidewalk, he first looked left but didn't see the Excursion, Bennie, or Carol. Running to the right side of the Starbucks onto Prospect Street, he saw the Excursion a half block up with the flashers on and quickly backing up towards him. Bennie was leaning out the backseat passenger window, frantically waving at Chase to run up to the SUV and jump in. Within a few seconds, Chase was jumping in the front seat, Susan put the truck into drive, and the four drove off, weaving through a number of streets and making their way over the Harvard Bridge and back into Boston.

Chapter 62
Celebration

OPENING THE LEATHER GYM BAG, Bennie pulled out the black receiver suitcase. He lifted it up in his right hand, as if his arm were a scale. "So this little suitcase is what all of this murder is all about? It doesn't seem possible. How can something so small and average-looking be the cause of so much mayhem and death?" Bennie asked, failing to fully realize the immense repercussions of what he held in his hand. "Although it isn't that big, it is kind of heavy."

Carol studied the small black suitcase and added, "It's really not that big. I could fit it in my handbag."

Chase turned around, leaned over the seat, and looked at the suitcase. "It shouldn't be that heavy. Let me see that."

Bennie handed Chase the suitcase, and Chase felt that the weight was considerably heavier than the two he had brought back from Boston the previous week He sat back in his seat and carefully opened it up. First running his fingers across the black felt lining that covered the top portion of the suitcase, he gently pulled off the velvety soft overlay that concealed the uranium and plutonium battery that made it possible to open up the receiving end of a wormhole. Susan looked over in horror and almost swerved across the center divider into incoming traffic. Two lead canisters along with wires and numerous circuit boards revealed the most frightening sight the four could ever imagine setting their eyes upon.

Bennie and Carol were looking over Chase's shoulder. Carol cried out, "My God, what is that, Chase? It looks like a bomb. And not just any bomb. This looks like it can be used as a weapon of mass destruction!"

Susan, Bennie, and Carol were leaning back into their seats and as far away from Chase as they possibly could. Chase was stunned. The day's events had transpired so quickly that he never stopped to consider the suitcase might contain a live battery.

"Okay, there's no need to panic. Everybody just stay calm. There's absolutely nothing to worry about." There wasn't much confidence in his tone, and the other three were still inching away from him, putting as much distance between themselves and Chase as physically possible without falling out of the Excursion.

"Um, Chase, honey, I think we need to get rid of that thing right now," Susan suggested in a whisper, as if the vibrations of her voice might set the battery off.

"Just pull over and look for a dumpster. Bennie will toss it in," Carol added, also talking in a whisper.

"We *can't* throw it away. I need to bring it back to Orange County."

"Are you crazy, Chase? Susan, pull over and drive behind those stores over there. There has to be a dumpster behind them," Bennie commanded in a shouted whisper.

"*No*. We can't do that," Chase countered, still whispering. "We need to get this back home right away." He put the black felt overlay back in place and closed the suitcase. "We can't just toss it in a dumpster. What if it ends up falling in the wrong hands? Come on, everybody, let's think this through."

"Chase is right. We can't just toss it in the trash. As much as I hate to admit it, we do need to get this suitcase back home. We can decide what to do with it once we get there," Bennie said, the voice of the negotiator taking control of the conversation as his voice returned to a normal tone.

"The problem now is that we cannot possibly get this through TSA at the airport," he continued. "So we'll have to drive back to California with it. If we drive straight through, each of us taking turns, then we can make the 3,000-mile trek in about two days."

There was silence for about a minute as Susan continued on Massachusetts Avenue, not sure if she should drive towards Logan International Airport or turn around and get on the Massachusetts Turnpike and head west. Finally she broke the silence. "Okay, call me crazy, but I think Bennie and Chase are right."

"But what about Nicky?" Carol asked. "He's sure to be able to trace our SUV and the plane and see that we're leaving Boston by car."

"I'll call my attorney, Matthew Ciralsky," Chase responded. "He can send the plane back empty tomorrow, and we can drive back in a different car. If Nicky traces our movements electronically, which I'm sure he will, then he'll see that the plane went back early. He'll be tracing a plane with no passengers. That should buy us enough time to get back home without any interference."

Pulling out his cell phone, Chase called his attorney who had made the original arrangements for the charter plane to Boston. Matthew had been Chase's parents' attorney for over twenty years and was a trusted family friend. Chase had retained his services after losing his parents a few years earlier.

"Matthew Ciralsky," answered the voice on the other end of the phone.

"Matthew, this is Chase."

"How's Beantown these days, Chase. Is it still cold enough that opticians give away free ice scrapers with each new pair of eyeglasses?"

"Yeah, it's plenty cold here. Listen, Matthew, I need you to reschedule the flight back to Orange County today. This afternoon, if possible."

"Okay, I'll see what I can do. Is everything okay with you in Boston, Chase?" Matthew was genuinely concerned for Chase's well-being and sensed that something was terribly wrong.

"Trust me, Matthew, everything's okay. We just need to get back home right away. Do you think you can get it done?"

"Sure, Chase. Just hang tight, and I'll call you with the time of the rescheduled flight. You sure everything's okay?"

"Yes, everything's just fine. Thanks for your concern. One more thing, Matthew, the plane will be empty. We're driving back home."

"Chase, what the hell are you up to? Do you need my help right now? I can provide you with a number of people who can help you right away."

"That won't be necessary, Matthew. Just please get the plane back to Orange County, and I'll see you in two days, okay?"

"Chase, you've got a lot of explaining to do. You're just as bad as your parents were when it comes to changing plans and spur-of-the-moment, crazy schemes, and that's going to get you into a lot of trouble. Do you understand?"

"It's a deal, Matthew. We'll discuss this over a steak dinner. My treat as soon as I get back. Thanks again. I have to go now. I'll call you as soon as I can." Chase ended the call before Matthew could offer a rebuttal.

"I'm going back to the hotel now. We need to get our things and get out of here right away," Susan said. Chase liked the way Susan took the initiative and organized everything with such ease. He was glad to have her back by his side. He made yet one more promise to himself that he would never lose her again. He thought back at that small moment in time in the Starbucks where he looked deep into Staci's green eyes and felt a fleeting, false sense of serenity. He shook his head and threw the thought out. She was a cold-blooded murderer.

"What are we going to tell Fred?" Bennie asked. "He gave us all of this hi-tech gadgetry that must cost a bundle, planned for a sophisticated breaking and entering into Professor Fischer's labs at MIT, and we end up doing a simple snatch-and-run."

That brought a few small laughs from everybody in the Excursion, and they began discussing what they would do as soon as they were back in Orange County. Fred and Nancy had made elaborate and meticulous plans to steal all six suitcases and battery packs, but now the four just wanted to get out of Boston as fast as they could, especially since they had a live suitcase. Under the circumstances, they considered retrieving one suitcase a success, and they knew Nicky would take additional precautions to safeguard the remaining suitcases from here on. Once they were back in Orange County, Chase was confident he could perform reverse engineering on the suitcase and battery pack, learn the secrets of how it worked, and move forward from there with a decision on what to do with the rest of the suitcases and batteries.

Chapter 63
Back at Starbucks

STACI PLACED HER HANDS on Nicky's chest while Nicky gently rubbed his jaw as he moved it back and forth. He cracked his neck on both sides, then rubbed his jaw some more.

"I'm okay, baby. No problem." Nicky looked around at the mess surrounding him. There were chairs tipped over, coffee spilled on tables and all over the floor, and baristas and customers gathering up their personal belongings that had scattered across the floor when some of the patrons made a mad dash out the door.

Nicky bent over and picked up a couple of chairs and set them upright. "What a mess. Can you believe that jerk coming all the way out here just to punch me?" He rubbed his jaw a few more times.

"I can't believe that he found us and found us so quickly, Nicky. I mean, how did he even know that we were here?"

"Good question, honey. I don't know, but I'm going to find out. Trust me, I will. He just walked right up to us with no hesitation, like he *knew* we were here. There's something going on. I'm asking myself the same question—how did he find us so fast?"

"*And* he knew my name. He called me Staci. How did he find out my identity so fast, Nicky?" Staci was truly worried now. She no longer felt safe, and safety and security were what Nicky had assured he could provide for her when he talked her into performing the acts that could land her in prison for the rest of her life.

One of the baristas walked up to Nicky's table and the table where the gothics had sat and wiped them clean with a couple of white towels. She then dropped them on the floor and soaked up the spilled coffee by using her feet and rubbing the towels in a circular motion.

"Hey, my laptop is broken," the short, fat, pasty-white guy with a bad haircut complained to Nicky. "Who's going to pay for a new one?"

Staci turned to him and quipped, "Ask your girlfriend to buy you a new one."

His friend laughed out loud. "Good one."

Nicky was looking around the bottom of his table for his black leather gym bag. At first he looked a bit puzzled, as he was still recovering from the punch Chase landed to his jaw. But his puzzlement quickly turned to utter confusion and then pure anger as he realized his gym bag was not in the café.

Staci saw what was now rage in his face. "What's the matter, Nicky? What's wrong?"

"My gym bag. My freakin' gym bag. It's gone!" Nicky was now breathing hard, his eyes wide open as he searched again under the tables and chairs. His head snapped up, and he looked desperately at Staci. "Do you have it?"

She shook her head and started looking around for the bag as well. "No, Nicky, I don't." She looked over at the two gothic guys trying to get back online. "Hey, guys, did you see a black leather gym bag?"

"No, not me. I'm still trying to get my laptop started," the one with the bad haircut said, hopelessly punching the keypad.

"I haven't seen one either," his friend answered.

Looking over to the four baristas who were behind the counter, Nicky asked, "Have any of you seen a black leather gym bag?"

They all responded no, and one of them came to help Staci look for it. By now, Nicky was gasping for air, and Staci knew he was hyperventilating. He savagely kicked two chairs over.

"Somebody grabbed it during the fight, Nicky. When all those people ran out the door, somebody grabbed it. Somebody either accidentally picked it up, or they purposely stole it."

Nicky was furious now, but more than that, he was scared. More scared than he had ever been in his life. Somebody out there on the streets had a receiver suitcase that was loaded with a live battery, and at the moment, he had no idea who had it.

"Chase! *He* must have taken it. That's why he showed up here today. He intended to steal the suitcase," Nicky said, still trying to regain his composure.

"Chase didn't have the bag, Nicky. He walked out of here empty-handed."

Nicky ran out the door and onto the street with Staci behind him. They looked up and down Massachusetts Avenue, then Prospect Street. The streets were bustling with cars and the sidewalks were filled with people as the lunch rush was just beginning.

Nicky pointed down Massachusetts Avenue. "You run that way. I'll take Prospect Street. We've got to find my gym bag."

Nicky took off running back and forth through traffic and onto the sidewalk on both sides of the street, looking at everyone, his long and lanky body almost being hit by a taxi, then by a UPS delivery truck. After three blocks, he stopped in the middle of the Prospect Street next to a manhole emitting off a funnel of steam, his hands on his hips and gasping for air. Uncaring, he stood between lanes, the recipient of numerous honks and choice words, and called Staci on her cell phone.

"Did you find the bag, Staci?"

"Nothing, Nicky. Absolutely nothing. I've run up and down the street on both sides, and I don't see it anywhere."

"Okay, meet me back at Starbucks," a dejected Nicky said after a long, deep sigh. He ended the call and placed his cell phone back in his pocket. He knew the suitcase was gone now. Nicky ran back to Starbucks where Staci was already there waiting for him inside. She was talking to Rhonda Prentice, the manager on duty.

"Nicky, come over here," she said with excitement and hope in her voice. "Rhonda tells me they have a security camera. She can look to see who picked up your gym bag."

Nicky's afternoon was starting to get better as a ray of hope flooded his racing heart. "Can you do that right now?" he asked Rhonda.

"Sure. I'll go in the back and look at the video. If I can see who walked off with your bag, I'll allow you to come back and take a look for yourself."

"I'd greatly appreciate it. I have my Blackberry in there with my entire life on it. I'm dead in the water without it," Nicky lied in his most sincere tone that Rhonda believed without hesitation.

She went to the back room, and one of the baristas offered to replace their drinks that were spilled in the ruckus. Staci ordered a Grande coffee and Nicky a tazo chi tea latte. Nicky was laughing now. His spirits were up. He felt that fate had smiled kindly upon him today.

"Maybe this is just a test," he said to Staci. "A test to see if we have the strength and fortitude to carry this through to the end."

Staci walked over to the station to pour some cream in her coffee. "Maybe. I don't know for sure. But we've got to get that gym bag back today, Nicky. No matter what."

Leaning against the station, Nicky looked over at the security camera behind the counter. "I hope that's not a camera that takes a frame every five seconds. I want to get a real good look at whoever walked out the door with it."

He paused for a moment to think. "I still can't believe that pinhead showed up here. You'd think the guy would be thankful that he's still alive. Why hunt us down and come all the way across the country. He couldn't have done it for only revenge."

"I don't know, Nicky. But Chase is turning out to be a worthy adversary. He almost killed me, although he did need a gun to accomplish that. And he tracked us down in a matter of days and showed up here. He even found out my true identity."

"He's a real pain in the ass, that's what he is. But don't you worry about him. I'll take care of Chase Manhattan soon enough, I promise you that." He wrapped his long, lanky arm around Staci's shoulder and gave her a quick kiss on top of her head.

Emerging from the back room, Rhonda motioned for Nicky and Staci to join her. She brought them back to her desk, where she showed them the events that just played out on her computer screen. Rhonda sat down in her chair while Nicky and Staci stood on either side of her and bent over to view the screen. They could see themselves sitting at the table. They could see the two gothic guys sitting on one side of them and the four chatty girls get up and leave the table next to them. Then they saw Bennie and Carol innocently sit down next to them.

"So far, so good. I see the gym bag on the floor when the four girls next to us got up to leave," Nicky said. "Then that new couple showed up and sat down."

They continued to watch the video showing Chase entering the café and walking up to Nicky and Staci. They watched Chase punching Nicky and the chaos that followed. People started to scatter, and some ran for the door. Then Nicky saw it happen.

"*There.* Right there! Do you see him? That man right there with the Red Sox cap stole my gym bag!" he shouted, pointing to the computer monitor.

The camera from behind the counter caught Bennie red-handed as he had to face that direction when he picked up the gym bag and put his back to Staci. Bennie's face was clearly visible. He was even smirking.

Nicky stood up straight and asked Rhonda, "Can I have a copy of that part of the video?"

"I can do better than that. I can copy that section of the video and e-mail it to you right now."

"That would be great!" Staci exclaimed. "Hopefully, we can use this to track him down."

Nicky wrote down his e-mail address on a piece of paper for Rhonda, and in less than five minutes, Nicky confirmed he received it with his iPhone.

"Thanks so much for your help, Rhonda," Staci said.

"Are you going to be okay?" she asked Nicky.

"I'll be fine," he said rubbing his jaw again and putting his arm around Staci. "He was just a jealous ex-boyfriend who can't accept the fact that this beautiful young lady is with me now."

Nicky and Staci walked out of the café and headed toward the parking lot where they had parked. "I'm going to forward this on to Khyati. Maybe she can find out who this guy with the Red Sox cap is." He pulled out his cell phone and forwarded the e-mail to one of the best hackers that MIT has ever produced, and some fine ones, indeed, have come out of that prestigious institution. Nicky also included a message for her to hack into Chase's credit card purchases in hopes of finding where he was staying in the city. Khyati had done a spectacular job at profiling Chase and his day-to-day routines a week ago, so he knew that she could easily find out where he was staying now.

Chapter 64
Khyati's House

NICKY AND STACI pulled into the driveway at 1132 Oakwood Drive in Cambridge. The two-story, red-brick house was an older home in a well-kept neighborhood built in the 1880s. Rent was not cheap, but the neighborhood was relatively safe, and a lot of students and faculty from MIT and Harvard lived there.

They walked up the front steps where Khyati Dasmunsi met them at her front door. "Hi, Nicky. Hi, Staci. Come in. Coffee's almost ready."

She led Nicky and Staci to the basement where a room the size of half the house held a complex labyrinth of tables and aisles containing servers, computers, screens, cables, and shelves of books large enough to rival the computer section of any bookstore.

"Have you decided on a name to call this place?" Staci asked as Khyati led them down a path past tables of computers and other equipment.

"I will call it The Basement. How's that?" she responded jokingly.

"I'll think of something for you. Something cute but sassy. Like you."

Khyati laughed at the comment, something she rarely did for anyone but Nicky and his group of cohorts who Khyati now considered her family.

"Bring a couple of chairs from over there," Khyati said, pointing to some folding chairs at a table with three computers and screens close by. "Gather around. I still have information coming in, and we should be able to find out what Chase has been up to very easily."

"I know you're good," Nicky said, "but how are you able to do this so quickly?"

"That's easy. The last time I was into his little network, I left a couple of back doors that I can easily open. His home security system is average at best."

"So, what's he been up to in the past few days? He already knows my name, and he shows up today at Starbucks because he knew that we were there," Staci asked, directing the question more to Nicky, even though she was looking at Khyati.

Khyati punched in a few commands in the keyboard. "That's the million-dollar question. He simply does not have the ability to do much more than e-mail, go online, and use Word documents from home. That's about it. He must have had help, some really good help, to find out your identity so fast and to know your whereabouts today."

"What about his computer at UC-Irvine?" Nicky asked. "Could he have used their network and their resources?"

"Possibly, although probably not from the college-issued computer in his office. I suspect that he employed professional help to pull this off in a matter of just a few days." She looked at Nicky, "What goes around comes around, I guess."

Khyati's words pierced Nicky's heart, and he couldn't think of a comeback for what she just said. "Fast forward to today. What do you have on Chase?"

Khyati pulled out the middle of three keyboards from the desk and pulled up a twenty-inch, flat-panel monitor from the back of the table in front of her and punched in a command.

"According to his recent credit card purchases, our friend Chase is staying at the Intercontinental Boston on Atlantic Avenue. He checked in this morning. Actually, he booked two rooms." She looked up at Nicky, who immediately made the connection that the guy in the camera who swiped his gym bag came with Chase to Boston. To say that Nicky had an anger management problem would be an understatement. The anger switch in his brain could turn itself on and off at will. It took him less than a few seconds to transition to rage.

"I *knew* it. That goofy-looking guy who stole my gym bag was with him. They're working together as a team," Nicky said through clenched teeth.

Staci interjected. "Who was that girl with him? She's in on this as well."

"That's why Chase booked a second room. They must be a couple," Nicky surmised.

"Maybe Chase has someone staying in his room. There could be four people altogether," Staci said.

"The new people could be computer geeks, no offense, Khyati, who have been able to track us down," Nicky said.

"In addition to discovering my identity, Nicky," Staci said in a tone that demanded he do something about the situation immediately. "Now we have at least two more people who we have to contend with."

Staci stood up and paced back and forth. "This is all wrong, Nicky. You promised me that *nothing* would go wrong. You assured me that you had all of the angles covered. What's your contingency plan? What's your exit strategy? Every great leader has one, you know."

Nicky was now standing too and doing a little pacing of his own. He thought of reminding Staci that had she succeeded in killing Chase, none of this would be happening right now and they could have moved directly into stage two of their plan. But he knew that would be most unwise as Staci had performed all of the dirty work so far. And Chase had, indeed, turned out to be a much worthier adversary than anyone in his group had anticipated. He had even managed to talk to his father in jail, which was no small accomplishment considering that he was in isolation and the authorities had only allowed the family to visit him once.

To Nicky, the answer was simple. They would go to the Intercontinental Boston Hotel and get the receiver suitcase back.

"Khyati, do you know what rooms they are staying in?"

"Not yet. All I have is the hotel and the itinerary for his plane so far. I'll have the hotel rooms shortly. But listen to this. He chartered a private jet to get here. His flight returns on Friday at 11:15 a.m."

"A chartered jet?" Staci asked with her mouth agape. "Are you *sure* about that?"

"Sure, I'm sure," Khyati said with a straight face. "And there's more. He paid $38,000 for the round-trip. He put it on his American Express credit card."

Staci was astonished at the way Chase had organized and mobilized a group so quickly. She understood now just how committed he was to stopping them at any cost.

"Nicky, Chase is really starting to creep me out. A *chartered jet*? Are you kidding me? This guy has completely turned the tables on us in just a few days. *What are you going to do about it?*" she demanded.

Khyati was also glaring at Nicky, and he didn't have to be a psychic to read their thoughts and facial expressions loud and clear.

He put his hands out in front of him, palms out and fingers spread as if he were trying to stop a speeding locomotive. "Okay, okay, listen up. Staci and I will go there now. We'll get the gym bag however we can. Khyati, I need you to have the Guu meet us there, too. I'm not too concerned with the goofy-looking guy and his female partner, and I think Staci and I can handle Chase. But we need the Guu in case things get messy."

Staci and Khyati agreed with Nicky's plan. They understood that time wasn't on their side. They needed to get over to the Intercontinental Boston Hotel right away if they stood a chance of retrieving the receiver suitcase.

Chapter 65
The Intercontinental Boston

CHASE, SUSAN, BENNIE, AND CAROL were packing the last of their belongings and placing their bags by the front door of Chase's room. Chase made one last check on the receiver suitcase that he had placed in a duffel bag. He disposed of Nicky's black leather gym bag along with its other miscellaneous contents in a trash can outside the lobby door.

"I should go downstairs and pay our bill. You three meet me in the lobby when you're finished packing," Chase said to the group.

Susan stepped forward, "Let me go, Chase. I wouldn't be surprised if they've been able to track us down by now. Since they haven't seen me yet, it would be safer for me to go downstairs and close out the rooms just in case they come into the lobby looking for you. They must be desperate and are probably out of their minds right now trying to get the suitcase back."

Chase thought for a few seconds. "That's a good idea, Susan. But take your cell phone and call me if you see them. You should be able to recognize them from the pictures Fred provided. Just remember, Staci will have shorter blonde hair. I'll call the front desk and let them know you'll be checking us out with my credit card."

"OK, honey." She planted a big kiss on Chase as she walked past him and out the door.

"You're one very fortunate guy, Chase," Bennie said.

"She's *smoking hot*, Chase," added Carol smiling.

"I'm one lucky guy, I know. Believe me, I won't mess this up with her," Chase replied.

Susan made it down to the lobby and walked up to the front desk. There was a small line ahead of her, but it was moving fast. After a few minutes of shuffling her feet and checking her watch three times, she was next. She pulled out Chase's American Express and closed out the two rooms.

She was putting the credit card back into her purse when the man in line behind her stepped up to the second clerk and asked him to call up to Chase Manhattan's room. Within a few seconds, the clerk was dialing the number.

Chase looked confused when the phone by his bed rang. If anything, he was expecting a call on his cell phone, not the hotel phone. He looked at Bennie, who shook his head no.

Back in the lobby, Susan's heart beat so hard she thought it would leave a permanent mark on the inside of her ribs. She looked at the man standing no more than two feet to her left. He was short and thick. Very thick. He was Asian. Probably Chinese. He had jet-black hair and a deliberate, almost diabolical voice.

She stepped away from the desk, pulled out her cell phone, and called Chase. He picked up on the first ring. "Susan, is everything okay?" Chase asked, already sensing something was wrong in the lobby. Bennie and Carol froze. They looked as if they were suspended in time, two mannequins bent over zipping up the last of their bags.

"Chase, there's a short, stocky Asian guy asking the front desk to call your room. He looks like bad news, Chase."

"OK, go out to the valet and get the Excursion. We'll take the stairs down. Meet us around back. Move now!" Chase ended the call and motioned to Bennie and Carol to get out the door.

While the clerk was calling Chase's room, he noticed on his monitor that both of his rooms had been simultaneously closed out. He muttered under his breath, "He just checked out. Just now. What are the odds of that?" But it was loud enough that the Guu made out the gist of it. He turned around and began breaking down the lobby into quadrants and scanning them in quick succession for Chase.

Breakthrough

Susan was halfway out of the lobby when she saw a young man and woman enter through the front door. Even though she had never seen Nicky or Staci in person, she was sure it was them. She turned around and saw the Guu now walking quickly towards Nicky.

"Khyati just called me. They're in rooms 1404 and 1405," Nicky called out to the Guu just loud enough for him to hear ten feet away.

The Guu met up with them. "He just checked out. Just as I was at the front desk. He's close by, I can feel it," he said, stretching out what little neck he had and looking around the lobby.

"Staci, you go out front and watch the valet area for him. I'll check out the lobby and the restaurant. Guu, you watch the stairs that lead out to the back. Whoever sees them first calls the rest of us. Let's go!" The three split up and walked away as fast as they could without drawing attention to themselves.

Susan was close enough that she could hear the conversation. She called Chase again. Chase, Bennie, and Carol had already made it down to the eighth floor of the stairwell when his cell phone rang. Before he could speak, Susan said, "Listen, Chase. They're here. Nicky's in the lobby looking for you, Staci is by the valet, and the mean-looking Chinese guy is going around back to the staircase where you're coming down. I heard them call him 'The Guu'."

Chase was always a quick thinker, and could make good decisions while under a high level of stress. "Listen to me, Susan. I want you to get the Excursion anyway. Staci doesn't know you. Act natural, get the SUV, and drive around to the back to pick us up. We'll have to get past the Guu. Be discreet and nonchalant when you pick up the SUV. Don't draw any attention to yourself from Staci."

"You be careful, too, Chase. I know you can take care of yourself." Chase felt the love and genuine concern in Susan's voice, and that was the extra motivation he needed to get past this next obstacle.

Chase looked over at Bennie and Carol. They were now on the fourth floor. "Let's go faster. One of Nicky's cohorts is on his way to cover the bottom of the stairs. Nicky's inside looking for us, and Staci's out front. It's a race for us to get to the bottom and out the door before this goon shows up."

With only three floors to go, they all heard the door at the bottom of the stairwell open and the sound of footsteps climbing the stairs at a very rapid pace. Chase knew he had no time to waste as he did not want to leave Susan alone outside with Staci. Jumping onto the second floor of the stairwell, he saw the Guu leaping three stairs at a time. He was much thicker than Chase anticipated, and he definitely did not want this monster of a man to get his hands on him. Without breaking stride, and with Bennie and Carol behind him, Chase got within three stair steps of the Guu and violently planted his left foot squarely in the center of the hulk's chest, knocking him back down the stairs. Chase kept running, even stepping on the Guu's head as he raced to the bottom.

The Guu was momentarily stunned, and Bennie took advantage of his misfortune to kick him hard in the ribs as he closely followed Chase to the first floor. Carol was right behind Bennie and stopped to spray mace in the Guu's eyes before kicking him on the other side of the ribs as he screamed and covered his face. All three burst out of the door and into the back of the parking lot.

Staci jogged up to Susan as she waited for the valet to bring out the Excursion. Staci stood next to her and stared, looking her up and down. Susan returned the look and smiled.

"Well, hi, there. It sure is cold. I wish the valet would hurry up," Susan said, faking a slight Southern drawl to try and throw Staci off.

"It's cold, alright," Staci said with folded arms and a feigned smile. "So, what are you staying here for? Business or pleasure?" she asked, still smiling with a façade of interest and friendliness.

"Business. I'm with a private equity firm in Raleigh here to work on a merger deal. Right now, I'm on my way to a meeting to work on some integration projects."

"I see," Staci replied, still staring Susan directly in the eyes. Susan didn't flinch. She was not a natural liar, but in this scenario, she felt stronger than she ever had in her life. She felt confident to stand up to this assassin without any fear. She was going to be the one in control. She wasn't afraid of standing next to the animal who tried to kill her man and who had murdered all of those other innocent people.

"And yourself? What's your business here?" Susan asked, as if she were a manager demanding an account from a subordinate.

Staci wasn't prepared to be put on the defensive and stammered for a response. "Oh, me? I'm here for a sales convention for ... um ... for a new winter clothing line."

Susan looked down at her and smiled. "Are you wearing the new line of clothes?"

Staci looked at her new, white, athletic shoes, faded blue jeans, and a blue down-filled coat. "Yes, this is part of the line we're selling."

"Shouldn't you be preparing for the summer line? Spring is only a month or so away. It would seem you're a little late to introduce a new line of winter clothing."

The valet pulled up to the curb in front of the hotel and stepped out of the Excursion. Susan handed the young man a ten-dollar bill, then turned to Staci. "Have a nice day. Good luck with your clothing venture."

Staci watched as Susan turned the Excursion around and drove to the back of the hotel instead of straight out onto Atlantic Avenue. Susan spotted Chase, Bennie, and Carol and picked them up. She then turned around and slowly drove the Excursion over the speed bumps and around the side of the hotel to the front where Staci was still standing and looking around with her hands on her hips.

"Everybody bend down. I can see Staci at the valet station," Susan said. The three complied. They all just wanted to get out of the hotel parking lot alive and back to Orange County.

Staci stared into the driver's side window as Susan drove by. Staci had her cell phone next to her left ear and pretended she was talking to someone. She laughed into the phone and waved as she passed Staci. Staci was suspicious. Why would this girl get in her car, drive around the back of the hotel, and then come out to the front entrance again? And why was she driving an Excursion if she was alone? She stepped out into the driveway of the hotel and memorized the license plate and called Nicky.

"Do you see them?" Nicky asked impatiently.

"Get to the car as fast as you can, Nicky. I'll meet you there. I think they just left in a Ford Excursion rental. I have the license plate number." Staci was already running as fast as she could and calling the Guu, who did not pick up his phone.

Nicky ran through the hotel lobby and down a hall that led to a back door to the parking lot. Staci was there moments after Nicky. "Where's the Guu?" Nicky asked, looking around.

"He didn't answer my call."

"Never mind. Chase must have taken him out. Call Khyati and get her over here to find him."

The valet pulled up with Nicky's truck. Nicky sped onto Atlantic Avenue and made a right. Now he felt that he had no choice. He had to bring this madness to a stop. At a red light before he got on the 93 Freeway, Nicky unlocked the secured center divider and pulled out the Browning Hi Power 9mm that they had confiscated from Rosie the previous week and laid it on the floorboard by his feet. The light turned green, and he merged onto the 93 South. "I'm not sure where to go. I'm assuming they got on the freeway to make a getaway." Nicky accelerated to almost ninety while dodging cars on his left and right.

A mile further up, Susan was also speeding south on the 93, weaving in and out of traffic, and looking in all three mirrors for any car behind her that might be driving as wildly as she was. Carol was looking out the back window as well.

By now, Nicky was accelerating to 120 mph.

"I don't see them, Nicky. I think they lost us," Staci said.

"Call Khyati. Give her the license plate number. She can tell us where the car was rented from."

"I bet it's under Chase's name," Staci added. "I just know it is. That blonde-haired girl has got to be the fourth person of their party. You wait and see. As soon as Khyati comes back with the names of the other people on his flight, I bet there will be a fourth person. A girl. *That* was her. I'm sure of it."

Staci was nervous as she was saying all of this, and even rocking slightly back and forth in the passenger seat. Her breathing was becoming sporadic, and she began to indiscriminately wheeze and gulp for air. Her chest tightened up, and she instinctively grabbed at it with her hands. Nicky calmly pulled over to the side of the freeway giving up the chase, turned on his emergency flashers, and pulled out a bronchodilator from the center divider and held it to her mouth, pumping three times. Within moments, the diameter of Staci's air passage increased and she soon began to breathe normally.

Breakthrough

Traffic was speeding by, and her life was unraveling before her very eyes. But for a few minutes, Staci felt warm, safe, and secure, cuddled up in Nicky's arms. Deep down inside, she believed that everything would turn out okay. It had to. It was their destiny. She knew it to be true. Why else would this breakthrough be dropped into their laps? She sobbed uncontrollably, but that was okay. She knew that somehow, someway, Nicky would make everything better.

Chapter 66
Back to Khyati

NICKY AND STACI drove back to Khyati's house to regroup. Both were tired, depressed, and wanted to eat a decent meal, take a hot shower, and get a good night's sleep. But the shower and sleep would have to wait. Staci was pretty sure that the good meal would have to wait as well, remembering the horrors of Khyati's refrigerator. Khyati again met them at the door and welcomed them in.

"You two look like shit." She sniffed her nose in the air and continued, "You smell even worse. Come into the kitchen and I'll get you something to eat." Khyati rarely swore. Nicky figured that she must be in a great mood and that she had been able to quickly identify Chase's friends.

The two sat down at her kitchen table that looked like something out of the 1960s. This was like opening a time capsule and getting sucked into a terrible nightmare that took a turn for the worse, a black hole of retro design from which there was no escape. The kitchen looked like it had been remodeled no sooner than half a century ago and left to defend itself against the dozens of fads and fashions that followed up and into the twenty-first century.

"No matter how many times I sit in here, I never really feel safe," Nicky stated as he cautiously sat down at the round oak table with a green tile top and looked around the kitchen at the teal laminate cabinets and burnt-orange Formica countertops with avocado-green highlights. Covering the walls was a country-themed wallpaper, complete with repeating pictures of freshly made corn bread, roosters, sunflowers, and other rural themes. The floor was covered with an off-white linoleum bearing a type of red-and-black pattern that he couldn't make sense of. Even the refrigerator and stove looked like they came straight out of an *I Love Lucy* episode.

Nicky also noticed how immaculately spotless the house was every time he came over. Khyati was a clean freak who could not tolerate a single dust particle on any surface, one picture slightly askew, or anything out of place. At least he could relate to this, being somewhat of a compulsive cleaner himself. Staci, on the other hand, thinking it humorous to torture Khyati in small ways, would leave her kitchen chair at an odd angle to the table, prompting Khyati to walk over and straighten it. Khyati would usually hold out as long as she could before straightening the chair, but never made it longer than two or three minutes.

Nicky thought she must spend literally hours each day cleaning and scrubbing the house spotlessly. Of all the times that he and Staci had been over, they had never seen her in the act of cleaning, yet the place was never dirty. He thought maybe Khyati was a night owl who stayed up to the wee hours of the morning with a bucket of Mr. Clean and a roll of paper towels, going from room to room, sterilizing the entire edifice.

"I know you don't like your food cold or nuked, Nicky," Khyati said, "so I'll warm it up for you on the stove."

Staci was already thinking that she would not like whatever it was that Khyati was warming up and unashamedly took out her cell phone to call the pizzeria down the street that she programmed into her phone for such an occasion.

Khyati brought out a Tupperware container of a carrot-based puree with sun-dried tomatoes, lentils, and chickpeas. After one sniff, Staci politely declined. She hit the pre-programmed phone number and ordered a large meat lover's pizza and a liter of Coke. Khyati shrugged her shoulders as if to say, "It's your loss, not mine." Then she scooped the contents from the Tupperware into a sauce pan and warmed it up, the pungent scent of curry filling the kitchen.

"I don't know what to do, Khyati. I can't believe they were able to steal the suitcase and get away. Any word on that SUV yet?" a dejected Nicky asked.

She turned her head while stirring the Indian concoction. "It's from Hertz, a 2007 Ford Excursion that was rented to Chase for three days. Again, on his American Express card. There's not much else I can do in that department."

"What about the other people with Chase? Have you been able to identify them?"

Khyati smiled triumphantly. "I sure did. Chase flew out on a Falcon 50 yesterday, and he purchased four tickets for the flight. It took a little bit longer to find the names, but I have them."

"I bet it was Chase, one guy, and two girls, right?" Staci asked, confident that Khyati would confirm her suspicion.

"That's right. The other three passengers are Susan Anderson, Bennie Knowles, and Carol Rodriguez. I'm searching for the DMV records and pictures. They should return any time now."

"I *knew* it," Staci exclaimed. "I should have made the connection as soon as I saw that blonde-haired girl, who would be Susan, at the valet station."

"And Carol Rodriquez is the Mediterranean-looking female with that pudgy-faced guy who stole my gym bag," Nicky said, nodding his head. "Chase not only wanted to confront us, he planned on punching me from the very start to cause a diversion so the other two could steal the gym bag. Somehow, they *knew* that I had the suitcase in it."

"I agree, Nicky. I think once we get the DMV pictures back, we'll match them up with the three amigos," Staci added.

"Do we know what happened to the Guu?" Nicky asked.

"He's alright. I was able to get a hold of him a few minutes after you called me. He said that he was about to break Chase's neck in the stairwell when a woman maced him in the eyes and the three pummeled him."

"Poor Guu," Staci remarked. "He's such a nice guy. Bad things just seem to wait for him around every corner."

"There's one more thing you should know," Khyati said directly to Nicky. "Judging from Chase's electronic conversations with the three amigos and a few other people, it looks like your father told him the piece of the puzzle that we are missing. He tried to code the messages, but I was able to decode it, and I am fairly certain that he, at least, has the basic building blocks of how your father was able to stabilize wormholes."

Nicky thought for a moment, then realized what Khyati was saying. "You mean, he *told* Chase the secret of how he was able to make the wormholes stable enough to safely pass through?" Nicky looked like he was about to blow a gasket when he, instead, took a few deep breaths in an attempt to calm himself down so he could think clearly. Nicky knew that he had to rid himself of emotion if he were to make the right decisions this afternoon.

He walked over to the stove and poured water into the teapot sitting on top of it. A few minutes later, the whistle from the steam forcing its way through the spout filled the air and broke the silence. Returning to the table, he sat down and silently sipped his tea. Staci and Khyati sat and patiently waited for their fearless leader to say something.

Finishing his cup of tea, Nicky returned to a state of homeostasis, and the three continued to discuss what they would do next. All three knew they needed to retrieve the receiver suitcase at any cost. To complicate matters once more, Chase was at the center of their focus as they had to bring him back, with the suitcase, so that Nicky could extract from him the secret of stabilizing wormholes. He was confident that he was at the point where he could build new suitcases and batteries that would be able to open and close a wormhole, but he knew that he could not stabilize them, which rendered the wormholes useless. As much as they hated to admit it, especially Staci, she would be the one to go back to Orange County if they were not able to retrieve the suitcase locally.

Khyati pulled out a stack of paper plates, some plastic silverware, and matching paper cups and placed them on the table. She brought over the pan of warm food and set it on a farm-themed pot holder in the center of the table. "I see you still hate doing dishes," Nicky smirked, as he scooped some of the warm food onto his paper plate and took a few bites. "This is great, Khyati. It's sweet, yet spicy at the same time."

"That's the beauty of Indian food. It's a contrast of the best things in life."

"We call that a pepperoni pizza here in America," Staci argued. "You balance out a sweet tomato sauce with spicy pepperoni."

Just like clockwork, Staci could hear a car pull up in front of the house. "That would be my pizza. I'll be right back." She returned less than a minute later holding the cardboard box, the smell of its contents overpowering the curry in the kitchen.

"Now *this* is what you call a meal."

"*That's* what you call an upset stomach and heartburn. But *bon appétit* just the same," Khyati said with a smile.

Chapter 67
Three Amigos Identified

AFTER ALL THREE had their fill of their respective foods, they went down to the basement. Khyati led the way down a different trail to the other side of the basement and sat at a table. On the computer screen were three different files in alphabetical order. She opened the first: Susan Anderson. Her driver's license filled most of the screen.

"That's the girl at the valet station. No doubt about it," Staci said, looking over the face and physical information. "Five feet nine inches and 125 five pounds. That's her, alright."

Khyati opened the second file. It was Bennie Knowles. He was wearing a suit and a yellow power tie, and he posed as if he were having his picture taken professionally. Nicky still thought he looked like a dork.

"That's the guy in the Starbucks video," Khyati said. Next was Carol Rodriguez. She opened the third file and Carol's image and other information from her driver's license filled the screen.

"She looks exotic, like she has Mediterranean features," Nicky said. "She's probably a Spaniard."

"I'll get started profiling them, where they work, where they live, what they like to eat. You know, the whole shebang."

Nicky wasn't happy about the state of his plan. He had to postpone phase two that would escalate events to the next level—a phase that included murdering two captains of global banking in New York and a U.S. senator. Chase and his group of friends had proven to be more than competent in thwarting his plans. He needed to end this escapade with Chase quickly and bring closure to the California connection that threatened to derail his mission and expose him and his followers to the authorities.

Chapter 68
Cheung Yu Shiquin

CHASE KNEW HE COULDN'T STORE the receiver suitcase at his house. He knew Staci would be back soon. He also felt there was a good chance that Nicky and possibly the Guu would be with her. He wondered if he should hide it somewhere at UC-Irvine, but they would eventually look there, and he couldn't take the chance of a maintenance worker or another faculty member finding it. Chase scoured his brain for people who could help him and places where Nicky would not look—but hopefully someplace close to his home in Laguna Beach.

Chase also needed time to sort through the events of the past couple weeks and decide if he needed to actually destroy the suitcases altogether as he had agreed to do with Prof. Fischer. Going back for the other five suitcases would certainly be the most dangerous job he had ever tried. It might even be impossible. He doubted whether Susan, Fred, and the rest would even support him in another trip back to Cambridge.

Chase wavered on what to do. Although he knew destroying the suitcases and batteries ultimately would be best, he still wanted to reverse engineer the suitcase and understand how Prof. Fischer made it. He knew Nicky only had a limited number of uses left with the five remaining batteries. He also realized Nicky lacked the secret of stabilizing wormholes.

He also needed to take care of business with Nicky, Staci, the Guu, and whoever else was a part of Nicky's little group of psychotic graduate students. He feared for Susan's, Bennie's, and Carol's safety. Fred's and Nancy's too. Chase correctly assumed that Nicky would be able to track them down fairly easily. After all, they found him before and set an elaborate trap. *Well, maybe not elaborate,* he thought, *but they did a good job of quickly locating me, deceiving me with the oldest trick in the book, and retrieving the original two suitcases I took from Nicky in Cambridge.*

The only person Chase could think of who could hold onto the receiver suitcase and defend himself against someone like Staci or the Guu was Cheung Yu Shiquin. The sixty-four-year-old Chinese master mentored Chase years ago when he was in junior high and high school, and more recently, when Chase decided to get back into shape and revisit the passion of his youth. Chase knew he could trust his master, and he trusted that his master could take care of himself.

Chase drove down Coast Highway with the top down, thankful for the blue skies, warm weather, and the girls walking on the sidewalks in shorts and that showed off their tanned legs. He shivered just thinking of the unforgiving cold in Boston. He loved the city and its people, but he was no match for the subfreezing temperatures.

Chase pulled into Cheung Yu Shiquin's studio, a nondescript, white, one-story building with no sign or advertisement on the front. There was a door and a single window—nothing else. Cheung Yu Shiquin never advertised. At his age, he only worked with younger, experienced black belts who wanted to go deeper into their art but were having difficulty finding someone who was significantly better than they were.

The door was unlocked. Chase let himself in, carrying a gym bag that contained the receiver suitcase in his right hand. The entry room was small with a desk and a few chairs on top of a worn blue carpet. A few Asian-themed watercolor paintings graced the wall. Two pandas hugging beneath a bamboo tree. A dragon in the air and a tiger on the ground, set in battle. A serene landscape of a forest emerging out of a mountain range from Au Ho-nien. Erik Chang, a part-time assistant to Cheung Yu Shiquin, sat at the desk and welcomed Chase as he entered.

Breakthrough

Chase could hear people in the training room through the door behind the desk.

He walked in to find Cheung Yu Shiquin observing five men and one woman sparring in various positions throughout the room. The master took his time strolling from couple to couple, interjecting while they sparred, identifying errors in techniques and decision making, and even stepping in to show one student how to perform a particular movement. At sixty-four, the teacher was still quick, strong, and decisive—and wouldn't hesitate to throw one of his students hard to the floor if it would help to teach him or them something new.

Chase previously sparred with two of the students and nodded to them as he walked around the mat to the back of the room where Cheung Yu Shiquin's office was located. Chase waited patiently as the master lined up his six students, and one by one, attacked them. Each student was free to defend himself as he saw fit. Cheung Yu Shiquin was like a chess master who challenges half a dozen players at once, and rotates around the circle making his moves within seconds. In a matter of minutes, he had checkmated all of his opponents.

Cheung Yu Shiquin bowed and went through the six black-belt students in humiliating fashion, all six landing squarely on their backs with a loud thud. He bowed to his six defeated students, and then walked over to meet Chase in front of his office. Chase bowed. "Thank you for meeting me on short notice, Master," Chase humbly said, happy that it wasn't his day to spar. Looking over to the six students rising up off the mat and rubbing their backs, he knew the same fate awaited him the following evening.

Cheung Yu Shiquin opened his door and Chase followed him into his office, a twenty by twenty space with plush, red carpet and a large gold rug with black trim depicting a nature scene with a small river, a bridge, trees, and mountains. A large desk sat off to the side and a 160-year-old hand-painted elm armoire, a trunk, an altar table, and three chairs balanced out the room.

"So, you would like me to hold onto an item for you, Chase? What exactly is it, and why is it you want me to hold onto it for you?"

Chase could see that he would have to be honest with the master. What else could he say? He was beyond making up stories as he tried to do with Fred, Bennie, and the girls. "Master, this suitcase contains the ability to alter our world as we know it today. Everything you think about reality and the limits of the laws of nature as we understand them have been drastically transformed. Everything changes as of today."

Cheung Yu Shiquin looked at the bruises still on Chase's face, and the way he was favoring his ribs and his left arm when he moved. "Your injuries look to be about a week old, Chase. Somebody must have wanted you dead."

"Yes, Master, somebody tried to kill me. And there is a good chance they will try again very soon. They want this suitcase that I took from them in Boston." Chase bent over and pulled out the receiver suitcase from his gym bag and showed it to him.

Cheung Yu Shiquin held the black case in his hands. It had some size and weight to it, but all in all, looked rather harmless. "Hmmmmm," he said as he cautiously tugged on his silver goatee. "Change the limits of the laws of nature as we understand them? This sounds like the greatest scientific discovery since the splitting of the atom."

Chase looked his master in the eye. "You don't know how right you are, Master. I need your help right now. I can't keep this at my house."

Chase hesitated as he retraced his steps over the past week. "I actually took two of these suitcases a week ago in Boston from a group of students at MIT, and they sent an assassin out to retrieve them and kill me. I went back to Boston and was able to bring back one suitcase. I need someone to hold onto it for me while I wait for the assassin to return. Regardless of what happens, she cannot get this suitcase back."

Walking back and forth across the red carpet, Cheung Yu Shiquin held the small silver rectangular box in front of him, raising it up and down and weighing it in his hands. In his mind, he was also weighing his options and the repercussions of his decision. He realized with this new information, he was already in too deep, and that he was one of the few people in history who truly had the mantle of greatness thrust upon him through cosmic choices. He didn't ask for this, but he understood that he was now playing a major role in the fight between good and evil, a fight that could very well determine the fate of countless innocent people.

The discovery of splitting the atom also contained major repercussions, depending on who held the power. If Hitler had been the first to harness the immense power of nuclear fission, then the world would be much different than what we know it to be today. Likewise, he reasoned, if this technology fell into the wrong hands today, such as terrorists or a rogue nation, and they successfully targeted major Western cities with nuclear weapons, the way of life as we perceive it to be today would be severely altered.

The decision for Cheung Yu Shiquin was easy. He always knew that he was put on earth for a higher cause. He just didn't know what it was until today. The decision was easier to make since he recently discovered that he only had less than a year to live. Regardless of the outcome of his decision, he now knew that he would contribute something of significance to the world that was far more noble than anything he could possibly have imagined. He faced Chase, still holding the silver suitcase in his hands. "I will do it, Chase. I will hide this here for you. You have my word."

Chapter 69
Staci's Back

NICKY WAS FINALIZING the finer details of the next stage of his plan in his head, occasionally pantomiming when he had a new thought. Staci sat on the right side of Khyati's living-room sofa dressed in her *shinobi shozoku*, minus the mask and hood. She leaned against the arm, her right leg lazily hanging off the side and her left leg folded underneath her. She played paddle ball with incredible speed and accuracy, annoying everyone else in the room.

Khyati sat in a chair that didn't match the fabric of the sofa next to her or the carpet, but somehow the mismatched and dated décor had a particular flow to it that gave off a sense of continuity. She was constructing an algorithm on her laptop for a new application she was developing that would help her identify her counterpart in Orange County who was helping Chase track Nicky and Staci. She was also waiting for a signal that someone had opened the missing suitcase.

The Guu stood in the center of the living room, stretching and going through the motions of advanced martial arts form he had recently learned. Mina Nguyen and Christopher Thompson, Nicky's other followers who formed his group of modern-day zealot revolutionaries and who drove Staci back to Cambridge from New Haven after she killed Gloria Newcombe, sat nearby. They were in two smaller but comfortable chairs, the only two matching items in the living room, passing time playing video games on Khyati's combination TV/stereo.

It was 11:40 p.m. in Cambridge, and the six graduate students from MIT could only sit and wait for something to happen. Nicky had convinced the group that Chase would soon open the suitcase out of sheer curiosity. All they had to do was to wait for Khyati to pick up the telltale signal, and the game was on.

Nicky was about to let Staci and the Guu sleep for a few of hours when Khyati suddenly jumped up out of her chair. "It's open! Someone opened the suitcase, Nicky," she said with excitement that woke the others out of their doldrums.

"Are you sure?" Nicky asked.

"Yes. I'm sure. It's open right now as we speak."

Staci tossed her wooden and rubber toy aside and jumped up off the sofa. She tied her mask around her face and put the hood on her head. Now she was fully dressed in her black *shinobi shozoku*, only this time, she did not bring her sword. Instead, she brought Rosie's Browning 9mm equipped with a detachable silencer, two knives, a handful of throwing stars, and a syringe containing a sedative. She didn't have time to chase people around like she had with Dr. Newcombe. She had to get in and get out as quickly as possible. In fact, she didn't even bother to holster the handgun to her thigh. She held it in her right hand down at her side, a bullet in the chamber. Nicky strapped a backpack on her containing a live transporter suitcase so that she could open up a new wormhole and return home quickly.

He held her by the shoulders and kissed her on the forehead. "You'll be OK, honey, I promise. Remember, get the suitcase and bring Chase back. In and out. Amy, Tory, and Phil from UC, Santa Barbara are already in the area and will pick up the transporter that you'll use to send yourself back. Eventually we'll get it back from them."

Nicky's voice was reassuring, and Staci believed that he was sincere in his intent to safely send her through a wormhole with a suitcase equipped with a nuclear-powered battery. A lot of things could go wrong on the way there and back. There were still a lot of unexplained phenomena that needed to be tested and proved when traveling through a wormhole, but she felt destiny would bring her back alive and in one piece. She would live to breathe another day, and eventually, settle down with Nicky, have children, and raise a family in a world that would soon be a far different and better place to live for everybody.

Nicky entered the final coordinates into his transporter suitcase, took a few steps back, and smiled at Staci. She forced a smile back and took a deep breath. In an instant, an orange and yellow corona appeared. Staci boldly stepped into the conduit, and in a moment, they both disappeared.

In less than a blink of an eye, Staci appeared in Cheung Yu Shiquin's office, where the master and one of his most trusted students who he had mentored since he was a youth, Bobby Kwan, discussed the suitcase Chase had left. They debated whether to open it, and if they did, whether anything would even happen. Within moments of their opening the suitcase, a bright corona of yellow and orange light materialized, and the dark figure stepped out of it.

Although Chase explained to Cheung Yu Shiquin how the suitcases and wormholes worked, and the dangers that could instantly materialize when they are used, the sage still couldn't resist the urge to open it. The suitcase looked harmless enough. His philosophically gifted student argued that Chase could not possibly be right in what he was claiming. Cheung Yu Shiquin wasn't sure who to believe. Curiosity and skepticism soon overcame common sense.

The master took a leap of faith. He felt prepared to deal with whatever might happen next after opening the innocent-looking suitcase. Yet the master still was astonished when he first saw the corona form right before his eyes and the assassin step out of it a few feet in front of him. The awe of seeing the corona caused the master to step back a few feet. It gave Staci the extra room—and the advantage—she needed to strike first.

She quickly raised the Browning 9mm semiautomatic handgun along with its silencer and without hesitation, placed the bullet that was in the chamber in the center of the master's right eye, ending his life one year early. Had Cheung Yu Shiquin not stepped back at the sight of the corona miraculously appearing in front of him, Staci would have ended up face to face with the master, and he would have had the opportunity to disarm her, or at least hold her for a few moments until Bobby Kwan could help.

Cheung Yu Shiquin dropped to the floor, a red splotch of blood, skull fragments, and gray matter leaving a trail on the carpet before splattering in an asymmetrical circle on the wall a few feet behind him. Staci shifted her aim slightly to the right and placed a second bullet in Bobby Kwan's left eye. He, too, fell to the floor and left a similar red chunky splotch on the wall directly behind him.

Erik Chang, sitting at the desk in the foyer, heard the commotion on the other side of the studio. He jumped up from his chair and walked briskly across the blue mats of the dimly lit training room. The light from Cheung Yu Shiquin's office sliced through the three-inch opening of the door which stood slightly ajar. Erik called out to the teacher, but there was no answer. He knew the master was sick. His walk turned into a run as he rushed to make sure he was safe. Once inside the door, he stared in horror at the unspeakable mess that lay before him. Cheung Yu Shiquin and Bobby Kwan both lay dead on the carpet directly in front of him, the wall behind the master's desk displayed the perverse design of dark scarlet fragments of what were once the contents of their heads. He turned around and started to step back when Staci stepped out from behind the open door and planted a bullet between Erik's shocked eyes, continuing the bloody pattern.

She looked up at the clock on the wall. It read 8:45 p.m. Chase would be here in fifteen minutes for his personal, hour-long workout. Khyati was still able to track Chase's every move by monitoring his phone calls, e-mail, and text messages. Nicky and his cohorts knew Chase's schedule. Staci couldn't believe her luck. In fifteen minutes, she would meet Chase again and bring him and the suitcase back to Cambridge. She thought she could actually get a decent night's sleep, too.

Earlier that day, Nicky had called his West Coast cohorts, Amy Leong, Tory Richmond, and Phil Turnquist, from the University of California, Santa Barbara, who had helped arrange Staci's first trip to California the week before, and had them drive to Laguna Beach and offer support. They remained in the area since late afternoon, awaiting specific instructions.

Staci walked over to the dead sage's desk and pulled out a pile of letters and utility bills from his desk drawer. Then she called Nicky on her cell phone and read him the address of the studio from the letters, and Nicky called the UC, Santa Barbara students with the location of the studio where Staci and the suitcase were.

After the conversation, she unstrapped the transporter suitcase from her back and set it down beside the receiver suitcase that Chase had entrusted his master with. She then took out the knives and set them next to the suitcases. She didn't think that she needed them for her rematch with Chase. She also untied her hood and mask and laid them down on the floor with the knives. She kept the stars in a pocket on her right thigh, just in case. She also kept the handgun in her belt. She then pulled out a set of keys from the desk drawer and placed them in her right thigh pocket.

Staci closed the door of the office and walked across the blue mats to the center of the training room where she stopped. She looked around to get a feel for the place and familiarize herself with dimensions of the room. There were no weapons on the wall like the combat room in Santa Barbara. There were no household objects that could be used as weapons like in Chase's house. It was just a large room with off-white cinder block walls, mirrors lining one of the walls, and a series of blue pads covering the entire floor. This would be an ideal place to have her rematch with Chase. Winner takes all. If she wins, she gets to take Chase back to Cambridge, where Nicky would extract from him the information that he needs, and she will never have to see him again. However, if Chase wins, she would end up in prison for the rest of her life. Or dead. And Chase would keep the two suitcases and continue the battle with Nicky.

Staci paced the floor in all four directions to get a sense of the depth and breadth of the room. She performed a few stretches and jumped in place to limber up and get her blood flowing a little bit faster, but not enough to considerably raise her heart rate.

Then she heard a car pull up, the engine stop, and the car door open and close. Chase entered the front door of the studio. Staci readied the handgun. She had Chase right where she wanted him. He stood just inside of the doorway in the training room wearing a simple white double-weave two-piece karate uniform, frozen in time, staring down the barrel of the Browning 9mm semiautomatic handgun.

Chapter 70
The Rematch

CHASE KNEW HE WAS A DEAD MAN if he attempted to run back out the door and into the front entry room. But he didn't want to just stand there and allow Staci to dictate the parameters either. Placing both hands in front of him, he slowly took a few steps toward the center of the room.

Aiming the semiautomatic handgun directly at his head, Staci began to circle Chase from a distance of twenty feet. Setting foot over foot while bending her posture slightly and controlling her breathing as she moved in an arc, Staci looked confident and steady with her aim.

"Chase," she said in a mild, low-key tone, "do you know what I want right now? I want a rematch of our previous encounter."

"Um …. that wouldn't happen to be in bed, would it?" was all Chase could think to reply.

"You're a funny guy, Chase. I really liked you. Out of all the men I have ever met, you are one of the few I felt I could build something nice with."

"It's not too late, Staci. We're both still young, and we have all that this newly discovered world has to offer us. Together we can—"

"That's enough, Chase. Please, no more. That's not going to work with me. Now, I want you to drop your gun on the floor. I can see the outline of it underneath your shirt. Do it. NOW!"

Chase hesitated and tried to say something else.

"Drop it, *now*," Stacy demanded, "or I will shoot you in the head. I'm good enough to shoot you in the eye. Either eye. In fact, I'm pretty sure I can shoot you in each eye and then between the eyes before your body even hits the floor. I've never tried that before, but I'm eager to try right now." Still slowly circling Chase, Staci continued to hold the gun steady.

Chase pulled out the Glock 9mm from his belt, slowly bent over, and gently laid it on the mat in front of him.

"You know the procedure, Chase. Step back now."

Chase complied, and Staci stepped forward and picked up his gun. She aimed both handguns at him, one at each eye. She then stepped toward him as he backed up to the far side of the room. Staring down the barrels of two semiautomatic handguns, he heard the front door of the studio open. Three people entered and stood in the doorway of the training room. Chase did not recognize the two young Caucasian males or the Asian female who stood side by side, arms folded, staring at him.

"Don't worry about them, Chase. They're with me." Staci walked over to the young female and handed her Cheung Yu Shiquin's keys, then handed each of the men a gun. Amy Leong turned around and walked to the front door of the building and locked it. She then turned off the light to the entry room, came back to the training room, and shut the door behind her.

Staci looked over at the three UC, Santa Barbara graduate students standing off to the side of the mats. "Whatever happens, I don't want you three interfering with our little rematch here. This is between Chase and me." The three graduate students nodded in unison.

Staci immediately initiated the fight with three quick spin kicks that were designed to force Chase to retreat. Standing his ground, he blocked all three kicks with his forearms. He followed with a front snap kick to her upper chest that forced Staci to take a few steps back and almost caused her to lose her balance. Chase countered with an aggressive assault of his own and faked a punch to the right side of Staci's head that forced her to step to her left, placing her weight on her left knee. Chase then followed with an axe kick directly to her left knee. Staci was able to move out of the way, but the heel of his foot glanced off the outside of her knee. Had the kick found its mark, it surely would have completely crippled her left leg.

Staci responded with a sweeping side kick to the inside of Chase's left thigh just below the groin and knocked him hard onto the mats. Lying on his back, he struck at Staci with a hook kick—again aimed at her left knee. She managed to jump up and avoid direct contact to her knee, but her ankle caught the brunt of the strike and she fell to the mat while Chase stood back up and regained his composure.

Chase stomped hard at both of her ankles, trying to break one or both. Staci backpedaled on all fours but could not escape his onslaught. She could only roll directly into and under him. Being almost a foot shorter and fifty pounds lighter than an opponent has its advantages. She easily rolled between his legs, stood up directly behind him, and prepared to strike a decisive blow.

But Chase was ready for her strategy. Now aware that Staci had once been a world-class gymnast, he anticipated Staci incorporating these methods into her moves. She confused him with these techniques in her fighting style at his house the week before, and he wasn't prepared to react to her style then. But now, he expected to see them mixed in with her kung fu moves. He was ready to defend himself.

As Staci stood behind Chase and set herself to deliver a series of punches to his lower back, he spun around to deliver a powerful midlevel reverse side kick and planting the sole of his foot squarely in Staci's stomach, sent her staggering backwards. He faked a frontal kick and followed with a crescent kick to the side of her head. Off balance and reeling from the effects, Staci could only retreat in a circular motion and try to block the volley of punches and kicks that Chase threw at her. Amy, Tory, and Phil could only watch as the two combatants passed within a few feet. Chase looked in control, and Tory wondered if he would have to use Chase's own gun on him.

Every second or third kick was now directed at Staci's left knee. She realized Chase knew she had torn ligaments in her left knee and he was targeting her main weakness. Staci originally wanted to play with Chase and make the fight last a while. She still respected him and felt a sense of honor that she could fight with someone who had studied under sages from across the globe.

But now she needed to end this fight quickly. She knew that Chase was a very smart man, and he could have a few more surprises up his sleeve. She set him up for the final barrage that would knock him unconscious, or at least weaken him to the point that she could inject him with the sedative she had in a pocket on her right thigh.

Staci retreated to the center of the mats—a maneuver that was actually the beginning of her final attack. She wanted Chase to continue to expend valuable energy and feigned fear and confusion while evading and blocking his punches and kicks. But avoiding his strikes was becoming dangerous for her. The more Chase attacked, the faster and stronger he became. Staci had to abandon her favorite strategy of hand-to-hand combat and keep her distance by using an array of backward flips, handsprings, cartwheels, and backward summersaults, incorporating what punches and kicks she could.

Finally, Staci connected with a sweeping hook kick that caught Chase behind the right knee and he crumpled over backward onto the mat. She reached for the syringe and pulled it out. With one very smooth movement, she brought the syringe out, pulled off the cap, and thrust it at Chase's abdomen. But Chase rolled to the side and kicked her hand, knocking the syringe out of her hand and sending it across the mat. It landed ten feet from the three UC, Santa Barbara students. Amy ran over and picked it up.

Chase jumped to his feet and was setting up into a bow stance when Staci stepped straight into him, planted her right foot on his leg just above his left knee that was bent forward, leaped up and into him and connected with the inside of her left thigh to the right side of Chase's head. Chase went down hard, and Staci took advantage of the moment.

She looked over at Amy and extended her right arm. Amy tossed her the syringe and Staci caught it by the handle. She quickly shoved it into Chase's right thigh, injecting the sedative. Then she quickly stepped aside, correctly anticipating that he would make one last desperate attempt to take her out. Chase managed to spin over onto his side and whip his left leg around in a sweeping arc, his foot catching Staci's ankle and flipping her over onto her back.

Had she not been able to inject Chase with the sedative, it would have been disastrous for Staci as she was momentarily in a compromising position. But the sedative was already in Chase's bloodstream, infiltrating his brain and shutting down his five senses. He began to lift himself up onto all fours but quickly collapsed back onto the mats.

Physically, mentally, and emotionally spent, Staci walked around the edges of the training room. She left Chase on the center of the mats. He was breathing fast and his head spun, while his mind moved back and forth between consciousness and darkness. Staci was breathing hard and trying to shake off the effects of Chase's punches and kicks. She still hadn't fully healed from their previous encounter a week earlier, and Chase had targeted the same areas of her body he had hit back at his house, along with her left knee this time.

"That was a great fight, Staci," Amy shouted out as Staci circled around toward her and her fellow students.

"I have to admit, I was getting worried," Tory said. "A few times I thought I might have to shoot Chase with his own gun."

"Are you alright?" Phil asked. "Is there anything we can do?"

"No, thanks. I have the situation well under control," she replied, still walking around the outer edges of the mats, her hands on her hips, trying to slow her heart rate and breathing to normal levels.

Staci walked back to Cheung Yu Shiquin's office, stepping over the three dead men that sprawled on the red carpet, and retrieved her knives, hood, mask, and the two suitcases. Reappearing in the training room, she walked back to Chase at the center of the mats.

"Thanks for showing up, Amy. We could not possibly do this without you. And I'm glad to finally meet all of you in person."

"No worries. Glad we could help," she replied with alacrity, her eyes wide open with a look of excitement and fascination as she stared at the two suitcases Staci held in her hands. "Tory, Phil, and I have waited so long to get a look at all of our hard work."

Staci smiled back, her sea-green eyes glistening with anticipation at finally being able to demonstrate the power of their cumulative hard work, sacrifices, and countless sleepless nights. "You won't believe your eyes. Trust me on this one. You couldn't possibly imagine what we've accomplished together without seeing a demonstration of the breakthrough."

She punched a few coordinates into the keypad and laid the transporter on the floor. Then she grabbed Chase's keys out of his pocket and tossed them to Amy. In her right hand she held the receiver that Chase had taken from Nicky at the Starbucks in Cambridge and bent down and picked Chase up with her free arm around his waist. Chase was still too groggy to resist, let alone stop her from transporting him back to Massachusetts.

Staci looked over at her cross-country colleagues. "I wish we had time to talk more, but I really need to get Chase and this suitcase back to Cambridge."

"We understand," Amy replied. "I'm sure we'll meet up again."

"Be careful with the receiver suitcase, Amy. Of course, you know it's loaded with a live battery. Again, I really wish we could spend more time together and talk about things."

"No worries, sister. We'll take care of the suitcase along with the two guns and Chase's car."

Amy stepped back and took her place in the middle of Tory and Phil, and they watched in utter amazement as an orange and yellow corona appeared and Staci stepped into it dragging Chase along with her. In a moment, they and the corona vanished. They simply ceased to be there anymore. All Amy and her two male friends could do was stand in place for a few minutes, totally stunned, staring straight ahead, not uttering a word.

Meanwhile, at the exact same moment in time that Staci and Chase left Laguna Beach, Calif., they appeared in the middle of Khyati's living room in Cambridge, Mass. Nicholas Fischer Jr., Khyati Dasmunsi, the Guu, Mina Nguyen, and Christopher Thompson anxiously sat on the sofa and chairs in the living room. All of the drapes and curtains were closed, but the lights remained on so the corona of light appearing with Staci and Chase would not look so bright that it would attract the attention of anyone who might be passing by the house.

Staci stood in the center of Khyati's living room. Dropping Chase to the floor, he fell into a sprawling heap of limp limbs. In her arms, she held the black receiver suitcase that Chase took from them at the Starbucks a few days earlier. Three feet in front of her was the other receiver suitcase Nicky employed to bring her back. The five observers paused in total wonder and amazement, then began clapping as they stood up and approached Staci and Chase.

Nicky was the first to reach Staci. Taking the suitcase from her hand, he set it down on the floor and gave her a long hug that she received with a glad heart. The Guu picked up both receiver suitcases and set them aside. "I'll make sure these don't fall into anyone else's hands again," he said glaring at Chase, trying to contain the anger that had built up inside of him since their first encounter a few days earlier in the stairwell at the Intercontinental Boston Hotel.

Chase was still groggy. He was barely cognizant of his surroundings, but he was aware that he was with Staci and Nicky. He had to concentrate with all of his remaining faculties to make out the Guu's voice, which sounded distant and garbled. Looking up, Chase saw more shadows of erect bodies than the number of blended voices that he heard. He tried to estimate how many people were in the room, but just raising his head up invoked a sea of dizziness and nausea. Light and darkness took turns replacing each other as he tried to balance himself on the floor against the spinning sensations that threatened to overwhelm him.

Chase sincerely thought he was going to die right there on the living-room floor. The other people in the room gathered around him in a tight circle. Someone had bent over, grabbed him by his shirt, and picked him up. Chase struggled to plant his feet on the floor. It was easier than he thought it would be as the guy lifting him up was considerably shorter than he was. Chase looked at the oversized head with no neck sitting on a pair of thick shoulders. *"This has to be the Guu,"* Chase thought, *"and this can't be good."*

Planting his feet firmly on the floor, Chase bent his knees and lunged forward in one move, head butting the Guu on the bridge of his nose. Although Chase was in no position to judge the extent of the Guu's injury, he knew that the force of the blow had caused serious damage and it must have hurt like hell. The others in the group jumped on him from all sides. On his way to the floor, Chase thrust out his left hand, palm up and fingers folded in, connecting with somebody somewhere on their face. Once on the floor, facedown with four other people on top of him, Chase felt a needle penetrate his right thigh. He tried to fight back, but within moments, the blackness of the abyss of space and time overpowered his waking senses, and he quickly surrendered to the bottomless ocean of a deep sleep.

Chapter 71
Nicky's Pissed

CHASE WASN'T SURE how long he had been unconscious. It took a few minutes just to raise his head. His first waking sight was the same as his last one before he passed out: shadowy figures hovering over him and distant voices blending together. But within a few minutes, the blended shadows began to take singular forms and he was able to distinguish tones and pitches between the muffled voices.

His head rolled from side to side as his senses became more in tune with their environment. He knew he had been drooling. He could also feel a soft nylon rope wrapped tightly around his wrists that were tied to the back of the wooden chair he was sitting in. His ankles were also bound together.

Chase took a few controlled deep breaths. Soon, he was able to hold his head up straight. He did not recognize any of his physical surroundings. Looking at the wallpaper, Chase wondered if he had been transported back to a time long before he was born. The trim around the door and the crown molding were wide, ornate, and dark. The ceiling and walls looked like they were made from plaster rather than drywall. He began to make out doily ornamental heirlooms on the table next to him that he remembered seeing in his grandparents' house.

Chase understood he had been transported back to Boston, the place he left only a few days earlier with his best friends. Now he was back, alone, and with the most dangerous people he ever met. He saw Nicky bend down a couple of feet in front of him, hands on his knees, staring him straight in the eyes. Staci was there, too. So was the Guu. Three other people were also in the room that he had never seen before: a pretty young girl from India, another young girl with Asian features, and a white male about the same age as the Asian woman.

Nicky lightly slapped Chase a few times on his left cheek to expedite the waking process. "Hey there, hot shot. How are you feeling?"

Chase spit in Nicky's face. He was repulsed that the guy had touched him, let alone slapped him in the face. He tried to struggle free, but he was secured tightly to the solid oak chair.

Showing restraint and self-control, Nicky acted as if he were already prepared for such a reaction from his captive. He pulled out a handkerchief from his pocket and wiped the spittle off his nose and cheeks. "That's OK, Chase. No worries, as you Southern Californians like to say." Nicky smiled and took his time folding his handkerchief back up into a near-perfect small square and placing it back into his shirt pocket.

Staci wasn't sure if Nicky would explode at Chase for spitting in his face. She believed that, deep down, he was gentle and altruistic with a heart of gold for his fellow man. She knew that as a child, Nicky wanted to be a veterinarian and help animals. In high school, he was involved in local charity groups to help the less fortunate and deliver meals to the poor and the elderly during the holidays.

But Nicky detested Chase with a deep and passionate aversion. Chase stood up to him. He quickly figured out that Nicky was behind the murders and that he framed his father for the heinous crimes. Chase physically tracked him down at the Starbucks a few days ago. Nicky never suspected that any of that could possibly happen. Chase also found out that they had the means of opening and closing wormholes and had been successfully traveling through them. He flew across the country and arranged an interview with his jailed father. He punched Nicky in the face and stole two of his suitcases. And worst of all, Nicky allowed Staci to sleep with Chase, a decision that he now deeply regretted. Nicky despised Chase, and she could tell that he was beside himself with Chase sitting in front of him, bound in a chair, and still somewhat sedated and at his mercy.

"You know, Chase," Nicky said as he circled the chair in the center of Khyati's basement, enclosed and separated from her extensive and highly sophisticated computer room, "I used to think that you were just a fool. I thought you were acting out of stupidity when you first caught wind of what was happening here. I thought after Staci almost killed you that you would count your blessings and have the common sense to just walk away."

Chase listened to Nicky, pretending to be more sedated than he really was. At the same time, he tried to gather more of his faculties and his strength. He assessed how tightly his hands and feet were bound. He knew he would not be able to break the nylon rope or loosen the knots that fastened him securely to the chair.

The chair was old and made of solid oak. Chase would not be able to break the integrity of its strength. But it did sit on four casters and the flooring was made of smooth linoleum, and Chase thought that he could use his feet to give him at least one good push in any direction. He doubted if that would help him, but it was an option he could use if he felt that he was about to die.

Nicky continued, "But you're no fool, Chase. I realize that now. And you do have balls. You've got gonads of steel." Nicky had his hands behind his back as he continued to circle Chase. "I bet if I kicked you in the balls right now, I'd probably break all of my toes."

Most of the others in the room chuckled. One laugh that was missing was Staci's. Chase looked over to his right where she sat on a folding chair, her elbows on her knees and leaning into Chase. She stared intently at him without expression, her lips slightly parted and her sea-green eyes wide open. He looked back at Nicky, now pacing back and forth in front of him, still rambling, but the meaning of the words were not resonating in Chase's mind.

The Guu sat on a sofa behind Nicky and directly in front of Chase about ten feet away. He wore a scowl on his face, along with a very large patch of gauze taped across the bridge of his swollen, purple, broken nose. He was actually snarling. Chase noticed the dark brown-paneled walls directly behind the Guu and the green shag carpet. There was other furniture in the room, all of it old and nothing really matching, but it was spotless. He felt that he had been not only transported through space, but time as well. All Chase could do was smile at the Guu while the Asian strongman reciprocated with more snarls and extreme facial expressions of anger.

Meanwhile, Nicky continued to pace and ramble. Chase looked around the room, and saw the Indian girl with her right eye swollen shut sitting on a large sofa chair next to the Guu, typing away at a laptop. Obviously, she was the recipient of his left palm. Chase looked at the young petite woman sitting quietly, with a green, traditional, embroidered Kashmir shawl wrapped around her shoulders. He wondered how a nice-looking girl like her could end up with a group of psychotic misfits like this. She coldly glanced at Chase with her one good eye, then focused her attention back to her laptop.

The Asian girl and the Caucasian male sat together on a large sitting chair to Chase's left. They were clearly a couple. The girl spoke, "How are you feeling, Prof. Manhattan? The sedative should be wearing off by now. Don't be alarmed. I'm a chemist. You won't die from the dosage I administered."

Her boyfriend laughed darkly, "At least not from the sedative."

Nicky was still talking. "Do you know why we spared your life tonight, Chase? Please, don't try to answer. Allow me to explain. You see, we have only six suitcases, three transporters and three receivers. But due to the events of the past ten days, I realize these suitcases can be stolen by the right people with the proper motivation. We, and by 'we,' I mean my group of friends here, believe we are almost ready to make our own suitcases. The problem we have is that we do not know how to stabilize wormholes so they won't collapse. Translation: I still don't know how my father and Dr. Newcombe successfully transported objects through a stable wormhole. I don't have their secrets, and clearly my father isn't going to give them to me at this point."

Chase felt a shiver rise up his spine then descend back down. Nicky stopped pacing and bent over, nose to nose with his captive.

"But I now know that my father gave *you* the information regarding his breakthrough. He didn't give it *me*. No. Instead, he gave it to *you*."

Standing up straight, Nicky began pacing back and forth again. "For some unknown reason, you gained his trust, and he gave this information to you—you, an outsider from Southern California, of all people. Now, there are currently only two people on the face of this planet who know how all of this works: my father and *you*."

Nicky emphasized *you*. He stopped pacing again. Chase knew that the idea of Prof. Fischer confiding in Chase and not his only son ate away at Nicky from the inside. It was slowly manifesting itself in rage, jealousy, and hatred toward Chase.

"What the hell are you talking about?" Chase shouted loudly. "You're mad. Do you know that? You're absolutely nuts, Nicky."

"Oh, am I?" Nicky shouted back, his speech accelerating faster. He was once again up close in Chase's face. "I'm nuts? Let me tell you what's crazy and what isn't crazy. What's crazy is my father and Dr. Newcombe allowing this world-changing breakthrough to be used for corporate greed, to pad a publicly traded company's quarterly earnings, to make their shareholders happy, and to allow their top management to receive outlandish bonuses while much of the rest of the world suffers needlessly in poverty, Chase. *That's* what's crazy."

"You had a lot of people killed, Nicky. You're mad. You know it, I know it, and so does everyone else in this room."

Nicky slowed down and paused before speaking again, this time in a milder and more controlled tone, stepping away from Chase. "Let me tell you what else is wrong with this picture, Chase. My father wanted only glory and a stupid Nobel Peace Prize so he could parade that stupid medallion around his neck at social gatherings of the world's so-called greatest minds. Don't you think that's crazy, Chase?"

"Your father is a fine man, a very good man, who only has the best intentions for mankind to benefit from this breakthrough."

"*Pffhhhhhh*" Nicky said with a dismissive hand. "Are you as crazy as he is? Don't you get it? The only people who stood to benefit from this once-in-a-lifetime breakthrough were the investors who would gain billions. The only thing these greedy old bastards care about is making more money."

There was only silence in the room. Nobody said a word. Nobody moved. Every eye was fixated on Nicky. Chase noticed they all looked mesmerized as they watched him pace and talk, gesticulating with his hands and animated body motions to authenticate his diatribe. Chase now saw Nicky in a new light. He was a very charismatic leader, almost as a cult figure, with his followers hanging on every word that proceeded from his mouth.

Chase now asked the $64,000 question: "Tell me, Nicky, just what do *you* expect to gain from all of this?"

Nicky laughed below his breath and looked around at the others in the room who remained sitting silently, surprised that someone had the audacity to question his leadership. "I'll tell you what we're going to do, Chase. We're going to destroy the New World Order that has its tentacles in every society on earth today."

"What? What the hell are you talking about? What New World Order?"

"Are you so gullible? Look around you. There's a quest for global domination today, as there has been in every generation before us. It's nothing new. Alexander the Great wanted it, and he came pretty close to accomplishing his objective. So did Rome. Genghis Khan had the same vision. Napoleon had it, too. So did Hitler. Look at the age of imperialism and colonialism, Chase. The British once boasted that the sun never set on their empire. The list goes on and on." Nicky was now shouting again and flailing his arms up in the air.

Chase was trying to sort through what Nicky was saying, but the effects of the sedative were still present and he was beginning to get a massive headache.

"Who's trying to gain global domination now?" Chase asked with much skepticism.

"Don't you keep abreast of current events? Maybe you're not as smart as I gave you credit for. Listen to me. Look at how the world is shifting toward free trade. Look at the recent free trade agreements such as NAFTA that break down individual barriers such as tariffs and protectionism. Australia and Japan have a free-trade relationship. Look at the Asia Pacific Economic Cooperation. And I assume you've heard of the euro, haven't you. Do you see any patterns forming, *Einstein*?"

Chase was starting to comprehend where Nicky was going with this. "There have always been free-trade agreements since man first engaged in commerce. The Silk Road extended more than 5,000 miles and connected China with Asia Minor and the Mediterranean. That free-trade route helped to develop great civilizations such as China,

Persia, Mesopotamia, Egypt, and Rome. I think *you* need another course in history, *Einstein*."

"Hmm," Nicky slowly let out. "OK, so my opinion of your intelligence just rose a notch. But let's dig a little deeper, *Einstein*. Free-trade agreements lead us to more common and uniform currencies besides the euro. Do you know that in a few years, construction will begin on a NAFTA 10-lane superhighway that will extend from deep inside Mexico through the heartland of America and directly into Canada? How far off can a NAFTA common currency be? How far off can a global currency be, Chase?"

"So what does this all mean, Nicky? Why all the murders?"

"Collateral damage, that's all. Necessary for the greater good."

"And you'll obviously try to kill more people, isn't that right, Nicky? You're not finished, are you?"

"Listen to me. It's the world's central bankers that are behind this entire façade. They're the ones making the rules and wielding all the power. Remember the golden rule: he who has the most gold makes the rules. It's not just a catchy cliché, Chase. It's the way the world runs today. They have a monopoly over money and credit."

"You're not going to start talking about the Illuminati, are you? Spare me the conspiracy theories. I already know you're crazy."

"No conspiracy theories here, Chase. Maybe there really is an Illuminati, Free Masons, or a Bilderberg group. Maybe not. Call them what you want. But for the sake of conversation, let's just call them elitists and globalists. It's common knowledge these people already use their power to influence social and political power. The next step is to control it. In its least common denominator, it pits the families who control the world's money against the societies that they lend to. And guess who wins?"

"I'm waiting for the slave theory. We're all slaves to these central banks, right?"

Nicky smiled. "You say that facetiously, Chase, yet that's basically the truth. You believe in the Bible, don't you? I know you do. We've been profiling you for almost two weeks now. There's a verse in Proverbs that tells us a rich person rules over poor people, and a borrower is a slave to a lender. Not only do they use money and credit to make us their slaves, they're also the ones who instigate war, immorality, and the disintegration of the nuclear family."

"So what do you plan to do, Nicky? How are you going to stop all of this and make the world a better place?"

Nicky stood still for a few moments, shocked that Chase was not making the connections he was explaining. Chase, still bound to the oak chair, looked around the room at the rest of the group. They looked different than they had even a few minutes ago. Every soul in the room was fixated on Nicky. Chase was freaked out by realizing he was witnessing the beginning stages of a cult that could very well alter world events very quickly.

"You're about to witness what I'm going to do tomorrow, Chase. You'll see firsthand exactly how this all works. You're going to watch Staci use a wormhole to assassinate one of the most powerful and influential people in the world."

Chase couldn't believe what he was hearing. He was able to foil one of Nicky's plots by stealing the suitcase at Starbucks. However, he was now a prisoner. He was without the aid of his friends, and he was in no position to foil another murder scheme. He responded to Nicky's threat. "Who exactly is this person, Nicky? You've already killed a state senator. Are you going after the president this time?"

Nicky laughed in a most condescending manner. "No, *Einstein*, it isn't the president. I said we're going after someone who is one of the most powerful people in the world. In fact, you may have never even heard of him, but he sits atop one of the largest financial institutions known, and he finances urban development projects on a global scale for developing countries. To help these governments build these massive infrastructures, he also provides the necessary means to secure slave labor from around the world to build the roads, bridges, and massive skyscrapers—at less than a dollar an hour."

"What do you hope to accomplish by killing a few individuals? They'll quickly be replaced by somebody else. That's not going to alter world events."

"Not quite, Chase. The individual we assassinate will be difficult, if not impossible, to replace due to the networks that he's been able to maintain. True, killing him won't necessarily change the existing New World Order. But that's only *half* the plan." Nicky smiled triumphantly as he continued his discourse while his group of followers watched in silence. "We're also going to use a wormhole to deliver one of these suitcases to the World Trade Organization's headquarters in Geneva. Once the beautiful Staci Bevere hides a suitcase in one of the offices and returns home safely, the suitcase with the uranium and plutonium material will be set to explode." Staci briefly stood up and smiled and posed as if she were a showcase model on a daytime television game show.

Chase was horrified at the picture Nicky was painting. "You're going to blow up a city just to kill people and destroy a global organization? Is this what you consider *collateral damage?*"

Nicky laughed out loud. "Relax, Chase. We're not going to blow up the entire city of Geneva. Each suitcase has enough energy for six uses. Once five are used up, we'll plant it inside the WTO's headquarters and detonate it. The explosion will be small compared to what a fully loaded suitcase would be capable of. The blast will only destroy about one half of a square mile."

Chase quickly did the math in his head. He knew Geneva sat on a plateau and that a nuclear blast would not be hindered by the surrounding Jura Mountains. That was the bad news. Prof. Fischer told Chase that the suitcases contained the equivalent of one-kiloton of fissionable material. As a physicist, Chase understood that a ground blast would be less effective than an explosion in the air. That was the good news.

Chase concluded that one-sixth of the energy in the one-kiloton blast would vaporize everything within a 500-foot radius of the explosion. The blast wave would level or cause severe damage to buildings up to a quarter of a mile from ground zero. Damage and casualties would extend another quarter mile out. Although limited, there was the matter of the fallout. Depending on the time of day and weather conditions, the casualties could easily be in the hundreds or even the thousands.

"You'll never get away with it," Chase shouted, straining in vain to break the nylon ropes that bound his hands to the oak chair behind his back. "Someone will stop you. Just as I was able to stop you once, someone else will also find out what you're up to and stop you."

Nicky wasn't laughing any more. His countenance changed. He again bent down and directly stared in Chase's face. "You've been a real pain in the ass, you know that, Chase? As a matter of fact, you frustrated our previous assassination attempt when you stole my suitcase from Starbucks. We were going to carry out the assassination that day. But I can assure you, I won't allow that to happen a second time. We're going to carry this same assassination out tomorrow, and you are going to sit in that chair and witness Staci using a wormhole to kill our target and safely return. So just sit tight and behave, or Mina will have to administer another injection that will ensure you'll not foil my attempt a second time."

Chapter 72
Five Amigos Fight Back

SUSAN ANDERSON SAT at Chase's desk in his office. Call it women's intuition, but she knew something was not right. She called Chase's cell phone. Chase should have answered but didn't. She left a quick message and repeated the process a few minutes later.

She called Cheung Yu Shiquin's studio. No answer. She called it two more times. Still no answer. Chase told Susan that Cheung Yu Shiquin always had coverage, and that his assistant always picked up the phone. He *never* missed a call.

Susan dialed Bennie who was at home catching up on negotiations with a commercial real estate deal he was deeply involved with. Carol sat on the sofa watching the end of *Déjà Vu*. He picked up on the first ring.

"Bennie, Chase isn't answering his cell phone, and neither is anyone at the studio he went to about an hour ago."

Bennie stood up from his desk, grabbed his keys, and headed for the front door. "We're on our way over to the studio. It's only ten minutes from here. I'll meet you there. I'll also call Fred and let him know we're driving over there."

Bennie was the first to arrive. He pulled into the driveway, parked, and got out. He saw three parked cars, but Chase's Mercedes was ominously missing. He tried to enter the building, but the door was locked. Pounding loudly, he hoped someone would hear him and unlock the door. After a few more futile attempts, he walked around the small one-story building, failing to find another door. There were no windows on either side of the studio or on the back wall. He came back around the front and tried looking in the glass door and one small window. Someone had turned off all the lights inside. *That's strange,* he thought, as there were still three cars in the parking lot.

Nancy pulled in with Fred in the passenger seat, and Bennie filled them in. Susan arrived two minutes later. They suspected something was terribly wrong. "I'm going to call the police," Bennie said. "Maybe they can get inside."

Fred interjected. "I think at this point, we should call the police and leave an anonymous tip that there's foul play suspected here. I think it's best if we stay nameless at this point. We always keep a few prepaid disposable cell phones we buy from Wal-Mart. I can call them from one of those and then throw the phone away." Opening her trunk, Nancy pulled one out and gave it to Fred.

"Do you always carry those around with you?" Bennie asked, as if to say the extra precautions were unnecessary.

Fred smiled confidently, conveying he was right and Bennie was wrong. "You'd be surprised how often we have to use these."

Fred dialed the Laguna Beach Police Department and with sense of urgency told the police there was foul play inside the studio. The five then got in their cars and drove over to Fred's house.

Once inside, Fred led them to a very large furnished room with wall-to-wall electronic equipment that closely rivaled Khyati's basement.

"We'll use the simplest and least expensive device in here to follow the action—a police scanner." Fred knew exactly where to look for the frequency for the Laguna Beach Police Department.

They listened in horror as the officer that led the team of four police officers, Capt. Chappell, detailed what he saw over the police radio as he walked into Cheung Yu Shiquin's office. Susan was the most terrified at the news of three dead bodies. She knew that Cheung Yu Shiquin had an assistant, and assumed the worst about the third body.

However, after hearing the descriptions that all three were of Asian descent, her terror dissipated and she knew that Chase was still alive. Somewhere. Someplace. Just not in Laguna Beach. Fred had to remind

Susan and everyone else in the room that Staci had more than likely showed up and took Chase back to Boston through a wormhole. In other words, he was probably being held captive 3,000 miles away.

Nancy stayed behind to monitor the movements of Nicky and Staci while Fred, Bennie, Susan, and Carol all moved into the living room. Fred wore his lucky Detroit Tigers baseball cap and poked fun at Bennie for donning a Red Sox cap while in Boston. Carol volunteered to make coffee and tea. It was late in the evening, and everyone needed something to give them a little boost of energy as they strategized their next moves.

"It's clear to me what we have to do," Susan started. Of the five sitting in the living room, she, by far, looked the most haggard of the group. The stress from the events of the past week, coupled with the air travel and the daily fast food, had begun to take their toll on all of them. "We have to go back to Boston immediately. All the flights have left John Wayne Airport for tonight so we'll have to call Matthew Ciralsky and have him make arrangements to fly out tomorrow. If we can get the same charter plane, we will."

"You can count on us to go," Bennie said right away, placing his arm around Carol's shoulders.

"Absolutely. Bennie and I are here to do whatever we can, Susan," Carol added, walking over to Susan and putting her arm around her. "Don't you worry about a thing. We know Chase is still alive. Fred and Nancy will track down his exact whereabouts, and we'll get him back home safely, I promise you that."

Nancy, listening in on the conversation from the bedroom down the hall, appeared in the living room and walked over to Susan's other side. "That's right, Susan," she said with an assuring hug. "We'll bring Chase back."

Fred took the lead in outlining the strategy. "Nancy and I will find out who else is working with Nicky and Staci. They must have someone who is capable of hacking into Chase's personal information and tracking his whereabouts. They are our counterparts."

"I'd like to hack into Chase's computer at home and look for signs of a black hat. I should be able to do this discreetly and then trace it back to its original source," Nancy added.

Breakthrough

"Nancy and I have a long night ahead of us. Susan, you call Matthew Ciralsky and have him set up the earliest flight out of John Wayne Airport. Then get some sleep. There's nothing you can do now, and you'll need to be well rested for what you'll have to do in Boston," Fred advised.

Bennie looked at Susan, then at Fred. "We're going to Boston, too. The three of us." He again put his arm around Carol.

"The couch folds out into a sleeper. You can sleep there, Bennie. Susan, you and Carol can sleep in our bed. We'll wake you up at 5 a.m."

Fred and Nancy took control of the night's events and made sure that Susan, Bennie, and Carol slept while they organized the trip's logistics. Matthew had told them he was almost certain he could arrange the flight to Boston in the morning. Fred and Nancy now had to work through the night and set up a network of help in the Northeast that would provide support once Susan, Bennie, and Carol were in Boston.

Chapter 73
Back to Boston

IT WAS JUST AFTER 8:00 A.M., and the Falcon 50EX waited on the tarmac, its 3 Garrett TFE731-3-1C engines running. The same pilot, co-pilot, and flight attendants were on the plane executing their final tasks before takeoff. Matthew did a terrific job at pulling some late-night and early-morning strings to get the flight scheduled for takeoff so quickly. Susan had to let Matthew in on a few of the details and tell him that Chase's life was in danger. Matthew was more than willing to help, and made himself available to assist them in any other way possible.

Fred made sure that Matthew, Bennie, Susan, and Carol didn't use any of their credit cards or bank accounts to finance this trip. He knew that somebody in Boston would be monitoring at least Chase's accounts, if not the rest of the group's, so Fred fronted the bill, partly with Chase's retainer and partly from his own money that he funneled through an account he previously set up under a fictitious identity. People in his line of business couldn't be too careful. He couldn't use any of Chase's accounts that Matthew had access to since that would set off an immediate red flag with whoever was monitoring Chase. Fred trusted Chase to settle accounts later.

There was still one door left open that the black hat on the East Coast could conceivably use to monitor the Falcon 50EX and see the plane's itinerary, once again departing Orange County for Boston. They may even know of Bennie's, Susan's, and Carol's identity by now and see that they were booked again on this flight. Unfortunately, there was nothing Fred could do on short notice to alter their identities. However, he did book a different hotel for them under a second false identity. He was reluctant to use the Intercontinental Boston this time, even though that would have given the three a sense of familiarity and perhaps made their job a little easier.

Bennie, Susan, and Carol jogged out to the plane with nothing but the wrinkled clothes on their backs and two laptops that Fred provided. They didn't even have time to go home and get their coats. Nancy had a jacket and two sweaters that somewhat fit Carol, who carried them in a gym bag Fred let her use. They would have to do some shopping in Boston for clothes using cash that Fred provided. Chase's tab with Fred was rising by the minute.

Once in flight, the three, per Fred's orders, relaxed in their seats, closed their eyes, and tried to get some rest. At least they had a hearty breakfast prepared by Fred, the self-proclaimed master of pancakes. Nancy had prepared fresh fruit for them and packed turkey sandwiches and carrot sticks for the flight.

Not much was said during the first few hours. Flying at 42,000 feet and at 450 mph, they had almost seven hours to rest. By the time they were on the ground in Boston and set up in their hotel rooms, Fred and Nancy would have a step-by-step plan of action laid out for them.

Susan was the first to doze off as she took a Dramamine to help combat motion sickness. Carol saw her lying comfortably across two seats and soon followed her lead, lying across the two seats opposite Susan. Bennie leaned to the right of his seat and positioned a pillow between his head and the side of the fuselage. It took him longer to fall asleep as he faded in and out of consciousness, but he soon drifted off into slumberland.

Like the previous trip a few days ago, Bennie was the first to awaken, opening his eyes over the Allegheny Mountains in central Pennsylvania. He opened the visor and peeked out over the snow-white landscape. A shiver ran up his spine as he remembered he didn't have anything heavier than the long sleeve shirt and light jacket he was wearing. The lean and thin Fred Merrill didn't have anything in his closet that would come close to fitting Bennie. Closing his eyes again, he imagined taking the afternoon off from work and playing a couple of rounds at Pelican Hill with a cooler in the golf cart full of ice-cold Heinekens.

The Falcon 50EX touched down at 5:30 p.m. EST. Bennie, Susan, and Carol braved the frigid air of the Northeast one more time, making a mad dash for the terminal. They received numerous glares and a few snide remarks from just about everybody they passed, from the flight attendants to the airport employees working the tarmac, to the passengers who saw them enter the terminal severely underdressed for the mid-February weather. Susan made a quick call to Fred and Nancy to let them know they had arrived safely. Fred told her to go to the hotel and take a long hot bath as he and Nancy would need another hour to tie up things.

This time, Bennie led them to the National Car Rental counter. Although Fred changed the rental company from Hertz to National, he again rented a Ford Excursion because it could hold up under heavy winter conditions and provide a fast, roomy getaway vehicle for bringing Chase back to the hotel. They were out of the airport in a matter of a few minutes, and Bennie was driving to the brownstone Eliot Hotel on Commonwealth Avenue on the Boston side of the Charles River directly across from the MIT campus.

Leaving the Excursion with the valet, the three went to check in. The doorman ushered them into the split-level marble lobby that was decorated in a neo-Georgian style. The blend of historic glamour and traditional comfort was in direct contrast to the more modern Intercontinental Boston they stayed at earlier.

Bennie checked them in at the front desk, and they showed themselves up to their rooms on the eighth floor as they only had Carol's sole bag to carry along with their computer bags. Their deluxe suites overlooked the Back Bay and gave them a panoramic view of the MIT campus.

Bennie and Carol went to their room and took hot showers. Susan went to her room and took a long relaxing bath while trying to sort through the events of the past week and try to decipher how she had ended up in one of key roles of a transcontinental murder scheme that threatened life as she knew it.

Chapter 74
The War Room

Susan dressed and invited Bennie and Carol to her room, where they set up a speaker phone and called Fred and Nancy. Carol turned on Fred's two laptops.

"Thanks again, you two, for all that you've done. There is no way that we could do this without you," Susan said in a well rested and refreshed tone.

"No worries, everybody. We're all in this together, remember?" Fred replied.

"Okay, this is what we have so far," Nancy chimed in. "I've been able to find out who has been tracing Chase. It wasn't easy, and that's an understatement."

"That's great," Susan said, feeling a surge of hope well up in her heart.

"Well, don't get too excited. I don't have their names yet. But I did identify at least one back door they left on Chase's home computer. They could come and go as they pleased and pretty much record most, if not all, of Chase's movements. It's only a matter of time before I can backtrack, so to speak, and locate the exact location these people are using. Then I can get their names and profiles soon after."

"That's a good start. I'm feeling better already," Bennie said.

Fred quickly interjected. "Don't, Bennie. In fact, you should feel less safe than you did yesterday. Whoever hacked into Chase's computer also looked into the activity on his American Express card, along with all of his other accounts. We know that they are aware of the original chartered flight to Boston, and it only makes sense that they would want to know who else was booked on that plane."

Susan was stunned and felt like Fred had dropped a bomb in the midst of her room. "Fred, how can you be sure about this?"

"Think about it, Susan. They see a charge for more than $30,000 to book an immediate chartered flight from Orange County to Boston. Don't you think they'd make it a high priority to find out who else was with Chase on that plane?"

Carol's jaw dropped as she gasped. "You mean they *know* about the three of us? Our identities, what we look like, and where we live?"

"I'm sure of it, Carol," Nancy continued. "These people aren't stupid. We assume that whoever is connected with Nicky and Staci, they are most likely MIT students as well. That school has a reputation for producing some of the world's best computer hackers. They're bright, talented, and imaginative, and they're some of the best in the world at what they do."

Fred allowed the muted silence fill the conversation as there was a sense of fear and a loss of their personal well-being. Bennie finally broke the silence. "So what do we do now?"

"Fred and I will make it look like you three are still in Orange County. We made some, *ahem*, purchases on your ATM and credit cards today at some local gas stations and grocery stores."

"However, if they decide to follow up on the Falcon 50EX and see that it made another flight to Boston, then they'll know that you're back in town," Fred continued.

"And they'll also be looking for us, as they'll have to assume that someone back here has been making it look like you're still in Orange County," Nancy added. "We're sure that they know your profiles by now, and that none of you pose a threat as a computer hacker. So it's safe to assume they'll be looking to identify us, just as we are trying to identify them."

"So it's a foot race," Bennie said, "to see who finds who first. That means we need to find Chase tonight. Not tomorrow. *Tonight.*"

"I'm not confident that we can find his location by tonight, Bennie," Nancy explained. "Even with some of the most sophisticated equipment available, our expertise, and our network of friends, this still takes time. We have to be stealthy as we try and identify all the players and where they are. We can't just burst in. We'll give ourselves away, and then they'll disappear altogether."

Bennie was pacing now, but Susan noticed he looked confident, like he had a backup plan. "Out with it, Bennie," she said. "What's going on inside of your head right now?"

Bennie replied, "Fred, what are Nicky and Staci up to right now? Do you know what they'll be doing tonight?"

"I was just getting to that," Nancy said. "Nicky is at one of his father's labs at MIT, and Staci goes to her gym at eight o'clock every Tuesday and Thursday night for an intense, two-hour aerobic workout in Cambridge. She always goes home after her workout and orders Chinese food. She's done this same routine for eight months straight."

Bennie stopped in front of the desk where the speaker phone was set up and grabbed the edge with both hands. "OK, everybody, here's my plan." Bennie's harmless, pudgy face was gone, replaced with his best hard-line negotiator's countenance.

"Fred, I need your contact in Connecticut that you used to track Nicky and Staci last week to come to the hotel right away. I need two things from him." Bennie sighed as he looked at Carol, and then Susan. "I need a small handgun, and I need a stun gun. And I need them by nine o'clock. *Tonight.*"

There was more silence, and Susan and Carol looked at Bennie as if he were out of his mind.

"Forget it, Bennie. We can't go that route," Fred said emphatically.

"Just hear me out. I don't need the gun to be loaded. But I do need the stun gun to be capable of rendering a human helpless in a few seconds."

"What are you saying, Bennie?"

"I'm saying that we need to meet Staci as she's leaving her gym and take her as a hostage. Then we trade her straight-up for Chase."

Susan promptly stood up. "Bennie, that's a *really* bad idea. We can't just kidnap Staci. That's really crossing the line. We could go to prison for that."

"Not to mention that capturing a wild elephant would be easier than taking down Staci," Carol added.

More silence. Then Fred spoke. "Actually, this is probably the best plan, people. We really can't wait, as Chase probably does not have a long life span at this point. These people are desperate, and will do anything to extract the information they are looking for from him. And once they have that, they'll kill him."

Susan and Carol were still stunned. Bennie continued. "Can you do it, Fred? All I need is an unloaded handgun and the stun gun by nine o'clock. We'll handle the rest on our end."

"My guy's good, but I'm not sure about the stun gun. Let me get on this. I'll call you back as soon as I know."

"In the meantime, we'll go downstairs and get some dinner. By the way, great sandwiches today, Nancy. They really tied us over," Bennie added.

Nancy was glad that she could do more to help than merely perform research in a room behind closed doors with the shades drawn. Fred ended the call, and the three California transplants went downstairs to enjoy the cuisine at Clio's and map out their strategy.

Chapter 75
Mr. Bennett

Susan was enjoying her crunchy sautéed Atlantic halibut as best she could. She was thinking back two weeks when her biggest concern was what color to paint her condominium walls to compliment her hardwood floors and new area rugs. Now she was about to participate in a kidnapping that involved tasering the most dangerous person she had ever come across. It was still to be determined who would actually pull the trigger.

Bennie still had his game face on as he worked on his slow-roasted Kobe rib eye au poivre while Carol ate sweet butter-basted Maine lobster. The mood was somber and the conversation light. When they finished their meals, no one had an appetite for dessert, so they ordered coffee.

"So," Susan broke the ice, "who do you think should, you know, do it?"

"I've been thinking about that," Bennie replied. "I think I should be the one to pull the unloaded gun on her in the parking lot at her gym. I think she would be a little more intimidated by a man with a gun than a girl with one."

"Can you hold it steady, baby? I mean, have you ever shot a gun before?" Carol asked. On the surface, Bennie didn't look like the type to be confident with a handgun.

"Baby, I have a handgun at home, and I practice five or six times a year at a local firing range. I have a steady hand. And I have the perfect tough-guy negotiator face." Bennie made a series of hard-liner facial expressions that he had practiced countless times in the mirror over the years.

"Yeah, that is pretty good. Very convincing." She leaned over to give her big loveable teddy bear of a man a kiss.

Susan poured cream into her coffee and stirred it, all the while looking up at the ceiling, listening to Bennie and Carol, yet, at the same time, alone with her thoughts.

"I'll be the trigger woman with the stun gun. I'm a very good shot at close range."

Bennie and Carol both looked at Susan with more than a hint of skepticism. "No offense, Susan, but you don't look like the shooting type," Carol said, taking a sip of her coffee.

"I know. People look at me and see a sweet young thing whose greatest sin would be jaywalking. But I can assure you I can shoot straight. I have *two* handguns," she said with a smile of confidence. "I own a Smith and Wesson model 686 double action revolver, and a Glock .22 semiautomatic handgun. And unlike Bennie, my girlfriends and I practice about twice a month."

"Well, look at you," Carol said, finally accepting Susan as more of a sister than a friend. "You've got some spunk after all. I'm surprised, but I can believe it."

Susan's pre-paid disposable cell phone rang. It was Fred. "Hi, Fred, what do you have for us?"

Both Bennie and Carol saw a significant change in Susan's demeanor and tone. Now that she had accepted her role in all of this, she seemed more than confident. She came across as a little darker than the Sweet Pollyanna Purebred type who they had come to know and love. *Maybe she's "in the zone,"* Bennie thought.

"A Mr. Bennett is on his way over and should be at your room at a little past nine o'clock."

"Mr. Bennett? That's his name?" Susan asked in an alarmed tone and sitting up straight.

"No, but I found a bit of irony and humor in using that name," Fred replied. "He'll have what you're looking for and give you a quick rundown on how to use them. You'll still have enough time to get over to the gym since it's only about a ten-minute drive from where you're at."

Now Susan had *her* game face on. Bennie was impressed with her change of demeanor. "We'll expect him. Do you have anything else?"

"Not yet. Nancy is taking a well-deserved nap. We've both been up since early yesterday morning. She should be up in a few hours, and then I'll take a short nap. We'll work through the night and focus on identifying the black hat. That's our main objective right now."

"OK, Fred. I'll call you as soon as we leave with Chase."

Susan had the sound of confidence in her voice and began speaking in absolutes, as if there were only one possible outcome that she would accept. "OK, Bennie, leave some cash on the table. We've got to go up to my room now."

Bennie found himself taking yet another backseat in the leadership department. First to Fred, and now to Susan. He tried not to let his feelings of displeasure show and smiled gracefully as he left a $100 bill on the table.

The three waited in Susan's room for twenty minutes, then came a knock. Bennie jumped up and walked to the door, asking, "Who's there?"

"Mr. Bennett," a voice replied.

Bennie opened the door and in strolled an average-looking man in his mid-thirties, carrying what appeared to be a laptop computer travel bag. He was five feet six, weighing about 145 pounds, and looked to be in great shape. He was clean-shaven, his hair was beginning to thin at the top, and he had burning-hazel eyes. He wore pressed blue jeans, a red sweater with white snowflakes, and a light but warm blue coat. His face was plain, with a straight jaw line that sported a slightly crooked smile. Mr. Bennett displayed an aura of confidence and sophistication that translated into one very capable and dangerous man.

Susan stepped in front of Bennie and said in an authoritative tone, "Thank you for coming on such quick notice, Mr. Bennett. We're really in a jam, and are very short on time and options."

Mr. Bennett responded with his slightly crooked smile. "It's my pleasure, Ms. Anderson. Any friend of Fred is a friend of mine." He placed his bag on top of the king-sized bed and unzipped it. Susan,

Bennie, and Carol clustered around as he opened it up. Inside was an unloaded Smith and Wesson M&P .357 sig. Before Bennie could ask if he could hold it, Susan bent over and picked it up. She handled it like she knew what she was doing, checking the chamber, feeling the balanced weight of the gun in her hand, and even spinning it on her finger, then grasping the handle in midspin. She then handed it to Bennie, who was still trying to maintain the remnants of his male ego.

Mr. Bennett unzipped another compartment and pulled out a black tranquilizer pistol. He then opened up a black leather pouch containing three hypodermic darts. "Sorry, folks, but I could not come up with a stun gun on such short notice."

"Are you kidding me?" Bennie said. "You brought us a tranquilizer gun?"

"I have to admit, that sounds a bit unorthodox, Mr. Bennett," Carol said, echoing Bennie's surprise at the sight of the tranquilizer gun and the darts.

"My apologies. But trust me on this one," he said, pulling out one of the hypodermic darts. "Each dart contains a particular sedative measured out for Ms. Bevere's precise age, height, and weight. We also took into consideration that she would also be ending a two-hour high-intensity workout." His slightly cracked smile turned into a full ear-to-ear grin, showing a set of near-perfect teeth that were as white as modern-day dentistry laser technology would permit.

"I don't know," Susan said. "This will be my job, and I've never held one of these before, let alone fired one."

"Have you ever fired a stun gun before?"

Susan shook her head no.

"Well, then, if you were willing to fire a stun gun for the first time, then you can just as easily fire this tranquilizer gun."

"I have to admit, I think the tranquilizer gun is a better idea," Carol said.

"I think so, too, Ms. Rodriguez. A stun gun will only render a person incapacitated for less than a minute. You would have to have this nasty girl in your car, bound and gagged, during those few seconds. Otherwise, the effect would wear off and ..." Mr. Bennett let those words hang in the air briefly before he continued.

"However, this sedative delivered by this tranquilizer gun to the neck will render her unconscious almost instantly. Even if you shoot her in the arm, chest, or abdomen and she pulls the dart out, the sedative will take effect in about ten seconds."

Susan held the tranquilizer gun, getting used to the feel, balance, and the weight. She held it up and aimed it at the chest of a half-nude girl in a Romanesque picture on the wall. "I like it. I like this a lot better than the idea of a stun gun. I'll aim for the chest as I don't want to miss and have to reload."

"I thought so," Mr. Bennett said in a quiet, confident manner. "Even though you'll have three darts, you will probably only have the opportunity to fire off one. But this gun is very accurate up to fifty feet, so if you can get in close to her, say ten feet or less, you should have no problem."

"We need to leave now," Bennie said, looking at his watch that read 9:20 p.m. "Is there anything else we need to know?"

"That's it," replied Mr. Bennett, zipping up his laptop bag and then looking at the three. "Good luck to you all. And please, call Fred immediately regarding your progress and any other significant events tonight." With that, Mr. Bennett turned, walked out the door, and was gone.

So there they were, Susan, Bennie, and Carol, packing the unloaded Smith and Wesson .357 and the tranquilizer gun into the gym bag Fred had lent to Carol before they left Orange County. They huddled together, and Susan led them in a quick prayer.

"Lord, we give to you this evening. We are not sure what exactly it is we are doing, or if this is even the right thing to do. But we are doing the best we can, and ask that you honor our intentions and bring Chase and the rest of us home safely. Amen."

Bennie and Carol both squeezed Susan's hand and said, "Amen." Then the three resolutely walked out the door, went down the elevator, through the lobby, and out into the dark, freezing night to do something that none of them had ever imagined they would be doing. Bennie handed the valet his slip, and while they waited for the Excursion, they held hands, looked up at the stars, their breath streaming out like billows of smoke, and said more silent, personal prayers.

The valet returned with their SUV, Bennie handed him a ten-dollar bill, and the three headed off across the Harvard Bridge into Cambridge to look for Staci Bevere. The hunt was on. It was time to turn the tables. They would now take the fight directly to Nicky, Staci, and whoever else was helping them. And somehow, someway, moving forward on a flimsy game plan and a whole lot of blind faith, they were determined to bring Chase back home—alive.

If you enjoyed **Breakthrough**, Stephen Tremp's exciting first novel, then you will want to be sure to read his next thrilling installment, **Opening**. Look for **Opening** coming soon at your favorite bookstore.

OPENING
Coming Soon!

STACI ENTERED THE WORMHOLE and exited in a large closet in the lavish apartment that occupied the entire thirty-ninth, fortieth, and forty-first floors and 10,000 square feet. The Tudor-style high rise on Fifth Avenue in the Upper East Side of Manhattan was built in the 1930s. It covered the entire block and bordered the lower eastern corner of Central Park.

The closet was pitch-dark, with the exception of a sliver of light eking through the small space between the double doors and the carpeted floor. Standing alone in the enclosed recess, Staci was scared. No, she was *terrified*. She didn't realize her heart was racing, and she was breathing hard. She had experienced an event that was completely new to her, a sense of imminent evil when she stepped through the wormhole. Although her journey from Cambridge to Manhattan took only a moment in time, Staci felt as if she had spent a lifetime in the tunnel.

She also felt as if she had passed through a caliginous catacomb of decaying bodies and malodorous swamp water. Yet, somehow she sensed that the rotting bodies belonged to the living, if that were even conceivable. It was a place of agony and terrible suffering. Perhaps what she initially thought was a catacomb was, in reality, a prison of sorts. She wasn't able to fathom this with her sight, but somehow, she understood the nature of the event inwardly.

Yet, with another of her senses, she actually had *smelled* something that was more foul and bitter than she thought was possible. It was a mephitic stink that was clearly not from this world. The vile stench had permeated her nostrils and polluted her. She couldn't get rid of it. She wondered if it had saturated her *shinobi shozoku*.

After a minute of trying to recalibrate her senses, she realized she was shaking uncontrollably. She shook her head then held it steady, closed her eyes, and breathed deeply. Slowly. She was beyond confused at the occurrence of what had just transpired. The best way she could explain this event to herself was that she had skirted the edges of the very bowels of Hell itself. The stench and the sense of living death could not be explained any other way.

She thought back two weeks earlier when she returned from Senator O'Connor's office in Boston's State House to one of Prof. Fischer's labs. At that time, she had experienced euphoria and elation, a sense of the bliss that awaited people on the other side. She felt as if she had discerned an angelic host that existed in a place where there was no pain or suffering. It was different now. Terribly different.

Still disoriented, Staci knelt down, placed her hands on her knees, and sat erect. She cleared her mind of her immediate mission. She knew her gift in advanced mathematics and applied statistics would not be able to help her sort through the spiritual events she had just experienced. Although she couldn't prove with her five senses that another world existed, possibly a parallel universe in the same world she lived in, she began to understand deep in her heart that there is more to the macrocosm than what can be measured with the five senses. She saw reality in a new light, and her trust and faith in mathematics to explain the universe just went bankrupt.

She understood there could easily be another dimension much different than the one she existed in, where unexplainable phenomena happened. Yet, this was also a dimension containing similarities in that it contained living beings of a good and evil nature, locked in combat with earth as their battleground. She thought this would explain current events in the media.

After twenty minutes of meditating and bringing her heart rate back to a level of homeostasis, she felt able to return to her immediate mission. However, Staci promised herself that this would be the last time she would ever enter a wormhole. She now knew Nicky really did not understand any of the risks associated with traveling through wormholes. They were not prepared to deal with the countless unknown events that could occur. Nicky would have to find an alternative means of conducting his business.

Satisfied she was able to maintain her internal stability, Staci needed to confirm no one was outside the closet. After a few minutes of silence, she was convinced she was alone. Opening the closet door, she looked around at the furnishings and décor and quickly realized she was in the library and not the master bedroom. *At least Richard had been able to get me into the place without being seen by anyone*, she thought to herself.

She reached back to pick up the receiver suitcase that opened the wormhole that brought her here. She tried to pick it up, but it wouldn't budge. She opened the door to allow more light to enter the enclosure and saw that the suitcase was fastened securely with leather straps bolted to the cement floor beneath the carpet.

Staci sensed something was amiss. Her instincts were telling her everything was wrong. She asked herself why Richard would set up the receiver suitcase in a closet in the library rather than the senator's bedroom closet, and why it was secured to the floor. And why weren't there any people in the library? Surely, at a party this size, certain people would gravitate away from the wilds of the party and end up here where it is less noisy.

Staci pulled out her Browning Hi-Power 9mm and quickly moved about the dimly lit library without making a sound, the crackling fire in the fireplace giving off what little light there was. The flickering flame cast a dancing silhouette of an unwelcome assassin moving stealthily across the room as she quickly confirmed she was alone.

The library was over 800 square feet, and the adjoining parlor was 400 square feet. She stood by the massive ceiling-high carved oak double doors that led to the rest of the apartment and put her ear to the one of the panels. She could hear a cacophony of scores of voices off in the distance and feel the vibrations from the band in the ballroom one floor below. The senator's party was still in high gear.

Staci backed away and quickly shuffled to the door on the other side of the library that would open into a parlor. Looking back at the crack of light slicing its way into the library from the outside hall, she could see four sets of feet quickly gather and stand in unison. She had

Breakthrough

no choice but to enter the parlor, even though she hadn't had the time to confirm if it was empty of people.

Staci quickly opened the door, entered the parlor, and closed the door without making a sound. A moment later, she heard the double doors to the library burst open as four people entered. She could hear them quickly spread out. Staci understood these were not party guests trying to escape the main party. These were people who knew she was here. People, no doubt, with a military background. She assumed she was up against some type of special operations personnel. She knew she had fallen into a trap. The crafty old senator was waiting for her, and had brought hired goons to kill her.

Looking around the parlor, there was no place for her to hide, no place for her to run. She peered out the lone window at the street forty-one stories below and wondered if the rumors whispering out of MIT were true, that a group of extremely gifted professors and their graduate students had discovered a way that allowed people to defy gravity, or at least allow them to float safely to the ground from high elevations. Maybe Nicky could have stolen that technology as well. *It sure would have helped me now,* she thought to herself.

Staci noticed there was a ledge; however, it was only four inches wide, and the weather was bitterly cold and windy outside. Escape by this manner was certain suicide, but so was staying inside and attempting to fight four men, who were, no doubt, armed and trained killers.

She started to open the window, then heard the slow, crackling voice of the aged Republican senator. "I know you're in there. We've been waiting all day for you. I was wondering if you were going to bother showing up and gracing us with your presence. Won't you come out and join my party?"

Hands still grasping the open window above her head, Staci's head snapped back into the parlor, her heart pounding hard again. This wasn't supposed to happen. She knew she had to control her breathing as she did not want to risk an asthma attack. She pushed open the window and stuck her head out into the freezing elements. The frigid cold, whipping winds and the icy rain coming down in layered sheets immediately stung her exposed eyes. To her dismay, she looked down at a smooth, three-inch layer of ice covering the ledge.

The senator interrupted Staci's fleeting thoughts of escape. "You're probably wondering how we uncovered your little plot to kill me. Poor Richard selected the wrong person to be an accomplice to a murder scheme that included me. After my dear colleague, the late Sir Alexander Kizanis, was brutally murdered in the sanctity of his own home, the rest of our little group had to be concerned that any one of us could possibly be next."

No way, Staci thought, as she looked back out the window and down at the ledge. Even if she were able to make it around the corner of the building thirty feet away, where would she be able to go? The senator owned the entire floor. He could easily have her shot, if she didn't first fall to her death.

The senator's slow and confident dialogue continued. "So we looked for connections, connections that we each might have with Sir Kizanis that could allow for an assassin to enter his home, and who would, naturally, be able to enter any one of ours. The one connection that stood out for me was the recently departed Richard Zarahoff. He was an assistant to both myself and Sir Kizanis, and he had helped us negotiate numerous global projects that would be beyond the means of your comprehension. As it turns out, he obviously was not satisfied with the salaries we were paying him.

"You have to find this ironic," he continued with a hint of laughter. "Our little group actually met here, in my library, where I secured your suitcase to the adjoining closet floor and away from my party downstairs. Surely, you must find this as humorous as I do."

Staci was frantic. She was a realist. Being gifted in the area of applied statistics, she understood that any opportunity of escape were next to nil. But they weren't zero. She still had a chance to make it out of there alive, no matter how slim her chances were.

"We were watching you in the closet as you stepped out of the wormhole. I had a video camera set up. The brief yellow and orange lights from the wormhole, which, by the way, was the most fascinating thing I have ever seen in my life, revealed you are a female, and that you have a knapsack. I assume you are carrying another suitcase that will enable you to get back home. I'll gladly retrieve that from your dead carcass very shortly."

Staci left the window open and again looked over the study. There was a closet a mere five feet from her. *Maybe,* she reasoned, *there's something inside there that I can use to escape. Or maybe there's another armed goon waiting to cut me in half with an automatic rifle.* Regardless, at this point, she was desperate.

She stepped over to the door and opened it, holding her Browning up and ready to unload. She gasped as she saw the lone item hanging from a meat hook. Richard Zarahoff's *head* was wrapped in a single sheet of cellophane, his eyes wide open and a look of absolute terror engraved on his face. His naked body was badly beaten and bruised, and both legs were broken. The senator's goons must have taken their time torturing him and prying out information regarding the receiver suitcase, what it was for, and how it worked.

"Please come out, now," the senator slowly repeated with more laughter in his voice. "I want to see what you look like before my men slice you up into little pieces and feed them to the pigeons."

Staci could make out the distinct sounds of three men rushing up to the door, then the shuffling of the seventy-six-year-old senator following closely behind. Holding her breath, she heard the harsh, raspy voice say the words she desperately did *not* want to hear slowly leave the senator's lips. "Kill her. Kill her anyway you want. But kill her now!"

LaVergne, TN USA
21 September 2009
158563LV00002B/62/P